MW00427317

TASTE OF ADDICTION

ENTICE SERIES BOOK THREE

VICTORIA DAWSON

PAPER HEART PUBLISHING LLC

To the hopeless...may you find comfort in being seen.

1

I angrily wipe at the tears that cascade down my cheeks. "Why are you doing this?" I whisper, my voice trembling with each spoken syllable. The lump in my throat triples in size, and I cannot keep my eyes dry long enough to see Graham who is a foot in front of me.

He pulls me into him and my damp face presses into the softness of his sweater. Hands tangle in my hair and pull my head upward to look at him. I blink, and two steady rivers leak from my eyes, as if a dam has broken.

"I need you to trust that I love you and that I am doing everything for us. I'm preserving our future. No one can touch you here. You'll be safe. It'll buy me some time at the very least."

"You are locking me away?"

"Sweetheart, I am keeping you safe."

"By keeping me prisoner here?" I demand, glancing over to the fortress. Damn him. "I have classes. A job," I argue, tugging at the hem of his shirt in desperation to get him to listen. To reconsider whatever it is he has planned.

"You're on fall break for the next eleven days. The cafe will be running on limited staff and with limited hours. Essentially, you have nothing pressing that needs your attention back in Portland. Consider this a retreat."

I swallow hard. He is always one step ahead. He knows my schedule and exactly what to say. He almost sounds logical. Except he is forgetting about the big picture and the demands of my research project. How will I ever be able to have something to present to Dr. Williams that will wow him when I will be cooped up inside this dungeon for the foreseeable future?

"So this is it?" I look over at the house. "You're just dropping me off and then going back to Portland?"

"Dammit, Angela." His hands shake me. "This isn't fun for me! I'm going completely nuts over Tanner targeting you, and I need to remove you from the equation long enough so I can shut him down."

"And how are you going to do that, Graham? You think in eleven days, you're going to somehow come up with adequate intel to pass along to the FBI or to your brother or whomever—that will be sufficient enough to draw out all of the key players in the drug ring? Just because I'm not around to interfere? You're delusional! You need me more than you think you do. I can easily work undercover and be the agency girl who lures out all the bad guys."

"Me, delusional?" Graham steps back and pulls at his hair, looking up into the sky. "You still cannot wrap your head around the fact that you'll never be sacrificial bait. First, hell will have to freeze over for me to allow you to put yourself at risk like that. Second, you've been caught by them. They may not know why you have a personal interest in their corrupt organization, but they definitely know you're involved in trying to shut them down."

I sigh and look away. He's right. There is no longer a good way for me to continue gathering new information on Tanner—other than through Paul. He is my ticket. But eleven days stuck here?

"You don't have to keep me here for a week and a half, Graham. I can follow directions from the comfort of the penthouse or my townhouse."

His eyes burn holes in my resolve. He shakes his head. "You're staying here. I have to separate myself from you so I can think clearly and come up with a plan."

"I hate this," I choke out.

"Oh baby, this is all killing me inside. I hate seeing you sad. It guts me." He scoops me up into his arms and carries me toward the house. "Just trust me, okay?"

I nod through my cloudy vision of tears. I had gotten so used to having Graham around that the thoughts of not being able to be physically near him make me want to punch something. "I love you."

He squeezes me tighter to him and kisses my forehead. "I'm so utterly in love with you that I'm willing to break your heart now in order to gain your entire heart later."

With one hand he opens the front door and treads softly through the house. When he rounds the bend, we are confronted by his elite team of men, all standing at full posture and ready to meet their captive.

"What was that, sweetheart?"

I sigh. I must be muttering things under my breath again. "Is it time to meet my wardens?"

He ignores my snarky comments, setting me down on my feet. "Angie, you know Collins. You have been acquainted with Austin and Parker." Each man tips their head when addressed. "However, you have yet to meet Malcolm"—Graham gestures toward the biggest man out of the crew—"and Owen."

Everyone smiles politely at me, which makes me feel the pangs of guilt for being such a brat. I try to bite back the scowl that wants to form on my face. This isn't their fault they got assigned the worst babysitting job on the planet. "Nice to meet you all," I mutter, my tone that of indifference. It is all just too much to take in right now. I can't believe Graham is doing this to me.

I yelp as I get scooped back up and toted up the stairs. Graham meanders down the hallway to the room at the very end. I lift my head to look around. The walls are painted a soft shade of gray. The huge California king bed has a solid-black stained wooden frame. The drapes are open and the forest of trees takes up the entire span of windows. A deep lavender shade is the accent color in the room and provides a punch of color in the bedding set, the curtain ties, and in the artwork.

"What do you think?" he asks, placing me on the center of the bed and joining me at my side.

"Pretty nice for a jail cell."

"Angie…"

I narrow my eyes at him. "What? Don't like to call it what it essentially is? I'm your shackle-less prisoner."

He ignores my comment and moves over to the desk

4

along the edge of the room. "I have all of your electronics set up so we can video chat. You're allowed to contact Claire on these devices."

"Wow, thank you," I snap, my voice dripping with passive-aggressiveness.

"I know you're pissed at me. I get it. But please don't do anything stupid while you're here. You're connected to the Internet on an anonymous VPN that is located in the Netherlands. So all of your devices are safe and no one can trace you here. Treat the stay like a minivacation. Collins will be by periodically each day to check in. But Austin, Parker, Malcolm, and Owen will be around here to assist you with anything you may need."

I scoot my legs to the edge of the bed and sit up. I bite at my bottom lip as I watch Graham try to show me where my wardrobe and all of my hygiene essentials are. I can hear his staggered breathing and know that he is emotional about leaving me here too. I guess, in some small way, that makes it better. To know that he doesn't just want to send me away for the sake of simplicity.

"I'll be fine," I whisper. I stand in place and rub my forearm against my cheeks to dry the last free-falling tears that manage to escape.

Graham stalks toward me and grabs my hips to lift me into the air. I wrap my legs around him and grasp fistfuls of his hair.

"I freaking love you, Angela Renee McFee."

I burst out laughing through my watery eyes. "I freaking love you, Graham Xavier Hoffman."

We stay entwined in each other until Graham's arms start to quiver from fatigue. He tosses me back onto the bed and crawls up my body like he is about to feast on his prey.

He moans. "I want you so badly it hurts."

"Then have me."

Within seconds, my clothes are stripped away, and I am left wearing just my jewelry. The anticipation is the fore-play. Not knowing when or where he will touch me causes my nerve endings to ignite. He kisses down my jawline and rests his mouth against my neck. He lingers there, nipping at my sensitive spot, but then kneels up on the bed to unbutton his fly and free himself from his pants. Clothes get discarded to the floor, and his body is back on top of me again, like a heated blanket. I spread my legs to accommodate him and wiggle my hips to show him I am ready.

Graham leans his weight onto his elbows and looks down at me. A sadness washes over his eyes, and for a second I think he is going to stop and veer off course. I hold my breath and wait. Soft hands snake down between our bodies to pull my inner lips apart. He rubs himself along the length of me and lines up at my entrance. We have been in this position many times before, and yet, this time feels different. It is like he is touching me for the last time. His hands feel softer. His breathing labored.

His eyes stare into my soul. I am completely open and vulnerable to him. I have nothing left to hide.

I rock my hips up and Graham slips inside a measly inch. I groan over the sensation. He belongs inside me. We fit so well. The only sounds between us are the moans escaping our lips, as we thrust our hips and meet in the middle.

It doesn't take long before Graham is pumping his

release into me, and I am panting out his name with my own. He covers me up inside the warm blankets and gets himself dressed.

"I have to go, sweetheart," he says softly, bending at his waist to press a kiss to my lips.

I look up at him through sleepy eyes and see that he is hesitant to leave. I reach for his hand and give it a squeeze. "Please don't go."

Graham's sigh shudders through him. "I don't want to be apart from you, baby. Trust me, I don't. I just cannot come up with a better way to keep you safe."

I nod and look away. This sucks. I grip the silky comforter and tug it up to my neck. I am suddenly cold, and a wave of exhaustion crashes into me as I struggle to keep my eyes open. Graham places a chaste kiss on my forehead, and I watch silently as he retreats out the bedroom door, closing it quietly behind him. I flop back onto the pillow and pray that the next eleven days go by quickly.

———

I wake to the sound of my own labored breathing and the disappointment that my sexy dream starring Graham had to end so abruptly. I roll to my side and pull my knees up to my chest. Sunshine is beaming in through the open drapes, but it doesn't have the get-up-and-conquer-the-world effect it usually has on me. I slither out of bed but only to grab my new phone that is situated at the top of the electronics pyramid that consists of a laptop, iPad, and kindle. I snatch my phone from the stack and meander back to bed. I am still naked. And I just don't care.

I look over all of the icons on the home screen and see that everything is in its normal place. Even my phone number is the same. At least there is that. I find the text app and see the notification that I have three new messages. I click on the icon. All from "The Boyfriend." I smile at the title. Graham is my boyfriend. And I miss him.

The Boyfriend: Remember to trust me.

I sigh over his words. He can be so repetitive. I read the next two.

The Boyfriend: Feel free to one-day ship some things to entertain yourself. Just email or text Collins whatever you would like, and he'll be sure to get them sent there. His address is Collins_Stone@hoffmanhq.com and his phone number is saved into your phone again.

The Boyfriend: I love you.

I write out messages but keep deleting them because they sound sad and are only going to make him feel guiltier for leaving me here by myself. So, instead, I just settle for a simple one.

Angie: I love you too.

I put my phone down and meander about my new room. I find my new wardrobe in the closet. Feeling barely in the mood for clothes at all, I just settle for a pair of black fleece pants and a red shirt that has a big heart in the center.

A knock at the door makes me nearly jump out of my skin.

"Um, yes? Be right there," I call to the person on the other side. I pull the hem of my shirt down and move toward the door. I pull it open and see Collins standing with a tray of food.

"Mr. Hoffman wanted to make sure you had an early dinner, given that you slept through lunch."

"Oh." I stare down at the tray of Donna's leftovers, and my mouth waters at the memory of how good of a cook she is. "Thank you." My eyes wander behind him as I think about how long I napped. "What time is it?"

"Three thirty."

"Wow. I must have been really tired," I say, mainly to myself. I take the tray from Collins's hands and walk it over to my nightstand.

"Miss McFee?"

I turn back to look at the sheepish expression on Collins's face. Even after all this time together, he can still be a bit shy around me. The man lives and breathes confidence—except when he is filling the role of more-than-a-bodyguard or more-than-just-a-chauffeur.

"There's a minifridge tucked into the cupboard section of your nightstand. It is fully stocked with your favorite items. However, if you want something else, just text me and I'll get it for you."

"Thank you, Collins. I do appreciate it."

"You're free to roam the house. There's a library here and a media room for watching TV. And a fully stocked kitchen. Just don't leave the premises without notifying one of the security staff. And if you try," he says, looking me straight in the eyes for added emphasis, "Mr. Hoffman will be furious and sirens will be roaring through the house."

"Message received," I mutter. Sheesh. The entire property is gated. What more do they need here?

I wait for Collins to exit before flopping down on the bed and digging into my food. It is heated to the perfect temperature and tastes almost better than it did yesterday. I lean down and pop open the minifridge and select a bottle of cherry soda. I stare at the label. How does Graham even realize my love for this stuff? I haven't had it in years. I doubt it is just a coincidence. Nothing ever is.

I lazily scan through my shopping app and nibble at my food. I don't even know what I would order to entertain myself. It's not like this is a normal occurrence where I am forced to quarantine away from civilization. Typically, I would accompany Claire to the gym or go to work or have my research to gather. Instead, here I am. By myself. Without much to do other than slow down. I guess in a way it is peaceful to know that the pause button in my life is not broken. That I can actually use this time away from the rest of the world as a way to cleanse my mind and refocus my intentions.

I finish up my food and place all of my trash back on the tray. I slip on a pair of slippers that are still in the box at the bottom of the closet. Then, I head out into the hallway and down the stairs in search of the kitchen to drop off my tray. Each room of the house is dimly lit, and the only sound I hear is the buzzing of the appliances.

I grab a bottled water from the main fridge and walk room to room until I discover the library at the back of the house. Just like most things that Graham owns, it is massive and immaculate. Every bookshelf is organized and labeled based on subject.

I run my fingers along the bindings and breathe in the smell of leather and worn pages. Near the window, I find a shelf labeled "Just For Angie." I burst out laughing over the titles that fill the section—*Baby for the Sheikh*, *Mail Order Bride*, *When Handsome Meets Hopeless*, and *Alpha and the Beauty*. Graham's not that far off the mark. These are all books I would gladly read—even though half have some pretty cheesy covers. Seeing them lined up in vivid color makes me want to double over in laughter. They don't seem to fit with the other more worldly books that decorate the rest of the shelves. I guess my reading preferences are singular in topic.

I remove *When Handsome Meets Hopeless* and curl up into the overstuffed chair that is near the big bay window. The book looks like it is fresh off the press, without any visible blemishes. I turn the page until I find the prologue and begin reading. My shoulders relax, and I kick my feet up onto the window seat when my legs seem to want to fall asleep and slip into the make-believe world that the author describes thoroughly.

My phone rings. When I catch the time of seven o'clock on the screen, I am amazed that I missed the sun setting and the day turning into night—despite having a front row seat for watching. I answer the call and wait for his smooth voice on the other end. He does not disappoint.

"Sweetheart. I miss you."

"Then why did you lock me away?" I can hear him exhale and I instantly want to take back my question. So, I try to counter it with something light and add, "You know by the time this is all over, your staff will quit."

"Ha, doubtful. Especially because I pay them a fortune to be amazing at their jobs. Did you eat dinner?"

"Yeah, your mom's leftovers. Very delicious." I frown over the impact of today. Thursday. "Happy Thanksgiving."

"Happy Thanksgiving, baby. I'm glad you enjoyed dinner. Wish I could be there with you. What are you up to?"

"Oh, just reading in the library. Found my super-secret section and decided to crack a book open."

"How did I do?"

"Spot-on."

"Good."

I hear the tiredness in his yawn despite it not being that late and yearn to wrap my body around his while we both drift off to sleep. "You better get some rest."

"You too, sweetheart."

"Goodnight, Graham."

"Goodnight, Angie."

I place my phone on the windowsill and finish the chapter I was in the middle of before I got the call. I close the book, shut off the light, and tread through the house until I am up the stairs and back in my room.

I brush my teeth and hair and then lie in bed with my iPad. I open up my secret email and reread all of the notes and research topics I sent to the account. I still have an internship to strive toward—even if my dream is more of a distant fantasy at this moment in time.

I wake up to the sound of an unusual rhythmic ringing coming from my nightstand. I flip open the protective cover on my iPad and answer the video call from Claire.

"Oh wow, girl, you look like you are fresh out of prison. Quarantine hair, don't care?"

I look at the tiny box that contains a close-up of my face. Wow. She got the prison part correct; that is exactly what this place feels like. "Yeah, and a bunch of other things I don't care about either," I say with a shrug.

"Oh no, you don't. Don't do that." She looks down at her fingernails and back to me.

"Do what?"

"I can already see the signs."

"What the hell are you talking about, Claire? Just spit it out."

"You have let yourself go."

I look down at my fuzzy heart shirt and then back up to take note of my rat's nest hair. My eyes are swollen and reflect back defeat to me on the video chat screen. "Way to build up a girl's confidence."

"Listen to me, Angela Renee McFee. It has not even been twenty-four hours since you have been sent to prison without a key."

"How do you even—"

"Graham filled me in on your new crash pad, but that man only gives crumbs of information when all I really want is a damn sandwich."

I laugh. Claire has a way of always lightening the mood.

She snaps her fingers into the screen, making my focus return to her. "But you will not continue on with this I-don't-give-a-fuck attitude. It does not look good on you.

And all the frowning is just going to give you premature wrinkles. Plus, brighten up, it's the best day to shop out of the entire year. So that is what we're going to do."

"What? How?"

She clicks her tongue. "Together. Virtually."

"Now?"

"Yes, dammit. Now. I have these urges—"

"Sounds like a personal problem," I tease.

"Hush. So, I have these urges to buy something frivolous. And expensive."

"Okay."

Claire holds up a poster featuring the names of the stores she wants to shop at, including cutouts of generic items she plans to buy. "Look, I even made a vision board to help keep us focused."

"I am—"

"Thankful and impressed," she interrupts. "I know."

I can't keep from smiling. "Yes, those things."

"In all seriousness, why are we even locking ourselves down with rich and sexy-ass boyfriends if we're not going to at least take advantage of their bank accounts once in a while?" she asks, but quickly moves on to the next topic before I can even respond. "We already lost eleven valuable hours today. But do you see me holding a grudge? No. Do you see me sleeping in and pouting and feeling sorry for myself? No. You know why? Because I am an adult. Shit happens all the time, but we get up and dust ourselves off and push forward. So buck up, young panda bear, and let's grab the men by the balls and shop!"

"This is all too—"

"And before you ask—because I know you will—do not

read into my animal selection; it was the first thing that came to my mind and I forgot the original phrase and had no time to think. Because time is already a-wasting!"

I wait until Claire is done with her half-rant half-motivational speech before bursting into fits of giggles. She knows exactly what to say to make me laugh and cry at the same time. Her fierce loyalty to being on Team Angie is the reason why I can trust her with my secrets and my fears. She is an amazing best friend, and I want to hold on to that title with everything I have. Yet, I am realistic enough to realize that when we graduate and move forward with our careers, things might change. People grow apart. But for now, I want to embrace this friendship with everything I have.

"So, let's start shopping," I say with the biggest smile. "I have been really wanting a heat press so I can make cool shirts and personalized items."

"Oh yes! And one of those machines that cuts out the lettering and graphics. Gotta get one of those too."

"Sure, why not?"

Her smile is contagious. "Now, that's the attitude! Have you thought about what you're getting Graham for Christmas? Ethan basically says he has everything, so I'm struggling. The typical watch, suit tie, and glow-in-the-dark cock ring are out."

I shake my head and look down at my phone as I pull open websites to peruse. "No, not at all. If I do think of something, I'm definitely going to have you do the ordering. That man has tabs on everything I do. I know it's because he is megaparanoid right now, but holy cannoli, I need at least one layer of privacy."

"He's obsessed with you, Angie. While Lifetime usually features those kinds of movies and the girl ends up tied to a bed somewhere to die—"

"Claire!"

"No, no. What I'm saying is, his obsession is the sweet kind. It's a compliment."

"Gee, thanks."

She bursts out laughing and scans over her phone for shopping deals. "I think I want to get Ethan one of those fancy coffee makers and something that he can use to make bacon in the microwave in case I am at the gym. He is a complete slut for bacon."

"Sort of like you are a slut for pancakes and margies?"

"Hey, quit being judgmental. Everyone enjoys a good margarita."

"This is true," I admit.

Claire clears her throat and then furrows her brow. "So on a serious note…"

"Yeah?"

"The anniversary of your car accident is coming up."

Of course, I know this already. But this is Claire's way of testing the waters with the topic. "Yup, November 30th. I cannot believe it has been five years since it happened. I won't be able to take my annual trek back to Baker City to visit James's grave either."

She nods her head. "What can I do to help you through that day, Angie? Do you think you will want a distraction? Virtual shoulder to cry on? Me to leave you alone? I want to be what you need in the time you need it."

I give her a weak smile. "You're an amazing friend, Claire. I can't honestly tell you what I'll need until the day hits. Some years I have spent the entire day crying at James's grave site. Other years I've spent it in bed trying to sleep through the limited memories."

"I'm here for you in any way you need—even if you don't know what you need yet."

I turn my head off screen and wipe at the tears pooling in my eyes. "I appreciate it."

I hang up with Claire and send in my order requests to Collins, making the decision that I'm going to choose to have fun while I'm here. Maybe this stay away from home can be a retreat after all.

I decide that a shower and clean set of clothes will make me feel more human. I already slept through breakfast, but at least there is still time to eat lunch.

That's the thing about being quarantined. I now have all the time in the world.

2

It's five o'clock when I am pulled away from my trash TV binge fest by a series of knocks. It is just a courtesy, really, since the media room is doorless. I hit pause and turn in my reclined theater seat to see Collins's silhouette in the light filtering in from the hallway.

"Oh hey," I say, sitting upright and making a bit of a mess with the popcorn I popped. I toss loose kernels into the bowl and set it on the seat beside me. I close the leg rest and climb the stairs to the top of the room.

"Here are your requested items, Miss McFee," he says politely. "Want me to deliver them up to your room?"

My mouth gapes at the turnaround time for the delivery. I was expecting at least a day, if not two. Nope. Collins gets my list checked off within three hours.

"That'll be great. Thank you."

I go back to my seat and finish the episode of *Love Lockdown*. It seems like a fitting show to engage myself in. Before heading back to my room, I make a snack plate for

18

dinner instead of a real meal. In the kitchen, I find grapes, cheese, and artisan bread. I uncork a bottle of my favorite sparkling Moscato and carry everything back up to my nightstand.

I find the items that Collins picked up for me on the desk. He managed to get me a heat press, a huge selection of vinyl sheets, blank T-shirts, and the cutting machine. In a separate bag, he has my special requested item that could not be found in a store—Graham's worn T-shirt.

I pull the plain black shirt out of the bag and hold it up to my nose. I breathe in his scent of citrus and woods. I can barely smell the rainforest and that is only because I am searching for it. I fold the shirt back up and place it on the corner of the desk.

I open up all of the boxes to find the directions. I've watched enough YouTube tutorials to have a solid grasp of how to go about making personalized clothes and glass-ware; however, having the equipment at my disposal is still a bit daunting.

It takes me a couple of hours to be up and running with my first project. I start by feeding the vinyl through the machine and watch as the laser accurately cuts out the letters and design I want to press first. I smooth out the white T-shirt onto the metal platform of the press and place the vinyl decals in reverse onto the shirt. I put the safety sheet on top and then close the heat press, while setting the timer. Once the timer goes off, I carefully remove the shirt and allow it to cool.

I peel off the backing and smile at the pink glitter letters that say, "Graham Handled: The act of Graham having his way with you." The words are centered between handprint graphics, with them acting like parentheses. For a practice shirt, it turned out better than I ever expected. I am going to have way too much fun with this new hobby of mine.

Now that I understand the concept, I move to my next challenge of turning Graham's black T-shirt into something that I can wear to bed tonight. I use my laptop to design the message, get the vinyl cut out, and then press it to the shirt. I pull my current shirt over my head and exchange it for my new one that says, "Property of Graham Hoffman."

I walk over to the full-length mirror that is inside the closet and laugh at the image reflected back at me. I then work at making him one that says he is my property. When I am done, I make my way through the house in search of Collins. When I don't see him, I call out a simple, "Collins? You here?"

"Can I help you with something, ma'am?" a voice asks behind me.

"Holy shit!" I yell, jumping out of my skin and dropping the shirt onto the floor. I turn around and see Austin standing in the shadows.

"Didn't mean to scare you. Collins is not here at the moment. How can I help you?"

"I, um," I say, bending to pick up the T-shirt. "I was just wondering if someone could get this to Graham for me? It doesn't have to be done tonight. Was just—"

"Of course," Austin says, taking it from my outstretched hands. "I'll get it delivered, ma'am."

"Thank you."

"Anything else I can help you with?"

"Um, no, I don't think so."

"Okay, have a good night."

"Well, hold on," I say hesitantly. "I really wanted to thank you for rescuing me at The Shack. I was really scared and you kept me safe. For that, I am truly grateful."

Austin's head gives a single nod. "No thanks necessary, ma'am. I was happy to help."

I saunter back to the room and spend time making homemade Christmas gifts for everyone on my shopping list. I play holiday music and channel all my creative energy into my projects.

I love the moment where your brain hasn't figured out if it is asleep or awake yet. Where you stumble through visions, some imaginary and some real, not being able to tell the difference. Where your heart is settled, your muscles are relaxed, and your breathing is calm. And then there's the instant where your nose catches a scent—being the dominant sense of memory recall—completely catapulting you through the foggy haze to present time.

That's what Graham's T-shirt does to me.

It brings me back. Holds me close. And makes me want to open my eyes.

But when I do, the only thing I have of him is his memory that kisses my body and wraps me in the scent of him. I pull the collar up to my nose and breathe him in. I miss him. It is only Saturday—I think—and we have not been physically in each other's presence since Thursday morning. Seems way longer though.

I roll out of bed and make my way to the bathroom to do my morning routine. I guess not feeling forced to wear makeup or put on real clothes is, in a way, relaxing. I have zero people to impress right now, and my mind isn't drowning in an endless list of to-do tasks.

I unplug my phone, see it is actually morning and not afternoon, and find a text from Claire.

Claire: Do not watch the local news or read the newspaper.

Umm, okay? That just makes me want to do both of those things now. And she has to realize that, otherwise she would have said nothing. Great. What bombshell am I going to see that will inevitably ruin my entire day?

I start by googling Graham's name and look for the most recent articles—specifically with yesterday's or today's date. *The Headliner* secures the top article for the search and features another interview by Violet Storm, a reporter who has been following Graham since he ventured into the business world. I read the title and snarl. Dammit!

TAKING A CHANCE ON CHANTEL

BY VIOLET STORM - THE HEADLINER EXCLUSIVE INTERVIEW

CAN WE HAVE A MOMENT OF SILENCE WHILE WE MOURN THE LOSS OF THE CHANCE TO DATE THE SMOKIN' NO-LONGER-SINGLE, BUT STILL ELUSIVE GRAHAM "HOT STUFF" HOFFMAN?

IT SURELY FEELS LIKE THE WORLD IS PLAYING A JOKE ON ALL OF US, RIGHT LADIES? HOW CAN SOMEONE WHO HAS

BEEN ON THE DATING MARKET FOR SO MANY YEARS—
NEVER WANTING TO SETTLE OR LET GO OF HIS BACHELOR
TITLE—FINALLY GET SNAGGED BY THE SUPERMODEL WITH
A HEART OF GOLD? NEEDLESS TO SAY, SOPHIA CHANTEL IS
ONE LUCKY WOMAN. OR PERHAPS IT IS GRAHAM WHO IS
THE LUCKY ONE. PRETTY SURE EVERY TWENTY-SOMETHING
WOMAN IN THE ENTIRE CITY OF PORTLAND WANTS TO BE
HER RIGHT NOW. AND THE ROCK SHE IS WEARING ON HER
LEFT RING FINGER IS ENOUGH TO SINK HER TO THE BOTTOM
OF THE WILLAMETTE. NOT LIKE SHE WOULD EVER BE
FOUND SWIMMING IN ANYTHING OTHER THAN A LUXURY
RESORT OR PRIVATE POOL. BEING ENGAGED TO A MAN LIKE
HOFFMAN CAN ONLY BRING EVERY PRIVILEGE AND MODERN
CONVENIENCE TO YOUR DOORSTEP. ENJOY IT, SOPHIA! WE
ARE ALL LIVING VICARIOUSLY THROUGH YOU...

I CAUGHT UP WITH THE POWER COUPLE AND TWISTED
THEIR ARMS—IN THE MOST NONTHREATENING MANNER, OF
COURSE—TO TELL ME HOW IT ALL WENT DOWN. BECAUSE
IF WE ARE ALL GOING TO MOVE ON FROM OUR FANTASY
WORLD, WE HAVE TO FIRST FIND CLOSURE.

"SOPHIA AND I HAVE AN EVENTFUL PAST AND NOW A
PROFESSIONAL WORKING RELATIONSHIP, WHERE SHE'S THE
SIGNATURE MODEL FOR MY JEWELRY COMPANY CALLED
JEALOUSY. IT WAS ONLY A MATTER OF TIME BEFORE THE
ATTRACTION WE FEEL TOWARD ONE ANOTHER BECAME SO
POTENT THAT WE WOULDN'T BE ABLE TO KEEP IT UNDER
WRAPS," GRAHAM EXPLAINS, WITH A SMIRK THAT WAS
ENOUGH TO MELT THE PANTIES RIGHT OFF MY BODY.

AND LADIES, LET ME JUST SAY THAT THE PICTURE DOES NOT CAPTURE THE ENAMORED EXPRESSION THAT WAS WRITTEN ALL OVER HIS FACE IN REGARD TO CHANTEL. THE TWO ARE SMITTEN WITH EACH OTHER AND ABOUT TO CONQUER THE WORLD BY STORM WITH THEIR BUSINESS ENDEAVORS. WHO WOULDN'T WANT TO DATE THEIR SEXY BOSS? PRETTY SURE THIS IS THE MAIN INGREDIENT IN A RECIPE FOR ROMANCE. SO, CAN WE REALLY BE SHOCKED? NO. BUT STILL DEEPLY SAD? HECK YES. SO GO THROUGH THE PHASES OF GRIEF WHILE WE LET THIS NEWS SETTLE INTO OUR BRAINS.

WHILE TYPICALLY RESERVED IN INTERVIEWS, IT WAS NICE TO SEE CHANTEL OPEN UP ABOUT HER LOVE FOR HOFFMAN. "GRAHAM HAS ALWAYS BEEN MY FIRST LOVE," SHE ADMITS. HER SOFT SMILE AND GAZE UP AT HIM SAID MORE THAN HER SIMPLE WORDS. "HE PROPOSED TO ME ON THE BUSY STREET IN FRONT OF HOFFMAN HEADQUARTERS—THE LOCATION WHERE WE FIRST MET. IT WAS A BEAUTIFUL DAY. DEFINITELY A MEMORY I WON'T EVER FORGET."

FOLLOW THE ENCHANTING COUPLE ON SOCIAL MEDIA WHERE YOU CAN GET A GLIMPSE INTO THEIR DAILY LIFE. AND STAY TUNED FOR ANOTHER FOLLOW-UP ARTICLE WHERE I PLAN TO TAKE MY STALKING SKILLS TO THE NEXT LEVEL.

-V.S.

Damn them! I stare at the photo of Graham dipping Sophia back in the middle of the city street. I imagine traffic had to be stopped to capture such an image on such a busy section. I want to throw my phone across the room.

I scroll through the other links and then do an image search to see all of the engagement photos that were snapped. The Internet is saturated with the news, and it seems that it has even garnered national attention on some of the entertainment sites. Am I that naive to think that Graham isn't a celebrity in the business world? There are even sites that are dedicated to predicting what Sophia and Graham's future children will look like. I guess having future heirs and heiresses to his fortune has sparked an online frenzy within just hours of the engagement announcement.

While deep down, I know that Graham told me to trust him—repeatedly—I still can't help but wonder if Sophia is pregnant. There is still a sliver of doubt. Maybe I am inadvertently fulfilling the role of "the other woman" and have yet to fully understand the implications.

A text notification from Claire flashes across the top of the screen and I click on the bar.

Claire: This is all a joke. Has to be. Some plan to keep you safe.

Angie: I may be physically safe. But my heart is still broken over seeing them together.

Claire: Ugh!

Angie: Even if this is a fake relationship, it still cuts me.

I hate this. I throw myself back on the bed and close my eyes while my thoughts settle. I decide that there is no way to know the circumstances until I ask Graham directly. I roll out of bed and get my iPad. I open the video chat app and find his name on the list. I hit the green button to start the call.

It doesn't take long for Graham to answer—except he has muted his end of the call. I notice a wall of windows behind him and the backrest of a leather chair. He is wearing a suit and appears to be in the middle of a meeting, on a Saturday. So why did he answer if he is busy?

My phone buzzes with a text from him.

The Boyfriend: I can't talk. But I still want to see you. Meeting is boring. But I have to be in it.

Angie: I cannot believe you think that being engaged to Sophia is healthy for our current relationship.

I glare into the webcam as I send my message. I watch as Graham reads it and frowns back at me. He then notices my shirt—his shirt—and breaks out into the sexiest smile. My phone buzzes with an incoming message.

The Boyfriend: Damn right you are mine.

Angie: You better hope I still am after all this shit you have been putting me through.

He looks into the camera and mouths, "I love you." And

I believe it. But I can still hate his stupid plan. I type another message.

Angie: You have a lot of explaining to do.

The Boyfriend: I'll call you back after I finish this merger.

I swallow hard. How can he even multitask when he is in the middle of a big business transaction? That man never ceases to amaze me. I end the call and flop back onto the bed.

Today is going to be one of those days. I can already tell.

I declare that today is a mimosa morning and pop open a bottle of champagne to mix with my orange juice. Even I am impressed that I made it up for actual breakfast, despite still feeling emotionally drained. However, I think a liquid diet is the way to go on this shitty morning.

I throw on a sweats outfit and text Collins that I would like to go outside for a walk around the property. He immediately responds.

Collins: Austin will accompany you. I'm with Mr. Hoffman today.

Angie: I don't need a chaperone.

Angie: Was only letting you know so I can avoid setting off the security system.

VICTORIA DAWSON

A knock sounds at my door and I groan. I am so not in the mood for this. I feel like the walls are closing in on me. I just need to get out of the house for an hour or so. I reluctantly drag my body across the room and open the door to see an alert Austin waiting for me to talk.

"I need out of here."

"Okay. I'm ready when you are."

"No."

"Excuse me?" he asks. I am sure he has heard plenty of embellished stories about my antics, but he at least has the decency to look surprised at my rebelliousness.

"You can watch me from the window or the security cameras or from a wristlet tracking device. But I refuse to be shadowed while I make a few laps around the damn house for some exercise!"

"Okay, ma'am, just calm down."

"Listen. We're practically the same age. So stuff it with this whole ma'am shit. I am done with it. I'm moody and borderline about to break something. So, either let me have this one ounce of fake freedom or deal with me trying to escape this mad house at every turn. Deal?"

He stares into my eyes as he wrestles with the choices in his head. I honestly think he is trying to figure out if I am for real or just bluffing. Surely he knows how stubborn I am by now. Graham has probably highlighted that description about me and starred it on every document he has given his security staff.

"Okay. Just please do not veer off toward the entrance gates."

I smile big and push past him.

Victory.

Graham does not return my video call from earlier where he promised to contact me back after his meeting. In fact, he goes completely off the grid. No texts. No email. No phone calls. Nothing.

By six o'clock, I have a migraine so huge that the only thing I want to do is lie in the dark and pop ibuprofens like they are candy. I take two each hour until I am finally able to find relief. At eight o'clock, my iPad rings with an incoming call, and I dart off the bed to get the device from my desk. I peel back the cover and sigh when I see that it is Claire who is calling. Where is Graham?

I answer the call and relax on the bed.

"So, you have a doppelgänger," she says in greeting.

"Is she as hot as I am?" I laugh, looking down at my pajamas. My skin is pale and my hair needs taming. Quarantine life is a struggle.

"Impossible."

I laugh over her comment. "Pretty sure I'm unrecognizable right now."

Claire nods. "You do look a little haggard."

"It's one of those days," I admit.

"Naturally."

"So where did you see my twin?" I ask, only because I am curious.

"Welp...I think she is living in our townhouse."

I sit up in bed. "What?"

"So, you really need to start educating yourself during your lockdown and watch some news. I think Graham hired a body double for you. You know, to make your breakup look realistic."

"What are you talking about, Claire?"

"I think he hired someone who looks like you to come and go out of the townhouse but to look really rumpled and sad and hating life."

"How's this different from how I am currently feeling?"

She gives me a once-over with the limited viewing ability that she has from the camera angle. "Yeah, it is strikingly similar. Anyhoo, your double is all over the entertainment shows and in some of the tabloids as being 'The Woman Scorned.'"

"Oh lovely. That's exactly what I need right now. Rumors."

Claire does a half laugh and holds up her phone to her iPad screen so I can see the contents. I squint as the image slowly focuses. And I see it. The girl with sunglasses and wearing an "I Hate Men" shirt is walking up the steps leading to our shared townhouse. I give Graham credit. She does have a strong resemblance to me. I cannot see her eyes, but everything else is very spot-on.

"Your shirt is cute at least," Claire says passively. "And accurate most days out of the year."

"That's not me!" I yell at her, making her jerk her head up from her phone to look at the real me.

"Oh," she says, "yeah, I know. I just got confused for a second. I mean, that is a shirt you would be a fan of wearing. Right?"

"Yeah, sorry. Didn't mean to have an outburst. I literally have been going through my day with a migraine that has lasted two hours that's now down to a dull headache. I'm a bit out of sorts."

"No need to apologize," she says softly. "So, you know how I'm always telling you that bad decisions make the best stories?"

I nod. "Sure, I remember, but it doesn't mean I agree."

"Well, I may have done something impulsive a few weeks ago."

"Okay, go on," I encourage. I could use a distraction.

"Sooo, remember when you and Graham came back to the townhouse from the lake trip, and you found Ethan giving me make-up sex?"

"Yeah, I'm pretty sure that image is forever seared into my brain."

"You're welcome."

"Welcome?"

"Hey, there are worse things to walk in on. At least that round we were doing the sex pretty normally. No toys or swings or kink. Just straightforward, dick-in-vagina, good ol' sex."

I laugh at the casual attitude she seems to have surrounding the topic. "This has a point, right?"

"Oh yeah, my point. I'm getting there. Just chill. These types of stories cannot be rushed. Anyhoo, that weekend Ethan did a ton of groveling and gift buying and panty melt-ing. Well, he has been asking to make a video of us," she says, aiming the webcam lower so I can see her finger pointing toward her crotch for added emphasis—which is highly unnecessary. "In the act."

"Wow. So did you go through with it?"

Claire glances at something off screen. "Yuppers. So

that brings me to my next topic. What are your biggest regrets in life? Here, I'll start," she says, holding up a hand to stop me before I even get a chance to speak. "Hair removal cream and trying to keep up with all things posh."

I laugh. "Umm, why?"

"I burned my kitty."

"You, ah, what?"

She points animatedly down to her crotch—again. "It's fried. Like torched."

"Holy shit, no."

"Yeah, like chemical burned and now it's waiting for the itchy regrowth. I hated myself in the moment. And I still hate myself now."

"So, why did you even attempt this?"

"It all goes back to my sex video," she says with a shrug. "My honeypot was going to get lost in the grass if I didn't remove it. What's the point of making a recording if it doesn't show anything fun? Now everything looks sun scorched. And it ain't pretty."

"I can imagine."

"Yup. So I have been avoiding the sex with Ethan and he thinks I am just on my rag—which is never really a deal breaker for him. But I have been sending him bloody images I find online to pass off as my own. You know, to defer his *appetite* until I at least heal."

I shake my head at her in disbelief. "Of course. Makes perfect sense."

"I hurt."

"Maybe instead of looking up random pictures of vaginas online, you should search for scorched pussy remedies?"

32

"You always sound so logical. It's kinda annoying."

We end the call, and I curl up into bed with my romance novel. I snack on gummy worms and leftover champagne from the morning's mimosas. My stomach rumbles with hunger but I just ignore it.

I do not have enough energy to care.

3

The sound of my vibrating phone lurches me upward from my sleep. My laptop teeters over my thighs, landing on the cushioned surface of my bed. I reach for my buzzing device, just missing the call—sheesh—and apparently six others. I play with the screen, searching through the options to see who keeps calling and find that Graham has that honor. I scroll through the list of texts he left, stemming from his worry of me not picking up. As I continue to read, the same buzzing persists from the incoming call. I hit the "accept" button and wait for the scolding.

"Tell me you're all right," his exasperated voice resonates through the line. "I'm about ten seconds away from giving my men the order to break your door down just to verify you're alive." I can almost see him pacing and raking his fingers through his disheveled hair—most likely driving everyone in his vicinity up the wall.

"What day is it?"

"What *day* is it? Are you kidding me? What the hell, Angie! Have you lost all track of reality? It's Sunday!"

"Wow. I must have fallen asleep," I answer groggily. I try my best to sound competent to end his unnecessary worry. The days, however, are blurring together. I am starting to lose hope that he will ever let me leave here. What happens if he decides it isn't safe after eleven days? Will I just be locked up in my tower forever, waiting for my prince? "I'm sorry you're worried. Give me a second to wake up."

"It is two o'clock in the afternoon!" he growls.

Ugh. "Why are you so angry? The last time I checked, rest and sleep were essential parts of a balanced lifestyle. And I didn't get much last night..." Between the recurring migraine and a series of flipping nightmares, I don't feel rejuvenated at all.

"What would you like me to get you for lunch?"

"I'm not hungry," I whisper absentmindedly, trying to figure out how I completely missed it being Sunday or the afternoon. His snarl shakes me from my thoughts. "Okay, calm down," I whisper, hearing his voice boom through my phone's speaker. Apparently, I unknowingly said the one thing that could evoke such a strong reaction. I wait for the rant and he does not disappoint.

"You didn't eat breakfast, lunch, or dinner yesterday. No, do *not* interrupt me," he warns, making me shut my mouth so he can continue his spiel. "You refuse to even look in the fully stocked fridge and pantry for an entire day. Nor do you place any requests with my men. When offered a meal, you decline. You slept until now and probably haven't had anything to drink in over twelve hours."

"Graham—"

"No. This is pissing me off, Angie. Do I need to hire you a personal cook? Force you to sit at a table in front of my men? Make you video chat with me during every meal?"

But I really am *not* hungry. "You are being extreme," I whisper, trying to calm him down.

"Let me try this again. What would you like me to get you for lunch?" he asks for the second time.

"Umm," I mumble, knowing that I cannot win against the tyrant food police. "Fruit?"

"And?" he probes.

"Pico de gallo."

"And?"

"Pistachios." There, that should make him happy.

"What the hell? Those are like toppings or garnishes or I don't even the hell know," he snaps. "I'm ordering you those stupid-ass items and a steak. And some carbs, dammit. And if you keep this up, I'll send Dr. Saber over to you to monitor the situation."

"No, please," I beg. This is so embarrassing. "I'll eat."

"Good."

I end the call and hop to the bathroom for a quick shower and hygiene tuning. I take extra time to put leave-in conditioner into my hair, brushing through it with a wide-toothed comb. With a careful twist and a hair tie, I have it lifted up off my neck to continue drying in a well-contained heap. It is the most effort I have made with my hair since arriving here. That has to count for something.

I pull out my drawer with my stash of pajamas and find the "I Heart Chocolate" long-sleeve set. The pants have adorable chocolate bars printed all over the fabric. I slip them on and then search for a matching pair of socks.

It does feel weird putting on pajamas in the afternoon, but my days and nights are getting mixed up. And having nowhere to go has made it easier not to care.

I answer the knock at the door and find Collins holding a huge takeout bag of food.

"Mr. Hoffman wants you to video call him when you get everything situated."

My teeth itch with the need to make a snarky comment. But I resist.

My iPad is already ringing with an incoming call before I even get a chance to open all of the boxes in the bag. Graham can be so impatient. I answer the call and see him relaxing behind his desk with his Property of Angela McFee shirt on. It looks good on him.

"Nice shirt."

"My sizzling hot girlfriend made it for me."

"She must be super talented."

"Oh, she is," he says with a beaming smile. "Ready for our lunch date?"

I look down at all of the individual takeout containers, feeling a bit overwhelmed. "Umm, I think so. But there has to be a mistake. This seems like way more food than just for me." I open up the biggest container and reveal a huge porterhouse steak. My eyes grow wide at the size of it and quickly move the box to the side. No way in hell can I eat all of that.

"I'm going to enjoy watching you eat every bite of that meat." *Oh, he can't be serious!?* "Decide to go twenty-four

37

hours without eating again, and I'll bring the whole fucking cow to your door."

I swallow the lump in my throat. He is so unbelievable with his demands. I prop my iPad up on the nightstand to give myself extra room on the bed to spread out the food.

I line up the mixed fruit bowl, a bag of pistachios, and a container of pico de gallo with fresh tortilla chips.

"You have very unusual food requests, sweetheart. But I hope that it meets your needs." His smug smirk makes me want to scream as I eye the makeshift buffet with shock. "Dig in."

I scan over all of the piles and select the fruit first. I remove the wrapper from the plastic fork and spear a piece of watermelon into my mouth. It is delicious. I glance up at the screen and see Graham leaning back in his office chair, his hands folded over his chest, just watching me. I swallow my bite and feel the lump in my throat doubling in size. Is he going to just sit there and watch me eat the entire time? If so, I am going to make it worth his while.

I crack open a pistachio and place it on my tongue. I chew and then lick the salt off my finger, moaning over the taste. I glance up at the video screen between my eyelashes to catch his eyes darken to a deeper shade of blue. A smirk is barely playing on his lips. But I see it.

I grab a strawberry from the bowl and place the juicy fruit between my lips and take a small bite. I try to go as slow as I can, constantly stealing glances at his reaction while I do so.

He clears his throat. "Don't forget about the main course. I know how you love your meat."

"I sure love *your* meat." I smile a closed-mouth smile.

His eyes wiggle with humor. "It loves you too, sweetheart. Now quit stalling and eat."

"Fine," I huff. I take the packed steak knife and start cutting up my meat into little chunks. I arrange the dipping sauces onto the lid of my box and test out all of them until I settle on the chimichurri as my final decision.

When I take more than just a test bite, Graham opens up his carton of food and begins to join me in eating. We talk about nothing important in between bites, waiting for the end of the meal for the more complex topics.

"So, why did you think it was a good idea to tell the world you are engaged to Sophia?"

I watch his demeanor change from lighthearted to serious in a matter of seconds. "I needed to take the focus away from you entirely. Make it seem like we are not together anymore. That I ditched you. Dumped you. Ended everything we had together."

"So it was your idea? And Sophia thinks you two are back in love?"

"I was never in love with her, Angela. And yes, it was my idea to try to convince the world we aren't together, but I had the marketing manager at Jealousy spin the story to Sophia and me as if I was hearing it for the first time, when in fact—"

"It was your stupid idea!" I complete his statement.

"I'll do anything to protect you, even if it means pretending to be with someone I have no interest in being with."

"I bet she is eating this shit up. You're like a snack for an attention-starved whore like Sophia."

"Watch your mouth."

"No. I don't owe her any respect. None. I'm so over this and it has barely begun. You expect me to just sit back and learn about all of these grand ideas you are spinning in your head from the media? You know how that makes me feel, Graham? Well, I'll tell you. It makes me feel like shit."

He puts his fork down, covering his face with his hands. When he looks back at the screen, I can see the visible stress lines on his forehead. He isn't getting enough sleep. "I'm sorry. The last thing I want to do is hurt you. Everything I'm doing is for you. For us. Please just trust me to make these decisions."

"And how long do you think you can keep this up?"

"As long as it takes until the drug ring is brought down."

"That could take months, Graham. Years. This isn't an eleven-day thing. And you can't keep me here forever. I have a life to live. Friends. Classes. A job."

"I know this, Angela! Do you really think I take all of my decisions lightly? None of this is easy for me, either. But right now, it was my only viable choice to keep you out of harm's way—even if just for a week and a half."

"So why Sophia? Why not anyone else?"

"Because I had to make it believable. Sophia and I already have a past. We have already been documented in pictures throughout the past year. And there were rumors that started long before you came into my life. So, it was a natural choice. We work together. She is my model for my company. It won't be hard for anyone watching to see we are—"

"In love," I bite out.

"It's fake. I'm acting."

I huff. "She's not acting!"

"She knows the score."

He is delusional. "Isn't her life at risk?"

"Not like yours is."

"Why not?"

"Because she's a model. She is not involving herself in any affairs other than furthering her own modeling career."

"But I thought anyone close to you would be in danger."

"I have my men on her too. But there is no intel hinting that she is in any added danger."

"Not even now that she's engaged?"

"Not that we can tell. She is playing the self-absorbed fiancée and is making sure she is publicly seen doing wedding planning—not meddling in the crime world."

"She's not playing. This isn't acting for her. She probably thinks she has a chance with you and that this isn't a facade at all."

"Angela." His eyes stare straight into mine, possessing me with their intensity. "I want to be with you. Only you. If anything, that should be clear."

I nod then look off to the side of the room. I want to ask Graham why he had to propose to Sophia, versus just publicly announcing she was his girlfriend. But deep down, I don't want to know the answer. I know what Graham and I have is real. However, I think what he had with Sophia in the past was real too. And it may still be real in Sophia's eyes.

That doesn't sit well with me.

We finish up the call, and I clean up all of the food packages. I put the extra fruit in my minifridge and my pistachios on the desk. I feel so stuffed that I can barely move without feeling like an Oompa Loompa. I am going to gain fifteen pounds while I am here. I can feel it in how my thighs want to bump and grind with each other.

I grab a vitamin-infused water out of the fridge and mosey through the quiet house into the even quieter library. The room is completely soundproof—or so it seems—with the only noise coming from my own breathing. And my loud thoughts. I just cannot shut off my brain. But this is how it is when I have nothing really to do other than think.

Graham has given me plenty to consider in regard to his previous relationship with Sophia. What if it really is not over between them? What if I am just the rebound and he is buying time until he can commit to her? My heart knows that he loves me. My brain knows that she still loves him. So here I find myself in yet another love triangle. One I do not want to be in but don't have a clear exit strategy for either.

In true Angie fashion, I sink into the overstuffed chair and allow my negative thoughts to poison the well. *Momma, I wish you were here right now. You would know exactly what to say to make me stop mentally obsessing.*

But I am all alone. I don't have anyone here, other than the security staff who hide between the walls and only come out of the woodwork if I call or need one of them to fetch me something. Claire and I chat often enough to help my sanity, but it is not the same as having the physical contact that I yearn for and desperately need. I had no idea how much I needed it until it was taken away.

I miss you, James. In just two days, it will be five years since his death. It is also the five year observance of my life getting spared. And for the first time in those five years, I am actually glad it was spared. Maybe it took Graham forcing himself into my life to help me realize that I can find some level of happiness, despite all that I had to go through to get to this point. However, no matter how happy I am, a small part of me is still holding on to the thread of guilt for being able to express that emotion, given the pain that my family endured in the past. It is as if I shouldn't be able to be happy ever again. So when I am happy, there is sadness lingering in the background, waiting to come to the forefront.

———

It is not an easy way to go through life, having two emotions constantly competing with each other and finding superficial conflict at every bend in the road. I want to find meaning in my life, yet it is hard to go about my day when my heart is with Graham.

I feel like days are still blurring together, and if it wasn't for the sun, I would lose all track of time. It is Monday. I only know this because I made a little calendar that I attached to the wall where I mark off the days as they pass. The whole prison-vibe thing isn't lost on me. At least my toilet has its own room. Graham wouldn't have hired an entire fleet of guards if he didn't think I would pull a *Shawshank* and try to escape. I'd be lying if I said the thought never crossed my mind.

My phone buzzes with an incoming call, and I answer it on impulse without even checking the caller ID.

"Hello," I say into the receiver.

"Angela, I am glad I got ahold of you."

43

"Hey, Dad." I try to keep my voice from shaking. "How are you doing?"

"Not the best."

"I'm sorry." I have no idea why I apologize. None of his mistakes are my fault, but yet, I still feel compelled to offer those words of comfort.

"I really need your help this time."

Here I thought maybe, just maybe, he is calling to invite me to lunch or to act like he remembered James's anniversary tomorrow. Maybe he is calling to tell me he put flowers on the grave. Or that the inheritance he took from me and blew through without a care is unacceptable to do as a father. Maybe he is calling to say the same words I just told him. That he is sorry.

Nope. No. Never.

Instead I get the guilt packed upon my shoulders to bear once again and keep me bogged down.

"I can't help you, Dad. I have no money to give."

"Angela, you damn well know that's not true. You are dating a very powerful man who has enough money to spare. Ask him for help. I'm your father."

I swallow down the lump in my throat and pray it stays there. My pulse picks up at the phrases he spews at me. "A father is supposed to protect his daughter, not ask her for money to handle his gambling debts." I am surprised the words flutter out of my mouth so fluently. It is like I have been holding on to them for so long that they have been rehearsed and re-rehearsed over and over again in my head.

"Oh, you are so righteous and holier-than-thou."

Tears fall down my cheeks like pathetic little streams, joining at my chin and then becoming a steady river. I know he is hurting inside. I know that the past decade has not treated him kindly. But it is not my fault. Sadly, I really could have used a dad in my life when I was suffering the most. Instead, I had to continue to grow up a little more each passing day. I had to find ways to continue to take care of myself. And continue to make mistakes and deal with the fallout on my own.

"We broke up, Dad."

"That's a shame. Did he leave you a little parting gift at least? Surely a man like him set you up with a bit of a going-away gift."

I can feel my throat tightening up. "How much do you need, $75,000?"

"If you would have helped me when I asked weeks ago, I wouldn't have the added interest of an extra $25,000," he snaps.

I glance out the window as the sun begins to set. My lower lip cannot keep from trembling as I try to keep my anger at bay. One hundred thousand dollars. How does one even accrue that type of debt? He has to be in way over his head with his addiction or playing high stakes with the hope of gaining back his losses.

"I'll wire it to my Baker City Bank account...the one that has the bare minimum just to keep it open. I'm pretty sure you still have your name on it since I was a minor."

"Yup, I do. Thanks, hon. That sounds perfect." His tone takes a complete turn. His once rough and angry timbre is now soft and friendly. He is not the asshole he was a minute ago. Like Jekyll and Hyde.

Even though I know he is manipulating me, I still feel that embedded desire to please him. Maybe it's some biological preset need—one I have no control over. Or maybe it is just a personality flaw that I have developed over those fragile developmental years as a small child. Regardless, it sucks to be taken advantage of but have no backbone to prevent it or stop the cycle.

I hang up with him and try logging into my Entice account to see my accumulated money and if I can gain back any of the escrow funds with me now being laid off. I know if I ask Nic, he will just tell Graham—who will in turn be involved in more matters of my life that I would like to keep personal.

I cash out what I have saved and pray that no one notices or alerts Graham. Surely if he finds out, he will ask a ton of questions as to why I decided to withdraw the money now. Or what I am spending it on. Which would then lead to another round of questions about why I didn't come to him for help in the first place.

I deposit all of my earned money, including the obscene amount that Graham gave me in an attempt to get me to date only him, into my local Portland bank account. From there, I am able to wire the amount of $100,000 into the Baker City account. It feels like such a waste. Like I am throwing money away and it is not even going to a good cause. I am only helping the codependency that will likely lead to another phone call and another demand for more money.

I eat the bare minimum to not be sick. I drink some water to not be dehydrated. And I move about the house just enough to not cause any alarm among the security staff. I go through the motions, pretending to be okay, when deep down I am full of dread.

I must cry myself to sleep in the comfy chair in the

library because when I wake, it is midnight and officially November 30th—the day my life almost ended. I wish I could say I am doing amazing things with it, given the second chance and all, but I would be lying. My life is nowhere near where it should be.

I had to restart my freshman year due to the accident, and now I am repeating my last semester as a senior. It is the never-ending college experience, where I might technically graduate but with a degree I never chose.

The internship I have been working toward is now further out of my reach than it was last semester. I just wired money to my dad, who only contacts me when he needs more. And my current boyfriend is publicly engaged to his supermodel ex-girlfriend. Oh, and I am locked away all by myself.

No wonder why I just want to sleep away my days and nights. What do I have to get up for anyway?

But I do have to move. Because if I don't, I will be too sore to do much else tomorrow other than lie in bed with a bad back. Sleeping on the chair is not nearly as comfortable as my California king in my room.

I put my book back on the windowsill, grab a water from the main kitchen's fridge, and then walk back to my bedroom. I go through my bedtime routine and lie in bed with my iPad to stream a show to help me get tired. I am going stir-crazy. There are only so many books to read or shows to binge watch or rooms to explore before I just snap.

I miss the outside world.

I miss people.

4

I wake with a start from the middle of a nightmare. It was so real. James was alive, and he was picking me up from the Baker City Community College campus late at night. I needed him. I always needed him. Like always, he came to the rescue. But the rain and fog were too dense. We could barely see. And then...bam.

Just like that. He was gone.

I snatch my phone from the nightstand and see that it is eight in the morning. My head throbs from the stress of the night. I hate today. I was hoping that I would be able to sleep through most of it, but here I am for the first time in days actually awake before noon.

Like every year leading up to now, it gets worse and worse with time. Time heals nothing. The more time that goes by, the longer I have to agonize over that night. A night that is missing so many of my memories. How can I move on when I have so many unanswered questions?

I find my bag that I packed for the trip to Hillsboro and

dig out my handbag. Inside the hidden compartment with the secret zipper, I find my Altoids container and pop it open to find the last two pills. Two. How am I going to cope with just two tiny little pills that barely even work anymore? My head throbs and my heart is suffering from the impact of today. I pop one into my mouth and drown it with a sip from the bottled water on my nightstand. I close the case and place it back where it belongs.

The sound of muffled voices catches me off guard. Maybe Graham has decided to visit after all. I exit the bedroom and make my way into the kitchen as I get closer to the source of the chatter. The first thing I see is the backs of several men standing around the island. Am I interrupting a security meeting? Then I hear the melodic timbre of a female's voice and my jaw drops. I would know that tweeting sound anywhere. If she were a bird, she would be that annoying kind that doesn't shut up in the morning when you are trying to sleep in.

Sensing my presence, Collins, Austin, Owen, and Malcolm turn around in unison to acknowledge me with a professional nod of their heads. Collins's eye twitches and in this moment I know that everything is going to change.

"Oh, hi," Sophia says sweetly to me, peeking around Collins's back. Her smile is bright but her eyes are dull. Fake. Or she just had Botox done and can't express herself from her nose up.

I narrow my eyes at her. What the hell is going on? "Why are you here?"

She glares at me through her artificial ultra-black eyelashes. "Good morning to you too, Angela. I'm here because Graham was very worried about me and always tries to keep me safe. We go way back, as you know. And I've been dealing with a stalker which, quite frankly, is *very* serious."

I give her a nod. There's not too many things I dislike more than fake sweet. This applies to candy and a person's personality. I hate to be cavalier about her woes, but a small fraction of my mind thinks she fabricated her fear to gain Graham's attention. Do I have proof? Well, no. A strong suspicion? Absolutely.

"So you're staying here?" I ask dumbly.

"Yes, Angela. I'm staying here where it's safe for me. Trust me, I enjoy my space, so sharing a roof with you will definitely be challenging for me."

I want to yell that I was here first. I want to tell her to go sleep outside. And I want to strangle Graham for thinking that putting us together was a good idea. Can the day get any worse? Maybe if I was forced to watch videos of the two of them together, then maybe it just could.

Ugh, just the way she says his name—like she has some hold on him—just makes me want to claw her eyes out. I will, too, if she messes with me and causes me to break. Today, of all days, I am almost on the verge. The way things are progressing now, I give it forty-eight hours before I throw her down. That's being generous.

I let out a long labored breath. I guess I should have heeded the universal warning to be careful what you wish for. Because my desire to have company here has blown up in the form of the one person I would choose last to coexist with. Lovely.

I catch Collins's eyes as he disperses with the other men, and I think I see a glimmer of sympathy behind his otherwise stone-like expression. I imagine he has known Sophia longer than he has known me, assuming he has worked for Graham longer than three months. While I do not know his feelings toward her, I would like to hope he would choose my side in a fight. With the way my personality clashes with Sophia's, it is pretty much a guarantee that there will be a battle. Let the best girl win.

I turn on my heel and decide to skip the coffee I am craving and head back to my room to be alone. Before I can make it a couple of yards, Sophia is clicking her tongue and drawing attention to herself. I swallow and choose to ignore her. I can be the better person—at least in the first thirty minutes.

"Angela, darling?"

I roll my eyes and sigh. *Just let me leave.* I turn back around and see Sophia leaning her stick figure against the island. "What is it, Sophia?"

"I was just going to say that I'm glad you're back on your feet after the incident."

I furrow my brow. What is she talking about? "Which incident are you speaking of, Sophia?" I am genuinely confused. Is she referring to the drugging that Mark put me through in the hotel room? Or the riot at The Shack? I have no idea what information she is privy to so she will have to enlighten me.

"You know, the one where you tried to slit your wrists in some dramatic suicide attempt in front of Graham's building."

"What?" My question is barely audible to even my own ears. It is like I am stuck in an underwater tunnel and running out of my oxygen supply. My throat closes at a rapid speed until I can no longer breathe.

"You know, the stunt to gain his attention? I meant to say, *kudos*, it worked. He might be under your thumb now, but he won't stay there forever."

My stomach contracts and my jaw tics. Is that the rumor that is floating around? Or is she just nasty enough to construct it on her own? I want to defend myself. To share with her the truth about the picture frame breaking. But what good would it do? So I muster as much strength as I can to maintain my own composure and just leave. I head to my room to suffer alone.

And I do. As soon as the door slams shut, I fall to the floor with my back sliding down the smooth surface. Damn her. How can she be so flippant about me getting hurt? What happens if I *was* trying to cause self-harm? It was almost like she wished it.

It makes me really wonder what Graham ever saw in her. We are such polar opposites on looks and personality and how we see the world. It is a mindfuck to think that he can be attracted to each of us individually when we are so vastly different.

I allow my heart to break, but I do not shed a tear over Barbie Bitch. My mind goes to a dark place, and I stay there just long enough to remember how it feels. What it looks like. How alone I am. But then I climb out. I am strong— even when I am at my weakest. I cannot allow another person to push me down and gain power over me.

I move to my knees and pick myself up off the floor— metaphorically dusting myself off in the process. I walk over to my personal fridge and remove the bowl of leftover fruit. I drag myself into the bathroom and draw a bubble bath. I have the rest of the day to endure, so I might as well do it with a fresh body.

When my skin is wrinkly and my body is relaxed, I get out of the tub, dry off, and put on yoga pants and an oversized cable-knit sweater.

I flop down on the bed, pull the blankets over my body, and take a nap. Maybe when I wake up, the day will be over and I'll be one step closer to being able to leave.

The sound of an incoming video call wakes me up. It is now three o'clock and I missed lunch. I answer Claire's call and laugh when my screen focuses so I can see her face.

"Nice costume," I giggle. She is dressed like a unicorn.

"Ethan is really into dress-up."

"This is information I could afford not to know."

"Well, he is becoming very needy about it too," she adds, ignoring my comment entirely.

"I needed the laugh, so thanks," I say. She is wearing a horn headband, bright-colored makeup, and a rainbow tutu.

Claire straightens her headband which seems to be a bit top-heavy. "I figure at the very least, you would see this and it may brighten your day. Oh no, did I just wake you up? You were sleeping, weren't you? Do you even know what day of the week it is? I'm sure it feels like Blursday. You're completely living my dream life right now. Like soaking up this lifestyle of the Rich n' Lazy."

I yawn and prop myself onto a bunch of fluffy pillows. "I just want this day to end."

Claire frowns into the screen. "I know it sucks for you. I know you miss your brother. I just want to make sure you know I am there with you in spirit."

"Thanks. Today definitely sucks. And when I thought things couldn't get worse, they did."

"Oh no, what happened?"

"Claire, you won't believe who is here right now."

"The Easter bunny. Santa Claus. One of the guys from Thunder From Down Under," she rattles off, barely taking a breath. "The Kool-Aid Man that the old people reminisce about?"

I shake my head and look at her with such confusion. "No. Not even close."

"Don't tell me, don't tell me. I love guessing games."

"Okay…"

"Give me an itty-bitty clue though."

"Hmm, let me think of a good one."

"Don't give too much away," she warns, clapping her hands in excitement.

"Cartoon voice."

"Tweety Bird."

I burst out laughing. "Not a bad guess, if Tweety Bird was a person."

"Male or female?"

"Female."

"Okay, so not Zander or the Hulk." Her voice trails off and she stares up at the ceiling of her room, deep in thought. She says these things with such a straight face that I cannot even tell if she is being serious or not.

"Ready for another clue?"

"Yeah. So not a cartoon and not a man."

"Correct. Last clue. Barbie Bitch."

"Well, that's basically like giving it away," she huffs,

tossing her hands up in the air, knocking over her headband in the process. "Sophia. Final answer."

"Yup. Bingo."

"Does Graham have a death wish?"

"Perhaps. But so does Sophia if she continues to mess with me."

"Ugh. Can things get any worse?"

"Probably. We could be sharing bunk beds like they do in Girl Scout camp."

"This is true. But what is Graham thinking? He actually thinks it's a good idea to keep his ex and current girlfriend under the same roof?"

"I imagine he didn't have much choice considering we both are in danger, and if we were separated, so would his staff be."

"Yeah, I get that, but I feel like this could have been handled better. Ya know? Like hire a babysitting service…"

"Oh, I know. Anyway, how are things with you and Ethan?"

"Good so far. His ex-wife is a piece of work. But his son is super adorable, when he's not trying to bust down the bedroom door when we are trying to be"—she lowers her voice and leans into her device—"intimate."

"Is he there now?"

"No."

"Then why are you whispering?" I laugh.

"Oh, yeah, no idea. Maybe subconsciously I wanted dramatic effect." She shrugs. "Anyhoo, I have no idea how to fill the role of potential stepmom, but I guess with Ethan being commitment-phobic now after a failed marriage, I won't have to worry about that for a while."

I nod my head and just provide a listening ear. It is hard to believe we are reaching the chapter in our lives where settling down is the next natural step. I still feel so young and have a lot of life goals to reach before I would be ready to marry and have kids. Do I even want kids? I mean, I love them and all. But would I even know how to be a good mommy—especially when I went through half my childhood without one?

"Angie?"

"Hmm?"

"Feel like I lost you there."

"Oh, sorry, I was just thinking."

"Care to share?"

I look up at the screen and giggle over Claire eating a stalk of celery. No peanut butter, no ranch. Just plain old-fashioned celery. I might miss her, but I do not miss the weird eating rules that change based on her mood. "Oh, it wasn't anything worth sharing. Just that it feels weird to be thinking about what will happen after graduation. Seems like I have been in school forever. Ha. In a way I have been."

She sucks her top lip into her mouth, making it disappear.

"Have you decided what you'll do if you get offered the internship in Los Angeles?" I ask.

"No. Part of me wishes I don't get it, just so I don't have to make a decision—and potentially make the wrong one. I feel like if I don't go when given the opportunity, I'll have regrets. But I doubt Ethan's and my relationship can withstand the long distance. Plus, having partial custody of his son makes life tricky."

"Have you heard from your parents?"

"Hmmfph...yeah right. Well, if you count the stimulus check they send me monthly, then yeah, I heard from them."

"At least they are not asking you to bail them out of bad life decisions like my dad is doing to me."

"Again?"

"Yup. I caved this time and answered his plea."

She frowns. "I'm sorry."

"'Tis life. Messy, complicated, wish-there-was-a-hand-book life."

"No truer words have ever been spoken," Claire agrees.

A notification of another incoming video chat pops up on my screen. "Hey, can we chat tomorrow? Graham is calling me."

"Yeah, sure."

I wave goodbye and switch over to Graham. At the sight of his stern face, my heart drops into my stomach.

"Hey you, what's up?" I give him a half smile. "Why do you look so...angry?"

"You and Sophia have not even been together for nine total hours and you're already making her feel unwelcome with your attitude and snide comments?"

"What?" I snap. "She told you that?" *Oh, the nerve of her.* She is something else.

"She said that you were 'huffy and puffy' with her in the kitchen when she first arrived and were nasty when she asked you a question. Said she was very concerned over you and was just trying to be friendly."

"And you believed her?"

"I know how you get jealous—"

I end the call. Nope. Not a chance in hell am I dealing

with this right now. He didn't give me a chance to explain, and his hostility toward my apparent attitude is annoying. I never even had a bad attitude. But, if anyone deserves to have one right now, it is me. I am so over this place that I feel like the walls are going to close in and suffocate me.

My iPad buzzes with an incoming video call. My phone vibrates with a phone call and several text messages pop up on the screen. I ignore everything. He can spend the rest of the day coming up with a good apology. I don't care to hear from him until he can say he is sorry. How can he just take Sophia's word at face value? What kind of hold does she have on him still? And the nerve of her to even fabricate such lies. She was the one attacking me with her snide comments about me trying to hurt myself for attention in front of his building. I growl to myself as I throw on a jacket and shove my feet into sneakers without even bothering to untie them. My hair is still damp from the bath, and the nap only added to its wayward volume. I slide on a red knitted hat with a big pom-pom ball of fluff sewed into the top.

I stomp out of my room and work my way through a path to the nearest exit. Collins catches me at the bottom of the stairs and has his phone up to his ear—probably getting an earful from Big Boss Man. I push right past him and ignore his directives to stop. I unlock the series of deadbolts from the front door and turn the knob. Buzzers blare since I do not bother to put in the code on the keypad, but I just walk out into the fresh air with Collins at my heels.

"Miss McFee, stop. Please."

"No," I say, not even turning back. "I just want to go for

a walk. Please leave me alone. Today's not the day to mess with me. This is your one warning."

I feel his presence shadowing me, but he resists the need to carry on with his talking, for which I am glad. I do not want to talk to anyone right now. Everyone can just leave me the hell alone. And if Sophia has half a brain, she will hide somewhere and not show her face to me for the rest of today. I am not sure I am capable of exercising any self-control.

I walk along the perimeter of the house and find the stone walkway that leads to the back. I veer off and make my own path through the woods when I come across a field. I plop down in the grass and lie back to stare up at the sky. The earth is cold and unforgiving. The clouds refuse to part to make way for the sun and look like they could burst out in tears at any moment. *I know the feeling.*

I don't see Collins or even sense his presence. I know he is watching somewhere, but he is at least respecting my need for the illusion of privacy. I close my eyes and welcome the cold breeze that whips along my neck and exposed skin of my face and hands. I block out all of my thoughts and just revel in the calm serenity of being still.

And I breathe.

I just simply breathe.

Drifting in and out of my awake-and-sleep cycle, I allow my mind to empty. I turn on my side and feel the first droplets of water falling gracefully from the sky. For a second, I think they are my own. I look up and see the rolling gray clouds. Time to haul my butt back into the prison. I am barely to my feet when it starts to pour. I whip around and search for the opening to the patch of trees that border the house when I spot Collins running my way.

"Miss McFee, we've got to go now," he says, grabbing my elbow and guiding me back the way I came.

"You've been out here the entire time?" I ask, out of breath from the jog we are on, trying to get back before we are both entirely soaked.

"All two hours, yes."

Wow. Two hours? My skin is cold and my body aches from lying on the ground. It doesn't take us long to get to the main door, but by the time we do, I am drenched. My sneakers slosh out water with each step, and I kick them off outside and leave them there on the doormat to dry. Their newness is now covered in mud and pine needles.

I toe off my socks inside and hang up my jacket on the hook near the door. My red hat follows. I fluff out my matted damp hair, trying to spark life back into it.

"Sorry you had to stay out there so long. I just needed to clear my head."

"I understand, ma'am. Please call Mr. Hoffman. He's been worried about you since you left the house, and there is only so much I can relay over text."

I nod but only to appease him. "Okay." There is no way I am calling Graham back. He can deal with the limited information supplied to him with the safety reports. I am pissed at him. And I have no intention of trying to get unpissed.

"My shift ends soon, so if you need anything before I leave, let me know."

"Thank you, Collins."

I march back up the stairs and find my room at the end

of the hall. I peel off my damp clothes and hop into the steamy shower just to warm up my body. It feels like the coldness goes deep to my bones. I dry off and decide that it is never too early for pajamas. I select a soft cotton pair from the stash that is just a solid lavender color.

My stomach sends me another reminder to feed it. I haven't had anything to eat since my morning bath when I nibbled at fruit, and it has to be dinner time or later by now. I slide into a pair of fuzzy black slippers and go off in search of food.

The kitchen is fully stocked with all the ingredients to make a salad, a sandwich, or soup. It is six thirty and there is no sign of life in the house. I pull out a loaf of bread, the pimento cheese spread, and the already prepared bowl of salad mix. I use the toaster oven to toast two slices of bread and then smear on a thick layer of cheese spread. I add a balsamic vinaigrette dressing to my side salad and decide to eat at the dining table that is surrounded by windows. I move about the kitchen gathering utensils and a napkin when I bump into something.

"Ouch! Watch yourself."

I look up in confusion at Barbie Bitch. "Sorry, I didn't see you."

"Well, I live here too now. So get used to having to share the space. It is as much mine as it is yours."

"Got it."

"Graham won't tell me the details why you are hiding out here, but I'm sure he is blowing things out of proportion. I must give you credit, you really have him confused. Playing the victim and probably not in any real danger at all. But, that's Graham for you. He's always trying to put out the fires you seem to start."

I turn to walk away, not having any words that will penetrate her skull. I just want to get back to my food. I barely make it three steps when my arm is tugged, making me whip around. "Let go of me and never touch me again."

"Always so dramatic."

I pull my arm from her hold and ignore her comment. I don't have time for this right now. I just want to eat and go relax. I need to forget that Sophia is here and forget that Graham is an idiot to think that this was a viable solution for protecting us both. I would carry my food back up to my room but do not want to give her the satisfaction of believing she is forcing me out of my original plan. I sit down and take the first bite of my sandwich. It is delicious.

In my periphery, I see Sophia adding ingredients to the blender for her health shake. I munch on my food, but the saltiness makes my mouth yearn for something to quench it. I get up and search the fridge for something good and settle on a bottle of pineapple juice. I crack through the protective seal and take a sip to verify that it tastes as good as it looks on the label.

I shut the fridge and pivot. Coldness covers my torso, seeping into my clothes as I stare into Sophia's satisfied eyes. I look down at the green smoothie coating my pajama shirt. Dammit. My nose twitches. My heart races.

"Oops, sorry," she deadpans.

I look at the hand she uses to hold her cup, and the sparkle of her fake engagement ring nearly blinds me. Why is she wearing it around here, flaunting it in my face? She notices me eyeing it and smiles her knowing smile. My vision blurs and when it returns, I see only one color.

Red.

I take the hand not holding my juice and push her —hard.

"Ouch," she says, stumbling back.

"What's your problem?" I ask her. Push. "What have I done to you?" Push. "Why do you keep getting in my face?" Push.

"You're just a distraction to Graham," she blurts out, pushing me back this time. "A temporary one!" Her smoothie drops to my feet.

I have had enough of her shit. I throw my drink at her face, and it hits her nose and then splashes all over her hair, her dress, and her feet.

"This is cashmere," she whines. Then she darts toward me and grabs my hair.

"Bitch!"

I grab fistfuls of hers and tug as hard as I can, as we slide to the floor from the stickiness of the spilled drinks. Sophia lands on top of me and smacks my face with her open hand. I cry out and then flip her on her back, sit up while pinning her down with my weight, and then smack her back. Hard. Two hands pull me off her so fast that I don't even have a chance to execute another. She deserves one more.

"Hey!" I yell, as Austin sets me off to the side.

Owen helps Sophia up and she looks ragged. Good.

"Angela attacked me!" she lies. There she goes, always playing the victim. "I should sue her."

As soon as Austin lets his guard down, I charge forward

and knock her back again. We become a blob of arms and legs as the men try to separate us again. I hate that Sophia has turned me into a violent person, but I feel mentally rejuvenated after physically expressing my feelings toward her. My head is clear. My body is drenched in healthy slime. Yuck.

When the men are sure I am not going to go on another rampage, I am released and able to go upstairs to shower—again. This will make a total of three times today I have either taken a bath or shower. A new record. I snap a selfie of my appearance to send to Claire, with the caption —*Should have seen the other bitch.*

I see several notifications, all from Graham. And all that I choose to ignore. I am so over today.

I dry off and get dressed in yet another lounge outfit. At this rate, I am either going to have to start doing laundry or run out of clothes. Graham blows up my phone with what I'm assuming is his reaction to the report about me attacking Sophia in the kitchen. I hide his notifications and open up Claire's messages.

Claire: Wow. Why do I always miss all the fun?

Claire: How did Graham react? He better choose your side. Everyone needs to know how much of a bitch that woman is.

I message her back.

Angie: I'm ignoring that man.

Claire: Ohhh, ballsy you are.

Angie: He's on my last nerve.

I watch the three dots that indicate a new message and wait for it to be sent.

Claire: Let me know how that goes for you...

Angie: It was a last straw kind of day.

Claire: We both know how possessive he is of you.

True. But he better tread carefully around me. I have reached my threshold and have no intention of being walked on.

5

It takes another two full days of ignoring Graham and avoiding Sophia before I start to return to my normal self again. I needed the time off to gather enough strength to even find the desire to answer his pleas. All he wants me to do is pick up the phone. Slowly, I am mentally getting ready to answer him. I think a part of me is nervous to hear his view on the issues going on here at the house. Everything seems divided. Team Sophia or Team Angie. And quite frankly, I'm not sure where he stands.

Collins is back on the schedule for me and is in full overprotective mode. No longer is he blending in with the walls. Instead, he is waiting at my door like a loyal golden retriever, just in case I want to leave and move about the house. Then, he does what he does best—follows me around.

I think the whole not talking to Graham has gotten to both of them. Collins looks at me as if he is trying to psychoanalyze me. He is walking on eggshells, as if I am going to snap into some violent rage fest. It wears on me that I am now viewed in a different light—completely inaccurate of who I truly am at my core. But there is only so much I can take before I have to stick up for myself. Attacking Sophia was my way of sending a message. Don't piss with me. Don't spread lies. And don't dump nasty-ass smoothie on me.

I can count on one hand how many times Sophia's and my paths have crossed over the past forty-eight hours. But it is really thanks to me that the number is so low. Her bedroom is two doors down. I have learned her schedule enough to know when she likes to get up and where she likes to spend the majority of her time. I made the mistake of trying to visit the library midday. She was sitting in the overstuffed chair, doing her makeup. The angry part of me —that is still holding a grudge from the food fight—thinks she is using the room for other purposes just to annoy me. At no time have I ever seen her pick up a book. So, I have been sneaking books out and just reading them in my bed when I feel the urge.

Graham averages about twenty texts a day, three phone calls, and eight attempts at a video chat. I almost feel sorry for him and imagine he is not being his productive self while worrying over me. I know he is getting reports on my welfare here, but I assume it is not enough to keep him satisfied. When he accused me of not being nice to Sophia when she arrived, it set me on a spiraling path that ultimately made me pull away from him. He doesn't trust me. And that hurts.

My days and nights are no longer mixed up. I have been getting up around nine each morning, putting on semi-real clothes, and brushing my hair. For the first time in days, I am back to enjoying my favorite cup or two of coffee. My anxiety and headaches seem to be under control, despite having the last of my pills the night of the food fight when my shoulder was throbbing. It helped me to sleep and calm down. But now I have none. And the thought of needing the relief and having no means to get it makes me feel on edge. It feels like a giant shoe is going to drop, and I won't be able to lift it off in time to get my next breath in.

I still miss James. Another anniversary is not going to fix that. I often wonder how my life would be if my mom didn't die and James was still here. I doubt I would have ended up in Portland. I definitely wouldn't have met Claire, Zander, or Graham. Some days I feel strong and have pride in knowing how far I have come from the small-town girl from Baker City. Other days, I feel like a hypocrite or a failure. And at my lowest, both of those titles compete for first place.

I walk to the door and peek my head out. Collins is right where I expect to find him.

"How can I help you, Miss McFee?"

"For starters, I really wish you would just call me Angie." The corner of his mouth barely lifts. It is so subtle that if I wasn't already studying his reaction, I would have missed it. "I would like to know if Graham is having a busy day at work or not. I was going to—"

"Mr. Hoffman is never too busy for you, ma'am." Collins clears his throat.

Ugh. I am not sure which I dislike more—Miss McFee or the generic ma'am.

"I was just going to—"

"He would love to hear from you in any capacity. That I'm certain of."

"Okay." If Collins had a tail, he would be wagging it right now. I resist the snicker that wants to break loose from my throat.

"Also, he wanted me to give you this." He hands me an envelope with my name on it.

I take it from his hands and then turn it over and over again. "Thanks. I guess I will break the silent treatment," I say quietly, mainly to myself.

I close the door and get comfortable on my bed. I fluff pillows and smooth out the comforter. I rip open the envelope and pull out a neatly folded letter. My heart drops over his handwritten words.

Sweetheart, I am sorry. I should have trusted you from the start. Please forgive me. I just want to hear from you. I love you, baby. -GH

I read and reread his message. It's as if I can hear his gruff voice in my own ears. This quarantine has disconnected us and did not help us stay on the same page. I do miss him, and I refuse to allow Sophia to come between us. I fold the letter back up and place it on my nightstand. Then I grab my iPad and start the video call. Graham answers immediately.

"Hey sweetheart," he says, with a warm smile. I see his Adam's apple bob in his throat as he waits for me to respond. He is sitting at his private office desk, leaning back in his chair, and steepling his fingers at his chin. His body language says he is relaxed, but the subtle crinkle of his forehead lets me know otherwise. "Nice shirt."

"Hi. Thanks," I say, looking down at my own design that I made with my heat press. It is of a girl stick figure representation of myself. I am wearing a crown, with the word "Quaran-Queen" underneath the image.

"Did you get my letter?"

"Yeah."

"You mad at me?"

I shrug. "I'm hurt. But getting over it."

"I should've listened to your side before casting judgment. I was wrong. Please accept my apology."

"What are you thinking putting the two of us together here? Are you crazy?"

He sighs and sits up straighter in his leather chair. "I couldn't spare to separate my security resources. So having you both at one safe location seemed to make the most sense."

"Yeah, except that we hate each other."

"Sophia doesn't," he says with a shake of his head. "She speaks very fondly of you, baby."

My jaw drops and I just stare at his face for several seconds. "You know that's all a facade, right? She can't stand me, Graham. Whatever she says nice about me, she probably thinks the opposite."

"I get it. Two alpha females in the same house. You both are bound to clash on some issues."

"Or every issue," I correct. "You really don't get it."

"I don't want to argue about this. I want to see how you're doing. And I have more apologizing to do."

"Over what?"

"I completely lost track of time and forgot about the car accident anniversary. I really wish I could've been there for you. Hold you. Comfort you. I know that day must be hard on you."

I turn my attention away from the screen. I sniffle and wipe at my nose. "I'm fine."

Graham's eyes narrow at me, but he spares me by not doing a bunch of follow-up questions. Instead, his eyes start to soften, and I can tell he is affected by my mood—and my silence. "I messed up. And I'm sorry for not acknowledging James's anniversary. I know how profound the day is to you and"—his fingers tug at his hair—"I hate being away from you. I hate all of this shit. I'm frustrated that I can't see an end in sight with this whole drug ring. The closer I think I'm getting to discovering the truth, the more curveballs get thrown. I feel helpless. Like I keep jacking things up with us and that's the last thing I ever intend to do."

My eyes dry at seeing Graham so upset. So many times he has been my rock that it feels different trying to be his support system for once. "I forgive you," I whisper.

"Really?"

I nod. My body relaxes at his smile of relief. I could easily have made him grovel for the rest of the day, but where would that have gotten my mood? Plus, I've already punished him enough by ignoring him.

"Our bedroom floor misses your clothes."

My pussy instantly heats at the implication of his words. I swallow. "I'm so lonely here."

"I know, baby. We'll be together soon. It might just have to be in secret though once you come back into town."

I nod. If having the world think we are separated is a

way to keep everything balanced, then so be it. "I just want to be together. I don't care how."

"We're together, Angie. Nothing has changed in my feelings for you. I know the whole fake engagement to Sophia has not made things easier on your heart, but it is just that—fake. I'm sorry she is there with you, and sorry you two just cannot see eye to eye. And I'm sorry I never trusted you. I have failed you in so many ways. But just know that you have my heart. That's not fake."

"You know Sophia still very much thinks you two have some pull toward each other."

"It is one-sided then."

I sigh and push myself back into the pillows. "But don't you think her feelings toward you are going to impact our relationship?"

"Only if you allow it to."

"It is hard not to, Graham. She is in my face. Flaunting what the two of you had."

"Past. It is all in the past."

"For *you*." I raise my voice. "I wish you could see everything that I see. But you just think that since you don't have lingering feelings, that everything is okay. It's not."

"What are you wearing underneath your outfit today? What color panties and bra?"

Damn him. I would be mad at him for changing the subject if I was not accustomed to doing the same when I no longer want to talk about a topic.

"Hmm, maybe I'm not wearing any."

He exhales. "You better not be walking around that house half clothed. Unless you want my entire staff to be fired because of you."

I reach into my nightstand and grab the big rainbow lollipop that we bought together during our frozen pizza mission weeks ago. I have been saving it for the perfect time and now seems worthwhile. I packed it for the trip to Hillsboro but never used it.

I rip off the wrapper and can hear the squeak of Graham's chair as he leans back. "Playing with fire again, my little pyro?"

I swipe my tongue up the side of the spiral pop as slowly as I can. Graham's low groan spurs me on, making me want to have a little fun. I allow my tongue to extend past the top, flicking it out toward the screen. "Yum," I say, letting my eyes widen and return to normal. "Wish you were here to enjoy it with me."

"You would be enjoying a lot more than candy."

"Hmm, quit being a tease. You're the one who sent me away. Not the other way around."

His growl makes me giggle. "When we're together, I'm going to fuck you so thoroughly that you won't be able to walk normally for a week."

"I sure hope so," I say, with a click of my tongue. I continue licking my lollipop like it is the tastiest thing I have ever eaten. "I'm kind of tired of you playing it safe in the bedroom."

"Dammit, Angela. You're pushing every single one of my buttons right now. And I have conference meetings I need to sit through the rest of the day. How am I supposed to do that being this sexually on edge?"

"Better go to your bathroom and rub one out," I say with a giggle. "I know I'm going to enjoy myself here all alone on my bed. Hmm...wonder if sex toys can be delivered here while I wait out my time?" His dry cough lets me know he understands my message. "Oh, and Graham?"

"What?" he snaps, just making me sink farther into my pillows from laughing so hard.

I lift my shirt up over my head and toss it over the screen so he gets just a quick glimpse of my black bra, before he is shielded from seeing me at all. "Buh bye. Enjoy your day." I end the call as his growl bellows through the microphone.

"Well, that was surprisingly fun," I whisper to myself.

I check the weather on my phone app and see that the day is going to be chilly but dry. I put on my walking boots and dress in a warm jacket and hat. When I open the door to leave my bedroom, Collins is standing his post.

"I would like to walk up to the field again through the forest."

"Yes, ma'am."

I follow him to the main door where he grabs his own coat from the hook. The cold air awakens my senses as soon as it hits my exposed face. I can smell the hint of fresh pine needles, and it is a friendly reminder that winter is approaching.

"Do you ever get bored here just waiting for me to leave my room?" I ask, turning to Collins.

He opens his mouth and shuts it again, as if he is debating on whether or not to talk to me. It makes me sad to think that he could get in trouble with Graham for social-izing with me.

I offer him a weak smile and continue with my mumbling. "I'm bored here. I want to just go back to Portland. I don't even think staying here is making much of a difference anyway. Seems pretty pointless, actually."

"Doubt Mr. Hoffman sees it that way," he offers.

"Yeah? How so?"

"Ma'am, without divulging too much, being here is the safest you've been in months. It is necessary."

"I can't be here forever."

Collins's eyes twitch, and I stop walking to turn to him.

"Graham can't keep me here forever," I warn, propping my hands up on my hips. "That's not realistic."

He nods and keeps his pace, forcing me to keep moving forward as well. We approach the forest. The rustle of leaves and the crunch of twigs break beneath our feet. Naked trees sway with each gust of wind above us, creaking like the joints on an elderly person.

I am surprised Collins didn't give me much fuss when I told him I wanted to go for a walk. Maybe he is starting to accept that I need fresh air for my own sanity. If the walls were feeling like they were closing in on me before, the acceleration tripled with the introduction of Sophia to the house. I hate to think that Graham picked out her wardrobe and bedding and hygiene products. What I think is only special for me may not be at all. This might just be how he operates in general.

The patch of trees clears and the field opens up. It is peaceful here. I am able to think. I half expect to find Sophia lying in my spot, only because she has infiltrated most of my hangout places since she arrived here, tainting them with her nastiness. But I am alone out here, except for Collins, who stays along the border to give me my illusion of freedom.

I find the softest tuft of grass and lie down on my stomach to rest. I kick up my feet behind me and cross them at the ankle, resting my chin on my hands. I wonder what this place would look like in the spring. Would there be wildflowers and birds chirping a pretty melody? Would bunnies be frolicking through the field? Or would there be a crazy ton of mosquitos waiting for a human to arrive?

My phone buzzes with a new text message, and I pull it out of my coat pocket to see that Graham has sent me a picture—of his cock. Wow, my first real-life dick pic. I swallow hard at the sheer size of him. How could I forget? But I do. It has been a week since I have last seen him. Touched him. And my body is thirsty for a taste.

I roll to my back and hold my phone up into the air above me to snap a picture of my face. Then I snap another of my mouth making an O shape. I send him both. The first one I send with the caption—*Wish you were here.* The next one with—*I hope you still fit inside my mouth.*

I get a text back immediately.

The Boyfriend: Fuck, Angie. How can you be wearing layers upon layers and still be so fucking sexy that it makes me get even harder?

I smile over his message. I love that I have some effect on him still. He sure has one on me.

Angie: Why are you sending me dick pics while you are at work? Doesn't seem very productive.

I send him my message with an emoji with a tongue sticking out.

The Boyfriend: I am horny and hoping you will send me something to get me by until I can see you.

Angie: Maybe later. Busy enjoying the fresh air. Chat later.

The Boyfriend: I will be patiently waiting.

Angie: Ha, when have you been patient about anything in life?

I slide my phone back into my pocket and hang out in the grassy field until my teeth chatter from the cold. I pick myself up off the ground and make my way to Collins, who escorts me back to the house.

I amble to the kitchen and put a kettle on the stove for tea. I dig through the fridge and find some hummus when I hear the clicking sound of heels behind me on the tile. Who even walks around a house in dress shoes?

My eyes close for a few seconds. *Please, just leave me alone.*

I continue pulling out pita bread and raw veggies from the drawer, ignoring Sophia behind me. I move back to the stove to check on the kettle and measure out the appropriate amount of loose leaf tea for the diffuser. I add the metal contraption to my mug and pour the boiling water over it.

"Nice shirt," she sneers.

Like before, I choose to ignore her. I focus on making

myself something to eat and fixing my mug of tea. Movement from the corner of the room catches my eyes, and I turn to see Collins hovering in the shadows. My shoulders instantly relax. At least he will be able to act as referee if Sophia refuses to leave me alone.

"You're like beer and I'm like champagne," she says with a smirk.

Think I don't know this already? I have pretty much said the same thing to myself since the very beginning. I smile to myself. Mainly because I know it will piss her off. And if I am going to work hard at being the better person, I need to at least have a little fun while I make the effort.

"You think this is cute, huh? Keeping Graham tied to you but never letting him fully be himself?"

She marches toward me, grabs my elbow to turn me toward her, and yells into my face, "Answer me!"

Collins bolts from his corner and charges toward us, and right before he can separate us, I wind my arm back and swing it forward with as much force as I can get to—

Thwack!

"Ahhh!" she yells, as Austin, who seems to appear out of nowhere, pulls her back and away from me.

But I follow them, throwing my hand at her cheek again, this time open. I am about to get a third hit in when gentle hands bind around me, tugging me in reverse.

"Miss Chantel, go to your room and stay there until I tell you otherwise," Collins directs, his voice stern next to my ear.

Sophia starts to argue, but he just glares daggers at her.

"I'm injured!" she yells. "I need a doctor! Someone notify Graham!"

"Oh, he'll be notified," Collins says, his lack of patience showing in his tone. "Austin, please escort Miss Chantel to her room."

"I really wanted to take another swing at her," I say quietly to him. "She's going to make me lose all my control. Can you at least see how I'm trying my best not to engage with her?"

"You're doing better than I ever would be able to if I was in your position," Collins says, releasing his hold on me.

It is the first time he gives me a real answer and not some polite canned one that seems rehearsed. Then it occurs to me that he could have easily stopped me from attacking her but chose to let me have the chance to even out the score. I smile up at him and mouth a "thanks." I gather my plate and mug, cringing at how my hand is starting to throb now that the shock has worn off.

"I'll get something for your hand."

I watch as he moves over to the freezer and pulls out an ice pack. He then wraps it in a dish towel. "Thanks," I mutter, taking it from him and placing it over the tops of my knuckles. "I'm just glad I didn't break anything."

"You could have, though," he says softly. "The power of the punch needs to come from your middle and index fingers. They have the stronger of the bones. Next time keep your forearm and knuckles in alignment."

I look at Collins in disbelief. "Wow." I shake my head as if I am trying to wake myself up from a dream. "Never in a million years would I ever think we would be talking punching technique right now."

He shrugs, as if it is no big deal. It is like another wall

that he has built around himself has come crashing down. "I'll make sure Mr. Hoffman knows the entire situation."

I look down at the cloth-covered ice pack. "Thank you."

"Anything else I can do for you?"

I shift my weight from foot to foot. "Do you mind keeping the media room free for thirty minutes so I can watch a show without Sophia trying to get me to punch her again in the face?"

"Done," Collins says.

"I appreciate it."

I make my way through the house until I find the dark room with the leather reclining chairs. I grab the remotes and turn on the trashiest TV show series I can find. While I am seeking out something mindless, the dating show has the opposite effect by making me bursting at the seams with sexual tension. Watching these men and women making out and taking secret rendezvous is just making me miss Graham even more. I just want to go back to my room and take care of the itch between my legs.

I take my dishes back to the kitchen to be loaded into the dishwasher, then make my way upstairs to the bedroom. It is four o'clock and I'm not sure I can get through the day without taking the edge off. I take off my top layer of clothes and lean back onto the bed. I pull the comforter up to my neck and settle into the mound of pillows.

I close my eyes and snake my hand down into my satin panties. I am wet. I have been since the video call with Graham. I pull my folds apart and slip my finger inside my entrance, pumping it a few times before sliding it out to play with my clit. Everything feels good, like it usually does, but I am missing one important element—Graham. I need him. I reach for my phone and text him a simple message.

Angie: My body misses the feel of your cock in me.

The Boyfriend: Fuck.

I smile at his one-word answer and type out one of my own.

Angie: My fingers just don't satisfy me like you can.

The Boyfriend: In a meeting and all I can think about is you. And your needy pussy.

I bite my lower lip and feel my fingers get even wetter. This flirting is surprisingly fun, but I think I need to take it up a notch. Why have all of this technology and not utilize it to the max? Graham sends me another message before I can respond to his previous one. I know I have him hooked.

The Boyfriend: What are your hands doing baby? Send me a pic.

I ignore his request and decide to do something better. I grab my iPad and open up the video call app. Then I click his name. It takes several rings before he answers. Immediately I get a text from him on my phone.

The Boyfriend: My kitten wants to be a tiger? Sitting at the head of the conference room table. You're on

mute. Carry on with your fun.

I read over his message and can hear the chatter in the background about profit models and supply order deadlines. I smile seductively into the camera, fold over the comforter to reveal my black bra, and then pull my hand from my panties to lick each of my sticky fingers.

Graham clears his throat and narrows his eyes at the screen, watching every move I make. He looks on edge, almost angry. I prop my iPad up beside me so he can see me from my head down to my waist. I kick my legs on top of the bed and close my eyes as I pleasure myself. I lose myself to the motions, and if it wasn't for the buzz of my phone on the end table, I may have forgotten to check in on Graham. I look at his message and laugh.

The Boyfriend: My palm misses the feel of your ass cheeks warming under the smack of my hand.

The Boyfriend: You deserve to be tanned for pulling a stunt like this—while I'm at work!

I bite my lip into the webcam and type out a response.

Angie: No one is stopping you from jacking off under your conference table. Just keep it classy and discreet.

The look he gives me in the camera makes me burst into a fit of giggles.

The Boyfriend: It's a glass table dammit.

Angie: Hahaha. Maybe no one will notice.

I know this is all going to backfire on me someday. But until then, I am going to enjoy every second of this torture I am putting him through. I will call it compensation for all of the crap he has made me endure over the past few days.

I put the iPad between my legs and bend my knees up toward the ceiling. I pull over the side of my panties and go to work at pleasuring myself. I arch my back and make sure my face conveys how good it feels to have him watch me— while also commanding a room full of employees. It is like I am his dirty little secret.

The deprivation of not being able to be physical with Graham, coupled with the fear of someone getting up from their chair and witnessing me in my state of undress, makes me wild with sexual prowess. For the first time in forever, I am able to get there—on my own. I pull a pillow over my head and moan into the fabric case. After I settle down, I sit up and look straight into the eyes of Graham—who is rubbing himself. He looks huge on the screen, and I know that the size dimensions transfer into real life too.

"Holy shit."

"Holy shit is right," he growls.

"Are you alone?" I no longer hear the other people talking in the background.

"Meeting adjourned."

I smile a cheesy smile as I watch him kick his feet up onto the conference table. His erection springs to its full glory. "Amen for frosted windows," I say with a smirk.

"And for webcams," he says, wiggling his eyebrows. "Take off your bra."

I do as I am told. I pinch my nipples that harden under my touch. "Hmm, spread your legs more so I can see you better," I direct.

"Is this good, sweetheart?"

"Uh-huh. Wish I was there to climb on top of you and slide the whole way down. Just like a flagpole."

"Soon. And when I do finally get my hands on you, I'm going to teach you a lesson for seducing me."

"Promise?"

Graham's eyes darken at my forwardness. I am not usually so brazen. But that is what he does to me—makes me lose all my inhibitions. I lean back in the bed and easily play with my pussy and breasts at the same time—all while watching Graham pull his length. I bite my bottom lip and think about all the naughty things I want him to do to me.

My breath picks up over my own growing desire. I am shocked that my body is still climbing. Higher and higher. I moan and clench my thighs shut as another orgasm over-takes me, just as Graham reaches his. He fists a wad of tissues and explodes into them, throwing his head back as he growls out his release.

"What the hell do you do to me?"

"Exactly what you do to me."

"You make me wild, Angie."

"Feeling's mutual, Graham."

We sit in silence for several minutes, basking in the afterglow of our video sex. My breathing comes back to normal and the sweat on my face evaporates, leaving me a bit chilly.

"Show me your pussy, baby. Show me how it creams for me."

I point the webcam down to show proof of my two releases.

"Taste yourself and tell me what it's like. Remind me."

I drag my pointer finger along my folds and gather some moisture. I turn my finger so he can see and then suck it clean between my lips. "Hmm…" I moan. "I taste a bit sweeter than usual. Maybe from all of the pineapple and fruit I've been eating."

"Yum."

"When can I see you? In person," I specify.

"Baby…"

"Graham, you can't keep me locked up here forever."

"It is way more complicated than I originally thought. I'm working on a solution—even if just a temporary one."

"I'm not sure how much more I can take here without going crazy."

"Just give me a little more time and soon you can go back to Portland. But when you do, you're going to have to stay at the townhouse."

I nod. I hate being alone there. Claire will most certainly be at Ethan's place, and Graham will have to be keeping our relationship a secret until who knows when. He has already said as much.

I watch as Graham unbuttons his collared shirt to reveal the homemade heat pressed one that says "Property of Angela McFee" across the front center. I laugh at his silly expression. "Good…and make sure every single female there knows it!"

His smile is genuine. "I am yours, sweetheart. Just as you are mine."

6

After about a week of being a lazy scrub-a-bum, I decide that Friday is a good enough day to attempt to be productive. The sun is shining through my windows, I feel surprisingly rested, and I have a little pep in my step over being able to connect with Graham yesterday—despite it being short-lived by the inconvenience of him still being at the office.

I start my day with a largest-mug-I-can-find serving of coffee. Collins is in full-blown hover mode. I actually prefer it over the hide-and-seek mode that he was in the previous days leading up to the epic food fight. I think having him as company has helped my mental state. I have made a quarantine candy-eating game out of his stone-like expressions. If I can get him to blush or crack a smile, I can eat a piece of candy from my secret stash of peachy rings, gummy raspberries, and sour worms. It helps to have something to work toward. Because it is survival, I feel zero guilt over making Collins be part of my fun. 'Tis part of the territory for accepting the job of being Graham's Bodyguard Gofer Bitch.

While hanging out in the kitchen with my mug of joe, I check out the pantry and find that it is lacking the main ingredients to make Christmas cookies. Darn it.

"Collins?" I ask from the bottom of the pantry.

"Yes, ma'am?"

I turn around to see him hanging out at the island. He has moved from the shadows and looks to now be on edge more than he did a day ago. This all stems from Sophia being aggressive with her taunting. No one in this house trusts that one of us won't kill the other and then try to hide the body.

"I really would like to make some cookies today but this place has none of my ingredients."

"Start making a list, and I'll get Malcolm to get anything you need."

"Okay, thanks, I appreciate it." I pull open my favorite recipes that I have saved to my email and start jotting down everything I need onto a notepad that is lying on the counter beside the fridge. "What is your favorite type, Collins?"

He glances at me, and if I wasn't watching for a response, I would have missed the bare hint of a blush. Score! I just won a piece of candy.

"I really like gingerbread cookies," he says quietly.

"Okay."

"But the ones that are decorated with royal icing and a lot of sprinkles," he adds.

I laugh over his specifications. Never in a million years would I have guessed he would say what he just did. I guess I was expecting him to say something more rugged, like snickerdoodles or oatmeal raisin. I stare at him and make his blush warm his cheeks to an even darker shade of pink. I count this as a new piece of candy won—because, why not? My game, my rules.

When I finish with my list, I hand it over and then head back to my room to work on some heat press projects while I wait for my ingredient delivery. I find a trashy show to put on the iPad and just enjoy the mindless background noise while I get to work.

I lose myself in my projects, and it isn't until my stomach growls that I realize it is time to eat an early lunch. I shut off the press and walk down to the kitchen to make a sandwich.

"You want one, Collins?"

"Oh, thanks, but I'm good," he responds. "Appreciate it, though."

I wonder if anyone has offered to make him a sandwich—ever. And there it is. A smile! Barely would classify it as one, but a slight curl of the lips, nonetheless. Candy raspberry it is. I text myself a reminder of what candy I will be able to enjoy later, all at Collins's expense. I am up to three pieces already and the day is not nearly half over yet.

I am two bites away from being done with my food when Malcolm shows up with a huge delivery of baking supplies.

"Here you go, ma'am," he says, placing the six bags down on the island. "Enjoy."

Malcolm is a jolly man who has the most personality out of all of the security men who work for Graham. He has the southern gentleman appeal going on—but probably with a pistol attached to his ankle. He could take me to church and to a gun range all within the same day.

"Thank you. You are very efficient," I compliment.

"That's what Mr. Hoffman pays me for," he says with a Cheshire cat smile.

If I was playing the candy-eating game with him, I would have diabetes by now. Malcolm is a natural smiler.

I rinse my sandwich plate and put it into the dishwasher and then prepare my work area for my cookie baking marathon. I get the carols playing on the sound system and dance around the kitchen getting my bake on.

It is four o'clock when I put the finishing touches on my last cookie. I cleaned as I baked, so the only thing left to do is start packaging up my creations into translucent plastic gift bags. I made eight dozen of three different types and feel accomplished. Having a goal each day has kept me from slipping into the darkness, and making gifts for others always has a calming effect on my mood. Who would have thought I could be this productive?

I put six cookies into each bag and use a red ribbon to make a bow at the top. I then skip up to my room to bring down the personalized mugs that I pressed this morning—each with a different message. I add the cookies to each mug and attach a gift tag to the handles.

"Collins?" I call out when I don't see him in his usual location.

"Yes, ma'am," he says, moving into the room.

"I made this for you. Call it an early Christmas gift," I

say, handing him his mug that says *Boss's Main Sidekick* across the side. "I gave you a few extra of the iced gingerbread ones, since they are your fave."

"Wow," he says, turning the mug a few times in his hands and looking at the details, "this is really nice. No one has ever done this for me before."

"Well, you deserve something for you too," I say with a smile.

He reads the words out loud and laughs. "Very accurate."

"I know, right?" I giggle.

"I made Graham a set of mugs for Christmas but don't tell him, please."

"This is one secret I can keep," he promises. "Thanks again for my gift. Mr. Hoffman is a lucky man."

"Is it okay if I take a walk to the field before it gets too dark to see?"

"That's fine. Just dress warm—it is cold out there."

"Okay, let me go change and I'll be ready in ten minutes."

"Sounds good."

"Oh, can you pass out these gifts to the other men? I made everyone one. They are labeled."

"Of course," Collins says with a genuine smile. It is so pure that I have to count it as two pieces of candy.

I jog up to my room to put on warmer clothes. Pajama pants and a T-shirt will not cut it. I put on leggings under a pair of soft denim jeans. I layer a thermal shirt with a thick knit sweater and slide on wool socks. When I get downstairs, Collins is waiting for me—already dressed—with a black and red plaid fleece blanket in his hands.

"So you don't have to lie on the cold ground," he says, handing it to me.

I smile at him and nod. I really hope he doesn't work so hard for Graham that he is unable to have a life of his own. He would make a great catch for a lucky woman, assuming she is attracted to the strong and silent types. It would be fun trying to pair him up, but I assume Graham would be furious if I helped him lose his right-hand man to a woman.

As soon as the front door opens, I feel the drop in temperature. It is the coldest day so far since I arrived here, and the sky looks angry. No longer is the sun visible from this morning. It's like it went into hiding and refuses to come out again until spring.

I zip up my fur-lined coat, slide on my matching boots, and place the red pom-pom hat on top of my head. I adjust my long wavy hair along each side of my neck and slip on a pair of red gloves to complete my attire.

"I may have overdressed," I mutter to myself, as I look down at all of my gear.

I lead the way out of the house, and Collins follows at a safe distance behind me. We take the walkway around the house and then make the path through the woods. I have been frequenting the field for so many consecutive days that the brush and twigs are sunken in from our walking. It takes me a few minutes and then the trees part and the field comes into view.

I find the perfect spot to unroll the blanket and spread it out in the middle of the pasture. I fix the corners and smooth out the fabric. Then I lie down in the middle and look up at the dark clouds. I start my favorite love music playlist on my phone and relax on my back, with my knees bent upward.

I sing to myself and let my body mold into the ridges of the earth. It has been eight days since I arrived here. I miss...

Home.

I miss my life with Graham at the penthouse.

I feel it before I see it—the cold droplets of flaky snow fall peacefully from the sky. Each unique, but yet a relative to the next. I open my mouth and catch one on my tongue. And then another and another—each dissolving in the heated sauna of my mouth.

There is something magical about the first snowfall of the season. That even though plant life is dormant, there is still hope for upcoming new growth. I roll to my side and prop myself up on my elbow. The sky is darkening, and I can barely see the white specks on the red and black blocks of the fleece blanket. I look toward the woods and in the haze of falling snow, I see the image of the man I love. Walking slowly toward me.

I blink. And blink again. How can it be?

I move up to my knees and watch as his smile broadens at the sight of me. He is real. He has to be. I jump up and make a running dash across the field. My hair whips behind me at the suddenness of my movements, and when I am within reach of his open arms, I leap into them and wrap my arms around his neck. My lips crash into his, and I pull his hair at the nape of his neck, tugging him closer—becoming one.

His arms slide under my butt, and he hoists me up

higher into the air, as I continue kissing him with rigor and pent-up need. He growls and squeezes me tighter.

"Graham," I rasp out, as soon as I break away to get some air.

"Sweetheart, I missed you."

He places me down on my feet but keeps his hands on me at all times. I look up into his eyes with confusion. He kisses me on my forehead, then places his cheek in the same spot as he grips my body to his.

As the snow falls around us, his hand slides down to my lower back and rests comfortably in the valley of my curves.

I pull back to look up at him again, afraid that if I stop looking long enough, he will disappear. "I thought we couldn't be together right now," I whisper.

He smiles down at me. "We can't. But I couldn't stand it any longer. I had to see you. Check on you for myself. I have an image to keep up back in Portland, so I can't stay long." His brow furrows. "I miss you, baby."

With one hand on my back, his other hand pulls my neck forward as his lips connect with mine. He is like fire and ice, burning the memory of his touch into my brain. As if I could ever forget.

The hand that is on my neck moves down to capture my hand. He spins me and draws me back to him, dipping me down. I laugh up into the sky, never fearing that he will drop me. He is always there to catch my fall. His head buries itself into my chest and when we are upright again, with both feet on the ground, he captures my lips for another kiss.

I want to stay here, alone in this field, dancing in the snow—the *first* snow—forever.

His teeth tug at my bottom lip, tweaking it with the sharpness of a bite. "You are so beautiful. And all mine," he murmurs, making my insides warm from just his words of affirmation.

My lips pull up into a smile, as he slows down the movement with his grip. When he finally lets go, he reaches down for the big cloth bag at his feet. I never even noticed it until now.

"Up for a snack?" he asks.

"Mm hmm," I hum.

We walk hand in hand over to the blanket that is now damp with a thin layer of snow. I shake it out, as Graham pulls out a series of objects from his bag. I settle in on the freshly cleaned blanket and watch with eager anticipation over what he brought.

"Thought we could make some s'mores," he says proudly, pulling out a portable fire pit and all the fixings.

He places two battery operated lanterns on the edges of the blanket and turns them on for added light. Then he adds the wood to the pit and starts the fire with ease. He wraps us both in an oversized wool blanket and hands me a metal pole for toasting marshmallows.

"Wow, you're like the sexiest Boy Scout."

His huge grin makes me giggle. I rest my head on his shoulder as he sets out to make the best marshmallow. I watch as he slowly turns the stake until the white fluff ball is an even golden tone.

He places it on top of the chocolate square that rests between two graham crackers and smooshes it down. He places the sandwich between my lips, coaxing me to bite. I chomp down and chew the stringy goodness.

"It's delicious," I say with a moan, licking at all of the crumbs sticking to my lips.

"Here, I can help," Graham says, leaning over to suck at my lips, tasting me. "Yum. Good, huh?"

"Better than sex."

Graham stops midbite and stares at me in disbelief. "You wound me."

"Been so long, I hope I don't forget what to do."

He bursts out laughing, making me join him. We finish the s'more together, while I toast up another marshmallow over the tiny fire. Snowflakes fall on my nose, and I try to lick them up with my tongue. The lantern light, coupled with the flicker from the fire, makes the snow on the ground glisten with a beautiful sparkle. Like billions of little ice diamonds scattered across the field.

I pull out my phone and take a selfie of Graham feeding me a bite of s'more. I look hideous with white strings of marshmallow stuck to my chin. And the lighting from the fire casts a weird glow on my skin—and not the flattering kind. But I laugh anyway, because it feels damn good to be together again.

"Thank you for coming here," I say, resting my head on his shoulder. "I really missed you."

"Baby, I've been going insane being apart. I hate this just as much as you do. But I'm working with Nic and the field ops team to figure out a plan. You've been keeping Nic's FBI affiliation a secret, correct?"

"Of course. I would never want to jeopardize anything or put anyone's life in danger."

"Okay, good. Not many from my security staff even

know we are brothers. The fewer people who know, the better."

I nod and snuggle in closer to him, as he wraps the blanket around us tighter.

"It hasn't been easy here," I admit. "Some days are not good days."

Graham places a chaste kiss on my forehead. "We'll be together soon, sweetheart. And then nothing will touch us."

"I have classes to attend. I'm almost done with my last semester before I graduate. I'm scared about my future if I can't get the internship I want. I'm so used to failure, but for some reason I can't accept not being the type of journalist I am striving to be."

His body goes rigid. I know he is not happy with my choices. But they are my choices. My life. We stare at the dying flames and watch as the smoke blends in with the foggy exhales of our own mouths.

"Life isn't always black-and-white, Angie. Sometimes doors can open that you never thought you wanted. I really wish you would consider other options for your career choices. Because this stubbornness you have toward bringing down a drug ring isn't going to happen. I refuse to sit back and watch you run into the fire, when you know damn well that you're going to get burned."

"I know more about life than you give me credit for, Graham."

"I just want you to be safe. Is that so much to ask for?"

We sit in silence as we encounter the umpteenth stand-off. How are we ever going to move past this? This isn't a crossroad where I have multiple choices. This is basically the end of the road. I either turn around and go back to having a life, where English is my major and everything is uneventful and bland, or I push through to the end and go off the pavement, where the dirt road can lead me to amazing opportunities in my writing career. Play it safe or take the risk? Those are my only two options.

Sometimes it is just easier to lie. "I'll think about another topic to write about. I still have some time to figure it out."

My comment earns me a passionate kiss that pushes me back into the snow-covered blanket. A few flakes stick to my eyelashes and disappear with each blink. I roll so I am on top of him and nearly kick over the fire pit in the process. I smile down at Graham and kiss his cold, red nose. I rub my lower half along his, laughing at how it is possible to achieve the needed friction with this many layers of clothes.

"I want you," he says, each word drawn out.

"I fear you forgot how to take me."

And just like that, I am rolled over, tossed into the night air, and hoisted over Graham's shoulder.

"I'm going to show you just how much your body remembers mine," he says, smacking my ass as he saunters through the field. It is so dark out that the help of a solo lantern is the only thing that gets us back to the house.

"What about all the stuff we left behind?" I ask, out of breath from all of the bouncing I endured from Graham's eager stomping.

"It's being taken care of. Just worry about getting that pussy of yours wet enough to grant me easy access. Because, sweetheart?"

"Hmm?"

"I'm going to devour it."

"I sure hope so. I'm a bit tired of you always playing it safe." I smile as I stare at the back of Graham as he makes his way up to the front of the house. Suddenly fingers wiggle at my sides and I jerk upward, trying to get away from the tickling. I am asking for it; this I know. But it is too much fun to harass the man after over a week of not seeing him in person. I whip off my winter gear in a hurry but fall down in the process of trying to get my boots off. I land on my butt in the foyer into a small puddle created from all of the melting snow. "Ouch!" I yell at the suddenness of the fall. Then I burst into laughter as Graham stares at me. "I'm a hot mess."

He shakes his head in agreement. "But all mine." He pulls me from the floor and wraps me in his arms. His face buries itself into my hair, and he inhales my scent. "You smell so damn good."

"Oh, Graham, is that you?" Sophia's tinny voice ringing from behind us makes me cringe from the sheer, unnatural sound of it.

I tense in his arms but don't even bother to turn around to look at her. I half expect him to let go of me, but instead he kisses me hard on the lips and then glances at her in acknowledgment. "Hey Sophia, I came to see my girl."

"So nice," she says with an octave even higher than her normal squeak. "She hit me, you know? Twice."

Be glad it wasn't more.

"And every security guard here said you deserved it," he says casually, making me giggle.

"That she did," I mumble. "Bitch better be glad Collins rescued her from another flying fist."

"We'll have to catch up later, then." She is hinting, borderline flirting with her tone. "There are two sides to every story."

I want to be catty. I want to be aggressive with my PDA. But I choose not to. When she goes low, I want to go high. So, I keep the rebellious pent-up teenager living inside my head at bay. I am sure she'll break out sooner or later. Sophia seems to have that effect on her.

Graham says goodbye to her and drags me up the stairs by my hand. He pinches my butt cheek and makes me squeal at the shock of it.

"Get your ass undressed," he demands as soon as the door is slammed shut and locked.

I decide to have a little fun and take my time removing an item, then folding it perfectly. I start with my socks and then my first top layer. I make a show at the neck hole getting stuck over my head and then struggling to get my arms out—for at least twenty seconds. Pretty sure I look like a deranged octopus, but it is fun nonetheless—well, until Graham saunters over to me and starts pulling articles off of me.

He narrows his eyes when he gets the top layer off and then looks down at the bottom layer of leggings and thermal shirt. "Is this some kind of joke the universe is playing on me? Were you planning on a blizzard today?"

I giggle loudly at his exasperated expression. "You better hope there's not a chastity belt on underneath."

He chuckles at my facial expression and tosses his hands into the air. "Nothing surprises me anymore."

It takes seconds for the rest of my clothes to create a pile on the floor. And once his join mine, we are on each other.

VICTORIA DAWSON

My hands fly around his neck and I climb him like a tree, wrapping my legs around his naked waist. Graham walks us back to the bed, and every movement of his thighs sends his cock harder against my core. He tosses me onto the bed and then pulls me down so that my legs are spread and my bottom is resting against the edge. He slides to his knees and his mouth sucks the moisture from my apex greedily.

"You taste divine," he says between licks. "Like the most delicious cherry."

I writhe on the bed in pleasure. I am so horny that I know I won't make it— "Ahhh!" I scream out, pulling at the sheets. Graham's hands hold me still, and he continues with his beautiful assault. I pant and moan and twist and tremble as a powerful orgasm flutters through my body. I feel it from my head all the way to my toes. My entire body vibrates from the pleasure.

Graham pulls away, kisses each of my inner thighs, and then crawls up onto the bed to straddle me. His arms snake around me, and he hoists me up farther on the bed, so that my entire body is on the mattress. He lines his cock up at my entrance and pushes forward into the warmth. He swallows my moans with the seal of his mouth on my lips. His tongue dances with mine. When the rhythm he sets is too slow for my liking, I thrust up, trying to increase the pace.

"So greedy," he coos.

I bite his shoulder, and he growls over the pain. He pulls out, flips me onto my belly, and then helps me to get on all fours. I crane my neck back to see him in his full glory. Sweat beads on his forehead and his skin is flushed with need. I wiggle my ass back to try to get him to continue what he started. I don't have to wait long. Fingers dig into my hips, and I am jolted forward as he surges inside me, from tip to root. I am stuffed full and loving the feeling of this angle.

Graham pumps in and out of me from behind, while I meet him thrust for thrust. My knees start to get weak as my climax builds. I move to my elbows and press my cheek into the pillow, as I allow my body to succumb to the force of the orgasm.

"Ohhhh!" I call out. "Fuck me, hard!"

Graham tips his hips and hits my sweet spot, sending me straight into another wave. His cock hardens, and he takes one more push forward until I feel the warning twitch and then the flood of liquid heat. He pulses within me until the last drop is released. Then he pulls out and flops down beside me, curling me up into his chest to rest my back against his torso. His hands snake around me, and I am cradled in his love.

"That was overdue," he mutters, smiling against the shell of my ear.

"How long can you stay?"

"Just until early morning, right before dawn."

"I should be ready to go another round in a few minutes."

"You are insatiable."

7

Graham stays true to his word and is throwing on clothes in a hurry at five in the morning. I want to wrap my body around him and beg him to stay. I know he wants to, and that is the only reason I am not trying to make him feel guilty for leaving me. Especially now...especially when I have had a taste of him. My body is the best kind of sore and I have not slept but maybe an hour—and that is being generous.

"I'm going to really miss you," I whimper, my lower lip trembling beyond my control.

He walks over to me, wraps me in his arms, and kisses my ear. His nose burrows into my hair, and he inhales my scent as if it is his oxygen, memorizing me in every way he can.

"Soon."

His one word gives me hope. As if him saying it makes it a possibility. I snake my hands around his waist and slide them up under the back of his collared dress shirt. Then it dawns on me what day it is.

I look up at him with confusion and whisper, "It's Saturday."

He nods and then looks past my head to the artwork on the wall. "I have to take a trip."

"A trip? For business?"

He pulls away from me after a quick kiss on the lips. I throw on whatever clothes I find on the floor and follow him out of the room. Collins greets him in the hall, and they exchange their super-secret looks with just their eyes. They make me want to hit something. I stomp behind Graham as he sighs, pushes hair back from his forehead, and then proceeds to walk down the stairs.

"What's going on, Collins?" I ask, since Graham is not helping to clue me in on the plan.

The smell of lavender and musk fills my nostrils before I see the source. But I don't have to look. I know who it belongs to, and the thought of what I think is about to happen makes me want to vomit.

"I'm all ready to go, Graham," she says sweetly in the foyer.

Graham's body whips around to shoot Sophia with daggers. "You were told to wait in the car."

She has the nerve to feign innocence. "I had to use the restroom before our drive to the airport. If we go now, we might be able to catch the sunrise. You remember how much I love watching the sun rise up to—"

"You guys are going on a vacation?" I ask stupidly.

"Just get in the car, Sophia." Graham's temper is exacerbated every time she opens her damn piehole.

Why he thinks her being in the car would erase the fact they are going on a trip together is plain stupid.

"Florida is going to be amazing this time of year. I hope we can go snorkeling. I've always wanted to try that, or maybe we can swim with turtles? You know, for the press."

Collins steps from the sidelines and opens the front door for her to step through, but she doesn't budge. Of course she doesn't.

Her attire is perfect for a jet-setting lifestyle that she is taking up with Graham. Her tailored ivory pants, designer shoes, and black silk shirt fit her persona and her body like a glove. Her hair is slicked back with a clear stone barrette, and her engagement ring is polished and ready for the world to see its beauty. Her luggage is resting at her feet. I don't even own luggage. Not even one suitcase. The contrast between our appearances, our personalities, and our lifestyles is night and day. Black-and-white. But here we are, pining after the same man. How can we be worlds apart and still find the same person attractive? How can he ever do the same with us?

Tears well in my eyes as Graham groans and turns to look at me. My vision blurs as I look up at his pained expression. Did he think I wouldn't find out? Was he just going to sneak into the car and hope I didn't notice Sophia accompanying him? I get that they are faking an engage-ment—but this? A vacation? And to go to Florida? Is he taking her to his family's home?

I swallow down the stomach acid that keeps rising into my throat. Damn him. The look written all over Sophia's face is that of pure joy. She smiles over at me, and I want to gouge her eyes out with her own stilettos. Because who dresses in stilettos when there is snow and ice on the ground?

She won. She knows it. She is already getting every-thing from Graham—albeit fake—that I have always wished for from someone I love.

I turn to walk back to my room and Graham calls to me, hot on my trail. I make it up to my room and lock the door before he can enter.

"Angie! Open up!"

"No!"

"Come on, baby!"

"No!"

I am too old for this high school jealousy drama, but I guess I am just that—jealous. I stomp into the bathroom and slam the door. I have a splitting headache and I just need to find some ibuprofen or Tylenol to take the edge off the pain. I dig under the sink but only find cleaning products. Then I try the storage closet. Nothing. Shit! I cannot survive the day without anything to cope.

I splash my face with cold water and glance up into the mirror to see the reflection of a girl in pain. Physical and emotional pain.

I hear the sound of the doorknob turning and see Graham lean into the doorway.

"I'm sorry, baby."

"You happen to say that a lot these days, Graham. Always sorry. Yet no real solution on ending the cycle. I'm not sure how much I can take before breaking."

He exhales. "Everything I'm doing right now is for appearance purposes. To keep you safe. This is all for you."

"Appearance purposes?" I ask, feeling more and more stupid with every word he speaks.

"Angela, I have to publicly make it known that I'm with Sophia. I may not have the paparazzi setting up camp outside the door, but there are reporters following me around and trying to catch Sophia and me together."

"America's favorite couple," I mumble, leaning my butt against the vanity. "Hottest bachelor in Portland engaged to America's sweetheart. You guys are basically the power couple everyone wants to live vicariously through." Lovely.

"You are the only woman I ever want," he says, stalking toward me. "Ever. But I need to take this trip and get Sophia out of the state. So a fake vacation is what's necessary."

"Why not get me out of the state?"

"I can't be away from you."

"How do you even figure that if you're going on the plane with her?"

"I'm coming right back. We won't be gone long."

"I just don't get it, Graham. Why do you have to go through all of these extravagant gestures…with her?"

"I would love to hide you away from the world and keep you safely in a box where no one can hurt you, baby. But you withdrawing from classes would not be the natural thing you would do. So you have to be in Portland in some capacity."

It's true. But I don't like this plan of his—at all. He basically came here to escort Sophia for a rendezvous trip to who knows where. And even if that is not technically true, that is how I feel, and he can't make me change my mind otherwise.

"Enjoy your trip," I bite out.

Graham steps closer to me, pulls me into his arms despite my reluctance, and kisses me hard on the lips. "I"—kiss—"love"—kiss—"you."

"If only love was enough," I choke out. Tears fall from my eyes, and I push him away to get him to leave. "You're going to miss your flight, I assume. So go." *Enjoy the damn sunrise.*

I follow him out of the room, and we make our way to the front door of the house. Sophia is leaning against the front door, reapplying her powder foundation with a little cosmetic mirror. She looks flawless.

I give Graham one last kiss and hug before he slips out the door with Sophia. She grips his elbow for support, so as not to fall on the slick surface with her sky-high heels. I wipe at my tears, and Collins offers me a tissue from beside me. I didn't even realize he was there.

"Thanks, Collins," I sniffle.

"Of course, Miss McFee. For what it's worth—and you know I never interfere or say too much—but you are *it* for the boss. Don't doubt that."

I nod and continue my silent crying as I watch the car pull away with a part of my heart inside. How can I continue to keep going about my day when my thoughts are going to be tainted with the image of Sophia trying to get her hands on my man? I may trust Graham, but I sure as hell don't trust her.

Collins waits beside me, probably in fear that I will crumble to the floor in a sobbing mess. I pull myself together, roll my shoulders, and seek out some relief for the tension building behind my eyes.

"I have a splitting headache over all of this. I really need some medicine. Can you please get me some?"

"Of course, ma'am. I'll call Dr. Saber and see what I can do."

"He's not my physician, Collins." And he already was reluctant to give me anything after I hurt my palm and after the hotel debacle. There's no getting him to cave and prescribe me something more powerful than the watered-down drugstore shelf bottles—which I've already depleted. "I just need something OTC right now. Maybe something extra strength? Do you have anything here or do any of the men have anything?"

"I'll ask, ma'am. And if there is nothing, I will send out for it immediately."

"Thank you."

It doesn't take Collins long to knock at my bedroom door. I squint from the light filtering into my dark room from the hallway. It makes my eyes burn and my forehead pulse from the ache. I look into his hands that hold three bottles of painkillers and smile weakly.

"You're in luck. Owen has a full stock here after he had some dental surgery done last week."

"Thank you," I say, taking the Motrin, Extra Strength Tylenol, and Aleve out of his hands. "This should give me some relief."

"He said you can just keep them. He had a prescription for Tylenol with Codeine so he ended up not needing these. Had them just in case."

I give him a single nod, extending my hands to collect the bottles. My head is throbbing, and I need to get the pain under control before I can feel human again. I close the door, not bothering to turn the light on.

I pop off the lids to the pill bottles and take one of each. Surely something will start to work soon. I crawl back onto my bed and rest my eyes, hoping for some relief.

It is just after eight in the morning, and I'm already frustrated with the day. But today is Saturday, and if I'm going to transition back to real life on Monday, I better have something to show for it.

When the tension in my head starts to ease marginally, I roll to my side and turn on my phone. No new messages. No new voicemails. Nothing.

I log in to my Bad Advice email and scan through the messages until I find one that is intriguing.

Dear Bad Advice,

I think I may be in love with a figment of my imagination. I have been infatuated with a girl online for eight months. But we never met. She always has an excuse as to why it is not possible. I want to just give up on her. But what happens if this is the love of my life, and she is just being shy?

-Potential Victim of a Catfish

Hmm… This one is tricky and super interesting to me. I can understand the need to physically see a person in order to verify love. But to start falling for it initially? It would be realistic to think that it starts in the mind and the heart first —before physical attraction takes root. It is hard to be my sarcastic self on this one, but I try. It's the theme of my blog, and I have to stay in character. However, I really want to follow up with the question asker and see how this all gets resolved. The obvious solution would be to make the girl video chat.

> **Dear Potential Victim of a Catfish,**
> **This girl (or dude) may be playing you, but why not have some fun and play her back?** Add some fun filters to your pictures and jazz up the upper body muscle virtually. Face swaps can be fun too. Get her to buy into the new revised version of you... So when she breaks up with you before seeing you or reveals she really is a man, then at least you have some amazing photos—and the experience—to use on the next girl.
> -Bad Advice

Knowing that Sophia is no longer lurking in the house, taking over my favorite rooms, I am able to move about freely once again. I carry my laptop into the library and set up shop on the desk in the middle of the room. I walk back to the kitchen to prepare a mug of coffee and use it to help with the swallowing of three Tylenols and one Motrin. Surely the caffeine coupled with the painkillers will help me cope. I have a lot of work to get done and lost time to make up for.

I wonder what Graham and Sophia are doing right now. It's like he went off the grid, and I'm too stubborn to reach out first. Are they sharing a mimosa on the private plane? Reminiscing about old times? Talking about the jewelry industry? I think the not knowing aspect is the hardest part.

My mind jumps to worst-case scenarios easily when she is involved. So, maybe she is napping on his shoulder, or moved down into resting her head on his lap. Ugh.

When I get back to the library, I decide to start consolidating all of my research into one document. I need to have something solid to show to Dr. Williams if I want to pass the class. I open up my secret email and copy and paste all of the photos I have taken into one blank document. This helps me to analyze any similarities between them. I will not be able to include the photos of people in my printed article, but I can at least use them to help me to push forward with my investigation.

Graham already thinks that Mark is not the only key player in all of this drug mess. He thinks someone else is pulling the strings. I doubt it is Paul. He seems too young to have that type of authority. After all, he is a frat boy in college. I am nearly positive he is just the middle guy, helping to drug the girls, run interference, or act like the hero to push suspicion away from himself. However, it is best not to completely eliminate him from my prime suspects list.

The series of photos involving Benjamin, Samson, and Edward all seem bland. Nothing stands out. They are the men who like to speak in non-English languages. I type in voice translators into my Google search engine and try to find the best one that may help me transcribe the low quality audio tracks of the video recordings I took when I would go on dates with Mark. Graham confiscated some of my footage that I was trying to collect from the Halloween party and the Maylord Hotel incident, so I am missing a lot of data as is.

Through my random research, I come across a blog post that catches my eye and reminds me of the *Bad Advice* post I just published. This particular one is on how a US citizen discovered that her foreign boyfriend was catfishing her for a year on the Internet. He was getting her to send him nude photos by sending her some of his own for encouragement —except they were not his. They were stock images that were boosted from a porn site. Her post talks about the devastation she went through and how she wasted eleven months of her life by believing the person she was messaging was someone he was not. She proceeds to share how she used a reverse image search to discover that the photos her supposed boyfriend was sending her were, in fact, fake.

I type out some personal notes on how a picture can be uploaded online and searched on the web to see if there are matches. I can feel the break of her heart in her personal blog post where she bares her soul for anyone willing to read it. Ugh, that sucks.

I doubt I would be able to do the same thing she did with the photos I gathered. For one, I know they are not stock images. For two, the quality is mediocre at best. However, this whole searching the web for similar photos has driven me to the idea that maybe I could use software to see if facial features match with any other photos from the Internet.

I google the words "facial recognition" in quotes and get a dozen search topics on software that specializes in analyzing faces in photos and pairing them with already stored images on the web. This is a potential game changer, assuming the quality of mine are good enough.

I sit back in my chair and kick my feet up to ponder over this revelation for a minute. I take a sip of my coffee and pinch the space between my brows with my fingers. My headache is still present, but not nearly as painful as it was an hour ago.

I grab my phone and open the App Store to see if this type of software is readily available to the basic consumer. I type in the search bar and discover that twenty different apps exist. I find the one with the highest star rating, but also with a decent amount of reviews, and then I click on it to download to my phone. I walk myself through the tutorial, then start putting photos into the database. The software targets each face individually and then scours the Internet for potential matches.

I start with Mark Tanner. I use one of my personal photos for the search, but I also retrieve one of him from the web that is of higher quality. The app spends several minutes processing the match and buzzes when the search is over. Ten photos supposedly match his face—which doesn't seem like many. I guess Mark keeps a low profile and tries to avoid much of an online presence.

I really wish Zander was here right now to help me navigate this challenge. He would know the best way to organize all of the information I am digging up. Instead, I have to go back to basics and just copy and paste the images I gather into a blank document, taking notes as I go. Doing things this way helps me to see them all on one screen, instead of having to flip through each individually.

Half of the photos I gather on Mark are solo images where he is attending a charity event or a headshot for his online resume page. The other half are images where he appears to be chatting with a group of men. Some are of high quality, some grainy, and some are mistakes—featuring someone who is not Mark at all. I stare at each person in the photos, and for the clear ones, I run searches on the participants' faces, just to see if something else stands out. I need to catch a break. Just one small break.

The last photo I look at from the Mark Tanner group has a girl on his arm. Oh no. Penny. According to Graham, Mark used Penny as one of his escorts. Then, when she got drugged, Graham worked at dismantling his escort service. He didn't actually need to though because when three girls died from overdoses, it was a natural event to shut everything down.

I run Penny's face through the software and come up empty. For a girl barely younger than I, I'm shocked she doesn't have a social media page, at the very least. Maybe she did at one point and her older brother scrubbed the Internet free of her face. I wouldn't put it past him.

In one of the photos Claire took and sent me, I have a decent view of Paul. His face also appears in the banner for the Campus Smoothie Cafe's social media page. I use that photo first and run it through the software.

While the images load, I take a break and exit the library to go make some pasta salad with the veggies, meat, and cheese that are in containers in the fridge. I boil some water on the stove and add the dry pasta from the pantry to get it soft. While I wait for the food to be ready, I crack open a can of Coke and swallow two more extra strength Tylenol.

I am used to walking around with a headache, but this one is particularly bad. Maybe the added stress of knowing that Graham and Sophia are spending the weekend together has made my brain swell with the thoughts of them making memories as a fake couple. I wonder why he is not texting me or calling. I doubt it is due to a lack of Wi-Fi connection. The longer he goes without contacting me, the more my mind drifts to a place where my worst fears congregate and rally against me.

I plate up my pasta and add some salad dressing. Then I make my way back to the library. I turn to walk into the room and nearly crash into Owen.

"Oh, I'm sorry," I say loudly, placing a hand over my heart to try to calm it.

"Didn't see you there, ma'am. It's me who should be apologizing for scaring you."

Owen and Malcolm are the least familiar men to me who have been frequenting this safe house. However, both are nice and respectful. I wonder if Collins is on a break or chatting with Graham. I am sure with Sophia gone, there is less need to hover over me like he has been for days. I can't get into a fight with the air.

"No problem. Just taking a break to make some lunch," I explain, pointing down to my food.

"Looks good too," he says with a friendly smile. "Oh, and Miss McFee?"

"Yeah?"

"My mug of cookies was a real nice surprise. I really do appreciate you including me on your gift list this year."

"Oh, of course! Glad you liked everything."

When I get back to my desk, I see the search is complete, and eight photos match for Paul. Several are from when he was at a different university. One is of him graduating from a school in upstate New York. His degrees?

Forensic science and international studies. His name? Not Paul. It is listed as Carson Tillman. He was a lacrosse star and honor student.

I knew he transferred to River Valley U, but why would he be attending my school if he already is done and using a different name? Something is not adding up. Plus, he told me during the night of the Halloween party that he was studying communications. This was after Skeleton Man gave me a completely different story.

I am not surprised Paul lied to me. He has been lying about everything from the first moment we met. The switch of the skeleton costume was enough of a red flag. I found language books in his closet when I went snooping around that night. They were of the same languages I heard Mark speaking with Benjamin, Samson, and Edward.

I place my head down on the desk and sigh into my forearms. Why is everything so complicated? Paul doesn't even bring books with him to the Smoothie Cafe. Agency girls are getting drugged, and Paul seems to have rescued a few. Or acted like he is being the hero. Maybe he is the Dark Hero.

When my eyes start to blur, I run back to my room to get my flash drive that I carry in my purse. I pop it into the port and save my consolidated work. Then I text Claire to help me get the names for every agency girl she knows who has been drugged. She must be bored because even on a Saturday evening, she responds immediately with a list. I scroll through the university database and find the email addresses I need. I type out my request using my private account that has no attachment to my real name.

Hello,

I am a reporter trying to gain insight on your recent incident on campus or near campus regarding being drugged. If you can provide any details about the moments leading up to the incident, please do so. I will preserve your anonymity. I am simply trying to figure out if there are any similarities to try to help stop this from ever happening again. We are women. We have a voice. We will not be just another number or statistic. Let's stick together.

Feel free to email me back with another address, if you are more comfortable doing so.

Sincerely,

A Victim Too

I log out of my account and carry everything out of the library. I take a stop in the kitchen and find Owen grabbing a bottled water.

"Need anything, ma'am?" he asks politely.

"My head hurts so badly. I keep getting these horrible migraines that are nearly debilitating. Makes me nauseous and sensitive to light."

"That doesn't sound fun."

"No, not at all. Any chance you have something stronger?" I know he does, since Collins basically shared that he did. I inwardly pray that he will cut me a break and give me something for this pain.

"I do, actually. They are a prescription, though, so be careful with them. I never needed them for my dental surgery but had them as backup just in case. Wait here, and I'll go grab the bottle."

"Thank you so much."

"Yeah, of course. Hope you feel better."

I fix myself a snack of veggies and dip. Owen is back within minutes and hands me the little orange bottle that has Tylenol-Codeine printed on a label around the side.

"This should be perfect," I respond with a smile.

I glance down at the directions, while carrying my laptop and snack back up to my room. I swallow two and then seal the bottle up for safekeeping. I use the bathroom and take a quick shower. Once my hair is partially dried with the hair dryer, I saunter back into the bedroom and put on a pair of pajamas that have donuts all over them. I relax back on the bed and munch on a piece of cauliflower that is doused in ranch dip.

I glance at my phone for the hundredth time and finally see the missed calls from Graham. Darn it! I look at the time stamp and must have just missed him. I listen to the voice-mails asking how I am doing, telling me he misses me, and requesting to video chat when I get a chance.

I prop up the iPad and click on his name to dial the call.

"Hey sweetheart," he says smoothly as the call connects.

We are in different time zones so it must be night there. "How are you doing?" I ask. "Flight okay?" He would have landed hours ago, but this is the first time I am able to chat with him since I watched him leave this morning.

"Everything worked out well. Uneventful," he says with a smile. "I miss you."

I try to see where he is but can only see the headboard and the pillows.

"You aren't sharing a room with Sophia, right?" If she is lying in the bed beside him, I may murder my iPad.

"Of course not, baby. I have a suite here at the hotel, but we have separate bedrooms. Plus, I should be back tomorrow but late."

"But we still have to stay away from each other?"

"For now, yes. But sneaking into your bed will be half the fun."

"I hate living by myself. I really got used to having Claire around, but she is playing house with Ethan, and I can't guilt her to come back and stay with me at the townhouse. Not when things are working out well between them again."

"I'm not a fan of leaving you there alone either. Trust me. But I need more time to figure things out."

I swallow hard. I have no idea if he is being honest with me. Or himself. It seems like as long as I have been involved in trying to figure out the whole drug ring thing, I have only gotten myself more and more confused. So, maybe all of his I-just-need-a-little-more-time lines are just that—lines.

I don't want to give him a hard time. I can tell he is trying his best to keep me safe. "Okay. I'll figure out how to deal." A yawn escapes my mouth, and I stifle it with my arm. "Ah, I must be more tired than I thought."

"It's only seven there," he says with a frown.

I bite into a piece of broccoli and rest my head back against the pillow. "I'm just so tired."

"Well, maybe we can chat more tomorrow," he says with a smile. "Finish up your food and get to bed."

"Sounds good," I agree, then end the call and close my eyes for a few seconds.

8

I startle awake to the sound of a plate hitting the floor. I roll to my side and squint as I look down at the veggies and ranch splattered all over the hardwood. I stare at the mess in confusion, while my brain catches up to reality. I vaguely remember talking with Graham and being so tired that I just wanted to sleep.

I pick up my phone and see that it is four in the morning. The light from my lamp casts a warm glow, but it does a number on my head. The throbbing. I move into the bathroom to get a damp towel to clean up my mess. I throw away all of the food and find my purse where I have the pill bottle. I shake out two more and swallow them down with some water. My mouth is so dry that it feels like I ate a bunch of cotton, so I down the rest of the bottled water until it is empty.

I sit on the edge of the bed and rest my elbows on my thighs, bending over. My head feels like a bowling ball, and I can only hope that the pills take effect soon.

I stumble into the bathroom and glance up into the mirror. My eyes are bloodshot, my skin pale and sweaty. I don't feel warm. I feel the opposite. I splash some cold water onto my face to wake myself up from my haze. But that's what does it. My stomach flips, and I feel the rising acid first. I double over the sink and brace myself on my outstretched hands. Then the rolling and rumbling and—

"Ahhh," I retch.

Yellow chunks fly from my throat, collecting in the bottom of the sink. I don't want to look. But I do. I can't *not* look.

I jerk forward four more times until everything in my stomach is expelled.

I run the water and pray it all goes down. I don't want to have to wipe it out. I don't want to touch it.

I sit on the closed toilet seat, my hands resting in my lap. My head pulses and I know that the relief I just swallowed moments before is now trapped in the contents I threw up.

I hobble into the bedroom and find my pill bottle. I swallow two more. Two more to take the edge off this headache. I lean my hip against the desk and lose my balance, falling into the chair. I cry out as I plummet to the floor, and my vision spots with flashes of light, then everything fades to black.

"Miss McFee, Miss McFee, you're worrying me."

I open my eyes to Owen hovering over me on the bed. Malcolm is beside him. Austin is hovering in back, his phone to his ear. I sit up on the bed and rub at my forehead. I reach for my bottled water with a shaky hand. Owen helps me unscrew the cap, and I manage to take a swig.

My head feels so much better and for that I am relieved. "I'm fine. I think my migraine just got so bad last night that I must have missed a step and fallen."

I can hear Austin in the background talking to Graham, I assume. He walks closer to me and hands me the phone. I look up in confusion and he mouths, "Graham." I nod and take the device.

"Hello."

"Sweetheart, I was so worried about you. Austin came to check on you when he heard a thump and found you lying on the floor. What happened?"

I glance at the clock and see that it is almost eight. I must have been out of it for a while. "I think I'm just getting some tension headaches. Probably from not getting as much caffeine as I'm used to back at home."

"Dr. Saber is on vacation for another day. As soon as he is back in town, I'm having him check you out. If he needs to outsource to a specialist, so be it. My men have been telling me your headaches seem to be getting worse. I'm sorry you are dealing with this, baby. We'll come up with a solution."

I really do not want to see a doctor. There hasn't been a doctor to help me with my shoulder pain, so why would one help me with my headaches? Seems pointless, but there is no stopping Graham when he gets an idea in his head. I imagine he is stressed out over me right now. "Okay. Thank you."

I end the call and shoo everyone out of the room. I really

need some space. I want to shower and get ready for the day. I have a crazy amount of work to do on my article, and I haven't even started writing it. Do I have a title? Nope. A clear objective? Nope. Anything that will make Dr. Williams happy? Not sure, but definitely leaning toward a "no."

Will I give up hope? No.

Sometimes my best writing comes from unexpected places, deep within the caverns of my soul. The loss of hope is simply my own fear of failure.

I log in to my secret email account—the one I used to email drugging victims from the agency. I am losing track of how many accounts I have created within a few months. Seems like this is just the normal territory for any investigative journalist. I like having an avenue though for people to reach out to me and be able to share their stories without the stigma. We all deserve to have a voice, especially women who often get overshadowed by a male-dominated society.

There are six new emails, all from accounts that are unknown and not registered under a specific name. I shuffle through each one and add my own label of Victim # ___ to separate their testimonies. I read the accounts of their experiences through their own eyes and shudder over the emotional toll each girl went through. Even if the case goes to trial, there is nowhere in the courtroom that these words would be allowed to be expressed.

They are raw. They are real. They are reflective.

I copy and paste the quotes that hurt my heart the most and include each woman's assigned victim number. We are more than a number. But yet, the number makes it even more…effective. As if using one makes it clear that society sees us this way. Bodiless. Mindless.

"I woke up to a stranger standing over me." -Victim #1

"I felt helpless." -Victim #2

"I worried what my parents would think if they knew I was dating an older man for money. No one would believe me if I cried victim to a completely different crime. But defending lawyers would dig up every skeleton from every one of my closets." -Victim #3

"I woke up in a hospital bed. Alone. I was at my lowest." -Victim #4

"I am nothing. Just a shell of who I once was. With a mind full of what-ifs and regrets." -Victim #5

"I may not have been raped. But I was assaulted. Taking away my memory is a crime. I never had a drug in my system until that night. Now I have a craving for more." -Victim #6

I read Victim #6's statement and frown. How horrible! Did the dose she received cause her to have an addiction? That is so wrong. I am angry. Raging. All of these women have lasting effects from that one night where they were used as human test dummies. Expendable in the eyes of evil men.

My mind drifts to Resa, remembering her terrorized face

the night she busted through the door of the townhouse. She was in shock. I know she left school, but I still want her to know that I'm thinking of her. Picking up my phone, I dial her number and hope she has enough strength to answer it.

"Hi, Angie."

"Resa, so good to hear your voice." The sniffles start and I know she's crying. "I didn't call to make things worse for you. I just wanted to reach out and let you know that I'm here for you if you ever want to talk." Despite not being drugged, she is a victim too.

"I'm doing better each day," she says with a whimper. "I just have a lot of nightmares. Being chased. Running... I close my eyes and I remember those moments of utter petrified fear."

"I'm very familiar with nightmares, Resa. And they suck."

"Sure do."

"Things are getting crazy here with druggings and girls being hurt. I'm so glad you are coping with your scare as well as you can."

"I resisted therapy for so long. Thought I could do life without it. But I was wrong. So wrong. It has been monumental."

"Great news." I smile. I'm so glad she is getting the help she needs. The brain can do crazy things—fragmenting memories and distorting the truth. Having a support system is exactly what Resa needs.

We hang up and I try to focus my energy toward doing something worthwhile. I open up my journalism software that allows me to see what my article could look like in print. I title it, "A Victim's Journey." I may not be able to find the ring leaders in time for the due date for my assignment for Dr. Williams, but at least I can produce a worthwhile article that still has investigative elements on a meaningful topic. I just hope it is enough to pass with the degree I have been longing for.

As for the internship? I still can prove myself postgraduation. I just need to get to graduation first.

I check my school email and see that Dr. Williams messaged me about seeing my article draft on Monday. The email is dated back a week ago. I just forgot to check my account. Well, at least I now know how I am spending my Sunday. I have a crazy amount of notes to add into my article, as well as all of the work I typed out yesterday.

This is just a draft. So, all of the polishing details can wait until the final hand-in period. Having little to no parameters for an assignment is daunting, but this is how most senior undergrad projects seem to be. A true test to how we will be able to handle the real-world workforce tasks.

I grab my flash drive and save my work. When my eyes start to twitch from the screen's light, I lie down in bed to close my eyes for a few minutes. It is now ten o'clock, and I feel the telltale signs of a headache brewing. I reach for my purse, and the movement causes my stomach to cramp with pain. I massage my soft abdomen and frown at how bad my fingernails look. I hold them up to examine their blueish color under the nail bed. Weird.

Maybe all of these occurrences are my body's way of telling me it wants to go back to Portland. I take out a couple of the prescription pills Owen gave me and swallow two. Maybe Dr. Saber will be able to help me—maybe even prescribe something more powerful.

There is a knock at the door, and I open it to find Collins standing in the entrance.

"Ma'am, it's time to go back to Portland."

"Oh, thank God."

"Leave all of your stuff. I'll have someone pack everything up for you—even your new wardrobe items. It can get delivered to your townhouse later this afternoon."

"Okay, but I need my electronics and my purse."

He nods and waits for me in the hallway. I bend to get my phone and laptop and drift forward into the end table. The lamp shakes from me bracing myself with an outstretched arm. Shit. I am so exhausted.

Collins escorts me outside, and I turn back to the house to look at it. It was my home for over a week, and a tiny part of me will miss it.

"Do you mind if I run up to the field just to take one more look?"

Collins gives me a weak smile and a nod. I take off in a slow jog, and he follows behind me. I hate running, but feeling the cold air beat against my flushed skin takes the edge off my headache or at least provides me a distraction from the pain.

When I get to the field, I look up at the sky and breathe in the clean smell of the fresh pine. I will miss my sanctuary, my place to rest and clear my head. Maybe I can find a substitute in Portland—perhaps a spot near the river that is less frequented by joggers and dog walkers. The typical park I love is now tainted with the memory of me breaking Zander's heart. Going there won't ever feel the same.

I pat the ground with three taps. Then I stand up and

make my way over to Collins who is waiting for me at the tree line.

"I think I'm ready now," I say softly.

He doesn't waste his breath with any words. I can tell he understands me and my eccentric need to find closure with a farewell goodbye.

We walk back to the front of the house where the car is idling. Owen and Austin are loading up bags of my clothes and hygiene products that must have been bought just for me and for my purpose of staying here. I was definitely gone longer than I'd expected.

I slide into the backseat and am relieved the privacy screen is down, just so I don't feel so alone. Austin joins Collins in the front, and we cruise down the driveway that takes us to the front security gate. We exit with a code and are on our way back to Portland.

I must have drifted off because I wake to the car stopping in a grocery store's parking lot in the suburbs. Collins cuts the engine and turns in his seat to look back at me.

I rub the sleep out of my eyes and try to get my eyes to focus.

"You okay, Miss McFee?" he asks, his voice full of concern.

"Yeah, I just dozed off. I'm still waking up."

Collins's eyes narrow, and I try my best not to make him worry. I sit up in my seat and clear my throat.

"Inside near the seafood section, you're going to see a woman your height, your weight, and with your hair color. She is going to be wearing a 'Feminist AF' hoodie. She also has your set of car keys. Are you following me so far?"

"Yes, I think so." This girl must be my body double.

"Put on her hoodie, take your car keys, and find your car parked in row D, the second spot. We will put all of your belongings in the trunk when you go into the store. The townhouse is about fifteen minutes away from here. Just plug in the address on the GPS on your phone. I'll have Austin follow you back discreetly in a nondescript car to make sure you get back safely."

"I can go to classes as usual tomorrow?"

"Yes. You just need to not contact Mr. Hoffman in public or try to see him. Act like you are not together anymore. Oh, and here," he says, passing me back a pair of sunglasses, "wear these."

"Okay. I think I got it."

I say my goodbyes and slip out of the backseat, with just my purse in hand. I roll my shoulders and rub the tension out of my neck with my free hand. I walk toward the automatic doors and look at the big signs along the wall until I find "Seafood." I make my way to the back corner of the store and see my doppelgänger.

"Hi," I whisper to her, making her look up at me with a smile.

"Let's go find the restroom."

I nod and follow beside her until we see the sign in the back center of the store—between the ground beef and poultry sections. My twin does resemble me. She isn't a dead ringer or anything, but with sunglasses on, I can see why Graham would have selected her. I want to ask her what her real job is. Her hobbies. I giggle to myself as I think about how absurd I sound—even if it is just in my head.

We select adjacent stalls. I grab the hoodie over the

privacy panel and slip it on over my shirt. It is definitely something I would own. In fact, I think I have the exact one —but in a different color—hung up in my closet at the townhouse.

"Thanks," I call back over to her.

"No problem. The keys should be in the front pocket."

I reach inside and fish them out. "Got 'em."

"I'm going to hang out in here for another ten or so minutes. So, you should be good to go. Good luck."

"You too," I say. "Thank you." For your service? I have no idea really what to say. This is all a bit awkward.

I walk out of the store and find my car in the second spot in row D, exactly where I was told it would be. It feels weird to be behind the wheel, nostalgic even. I can't even remember the last time I drove myself anywhere. I adjust my seat and mirrors, then pull out of the parking spot. I glance periodically at my GPS to make sure I am on the correct road. Once I get to a familiar section, I shut it off and place the device into my cupholder.

I park my car in the empty spot that is assigned to me and then walk up the stairs to unlock the door. I trot back to the car and unload the trunk. It takes me just two trips to have everything inside. The house feels cold, as if it has not seen life in weeks. I adjust the thermostat to the heat setting and move about the house, putting things back where they go. This is my home for the foreseeable future.

I should be used to not having a permanent home. I should be used to having to move around my whole life. But despite being familiar with the emotions, it doesn't mean I like it.

I jog upstairs to see my room. It feels dull. All of my

sewing materials are gone. While my bed is in the same place, I don't want to sleep in it. I miss the penthouse bed I share with Graham. I miss Graham.

Collins must have sent for some of my items to get cleaned from the safe house, because I see everything I already wore there neatly folded in my bag. I add my new wardrobe to my closet.

As I bend, I catch a glimpse of the cardboard box in the back corner on the floor. It is hidden behind a pile of clothes that need to be donated to the local women's shelter. I scoot to the floor and pull the box toward me. I finger the lid and read the label description—McFee-McFee Baker City General Hospital.

I take deep breaths to calm my heart and lift the lid a crack, peering inside for the first time since the accident. I have transported this box from bedroom to bedroom, during every move that I have endured over the last five years, never having the desire or the courage to look inside.

I place the lid on the floor beside the box and look at the ziplock bags that hold James's and my bloodstained clothes. I remember the outfit I wore. It was my favorite white shirt with the lace. I stare through the bag and see that the color is now a burnt red color, almost black. My denim skirt? Ruined. I push the bag to the side and look at my purse and broken jewelry and the ball cap that James would live in.

And just like that.

I am there.

I cry as James reaches over the center console to squeeze my left hand. His brown hair sneaks out from the confines of his hat like whispering feathers.

"Are we being followed?" I ask, turning around in the seat to look out the back window into the night.

James swallows hard and turns on the defrost to clear the fog from the windshield. "No."

My legs sprout goose bumps. I chose the wrong outfit for the last day of November—clearly.

"Thank you for getting me," I whimper, holding my ripped lace shirt in place with one hand.

He glances my way and gives me the most pitiful look. "Did he—"

"No, but he would have if you hadn't shown up. He was so pissed off that I wouldn't take the drink he made for me. I know he put something in it. And then he got super pissed off. He knew I knew. Said I was going to ruin his reputation by squealing. He broke down the bathroom door. And I just fought and fought, unable to see anything through the red of my anger. Then when the anger tamed and it was safe, I ran."

"You should never be afraid to call me. Ever. And you always fight. You did the right thing, Ang."

"I'm not so sure." I look back behind us. "Look where it has gotten us."

"None of this is your fault."

I cry harder and shudder at the thought of him raping me. That was the plan. Why else would he want to slip something into my drink? I almost lost my virginity to a dude at a party and would have had no memory of it. I would have woken up with a headache and blood between my legs. I could have gotten a disease or gotten pregnant.

"Angie, don't cry. The police are going to take care of

this. We are only—" He halts his sentence as he glances in the rearview mirror. "Fuck!"

I spin around under the confines of my seatbelt and see the headlights. They are blinding. I squint as James speeds down the country road toward the center of town.

The lights behind us get closer. And closer.

James curses under his breath as the back of our bumper gets hit. The car skids to the gravel shoulder and starts to spin to the left. Smoke and dust clouds the night sky.

CRASH!

BEEEEEEEEEEEEEEEEEEEP—

HISSSSSSSSSSSSS—

I shake off the glass from my hair and push at the airbags. I look over to see—

"James? James! JAMES!"

Blood gushes from his head, and I freak out over the sight of his broken body.

My fingers tremble as I realize I am not experiencing another nightmare, but rather a series of memories. Holy shit. Flashes of that night's truth flood my thoughts. And for the first time since the accident, I have actual memories.

James was coming to rescue me.

Flash.

I was at a college party and about to get drugged.

Flash.

I locked myself inside the bathroom and when my predator broke the lock to get to me, I fought and fought and fought.

Flash.

I can see his silhouette in my head but no clear face.

Flash.

James burst into the scene and got me out of there. But we were being hunted down. This was not a hit-and-run because someone was drunk. Instead, this was a premeditated car accident to keep us from going to the police with the information.

It was on purpose that we got hit. It was vehicular manslaughter.

However, me surviving was probably never in the plan. Not remembering helped me move on without the haunting of the truth. Instead, I'm being haunted by the unknown.

I squeeze the bridge of my nose and lean my head back to look at the ceiling of my closet. How could I get these facts so wrong for so long? It is like my brain completely shut out the truth.

It was all my fault for getting James involved. He was the collateral damage. The sacrificial lamb that went to slaughter—decades before he was supposed to die. And I will carry that burden the rest of my life. There is no overcoming it. There is no getting better. I just have to learn to live through the pain of the realization that if I would have either not gone to the stupid party or not have called him, then he would be alive.

Or maybe I would have been the only victim.

Tears flush out of my eyes, and I close them to keep them at bay. I lie beside the box and curl my body around it. It is like I have a piece of James inside. His tattered clothes that were cut off him. His favorite ball cap.

After several tremors that shake my entire body, I pick myself back up to dig further into the box. At the bottom, I find the tree air freshener, which has lost all of its appeal.

James loved those stupid things. He always said that they spiced up even an older looking car. Next to it, I find the blanket we would keep in the backseat, often using it as a pillow on longer trips. I brush my hands across the fleece fabric, only stopping whenever the specks of blood halt my caress. The spots are so small that I am not even sure if I am actually seeing them or if my mind is playing tricks on me. I move my hand away swiftly, knocking into a cold metal object. I pull the object out of the box, staring at it in my palm for what seems like an eternity. A Swiss Army Knife?

It looks so familiar, yet I cannot remember it. Where did it come from? It's pink. Pink? James would have never been caught with something pink. But out of all the things in the box, why can't I find a connection to this one object?

I swing open the blade with a flick, examining the sharpness against the pad of my thumb. The heat from the metal jolts my arm away, dropping the knife into the box with a thud. I jerk away from the box and then quickly slap the lid on and kick it into the corner.

Fuck.

What the hell just happened? I squeeze my eyes shut and can picture the knife inside the cup holder of the car. The same car that—

I can see James's eyes on me. I can feel them. In my memory, I glance back at the pink shell of the tool, forcing myself to piece together the flashes to—

Pink knife.

Car.

James. Me. James driving. Me crying.

James is upset and—

Do I want this? Do I really want to remember that day?

No. It is night.

I see flashes of another guy. The one from the party. And then the bloody forehead and eyebrow from where I cut him. I was trying to get away from him and I used the knife on him. The same one he used to threaten me.

The knife is not mine.

It is *his*.

9

After we buried James, I lost my will to live. It was during that time I started to cut my legs, not so much to kill myself, but as a way to gain control of a situation I had little control over. It wasn't until I started investigating what happened to him that I found my purpose. While I never figured it out, and the police never took any of my testimonies seriously enough to conduct their own investigation, I was pushed into a new academic track once I restarted my freshman year at River Valley U.

And here I am, five years later with a clue that I overlooked the whole time. If I can find the owner of the pink Swiss Army Knife, I can find the man who killed James and tried to rape me.

I crawl on all fours back to the box and fish for the dreaded knife. I am afraid that the memories surrounding the knife will cut me deeper than the blunt force of it ever could. Maybe I have resisted remembering the night of the accident for all of these years because all along the truth would have put me in grave danger.

I am tired of not having the answers. I am tired of living with the dull ache in my heart that never quite goes away.

I turn the knife over and over in my hand and open the blade. There are blood dots on the shiny metal, and I wonder if I can get a private laboratory to analyze the results and then run a background check on the DNA to see if it matches anyone who is in the database.

The officers at the scene that night just assumed the blood was from me or James. I had the knife in the cupholder. It was a safe assumption. And the beer bottles surrounding the hit-and-run suggested that it was just a drunk teen whose car went across the double yellows.

Those beer bottles had to have been planted at the scene.

I know Nic would have connections with his whole privacy and security background. And maybe he would keep it a secret from Graham so he wouldn't worry. But either way, I need to find out who killed James. Then maybe I will be able to move forward with my life—even if just a few more steps. At least I would be moving in the right direction and not staying stagnant.

I close the rest of the box and push it to its home in the corner. I pick myself back up off the floor and slide the army knife into my purse for safekeeping. Maybe the more time I spend with it, the better my chances of remembering something of value.

With nothing else to do here other than watch stupid TV and work on my assignment, I decide it is best that I continue to push forward on my article. Classes start back in session tomorrow, and with my work shift at the cafe for the next two days, I will have limited time to contribute toward trying to impress Dr. Williams.

I trot downstairs, grab my laptop, and set up shop on the couch. I put my flash drive inside to pull up my draft. The little circle with the moving dots tells me that the machine is "thinking." I rest it on the coffee table and move into the kitchen to grab a drink. Water seems like the best choice, only because I have no idea what I am in the mood for. My brain hurts as is.

I lie back on the couch and place my laptop on my lap. I wait for my machine to recognize the new device and am presented with an error message. *E:\ is not accessible. The file or directory is corrupted and unreadable.* My breathing quickens to the point that I feel like the collar on my hoodie is attacking my throat in a choke hold. I nearly tip the laptop off my thighs as I read the message again. Tears well up in my eyes, as I try to think of what to do. Should I pull the flash drive out and try again? Maybe try a different machine instead? Is the library even open with classes not in session?

I double-click on the search engine and try to look for a message board that might supply me with a solution to the dilemma. My shaking hands have trouble steadying on the mouse keypad to even click on the blue links. When I come up empty-handed, incapable of understanding the tech lingo, I grab my cell and search through my list of contacts.

I find the number I need and click on the call button. I really hope he answers.

As soon as the doorbell rings, I put my laptop under my arm and rush to the door. I open it and want to launch myself into comforting arms, while sniffling and shamelessly rubbing my face into his shirt. But there are no welcoming arms. There are no words of affirmation to confirm I made the right decision by calling him. Instead I am greeted with indifference.

"Zander, I'm sorry for bothering you," I say softly, trying to get a better read on his mood. "I didn't know who else to call."

His shoulders soften, and the tension that he seems to hold there relaxes. "I wasn't busy."

"Thanks for coming. I'm so desperate."

"Angie, of course. You should have called me an hour ago when this first happened."

"It's not like we are talking these days, Z."

"I know," he whispers, rubbing his hand over his forehead to swipe some blond locks from his vision. He steps back to look at my face. "Is anything else bothering you?"

Yeah, want a list? "No," I lie. I really want Graham here. But the world needs to believe we are broken up.

"Let me take a look at your flash drive."

I hand over my laptop and portable drive, pointing into the living room. "Let's go set things up in there so you can be more comfortable." In my anger and pain, I feel like knocking everything on the floor and jumping on the screen. I spent weeks preparing my research—months even. I finally had consolidated my information and started the writing process at the safe house, only to have everything potentially be lost. The thought of it all being gone, just a day before the due date, makes me want to throw up.

Zander plops down onto the sofa and pulls out several items from his messenger bag and then leaves to run out to his car to retrieve more items. I watch him work but know that hovering is not going to help him. I supply him with a soda and crunchy-salty snacks, thanking him over and over again for his assistance. Graham's men must have proactively stocked my fridge and pantry knowing that I was going to be staying here once again. The food inside is definitely not Claire-approved. Plus, she has probably been here the past few weeks as much as I have been—which is not much at all.

My migraine builds with the fear of losing my work, so I excuse myself to pop some more pills upstairs in the bathroom, deciding that upping the dosage is the only way to manage the pain.

This is just temporary and things will go back to normal, and I won't have to rely on the pills to help me cope.

I stare at my sunken face in the mirror and know that the stress and the pain are taking a toll on my body. I double over the sink when a particularly painful surge hits my temple region, and I breathe through it, thinking about melted chocolate and pretty seashells to provide a distraction. As I make my way toward the steps, my vision blurs and the stairs appear to move like an escalator. Holy cannoli. They are alive.

"Zander? Zander! Help!"

He jogs up the stairs and helps my swaying body stay steady.

"Angie, you are worrying me. What's going on?"

"I've been getting these migraines. Can you help me down the steps so I don't fall?" I lean into him but he scoops me up instead. My head bounces as he walks down with me in his arms. He smells like the beach.

"I heard you broke up with Graham," he says, placing a gentle kiss on my shoulder. He lingers there way longer than a friend would do. But are we even friends anymore? "Does that mean you are back on the free market for dating?"

I cringe over his words. I really do not want to deal with this again. He places me down on the couch beside him. My laptop is open and he has his hooked up beside my device, running what looks like a series of tests.

"I need to be single right now and focus on graduation." It's not exactly a lie, but it isn't the whole truth either. I am very much involved with Graham—secret or not. I know where we stand.

"His face is splashed all over the tabloids and Internet," Zander adds. "Hooking up with some model who works for him. I think her name is Sophie? Or Sophia?"

His words are matter-of-fact, but I doubt with the intention to cause me unnecessary hurt. Zander is not an asshole. He is just reminding me of how shitty the situation is. Like I need reminding.

I get up from the couch and pace the room. My vision is off but I just suffer through the flashes from the migraine. "Are you saying this just to make me upset? Do you think I don't know all of this already?"

"I'm just pointing out that if you were with me, I wouldn't just dump you and break your heart like that. I wouldn't just hop to the next girl, because you are it for me."

I sigh and push my hair behind my shoulders. "I can't be what you need, Zander. It was a mistake asking you here."

"I can't do anything with your flash drive anyway. The device is corrupt, and everything you saved on your hard drive is corrupt too. You have a pretty serious virus, maybe even some malware. Would probably be best for you to just get a new device or reformat the entire thing to the basics. It's just hard to gut a laptop. So I would lean toward getting a new one."

"Fuck!" I yell. "I have a draft due tomorrow."

"I'm sorry," he says, but the apology is flat. "Let me know if you want to rekindle our *friendship*."

"Don't you mean, *date* you?" I correct.

"Yeah, that's exactly what I mean," he says, walking out the front door.

Like a foundation built with cards, I crash to my knees, weeping. "I'm sorry!" I bellow. "I'm fucking sorry!"

Zander joins me on the floor, hugging me to him. Tears run down his face, and for the first time in what feels like a month, I see him genuinely apologetic. "I'm sorry too."

"I never wanted to hurt you." My words come out in sniffles. "I miss being friends. Are we never going to move past this?"

He helps me off the floor and escorts me back to the couch, plopping down onto the cushions as well. He places his head into his hands, and I can tell he is struggling. I am struggling too.

"I'm sorry," I echo. I really am. I never expected to fall so hard for Graham that even when he pisses me off or does something to make me question his ethics, I still cannot deny the way he makes me feel.

Zander lifts his head, tears visibly forming in his eyes. "I'm the biggest jerk on the planet, Angie. I allowed what I wanted to supersede what you needed. I can see that now. I can see that despite being broken up with Graham, he still very much has your heart. Probably always will. Yeah, it sucks." He waves his hands into the air. "All of this sucks. But I'd have always regretted not making the effort—even if you were destined to reject me multiple times."

"I'm not rejecting you from my life, Z. There's room for you in it. I just cannot give you what you think your heart wants."

He nods, placing his face into his hands again. "I get it. It took me long enough, but I get it. I'm really sorry for making you feel so badly about all of this. I'm sorry about The Shack. About everything."

I wrap my arms around his back. "I forgive you."

"I'm not sure I deserve it."

"You're a good man, Zander. One day you're going to find a girl who wants exactly what you are willing to give."

He gets up from the couch, offering me a weak smile, while walking backward toward the front door. "I hope she's as amazing as you are to me."

As soon as he leaves, I feel the start of a nervous break-down. I stumble into the kitchen and dig out the hard stuff from the bottom cabinet that Claire and I used for our past Monday night rituals. Those days are over. Not only did the TV show end, but Resa left. And despite not really enjoying college, she was forced out by some men looking for their next victim.

And no matter how hard I try to give these girls a voice, it is like the world is trying to silence them.

I pour a shot of tequila into a glass and throw it back. I chase it down with a second. I have no idea if I measured them correctly, but the familiar burn makes me think I did something right.

I flop down onto the couch in the living room and stare at the message about the corrupt files that taunts me on the screen of the laptop. I kick my foot out and launch it to the floor.

My phone rings beside me, and I struggle to find it in the cushions of the couch. I wrestle it out and answer it with, "Wha?"

"Sweetheart?"

"Yup?"

"What's wrong, baby? I'm on the plane back to Oregon. Just called to check in on you."

"Oh, nothin' much here goin' on. Just my entire project that my grade departure. No, describes, nope." I giggle like a demented clown. "Depends, yes *depends* on is disappeared."

"Are you drunk?"

I pull the phone away from my ear and stare at the screen in disgust. Oh, the nerve of him. He is riding mighty high on his horse today.

"Shut up," I hiss into the phone. Then, I end the call and hide a pillow over my head to block out the light.

My phone buzzes on my chest, and I shut it completely off. I don't have time for any of this shit.

———

I wake from my stupor to someone picking me up. I scream at the unexpectedness and am quickly shushed.

"Angie, it's me."

"Graham, what are you doing here?" I ask, turning in his arms. It hurts to open my eyes but I do so anyway. He is wearing a River Valley U hoodie. His hair is tucked under a black ball cap. "We can't be together. That's what you said."

"I just landed and had to see you, baby. You hung up on me and refused to answer my calls. I parked down the street behind the row of homes and snuck in through the back door."

I hug him tighter; it feels good to see him. I sniff his neck and fall in love with the woodsy rainforest scent. I lose myself in the moment and then remember why I have been so stressed out. "My article I'm writing in order to graduate is gone."

"Gone?"

"The laptop you gave me has a virus, and my flash drive is now corrupt."

"I'll take a look at it. But I may have to call Nic to come here. He has way more experience with this type of thing than I do. But, first, let me look at you." He places me gently on the sofa and sits beside me, taking my hands in his. "You seemed out of it on the phone. What's going on?"

"I just got a little tipsy from the fear of losing my project. Just had a little drink and it went to my head faster than I was expecting."

"What did you have to eat today?"

I pause and look up at him. I honestly don't even remember if I ate anything today. The day itself seems impossibly long. Longest Sunday ever.

I brace myself for the inevitable. I am not in the mood. I try to hide my head into his muscular chest.

"For fuck's sake, Angela. This shit again?"

"I probably did eat, and I just forget what exactly, Graham."

He gets up from the couch and stomps into the kitchen. I rest my head in my hands and massage the back of my neck. He is giving me a headache. I hear the sound of cupboards opening and closing. The sound of bags crumpling. He returns minutes later with a chicken salad sandwich on toasted focaccia bread.

My stomach growls at the sight of food, and I take the plate from his hands and eat the entire sandwich with just a few bites.

"You drive me absolutely nuts," he barks.

"You drive me absolutely crazy too," I snap back.

Despite his pissed mood, my body reacts to the sound of his voice. I hate to admit it to myself—and refuse to let him know—but I missed his controlling nature while he was gone. His stalking and flirtatiousness and overbearing behavior—

Yeah, I missed that.

Graham takes my laptop and looks at the death screen. He fishes his phone from his pocket and places it to his ear. "I need your help. Angie's place. Come through the back door and disguise yourself." He places his phone down on the coffee table and grabs my feet to rub. "Nic's on his way. If he can't fix your machine, then no one can."

I nod. There is still hope. Does he even want to help me if he knows it may disrupt the FBI investigation? I guess I will cross that bridge when he gets here. They both probably think I chose a different topic. In a way, I did. But publishing emotional testimonies before the case fully goes to trial could be bad. The publicity alone may make it challenging for the key players in the ring to accidentally make a mistake and reveal themselves. I haven't even decided whether I am submitting the article to any media sources offering internships. I have to graduate first. And then apply for internships.

I moan and sink my body farther into the cushions as Graham's expert hands work out the stiffness in the bottoms of my feet.

"How was your Florida trip?" I ask. I just saw him yesterday morning, but so much has happened over the past forty-eight hours that it seems like it has been a week since we shared the same space.

"Next time I go, you're coming with me."

"Did you go to your family's home?"

He frowns. "No, sweetheart, I wouldn't take Sophia there. She hasn't even gone with me to Hillsboro. You are the woman in my life who I want to share with my family. Please know that this recent trip was just a facade. Nothing more."

"Why didn't you stay longer? I mean, I'm glad you didn't but..."

Graham sighs. "I just needed to take some pictures with Sophia and make it appear we were there longer than we were. I don't like being states away from you. I can't think and don't function as well as when we are closer in proximity."

"Okay," I whisper. I hate that I need this level of verbal reassurance, but I do. Sophia brings out the worst in me, and knowing that she wants Graham back makes my hairs stand on end.

Graham looks down at his phone and stops rubbing my

feet. "Zander was here?" he asks, venom dripping from his tone.

He must have just gotten word from his men who are watching my place and reporting back. "Yes, but only to tell me he couldn't fix my issues."

He narrows his eyes at me. "Just that?"

"And to see if I'm interested in dating him now that I am newly single."

Graham growls and sits up taller. "He doesn't waste time."

"I told him I wanted to be single."

"Good."

"And there may be a glimmer of hope that we can go back to being friends, which I would love because I hate all of this tension between us. He apologized. We both did."

"Why didn't you call me?"

"Because I got scared and panicked. Plus, you were on the other side of the country!"

The sound of a throat clearing causes Graham and me to look over to the kitchen area, where Nic is standing with a book bag draped over his shoulder. I look back and forth between the two men and am still kicking myself for not seeing it sooner. They have very distinct features. Between the chiseled jaws and clear blue eyes, I should have suspected their family ties months ago. Graham gets up and makes room for Nic to sit down to look over my device. I sit up and watch as he goes to work.

"Good to see you again, Angie. Wish it was under better circumstances."

I offer a weak smile. "Same."

I watch as Nic plugs several cables into my laptop and

sets up another device beside it. He seems to have more experience than Zander and that is saying a lot since Z is very skilled, despite not being able to deliver earlier.

"You sure you didn't save your work elsewhere? Email it to yourself? Save it on a different device?"

"I mean, I did. But everything was fragmented. I spent the past two days consolidating everything and deleting the scraps. Everything recently has been saved to this laptop or my flash drive."

"The flash drive has been tampered with," Nic explains, pulling it out of the side port.

"Tampered with?"

"Yeah. Did you accidentally dump it in water or step on it?"

"No. It was working this morning. Now it's not," I say in a rush.

"I can't be certain yet, but it also appears that someone has installed a keylogger on your laptop. Having both your portable flash drive and your hard drive acting up seems to hint at it being a purposeful attack."

"What's a keylogger?" I ask stupidly. Am I supposed to know this lingo?

Nic keeps typing away on his own device but glances to Graham.

"Software or just hardware?" Graham asks Nic.

"Looks to be both. But I need more time to diagnose that."

Graham frowns and then walks over to kiss my forehead.

"What's going on?" I demand.

"Someone has installed or got you to install malware on

your laptop that keeps track of your keystrokes. Whenever you type something into a document, on Google, or in your email," he says with a sigh, pausing to most likely think how to word a complex topic to someone who knows very little about it. "Basically, any time you use your keyboard to press keys, the malware sends back information to the malicious person on what you are typing. They can see everything. Documents you have typed, email, social media posts, etcetera."

"Why would someone even care?"

"Maybe to gain access to your accounts. Passwords in general. Anything."

"Shit," I exhale. "But it is safe to say my work stored on my laptop is gone?"

"Yes," Nic interjects. "You said you sent yourself some email."

"Yeah, I guess I can log into my accounts and try to rush writing my article."

"When is it due?" Graham asks.

"Tomorrow morning."

He rubs his hands over his forehead. "I'm sorry, baby."

"Let's just hope I can get into my email. I can whip something together," I say, my voice breaking. I sniffle. Who am I fooling? Even with the email, I would have to spend the entire night trying to organize all of my information. I feel the bile rising in my throat. There is no way I can recreate the authentic nature of what I already produced. Writing is organic and unique in that aspect. That is why saving your work is so damn important.

And I did save it, in two different locations.

The research, the graphics, the video footage, the

special elements I added to the journalism template. Everything I saved is gone. How can this be happening to me?

I watch as Nic cleans up his cables and stuffs them back into his book bag.

"Angie?" he says softly.

"Yeah?"

"Can you log into your email accounts on your phone and see if you can get in? If you can't, then we know that the person who is doing this to you has already made a move. If you can get in, we need to change all of your passwords."

I nod and grab my phone. I go to the host site for my victims email account and type in my address. Next, I put in my password. I click *sign in*. Nothing. I double check the address, making sure I didn't accidentally hit the wrong key. Then I methodically type in the password.

Denied.

I try my Bad Advice email account.

Denied.

I try my personal account.

Denied.

The secret account I was emailing myself voice recordings.

Denied.

"Fuck!" I yell, whipping my phone across the room. "I'm blocked out of all of my accounts. All of them. Do you guys even know what this means for me? Well, let me enlighten you... My future career is basically gone if I can't even freaking graduate with the degree I want!" Nic and Graham make eye contact with each other, and I spring up from the couch as if my butt is on fire. "Did you guys sabotage me?"

"What? No!" Graham yells. "Why would you even ask that?"

"You gave me a new laptop, a new phone! New everything when you quarantined me away from the world! And now this happens?"

"To keep you hidden, Angie, not to mess with your accounts or your work," Graham explains. "We had nothing to do with this. But someone *is* responsible. Someone did this to you with the intention to cause harm. This is not accidental."

"What? Why? Why would someone do that?" I ask. "You don't think this is a random act?"

"No," Nic says, his tone serious.

My stress level marinates and boils, going full force at maximum velocity. All of my work over the course of three months is now hidden away on a tiny flash drive that stores my now corrupt files or corrupt device or corrupt-whatever-the-hell. My throat clenches, sobs rolling over my upper body, quivering to fight my emotions back down into control. I forfeit round one. The unladylike crying is turned on to full blast.

"We'll figure out who did this," Nic tries to comfort, but it is useless.

"Finding the person who did this is not going to fix my work. It is gone. And recreating it will be next to impossible." In this moment, I wish Graham would ride in on his white horse and wave a magic wand and fix this nightmare. He always fixes my dilemmas—except this one. This one he can't fix. I would relish the white-knight behavior and

VICTORIA DAWSON

would even volunteer to groom and feed the stupid horse if I could just get my project back.

I get up from the sofa and try to find my phone. I stumble, nearly face planting. *You are so out of it.* My nerves, emotions, and motor skills are out of whack. My logical side goes on hiatus.

I start to crumble. My legs give out on my descent to the floor. I hear a curse vaguely echo in my ear. It feels like I am underwater, the air leaving my lungs in anger. Strong arms band around me at the waist and scoop me up like a small child. I get pressed to the chest of a muscular wall of steel, giving me a flicker of believable comfort. It is in this moment that I feel Graham's love radiate from his core. In the moment, I feel safe—a sensation that rarely surfaces.

My head sinks against Graham's shoulder, my mouth resting against his scruffy neck. I sniff the intoxicating aroma of mild soap. I will never tire of his scent. I snuggle in closer, like a kitten. His five o'clock shadow is my new favorite thing. I am center stage to enjoy it.

"Are you petting me?"

I let out a whimpering giggle. "Maybe."

He kisses my cheek and then my ear, making me shiver with the remembered feeling of his lips on me.

"I'm glad you are here." My words are barely a whisper. "I'm sorry I accused you and Nic of sabotaging my work."

"It's okay, baby," he says, placing me back on the couch. "Is there any way your professor will give you an extension?"

"No, he's a hard-ass. I had over an entire week off from classes for the fall break to work on this assignment. He won't cut me an ounce of slack because I should know better. It's my fault. I should have backed up my work in other ways. I'm a moron."

"It's not your fault someone maliciously attacked you, Angie," Nic defends. "I'm going to keep your laptop so I can figure out the point of entry for how someone was able to add the keylogger. I just need time to analyze it."

I nod. "Okay, but what am I supposed to use now if this machine is broken? I need to start writing something to hand in tomorrow." A huge percentage of my grade is this draft. I am in over my head.

"You can use mine," Graham suggests. "It's in my bag." He gets up from the couch and grabs his device out and then sets it on my lap. "It's late and you should be sleeping. But I understand your desire to get something on paper."

"Thank you," I mouth. I open the lid and a blank document and start typing. I lost all of my email accounts, so I also lost the victims' emotional testimonies that were the backbone to my article. This all just sucks.

"You're going to want to create new accounts and use strong passwords to secure the entry into them. If you use the same password to access any online banking or credit card management, you will want to log in to those accounts and change the password," Nic explains. "I would also suggest using a password keeper that uses a two-factor authentication to access it. But we can set that up at a later date. Just know that none of this will protect you from an actual keylogger if you are prone to clicking on links that could actually be harmful."

I nod to Nic. This is his thing. I thought Zander was nerdy for computers, but Nic takes it up a few more levels.

While the brothers talk amongst themselves, I lose

myself in my writing and get as much as I can on paper. Something is better than nothing. I can print it out at the lab in the morning before my early private appointment with Dr. Williams.

I must have dozed off because when I wake, Nic is gone and Graham is gently placing his laptop on the coffee table. I look up at him, and he bends to kiss my forehead.

Before I am able to protest, he lifts me like a small child, one hand under my knees and the other on my back. He carries me up the steps and puts me down on the vanity in the bathroom, with my back to the mirror.

He puts his fingers on my cheeks, igniting the blush that already is inflamed. "You called him first."

My eyes move to his. "Excuse me?"

His brow raises as his eyes narrow, studying my facial features in detail. "Zander. You called him first. Why?"

"It was a technical issue." My short explanation doesn't appease him.

"You know Nic and I have computer science backgrounds, albeit Nic's is way more extensive."

"You weren't here."

"I still don't like it, Angela."

I cannot fault Graham for having a jealous streak. I have one too. "What would you rather have me do? Fend for myself?"

"Simple, call me first. I gave you a number to reach me. You have it in your phone." His fingers tangle in my hair, pulling my attention back to him. "I thought about you every waking minute of every day. I can barely function when I'm away from you."

"I really missed you, Graham," I admit. "Do you have to leave to go back and get Sophia?"

He smooths a strand of hair behind my ears, leaning in to press a kiss to my forehead. "No. She'll come back alone tomorrow."

"Okay."

"It takes everything in me not to break down and just move you back in with me, sweetheart."

"I hate this fake relationship thing you have going on with her."

I turn my attention away from Graham and fumble with my toothbrush as I remain on the counter. I take care of my teeth. He brushes my hair back and cups my face in his hands, interfering slightly with my brushing technique.

"You've lost weight."

I turn to spit and rinse, adjusting to the position. His hands are on my sides and back again, and I cannot hold back the grimace as his hands touch over my flesh. How can I eat when I'm in so much pain? How am I supposed to chow down when my boyfriend keeps leaving me? When will things just be easy?

He continues to probe and squeeze my skin, and I try desperately to shift away from him and the evaluation. I suppose he is correct. My clothes are fitting a bit looser, my face less full. I didn't notice before now, but he is right.

"Angie?" he says my name, waiting for me to fill in the blanks.

"I keep having these headaches, and eating is the last thing on my mind."

"Fuck. You're going to make yourself even more sick by

skipping meals. Maybe some of your head pain is from low blood sugar."

"What time is it? I have to keep working on my project."

"Late. Just cut your losses and get a few hours' rest. No point meeting with your professor with eyes you can barely keep open."

I hate to admit it, but he is correct. I cannot be stumbling over my words when I meet with Dr. Williams. I need to go in with confidence. "Let me finish up in here, and I'll go lie down for a bit."

Graham hesitantly nods and walks out of the bathroom.

I slide off the vanity and wash my face. I dig under the sink and find a bottle of Tylenol and shake out three. They are the extra strength kind, which doesn't mean much, so three will be necessary to curb the pounding. I cup some water in the palms of my hand and swallow back the three white ovals.

"What did you just take?"

I look up with bloodshot eyes to see Graham standing in the doorway.

"Just some painkillers. For my headache."

"Names and amounts, Angie."

I prop my hands on my hips at his accusatory tone. His stance is rigid, almost like he is pissed off at me. "Why are you being so overbearing and bossy?"

"Something is going on with you. You are losing weight, popping who knows what, and—"

My eyes narrow and my nose twitches. I brush past him when he takes up too much of the doorway. "Just spit it out, Graham. Quit talking in code." I throw my hands up in the air in utter frustration. The last thing I need right now, the night before my draft is due, is to deal with his accusatory comments. "You think I am what?" I turn to look at him face-to-face. "A pill abuser? A drug addict? What? What do you think I am?"

"Sweetheart, just calm down and let's both take a deep breath."

"No. I am so mentally exhausted that I can't deal with you right now." I rip off my clothes and start changing into a pair of pajamas that I have to dig out of the bottom of my dresser drawer. I haven't been here in weeks it seems, and all of my clothes are wrinkled from the lack of wear.

"Angie..."

"You are so disengaged from the reality of all the things I'm going through right now," I rant, shoving my legs into the bottoms, "that you have to bring your judgmental eyes and lack of trust upon me too. Like I'm not dealing with enough."

His frown breaks my heart, and I can't stand to look at it happening. I am being harsh—even if I feel it is justified—but he basically is lacking a sensitive bone in his body at the moment.

"I saw you take three of something. I am worried that you are taking too many. If your head hurts this bad, then we need to go see a doctor." I can see his anger boiling. He is hiding it, but I can tell it is there. He has two emotions—mad and not mad. And right now, he is definitely mad. I don't deal with *mad* well, especially from him.

"Tylenol, Graham," I say in a huff, pulling a cotton shirt over my head. "Have you ever heard of it before? Know how mild Tylenol is? It basically does nothing for a headache. They allow pregnant people to have Tylenol, Graham. Babies can have Tylenol. It is like swallowing a piece of candy. That's what I took. Nothing crazy. Nothing really even effective."

He eyes me skeptically. "What else did you take?"

"Huh? What are you talking about?"

"Before I arrived," he clarifies. He stands over me while I put on a fresh pair of fuzzy socks.

I shake my head back and forth in shock. Is he for real?

He kneels down in front of me, while I sit on the edge of the bed. I think he is going to hug me or put his head on my lap like he has done in the past. Instead, he reaches up to steady my chin. "Your pupils are constricted. I can't believe I didn't notice this before. What else did you take?"

I swallow hard and brace myself.

"What else did you take, Angie!"

"Um. Well…" I look away and have trouble focusing.

"Tell me, Angie. Tell me!"

I pull my chin away from his touch. "I had a drink, Graham. I told you this downstairs already. A simple drink because my entire assignment that I need in order to graduate has been trashed."

He gets up from the floor and walks downstairs. I hear him rummaging around the kitchen. When he gets back up to the room, he hands me a giant glass of water. "Here, at least drink this."

I take the water out of his hand and mouth, "Thank you." It is like my vocal cords have stopped working. The glass hits my teeth as my trembling hand tries to steady it. Water dribbles down my chin, and I quickly wipe it up with the back of my free hand. I place the glass on the nightstand and climb into bed under the covers.

Graham leans over and places a gentle kiss on my lips. "I love you, sweetheart. We're going to get through all of this together."

I close my eyes and wonder what he means exactly, but I am too weak to ask him to clarify.

"I love you too."

10

At seven thirty, my alarm sounds, and I roll over to find the bed empty with just the imprint of where Graham's warm body once lay. I wasn't expecting him to stay. He said he couldn't, but he did anyway. Memories of the night filter through my head like a slideshow. Project failure. Pill accusation. Graham spooning me until the sun rose and then disappearing with the only sign he was even here being his scent he left behind. I can still smell him on my pillowcases. I'll never want to wash them.

Hmm. Despite being asleep most of the time, I can still feel his lips against my neck, breathing in the scent of my hair. His hips in line with mine, pressing his crotch into my butt. He must have told me how beautiful I was at least a dozen times.

My only regret is not being as coherent as I could have been. So that I could commit every word and every movement to my permanent memory.

I throw on clothes in a hurry and decide that professional attire is best. I settle for a bronze-colored pantsuit with a silk shirt in a soft ivory shade. I know I didn't buy it myself, and it looks too long to be Claire's. Regardless, I am thankful that I have options. I pin the back of my pants to keep them from falling down. I am sure with a little carbs, I will be filling them back in.

My headache is dull this morning and not nearly as bad as it has been over the past forty-eight hours. I swallow one of the special pills Owen gave me, just to help with the maintenance. I transfer the remaining ones to another container and throw away the bottle that has all of his information on the label. I am so thankful that he hooked me up, even if the pain is simply reduced and not actually cured.

I comb my hair back with some water and twist it into a low bun, securing it with several hair ties. My hair is thick and often has a mind of its own. I brush my teeth and dust on a layer of light makeup. I grab a pair of heels from the box in the closet and jog downstairs. If I am going to have time to print my work, I have to leave soon.

I slip on my shoes, pack my school bag, and lock up the house. The morning air is less fierce than it was at the safe house. I think being in the valley helps shield Portland from some of the winter elements typically seen in the mountains. For that I am glad. I much prefer warmer weather to the cold.

I start the engine and back out of the parking lot. I eat a granola bar to calm my angry stomach while I drive. Once on campus, I park and run up to the computer lab. I put my new flash drive into the port and print my partial project. I look at the stark white paper feeding through the printer that gets inked with my mediocre words. It is sad to think that in this moment, I have let myself and my professor down.

I pull the sheets off the top and stuff them into a folder. I log out of the machine I was using and make my way out of the building and back to my car. I park at Harrison Hall, then walk through the main entrance and down the same hall I have walked down numerous times. I push some pieces of hair that have escaped the bun behind my ears.

Outside the door to his office, I lean my back up against the wall and close my eyes. *You can do this, Angie.* I swallow, clear my throat, and then knock on the door.

"Come in," a girl says.

I keep forgetting he has a work-study student. I peek my head in and give the sweet blonde girl a smile. "Hey, I'm here for the nine o'clock time slot for my journalism project."

The teen girl is squatted down behind her little desk, organizing file folders. It seems like such an ancient process since the invention of computers. But Dr. Williams definitely seems old-school.

"I'm Angie, by the way," I say softly.

She reaches her hand out for me to shake. "Beth."

As I take her hand in mine, her sleeve pulls back, and I see the identity bracelet on her wrist. It is the same one that I used to wear when I first joined the agency—the one Graham's company created with the ability to trace locations.

I try not to stare, but I can't take my eyes off her jewelry. She is new. The type of metal signifies it, plus she does not look to be anyone who I have met before.

A weird feeling washes over me. Isn't she too young to be dabbling in this type of lifestyle? Does she know what she is getting involved in? A part of me wants to lecture her and parent her. So much has changed for me since I joined Entice Escort Agency that it is hard to even consider myself as the same naive person.

"Is Dr. Williams having a good morning or a bad morning?" I ask softly, the slightest hint of humor present in my tone. I'm pretty sure his mood isn't going to affect my grade, but maybe if I catch him having a great morning, it can help?

I watch as Beth swallows and sits back on her heels. "I honestly have no idea. I've been here since the start of school, and I still can't read that man. But you know how he loves punctuality so go on back before you go from being early to being late."

I nod. She is wise. "I love your bracelet," I say casually, pointing down to her wrist.

Beth startles and fixes her sleeve over the metal band. "Thank you," she says quietly. "Sometimes I forget I am even wearing it."

"That's what good jewelry does, right?" I call back over my shoulder as I knock on Dr. Williams's private door.

"Yes?" His voice is gravelly and stern.

Shit. I pull open the door a crack and peek my head through. "I'm here for the nine o'clock."

"Come on in, Miss McFee. I scheduled you first so that you can set the bar for everyone else," he says, motioning with his hand for me to sit down. "Let's see if you took my advice from the last meeting. The suspense is killing me."

I clear my throat and want to pass out. At least if I am

unconscious, then I won't have to witness this turning point in my life.

"Don't keep me waiting. Let's see what you have so far."

"Dr. Williams, I had a crisis happen yesterday when I went to pull up my work off my flash drive," I start. It sounds so hideous and unconvincing, even to my own ears. I pull my folder out of my bag and hand over the three pieces of paper that contain my typed draft. It is not neat or professional or memorable.

Dr. Williams takes my documents and scans through them, pulling his wire-rims higher on his face. "Due dates are not suggestions, Miss McFee."

I sink into the leather of the seat as his words deflate me. "I know. I am sorry." I want to cry. I have come full circle. Seven months ago, I sat in the same leather chair and was delivered a similar verdict. Sadly, I was closer to my dream in the spring than I am now.

"What's to be sorry over? This is your life, not mine. But I cannot consciously pass you along to the next chapter without you earning it. This work is not up to par," he says, tossing my papers to the corner of his desk. "Not even close." His eyes level with mine. "Do you know how frustrating it is for me to sit back and watch this happen to you? I see potential. And it's wasted."

"I have been following the victims of the campus druggings. I even set up a private email for the girls to speak out. I had consolidated all of my information and used the journalism software program to organize it."

"Why are you even telling me this?" he asks, uninterested. "How does this benefit the huge portion of your grade right now? I told you months ago that the draft counts toward your final grade. Did you misunderstand, Miss McFee?"

I shake my head. "No."

"Very well, then. I'll read through your documents more and give you a grade for this portion. If you even want a chance to maintain the minimum grade for the course, I will"—he pauses and looks at me straight in the eyes— "once again tell you to stop interfering with a police investigation and defaming the university without concrete facts."

"Understood."

"Do you though? Because you don't seem to be hearing me at all."

I straighten my back. "I feel passionate about helping these girls, Dr. Williams. How do I just let that go?"

"You cut your losses."

Pretty sure Graham told me the same thing. "Okay."

"Want to hear a little fun fact?" he asks, and then continues on. "Women are inundating the journalism field with the number of graduates coming from top universities. They basically comprise two-thirds of the population holding the degrees. However, it is still very much a male-dominated career."

Society too.

He taps his fingers along the polished mahogany wood. "Those women are learning very quickly that they are not cut out for this line of work and change careers almost immediately. It's not too late to change your focus. But now you went from being in a marathon to being in a sprint.

Time is ticking, Miss McFee. And right now, you are on the road to failing my course—again."

"The journalism world could use some feminist reporters, don't you think?" I challenge. His fun fact is something I already know. It is why I'm so driven to prove myself.

"Of course, I'm sure there's a place for them in the workforce. But that is assuming they can put the time in at a university and actually graduate. My nine thirty should be here. I'll let you know the final submission date via email. But let's make this easy. If you plan to hand in anything even hinting at the topic of the druggings, expect to fail automatically. I am your advisor. Take my advice."

Ouch. I am going to be sick. All of the good graces I have received from Dr. Williams in the past are now nonexistent. I lift myself out of the chair and stumble toward the door. I wave a quick goodbye to Beth who frowns over my departure.

I run out of the building and lean against the stone siding as I try to catch my breath. It is over. I needed this meeting to be my closure. I have no fight left to give.

Groups of students filter into the building, and I watch as they enter. I feel out of control, and the only thing that I want right now is to lick my battle wounds in isolation. I walk back to my car and slam my hand down on the steering wheel.

"Dammit!"

I hear a tapping on my window and jerk up to see Bryce standing outside. He is finally back to good health with his ankle. I roll my window down.

"Hey, Teach."

I blink hard and squint at the sun. "Hi."

"Rough day? What's wrong? How was your holiday break?"

"I just have a headache," I say softly. "Hey, do you have any leftover pain pills from your ankle accident? I just have lame OTC kind, which basically works like a Tic Tac breath mint would."

I watch as Bryce digs in the bottom of the book bag draped over his shoulder. "You're in luck. I barely used these things. They make me hallucinate."

"Oh wow, that's not good."

"Totally not fun. Maybe if my head had a better Rolodex of images—maybe even sexy ones—I would have been more inclined to use them. You can keep them—there's only a handful left."

"Thank you so much."

"See you in class?"

I sigh and look out the front of my windshield. I am not feeling like sitting through a class today. I need to go lie down. "Can you please take notes today?"

"You know I rely on you for those," he chuckles.

"I need to skip today."

"Oh no, do you have senioritis?"

"Is it contagious?" I ask with a forced giggle. "If so, I had to have gotten it from you."

"Hey, if you're going to get anything from me, it's a good time."

I laugh at his lighthearted sense of humor. "I'll hopefully see you at the next class."

Bryce backs away from the car and waves goodbye. I pop open the little orange bottle and shake two into the palm of my hand. I toss them back and wince over the pain of the dry pills making their way down my throat without the flush of a beverage.

I grab my phone and scan through the contacts list until I find Larry's number for the Smoothie Cafe. I dial it and wait for him to answer.

"Hey, Larry, this is Angie McFee. I am so sorry but I need to call off today for my work shift. I am feeling a bit under the weather and just need a day off to rest."

"Sure, no problem. Hope to see you tomorrow."

I end the call and then start up the engine. I back out of the parking spot. My vision is blurry from the headache pain behind my eyes that keeps building. I keep one hand on the steering wheel and one on the bridge of my nose. If I can just get home and rest my eyes, I will hopefully feel a little better.

It is a short trip back to the townhouse. I cut the engine and walk up the stairs, then unlock the door and reset the alarm system. I need to get out of these stupid dress clothes. What good did looking professional do anyway?

When I get to my room, I start discarding clothes, tossing them on an armchair in the corner of the room. I will hang them back up later. In my closet, I find a simple pair of leggings and sweater to put on. My head throbs so I try to remember where I put the pills that Owen gave me. Maybe one of those, combined with the two Bryce let me have, will fix this pulsing in my head for a few hours. I need a break from it.

I try my nightstand. Nothing.

Maybe they are in the bathroom. I'm not usually this forgetful. I think the stress of the past couple of weeks has been wearing down my brain. I push open the bathroom door and nearly scream at Graham sitting on the closed toilet seat, looking like he is about to go to war.

"Whoa, what are you doing here?" I ask in a hurry. "Did you just let yourself inside? What's going on?"

"How long have you been using?"

"What?" I ask, staring at all of the bottles on the counter. There's not many and most are OTC.

"You heard me, dammit!" I see the panic in his eyes and he wrenches open the medicine cabinet and rummages through the hygiene supplies, trying to find more proof to add to his growing stash. I swing my hands up and try to stop him but he has already convinced himself.

He pushes past me and stomps into the bedroom. He finds my school bag and starts throwing things out of it into a pile on the bed.

"Stop!" I say, grabbing his forearm from behind. "What are you doing?"

I hear the rattling before I see what he has retrieved. "These are narcotics! Opioids!" he bellows, holding the container in front of my face. He shakes it and reads the label out loud, like I am a child. "That's assuming what's inside is actually what the label says!"

"I've told you I've been getting headaches, Graham." I try to keep my voice even-toned. He is spitting rage.

"T-3s with Codeine, Angela. Do you know how dangerous these are? And Lorazepam? For fuck's sake, what the hell have you been doing?" I hear his disgusted sigh, and I quickly go into defense mode.

"I don't even know what Lorazepam is." It's the truth. I really don't. "What are you talking about?"

"Lorazepam is a benzodiazepine."

"Oh, that explains everything," I huff. I look up at him with hatred. Why is he doing this to me right now?

"It is an anxiety medication that can cause drowsiness, weakness, dry mouth, nausea, changes in appetite, blurred vision. But the problem with this type of medication is that it is highly addictive."

"Where did you even find it, Graham? Is it even mine?"

"I found little rolled up foil balls with pills inside in your drawers, hidden in the back corners, Angie. Pretty sure they are yours."

Shit. I didn't even notice them or I would have used them when I was desperate to relieve the pain. I often used foil to protect them and could easily pocket one when I needed to have backup when I would go out. It's so easy for those that aren't living with agonizing pain to cast judgment. He just doesn't get it.

"Pretty sure you have violated so much of my privacy that there's no coming back from this. That's the bigger issue here, Graham, isn't it?"

His eyes twitch as he watches me stomp around my room. I am pacing and about to explode on him with an angered rage. Damn him.

"What about the T-3s? Who prescribed those to you?"

"You know that I was in a car accident, Graham. Why are you making such a big deal out of all of this?"

"The accident was five years ago."

"I have lingering injuries."

"What did you eat today?" he demands, pushing hair back from his sweaty forehead.

"Granola bar."

"That's not nearly enough," he scoffs, stalking me with his eyes. "And with all those meds—which I'm sure you were popping several doses today to help with your pain, going completely against the daily limit allowance—you *better* have taken them with a full glass of water because those damn things could rip the lining out of your stomach. Give you an ulcer. Not to mention your liver is working overtime to help filter."

"Wow. You have a vivid imagination."

"You claim you can take care of yourself. Well, right now, you pretty much suck at it."

My lower lip quivers, and I bite at it to keep from breaking down at his harshness. This *stress* is going to give me an ulcer—not the pills. He moves closer to me and grips my face to look at his. My gaze struggles to concentrate on his, more out of fear of getting yelled at than anything else. Make it stop, please, make it stop.

"Do you know how freaking annoying it is to be in pain from migraines?" I ask, breaking free and going back to my pacing.

"I'm getting you help. This all stops. I cannot believe I didn't see this sooner. The headaches and the lack of eating meals and the constricted eyes. Now you are stealing pills."

"Stealing? Oh wow, are you freaking kidding me?" I ask, stomping toward him. I push at his chest. "Get out. Get out of my house! Get out of my life with your attitude!"

"You're mixing them, aren't you?"

"Leave!" I scream, pointing toward the door.

"You aren't taking fucking pain medication until you see a specialist. These are highly addictive and dangerous. Some aren't even yours!"

"Get out, Graham!"

He turns away from me and my shoulders droop. I think he is going to leave but instead he storms into the bathroom and grabs the bottles of pills.

"What are you doing?" I ask.

"Gathering evidence." His jaw is clenched, and his nose is twitching from the control he is obviously trying to maintain.

"What? For whom? The police? Are you turning me in to the police?" The sound of the doorbell ringing fills my ears. I look toward the door leading out to the hallway. "Who's here?"

Graham fiddles with his phone, ignoring me for the moment.

"Graham! Answer me, dammit!"

"Dr. Saber is here."

"You fucking cannot just let me handle my own life, can you? Is that impossible for you? You butt into every little aspect of it and just try to control everything. I've been stressed out over my final journalism project and have been getting these horrible migraines. Nothing seems to work at fixing them. At most, I can take the edge off. I am not doing anything wrong. Just trying to cope."

"I want Dr. Saber to make that call."

"Fine. But give me a little privacy to finish getting dressed and go to the bathroom before you send him up here."

Graham pushes hair off his forehead and takes a deep breath. "Five minutes. I am so spitting mad at you right now that I need to cool off before I whisk you away again and never let you leave my side."

I watch with tear-filled eyes as he snatches away each anchor that helps me stay grounded. Without the help of the pills, I won't be able to survive the daily struggles of going through life in agonizing pain. Graham doesn't understand. It is like the eyes that used to see me in one light, now only see me in darkness.

He takes it all. That is what he is good at. Stripping me raw and leaving me with nothing left but my sins.

I wait until he is in the hallway before shutting my door, locking it, and then quickly going about packing a bag. I throw in some spare clothes, toiletries, and a wad of bills that I keep in a sandwich bag in my sock bin for emergency purposes. I need to get away from here—if just for the day. The last thing I need is him following a credit card trail.

I can hear Graham greeting Dr. Saber downstairs and know that there is no escaping this house easily. I say a silent *thank you* for thinking to bring my car keys upstairs, instead of leaving them on the hook near the front door. I pull my hair back into a ponytail, double check that I have the Swiss Army Knife in my bag, and slip on a pair of Chucks. I zip a light black jacket over my sweater and fix a ball cap on my head, pulling my gathered hair through the hole in the back.

I go into the bathroom and hoist myself up on the vanity. I pull open the little window and remove the screen. The half roof is an easy platform to use to access the back deck. I climb out of the window, dragging my bag behind me. I don't bother shutting it. Graham will figure everything out soon. I carefully walk along the shingles and then crawl on my belly to the edge. I let my feet drape over first and then slide down until I land semigracefully on the boards of the deck.

Victory.

11

It feels like I just broke the law, which is completely absurd. I just need to get away from here. I have been back in Portland for a day, and I already need to clear my head from all of the clutter. Graham does that to me. But I don't need him to point out my flaws and imperfections. I do that well enough on my own.

I run around the back of the houses and sneak into my car. I close my eyes for a moment as the engine purrs. I take a deep breath. It is time to face my fears head-on. I cannot hide anymore from the nightmares that haunt me. I need to go pay homage to my past. I need to go back to Baker City.

I blink a few times in hopes of getting my vision under control. I pull out the knife and place it in the cupholder—just as I remember from the night of the accident.

Glancing in my rearview mirror, I back out. I take a few side roads and then work my way north until I am entering the on-ramp for I-84 going east. I roll my shoulders and lean my head back on the headrest as I settle in for the five-hour trip back to my once home.

My phone buzzes with incoming calls and texts. Only one person in my life blows up my notifications like this. I groan and shut off my device. I really just need to decompress. Graham thinks I am some sort of addict. I don't need this type of negativity in my life right now. I already have so many other things on my mind.

Momma, I miss you. If she were here, I know she would know what to say to help me get through this chapter that seems to be titled, "Failure." It makes me nauseous when I think of all the hard work I put in over the past year with nothing to show for it. I am just wasting away the days. Living life on a hamster wheel with the destination being to nowhere.

I am alone in this world. And the revelation that I may stay in this limbo state is a hard pill to swallow. Graham accused me of being a druggie. Dad is guilting me for money to cover his growing debts. Claire might leave for L.A. Zander and I might never recover our friendship fully. Dr. Williams thinks I am a failure.

I am an hour into the trip when I think back to the maple tree that was situated in the large front yard. It was the same tree that helped to secure our playhouse. The same tree that was used for our tire swing. And it was the same tree that sheltered one of mom's last wishes—our treasure capsule. Seven weeks before she passed away, she made James and me promise to wait until after our eighteenth birthday to dig it up—preferably after the start of freshman year. She would ramble on and on from her home hospital bed about us having a lot of living to do and that we should experience our freshman year of college with full vivacious spirit without her illness influencing our big decisions. She knew her time on earth was limited. I knew it too. I just always thought I would have one more day.

Momma said that it was a gift to know that she was going to die ahead of time…that not everyone gets that privilege. While true, I can never be thankful for cancer. Cancer is *not* a gift. She wanted to prepare us for the chapters in our lives that would be tough without her in it. When James died, I couldn't bring myself to dig up the capsule without him being there to experience it with me. It is as much his as it is mine.

But James is gone.

Momma insisted that her life should be remembered and celebrated. She didn't want us to spend a lot of time mourning her. And here I am, not living out her wishes. Because every single day, I mourn her. I miss her.

Anger rises inside of me at the thoughts of my maple tree now belonging to another family. I remember the exact moment when I tried to go home and realized that it no longer could be called mine. I guess in a way, it died with Mom. James and I tried to hold it together, but that didn't last long. And when it was just me and Dad, I failed at it as well.

Now some other little kid has the blossoming memories of a big yard and a beautiful tree. But my capsule is still there—completely hidden from view. And today is the day I am going to go get it.

I glance in the rearview mirror as I enter the Baker City limits and am in uber-paranoia mode. Every car that takes the same turn or two that I take makes me question whether or not Graham is following me. Every dark car with a driver wearing a pair of sunglasses makes me think that they work for Graham.

I am afraid to even get out of my car before I reach my destination, but I really have to use the restroom. I swing into the parking lot of the gas station and hobble inside, trying not to pee myself. I am going to burst.

It feels weird being back in the town I grew up in. So much has changed. Many of the buildings that held an iconic place in my heart were gutted to keep up with the modern demands of society. Nothing stays the same.

My feet carry me down the sidewalk and into the little store that specializes in lawn and garden upkeep. If I'm going to make any effort at digging up the time capsule, I better have the right supplies.

When I'm behind the wheel again, I place my bag of snacks and the gardening tools beside me on the passenger seat. I check my phone and shoot Graham a quick text. It is unfair to make him worry. Even with telling him I am here, it will be impossible for him to get here before I check the items off my to-do list.

I drive through the center of town and look at all the architecture from the various shops and restaurants. Being a historic city, at least there is a level of preservation when it comes to maintaining the outward appeal.

My heart rate quickens as I get closer and closer to the house that helped raise me. I imagine that I will have to just look from afar as another family inhabits it. When I came back here with Claire, it was shocking at first to see another child running in the backyard. To see a dog prancing around the wraparound porch, guarding its territory—one I used to call my own. It wasn't a bittersweet moment. It was purely bitter. I cried the entire trip back to school. I vowed never to come back.

And here I am.

I turn onto the narrow road that my childhood house resides on. The houses in this section of the town are sparsely situated, with huge front- and backyards. The public water system doesn't stretch out this far, so everything is well and septic. However, the land is flat and the view of the mountains in the far distance is breathtaking. It is the perfect town to raise a family. We were the perfect family.

I see the "For Sale" sign with the little bar that states a foreclosure before I see the actual house. I pull up the gravel dirt driveway and park. I look up at the once light-blue exterior to see a dingy gray with badly painted black shutters. Boards line the upstairs windows, and it appears that the house is getting ready for a typhoon to hit. I stare in silence; even my own thoughts have quieted as I look at the skeleton of a house. Coming back after all of these years and witnessing the lack of life in a house I once loved is like trudging through a graveyard of memories.

I cut the engine and get out with my gardening tools. I guess I have little worry now of getting arrested for trespassing; looks like no one has been here in over a year. I walk along the side to get a closer look at the maple tree. No swing hangs from the strong branches. No names are carved into the side. To anyone, it is just a tree. But to me, this tree represents hope. It is the tree that we would take family pictures in front of. The tree that supported our swing that I would spend hours on. And at the back location, diagonal from the house, approximately three feet from the base, the time capsule is buried. I use my shoes to judge where to start digging. I sit down on the ground and spread my legs out on the cold grass. I take my little garden shop digger and start to pull up the earth.

I am about to start second-guessing my time capsule geography when I see the tattered piece of plastic poking through the soil. I continue digging and after several more minutes, I am resurrecting the old metal thermos that is sealed in a ziplock bag.

I hold the DIY capsule to my chest. The smell of the earth penetrates my nostrils. I scoot back to the tree and lean my back up against it. I sit for…

I don't even know how long.

When my breathing returns to normal, I remove the plastic shell from the thermos and twist off the cap. Inside, there are two envelopes that are rolled to fit along the edge of the container. One for James. One for me. These are the notes that Momma wrote and made us promise to wait to open them. We waited. Unfortunately, a bit too long.

I open the envelope with my name written in marker in Momma's beautiful handwriting on the front. She was always the most elegant woman I knew—even when she would wear an old apron when baking. It was all about how she carried herself. With dignity and grace. Everyone loved her. She was easy to love.

Unfolding the sheet of paper, I am thankful to see that the words are still legible after all these years.

Dear Angie,

By the time you read this, you will have already entered into the most exciting time of your life—the college years. It is not a natural part of life to go through it without a mom by your side. But you are strong. You are beautiful. You are made to persevere.

Ever since you were a little girl, you always doubted yourself. Did you know that you didn't take your first steps as a baby until you were close to seventeen months? I never wanted to compare you to your brother, but it was very clear early on how different you both were. You always wanted to make sure you could do something perfectly before taking the risk of failing. So, while James was walking and stumbling at a year, you were waiting until you were older. And when you finally did take those steps, you were so steady on your feet that you could easily walk on cement without giving me a heart attack that you were going to fall.

Why am I telling you this? Because I hope you realize now that it is okay to fall. Falling is a part of life's journey. Please do not walk into the trap of being so rigid (and stubborn) with blinders on that you miss out on your true talents. What brings you joy is what will bring you future sustainable success. Please do not set out to only follow Plan A, when Plan B or Plan C may open some amazing doors.

I am sorry I cannot be there with you and watch you shine. I am sorry that you have to go through this life without the love of a momma who always has your back. Let me live in your heart and in your memories. But only if you are able to live your life in the forefront and not allow the past to overtake the present.

I love you so much and even a little bit more,
   -Momma

My tears fall onto the words, darkening the lined paper with dots. Momma has always been insightful and wise. And even over a decade ago, she could see me. See my stubborn nature. See my need for perfection. She was right then. And if she were here today, she would still see that her words are exactly what I need to hear in this exact moment.

From the thermos, I dump out a pack of chewing gum, the front page of a local newspaper, a hair barrette, and five family photos. It is painful to look at the pictures, knowing that so much has changed since they were taken. I seal up everything into the container and carry my supplies back to the car.

I walk up the stairs to the wraparound porch and meander along the warped wooden planks, dragging my feet and kicking up peeling paint. I can't tell what I am sadder over—the house no longer being mine or the condition that it is in now. I pull at the front door and find that it is locked. I walk around the side of the house where there are vines and other plants growing up on some white lattice plat-forms. I look up and see my bedroom window open and decide that this is my point of entry.

I wish I could say that this is familiar territory for me—sneaking in and out of my bedroom window—but it's not. I was Goody-Two-Shoes Angela. I was the model daughter and the girl at school who would never cause problems.

While I had a voice, I never raised it or deliberately compromised the image that was instilled in me from early on. I was not confrontational.

But now, I am different. Life hardens the heart that way. Makes me know that bad things happen to the most amazing people. That no matter how perfect you can walk along a path, you can still fall and hurt your heart, even if there is nothing obvious in the way.

I look up at the height I need to climb in order to gain access. It's not so bad. I place my right foot into the slot and hoist my body up a few feet. My hands burn from gripping the warped wood, but I keep my eyes on the prize and keep on climbing. When I get to the roof that covers the porch, I crawl across it. The sound of breaking shingles echoes in my ears as I put further strain on the already-needs-replacing roof.

I remove the frayed screen and pull the window up farther, before climbing through feetfirst. I'm not sure what exactly I was expecting by coming back here. I definitely wasn't planning on going inside the house. But now that I am here, I don't want to stay. All of the good and bad and happy and ugly memories flood through me—highlighting everything I have lost.

I look around my empty room and see dust in the corners. The carpeting is ratty looking, and the smell of mold and stale cigarette smoke puffs out of the fibers with each step. My dull headache that never really got better from this morning builds over the nasty air I am forced to inhale. And what good is it to work my way through a house that is definitely no longer a home? I don't belong here. Not anymore, at least.

I get down the same way I arrived and back away from the front porch, saying a silent goodbye to the house. When I get into the car, I break down. Will this blanket of sadness ever go away? Am I destined to carry this burden for the rest of my life?

I drive to the local flower shop and pick up two bouquets of flowers—red roses for Momma and white roses for James. On the other side of town, situated on the hillside that has a beautiful border of trees, is the cemetery. I take the winding road up the brick pathway and find the row where half my family is buried. I park the car and carry the roses and time capsule through the grass until I find the neighboring headstones. I sit down between the two and place each bouquet in the corresponding locations.

"I could really use you both right now." I lay my head back and look up at the sky. "I really messed up my life, and while I would like to pass on the blame, it really is my own fault. I just"—my words catch in my throat—"can't seem to get over the loss. I doubt I ever will."

I don't visit here enough, but the few times I have been back to town, I always stop. It is peaceful. I stretch out my legs and watch as the sun starts to hover closer to the horizon.

How can I ever be happy when you both are not here with me? How can I find joy in my own life when your lives ended way too soon?

It is guilt holding me back. Guilt for being here on earth when they are not. Guilt for trying to make my life be more than just the pain, when they had to deal with so much themselves. It isn't fair. It isn't fair that I lived and they died. Why me? Why was I spared? And for what purpose? Just to fail again... Such a fucking waste.

When the cold air starts to make my teeth chatter, I sit back up and pull out the letter meant for James. Using my fingers, I dig up the earth, place the note into the soil, then arrange the grassy patch on top. I situate the bouquet and brush off his stone from the dusting of dirt and dry grass. I clean off momma's stone and then make my way back to the car.

It is five o'clock, and I still have two more stops to make. I start the engine. Then I travel up and around on the loop to exit to the main road. It only takes me ten minutes to get to the apartment complex. I find a free "guest" spot and park.

This may be one of my horrible ideas, but if I leave without making a valid attempt, I will most likely regret it. That's the thing about regrets, though—it usually takes time for them to occur. And being five hours away in Portland makes it harder to visit on a whim.

My fingers tremble as I ring the doorbell for the unit with the label of 5C. I have never been here before. The entire complex is only about ten years old. After a minute of waiting, I'm turning to walk back to the car when the door gets thrown open. I turn on my heel to look at the man standing in the frame. A man I barely recognize or even know anymore.

"Angela?" His voice is rough and broken. He sounds like he has chronic laryngitis.

I plaster a fake smile on my face. "Hi, Dad."

His eyes squint, and he stumbles into the door. "What

you doin' here? Thought ya said there ain't nothin' here for you."

There isn't. Not anymore at least. "I wanted to dig up the time capsule at the house."

"Place been vacant for months."

"Yeah, it was sad to see it that way." I fiddle with my fingers as I wait to see if he is going to invite me in.

"It was just a house," he says with a shrug.

One you sold without even running it past me. "Did you get the money I wired?"

His eyes narrow, and he coughs into his arm. "Yeah. I suppose there's no chance I can borrow some more."

"What's going on with you, Dad?"

"We are cut from the same cloth, Angela. It is part of our makeup and our personalities."

I sigh deeply. "What are you talking about?"

"We are both addicts."

I stumble back over his words. They are what Graham also implied this morning when he was rummaging through my pills. I get headaches. I am not a pill abuser. I am coping with pain. I am not a druggie. I am—

No. "How do you figure that?"

He laughs maniacally, and for a second I think he is just saying things to get a rise out of me. But then he continues, "Your boyfriend is worried about you."

"Oh," I say. Of course he would believe Graham. Graham is very convincing.

"But I see it with my own eyes. You are battling demons."

"Aren't we all?"

"Yeah, I guess you're right. But not everyone needs to

self-medicate while doing so. I know the signs. I have lived them myself. But you need to not be like me. You can be cured. I am too old to change now. But you can change."

"I get headaches, Dad," I say without an ounce of emotion. I am tired of explaining myself. "And I have residual shoulder pain from the accident."

"Play stupid games, win stupid prizes, Angela."

I look away. I'm not sure what I need right now, but a lecture is definitely not it.

Dad clears his throat and pulls at a piece of my hair. It is such a weird feeling. I can't even remember the last time he has touched me or hugged me. "How long are you in town for?"

"Not long," I say, looking at my cell for the time. "I need to get back to Portland for work tomorrow."

He gives me a single nod. "I guess you don't want to come in for dinner then?"

"Maybe another time." I turn to leave.

"Angie?"

"Yeah?" I call back over my shoulder.

"Thanks for stopping by."

12

It is pitch black when I get to the back road that leads from the community college to the town center. I park along the guardrails and walk along the gravel shoulder until I find the wooden cross nailed to a telephone pole with the initials JPM carved into the side.

I'm sorry, James. I'm sorry you came to rescue me, like you always did.

I close my eyes as I sit my butt on the edge of the rail. The person who hit us was at the party I attended. He was terrified of us going to the police. So he ran us over, killing James in the process. But James was just collateral damage. I'm the one who has the memories to unlock. I have the key to this mystery.

My phone buzzes with an incoming text message, and I glance down at it, half expecting it to be from Graham. He has texted or called me every thirty minutes since I left Portland. On the screen, I see the unknown number notification. I click to read the message.

Unknown: Stop interfering. Little girls like you never know when to stop.

My phone slips out of my hand and lands on my thighs before crashing to the ground. I scoop it back up and reread the words again. *Interfering?* By being here now or by trying to uncover the campus drug ring? I rush to the driver's side of the car, hop in, and lock the doors. I clutch my phone to my chest as the engine purrs. It is eerie out here all alone in the dark. My headlights beam on the cross I nailed to the pole.

After James died, I sought out any way to cope with the loss. I would use sleeping and journaling and cutting as self-help methods. At the time, I didn't know what I was doing. But looking back, I was just managing the grief my heart felt. When Momma passed, I had James to lean on. When James passed, I had no one. Maybe in a way I resent my dad for not stepping up. Maybe I resent him for coping with his grief in other ways. And how is that even fair of me to do that? Seems pretty hypocritical. But that's what sums me up these days. I *am* a hypocrite.

My phone vibrates, and I pull it away from my chest to look at yet another text message from the same sender.

Unknown: Your left taillight is burned out.

The words rattle through my body, sending a chill up my spine. How? I turn in my seat and look behind me in the darkness. No one is here. The sun is completely set, and I am basically on a barely used back road.

I have received text messages before that were threatening, but later discovered that they were from Graham to scare me into quitting the agency job. What happens if they were not all from Graham? What happens if I have had someone else following me and terrorizing me the whole time?

Whoever keeps sending me these messages has an axe to grind. The persistence alone is indication.

I wrestle with my seatbelt to get it untangled and clicked into place. I glance into the rearview mirror and then ease back onto the road. Two rays of light hit my mirror within seconds, warning me that I am being followed. My heart jumps into my throat, and I panic as the adrenaline surges through me.

I race down the road, every pothole making my car jump and jerk along the way. The headlights get brighter as the driver behind me closes the distance. It is like I am reliving my past—except I am the one driving. I barrel around a turn and my right tires go off the road, spattering shale up into the bottom of the car.

I glance to the passenger seat and there he is, plain as day. I blink and shake my head to exorcise the image from my reality. James. My vision blurs and when it returns, the only thing I see is the guardrail.

The car spins and spirals out of control until it hits the opposite side of the road's shoulder, barely missing the telephone pole. I look behind at the dusty cloud that is visible in the back lights of the car. No one is on the road but me. I rest my head back against the seat and take a deep breath. I am starting to wonder if I made up the chase in my head. I obviously saw James riding shotgun, and I know he is gone. I must be hallucinating. And every time I piece the fragments of memories together, the only thing clear is that I'm losing my mind.

I look at the dashboard light that indicates low tire pressure. Shit. It is only a mile to get back into town and find a gas station that has an air pump. I steer the car, driving well below the limit. My phone buzzes on the passenger seat, and I flip it over to see who is calling. A sense of relief overcomes me as I see the caller ID.

I slide the bar and answer out of breath, "Hi."

"I'm sick with worry. Are you okay?"

I'm not even sure how to answer the question. Am I okay? I pull into the gas station, get out of the car, and grab the pump hose for the tire. "No, not really."

"What's wrong? Where are you?"

I remove the valve stem cap and attach the hose, allowing the machine to start. "I went back to Baker City to take care of a few things," I say over the noise from the machine.

"Are you in any trouble?"

I imagine he has tabs on me. He always does. And given that my new phone came from him—coupled with his history of placing trackers on people—he probably knew all along I was here. Part of me wants to get mad. Part of me wants to demand my independence. However, the other part of me is thankful I have someone who loves me enough to want to protect me.

Maybe I do need some protection—even from myself.

"Talk to me, Angie. I'm worried about you."

"Are you sending me scary texts again?"

"What? No. Of course not. Baby, talk to me. What's going on?"

"I think I have a stalker."

"What? Since when?"

"I don't know," I say, putting the valve stem cap back on the tire and placing the hose back on the holder. I get back into the safety of my car and lock the door. "Remember when you were sending me texts to try to get me to quit Entice?"

"Yes."

"Well, I think during that time, I was getting texts that were not from you. And I just figured they were part of the whole plan you had so I never bothered to tell you about them."

"What kind of texts?"

"Ones stating my location. Or what I was wearing."

"Fuck!"

"So you never sent me texts like those?"

"No, Angela. I was trying to get you to willingly quit the agency, not terrify you. I wish you would have told me this before."

I snap my seatbelt on. "I obviously didn't know. The numbers were all different and when I found all of your burner phones, I just figured you were the only person who was fake threatening me. I never thought there was a second person trying to cause me real harm."

Graham sighs into the phone. "What do your recent texts say that you got while in Baker City?"

"A warning to stop interfering. And one about my back left taillight being burned out."

"Is it?"

"Yes."

"Dammit. Are you driving or in a safe location?"

"I'm at a gas station. I was visiting the location of the accident and was chased. Actually…" Tears burst out of my eyes, and I look to the passenger side to see James smiling at me. "Fuck. Make it stop."

"What? Make what stop?"

"The visions." I squeeze my eyes shut and lean forward to rest my head against the wheel.

"What's going on? Talk to me. I feel helpless."

I draw in a deep breath, then whisper, "I keep seeing him."

"Who? Seeing who?"

"My brother."

"How? He is dead."

"I know. And I need help. I have a problem and it's time for me to come clean with it."

"Oh sweetheart, I wish I could be there with you to drive you back here safely."

"I'm afraid to drive, Graham. I keep hallucinating. Seeing images that aren't real. I thought I was being chased by my stalker but cannot even separate visions from reality. My taillight could have been burned out for a while and the person trying to harass me just chose now to let me know. I'm scared," I cry out. "My head hurts. I'm a mess."

"Have you taken any pills recently?"

I think about this question. Have I? I go back and forth in my head over all of the places I have been while visiting my hometown. "I don't know. I can't remember. I'm going crazy. How can I not even remember?" He confiscated them. But did I have any lingering in my purse? My head hurts, and I think my body needs them. I am dependent on them. Like I can't even go now without having something to take the edge off the pain.

"Oh baby, just take a deep breath. This is all going to be okay. You are not alone. We are going to deal with this together. I have one of my men almost there in Baker City."

"Did you track me?"

There's a long pause. "Yes."

I swallow hard. "I figured as much. How?"

"I use several different ways."

I am surprised he is being open with me about this. I mean, I knew it already, but usually he shelters me in every way possible. "My car? My phone?"

"Mainly phone. I didn't want to risk your car's tracker box being spotted."

"Okay."

"The poor cell reception kept me from following your path in the beginning, so I had a late start at finding you. Remember Owen? You guys met at the safe house."

"Yeah."

"I don't want you to be scared, but I want you to stay where you are and wait for him. Don't get out of your car. I'm going to drive toward you, and you both are going to meet me. I'll escort you the rest of the way back to Portland. Then we will come up with a plan to get you back to good health. Okay?"

"Okay. So just stay here?"

"Yes. Let me get ahold of Owen who should be there in a bit. Just hang tight."

The call ends, and I sit shaking behind the steering wheel. So much has happened here. So many revelations and enlightenment. Sometimes it takes hitting rock bottom in order to make a change.

My phone buzzes, and I answer Graham's call.

"Baby? Go park near the storefront and get a drink or snack. Use the restroom. Owen should be there in twenty minutes."

"Okay," I say hesitantly.

We hang up, and I start the engine. I pull around to the front of the store, park, and hop out. My head hurts, and maybe some caffeine will take the edge off. I walk into the store and find the restroom in the very back. For a small-town gas station, the inside is very nice.

When I am done freshening up, I grab a pack of crackers off the shelf and a bottle of iced coffee from the cooler. I pay and then make my way out to the safety of my car.

It doesn't take long for Owen to pull up beside me and get out of the driver's seat. His warm smile makes me relax for the first time since I arrived here. He helps me out and escorts me to the backseat of his car.

"Feel free to rest, Miss McFee. If you want to get something to eat from inside, I can run in and grab it for you," he offers with a warm smile.

"Thank you, Owen. I actually just finished my snack."

"Okay," he says, slipping into the driver's seat.

"What about my car?" I ask, looking back at it.

"Mr. Hoffman will get it back to Portland. Don't worry about anything. It's all taken care of."

That's the thing with Graham... He's super thorough. He thinks of everything.

I feel his touch before I see him. His warm arms wrap around me and hold me close to his muscular body. It's as if I am in a dream. Except in my dreams I cannot smell, and his smell coating my body is intoxicating.

"Hmm..." I moan into his neck, as I breathe him in. "I've missed you."

He kisses my ear and then rubs his nose into my hair. I get lifted and the cool air wakes me. I open my eyes to stare straight into the blues of Graham. He bends to kiss my lips and I accept, opening mine to let him inside. I want to be mad at him. I want to scream at him for rummaging through my belongings earlier today. But I can't.

I am in trouble.

I am abusing pills.

I need help.

My vision isn't the best right now, but I can tell even in the darkness that he is relieved to be with me. The feeling is mutual. Graham is my lifeline. My anchor. While it used to bother me in the past to be so wrapped up in a man's life, it is the one thing that is providing me with a steady comfort during a time of uncertainty.

"Sweetheart, I never want to let you go."

"But we have to keep being apart?"

"No. Not anymore. This changes things. You are way safer with me than without me. I can barely function away from you, and that leaves me vulnerable as well. I've been going about this all wrong. I'm tired of being apart. I love you."

I squeeze him tighter. "I needed to come back to Baker City. I'm glad I did. It helped me to heal a bit more and face some of my demons."

Graham looks down at me and nods. "I didn't want to stop you from going there. I never want to stop you from growing and dealing with things on your own timeline, Angie. I just want to protect you from unnecessary pain."

He places me on the passenger seat and straps me into his car. He rounds the front of the car, strumming his fingers along the hood, before entering his side. He glances over at me and gives me a half smile. "Ready to go back home?"

His words penetrate my ears. It is ironic for him to use the word "home" as he does—especially after my visit to Baker City. But I no longer have a home there. My home is with Graham. Wherever he is, so is my heart.

"Yes."

He shifts the car into drive and pulls off the shoulder back onto the highway. We are in the middle of nowhere and I am anxious to be in bed, where I can rest. My head hurts and I try to rub the pain out with my fingertips.

"Are you in a lot of discomfort?" he asks.

"Yes."

A frown mars his features, and he reaches across the center console to rub my left thigh.

"I need you to promise me that you will stop taking pills. None. You have to stop them all right now. Even the ones that are just over-the-counter."

I know his fears. I have fears too. "Okay."

"How long have you been doing this?"

I turn to look at him and then shrug. "I think sometime in the spring. It didn't start out as a problem, or at least looking back, I didn't think it was one. I failed my last semester as a senior and was devastated. I didn't initially plan to try again. But I had old pills from when I hurt my shoulder and leg. I never really took them after the accident. I wanted to be in pain then. Pain felt good. I thought I deserved it."

Graham squeezes my hand and continues to listen to me ramble. It feels good to bare my soul and reveal my sins. I used to think that my flaws would keep him from loving me, but now I'm realizing that he loves me despite my flaws. And that makes me love him a tad bit more. I have a lot of baggage, but he doesn't seem to mind.

He lets go of my hand to pull out his phone from his pants pocket. He glances at the screen, puts in his earpiece, then answers the call.

"Hey," he says. I glance over as he listens to the caller. "Plans have changed." He runs the fingers of his right hand through his hair. "Soph, I'm not kicking you out. I'm relocating you. This was always temporary."

I can hear her side of the conversation through the other end because she talks so damn loudly—in that high-pitched squeak she calls a voice. She's been staying at the penthouse. Oh, hell no. I can hear her argue that there is plenty of room for her to be there too. She is scared and alone, blah blah.

I'm not stupid enough to miss the irony that I have similar fears as Sophia. However, I'm not the one trying to manipulate a man to take pity on me.

Graham sighs and the tic of his jaw increases as she rattles on and on about her safety and her stalker and how they are supposed to be keeping up the appearance of a fake relationship. I start to wonder whose idea this whole fake engagement thing really was. Graham made it seem like it was his, but I wouldn't be surprised if she didn't orchestrate the whole thing—or at least plant the original idea inside Graham's head. Sure, back at the safe house, he told me that the marketing director spun the idea to him and Sophia, but this has Barbie Bitch's name all over it.

He doesn't see her the same way I see her. Like he has some pretty image of her inside of his head and cannot see past this illusion to discover the real truth. For someone who doesn't seem to give people the benefit of the doubt, he sure does for her.

I shift in my seat and look out the window. We are entering the Portland city limits. It's after midnight, and all I want to do is curl up with Graham in bed. I am emotionally exhausted, and even my bones ache for rest. That's what stress does to a person—it ages you.

Once again, Graham's hand is on my thigh, reaching for mine to hold. I must have missed when he ended the call, absorbed in my own thoughts.

"Everything okay with Sophia?" I ask, not even wanting to say her name. I feel like I am in middle school with this newly released jealousy I have exhibited over the past month. I guess I never really had anything to be jealous over before Graham. There is something very primal inside me that wants to fight for him—especially when it comes to Sophia. She wants to sink her teeth into him and has no problem vocalizing her desires to me. I just wish he wasn't so oblivious. Sweet Sophia is more like Snake Sophia. Slimy and seductive.

"Yes."

"Is she sleeping in our—"

"For fuck's sake, no. She is sleeping in the second guest

room, on a completely different floor as me. I'm so ready for this all to be done."

Graham's terse response makes me want to ask a follow-up question but I resist. Maybe I don't want to know if she is prancing around wearing skimpy lace pajamas, hoping he notices her. The last thing I need right now is for him to keep thinking about Sophia.

"You're not going to send me away again, are you?"

"No, baby."

"Good."

"You know I was only doing that to protect you, right?"

"Yes. But I'm still in danger."

"You are," he agrees, with an angry edge to his voice. "And Nic is working with the FBI to ramp up internal protection while he remains an informant. But these things take time. This is not a black-and-white situation. So many variables make for a lot of gray areas."

"I'm going to either fail this semester again or have to graduate with a degree I don't want."

"I need you to trust yourself."

I glance over to him. The lights from the oncoming cars make my head pulse with the growing pain that radiates from behind my eyes. "What do you mean?"

"*So what* if you fail. *So what* if you have a different degree. You'll figure out how to push forward, and maybe the dream you thought you've been working toward was always a consolation prize or a default or an I-need-to-pick-a-major decision."

I open and close my mouth at his words. I think back to my short time at the community college, where I was taking general education courses. I really didn't know what I wanted to do with my life. Then James died, and I lost hope in living. I then became engrossed with trying to find out what happened to him. That was how my compulsion to be an investigative journalist began. I was tired of all of the stories in the press about the accident only skimming the surface. I wanted to know what happened to James.

But would I have still wanted to go that route if it wasn't for the lack of closure on the case? What would have happened if James did not die? Would I have been happy studying general education at BCCC?

I am a senior. I cannot be this undecided. And yet, here I am without a clear path to travel down. Have I allowed situations to dictate my journey instead of really looking inward at myself and discovering my own passions?

After Momma died, I very much hung out in the shadow of James. It was one hundred percent by choice, and I would have stayed there longer because it was comfortable. He would try to bring me out of my shell and on several occasions did, but I was timid and lacked confidence. Then when James died, I struggled to find a new identity. Perhaps all this time I never really discovered anything.

Graham pulls into the parking garage, cuts the engine, and turns his attention to me. He fixes a piece of my hair behind my ear. "I wish you would have the confidence in yourself that I have in you."

"Why do you even have confidence? It's not like I have done anything wonderful that proves myself."

"I've seen enough in the past few months of knowing you to say that you are one of the most insightful people I have encountered. You see the world differently and not necessarily in a bad way, Angie. Just different. When you visited HH for the day, you were able to completely command teams with your understated intelligence. You are not flashy and cocky. Instead you are creative and articulate. And that quiet confidence is powerful. If you could just trust in it, you can do amazing things."

"Thanks." When he talks like this, with compliments, I sometimes think he is referring to someone else.

"The fact that you have zero clue how impactful you are makes you relatable to others. And that is a gift you cannot learn or teach to someone."

"I must get it from my momma," I say softly. She exemplified elegance and grace with how she spoke to others. Everyone liked her. She had the charisma that people gravitated toward.

"I really wish I could have met her."

"She would have liked you," I say thoughtfully. "Would have told me you were the type of man women should wait a lifetime for."

Graham's huge smile is genuine and makes me sprout one of my own. I don't even think I have really smiled today.

"Let's get inside," he says, exiting the driver's side and opening the door to my side. "It is going to feel amazing to have you back in my bed."

I link my arm in his and we walk toward the elevator. "Feels good to be home."

Graham stops midstride, turns toward me, and cups my face. His kiss is so powerful that my spine dips backward. His arms brace me, while he leans over to maintain contact. "You"—kiss—"are"—kiss—"my"—kiss—"home."

13

We are barely inside the foyer when Sophia comes bursting through the door to greet us—no, correction, *just* Graham. She is wearing satin pajama shorts and a fitted white spaghetti-strap top. No bra. And she clearly needs one. It is like my nightmare has come to life in full technicolor.

I narrow my eyes at her, but she doesn't even address me with a glance to notice my expression. For December, her outfit seems very impractical. Pretty sure if I move closer, I may get sliced by one of her nipples.

"I'm so glad you're back." She is breathless. "Here, look," she says, thrusting her cell phone at Graham. "See? This is what scares me."

He tenses at my side and reads the texts she has received —from her stalker I am assuming.

"He's getting sloppy, and it's only a matter of time until an arrest is made. I have my men acquiring the street view cameras. Between those and the cafe's security footage, I bet we'll know soon who keeps trying to terrorize you."

Sophia nods and then looks up at him with the saddest puppy dog eyes. "I'm so thankful you're in my life to protect me. You always do. I'm scared."

"I know, Soph," Graham says softly. "But this will all be over. I just need you to stay elsewhere right now."

"Why? I've been doing exactly what you say, and now you're kicking me out because of her?"

"Watch your tone," he warns sternly. "Angie and I have always been together. We were all going along with the ruse for publicity, but—"

"You're kicking me out."

Graham's body tenses at my side as he lets out an exhale. "I'm relocating you. This was all temporary and just for appearances anyway," he says, brushing hair off his forehead.

"We can all stay here," she says sweetly.

I cough, trying to cover my shock. She's nuts.

Graham wraps an arm around me, kissing my forehead. He must sense my heart dropping. "That's not going to happen, Soph."

I can't look a second longer at her pouty face without punching it. I just want to shower and get ready for bed, so I slide my hand out of Graham's and make my way into the main part of the penthouse to get settled in for the rest of the night. They can figure this out without me being a witness.

I walk up the stairs and make a beeline for the bathroom. I turn the shower on and start stripping off my clothes. I step into the spray and slick my hair back as it absorbs the water. I close my eyes and try to think about anything other than my brain pulsing with the need for a pill —a pill I do not have. How am I going to get through the next twenty-four hours? How am I going to survive the week?

I finish washing my hair and body, then I shut off the water and dry off. Graham's warm hands turn me and help me to finish the drying process. He grabs my brush from the drawer and runs it through my damp locks to get out the tangles.

"Is she gone?" I ask.

"Against her will, yes," he replies curtly.

I think he is irritated with me, but his loving actions tell me his frustration is really directed at her. I mean, who walks around in lingerie like she did unless she is trying to make me jealous or gain the attention of Graham? Oh, the nerve of her. Are we destined to always coexist with each other? Or will she eventually piss Graham off and get kicked out of his life for good?

I let out a sigh. "I just need a night of peace."

"And you'll get it. How are you feeling?"

I look up into the mirror and catch his eyes. "Like my head is repeatedly being run over by a Mack truck."

"Have you always gotten migraines or do you think it is just a side effect of taking the pills?"

"The headaches seemed to have come out of nowhere. So, I assume there is a link between them and the pills." I turn in his arms and hug him tight. "I'm struggling. I never intended to get…" The word "addicted" hangs on the end of my tongue.

His hands wind into my hair. "I know, baby. And I'm going to help you through all of this. You will be okay. We are in this together."

He guides me into the bedroom and helps me into a pair

of pajamas. On the bed, there is a huge snack plate of fruit, nuts, cold slices of meats, and a variety of cheeses. It is like a picnic. I stare at the little plates he set out and the candles he lit on the dresser. It is nearly one in the morning and here he is, trying to take care of me.

"Wow, this is impressive."

"Let's have a snack before bed."

"This is basically a meal to me."

He smirks. "Well, then let's have a meal together."

We take our respective sides, and I cross my legs and settle in against a mound of pillows. I fix my plate, and despite not really feeling like eating, the food looks amazing. On my nightstand, there is a huge glass of ice water, and I reach over to take a few sips. My trembling hand shakes the ice around, nearly sloshing some of the liquid up and over the side of the glass.

"Drink it all. I can get you more," Graham says. "Staying hydrated and getting something in your stomach will help. Plus, I have this for you." He pulls out a little tube from his drawer and hands it to me.

I take the bottle and examine the name on the side. Peppermint oil. "Okay?"

"Rub it on your forehead. It's supposed to help with headaches."

I turn the cap and roll the little ball dispenser over my forehead. I know that the headaches are a side effect of stopping the pills. However, any ease of the pain is welcome— even if they are old wives' tales.

"Thank you, Graham. You always take such good care of me. I used to hate it, actually. But now it's one of the reasons why I love you so much."

He leans over on his right arm and gives me a sweet kiss on my cheek. His nose nestles into my neck, and he breathes in my scent. I want these moments to last forever. Where everything is relatively at peace and we are getting along.

I fill my plate and start noshing. It is weird to eat when I don't physically feel hungry. As soon as the first bite comes to rest in my stomach, the cramping starts. I drink a sip of water and try my best to chew the food and slowly pace myself. Everything tastes delicious. It's not that… It is just that I went so long without really eating that the first couple of bites feel like I just swallowed a bowling ball.

"I'm always going to take care of you, sweetheart. And going to do a better job than I have been. I failed you."

I look over at him, and the sadness that washes over his features makes my heart stop. "Graham?"

"Hmm?"

"This is not your fault. You're not the reason why I got hooked on pills. This has been a slippery slope for many years."

"Why try to stop now? What made you realize you had a problem?"

"Honestly? It took you accusing me of this level of self-harm in order to have the epiphany that everything you were insinuating is true. Looking back, I didn't have a problem after the accident. I guess I coped with everything by cutting. But it easily became an issue when I decided to use pills to help my anxiety, which then evolved to using pills to alleviate pain. If I didn't have a pill, I would be in agony. So to avoid that feeling, I would self-medicate."

Graham serves himself some more nuts and cheese, while asking, "Is your pain more than just headaches?"

"I have residual shoulder pain from the accident. Certain times I get stiff and get a sharp stabbing pain if I am pushing myself too much or lifting something too heavy. I would medicate. Then I would need more and more." I shake my head at my carelessness. "I just didn't know what else to do. No one really understood…"

"I'm getting you the best support team to help you get through this, Angie."

My eyes grow wide. "I don't want to go to a facility." Like Penny…

"Outpatient."

I nod my head and look away. "Okay."

Graham's fingers guide my chin back to him. "I promise."

We finish eating and I go into the bathroom to do my bedtime routine, while Graham takes the leftovers and dirty dishes back down to the kitchen. I stand over the sink and look at my sunken in eyes and pale gray skin. I have seen better days. I have also seen way worse. I just have to keep on, keeping on.

When I return to the bedroom, Graham has my side's covers pulled back and ready for me. I smile at him and crawl into bed, curling into his side like a kitten.

"You feel so good," I moan, as he draws me closer. It is like he wants to blend our bodies together to become one.

"I've missed you so much, Angie. I'm never letting you go."

I wake up to an empty bed and check my phone for the time. Eight o'clock. My head feels like it could not possibly be supported by my neck, it is that heavy. I roll out from under the warm blankets and sit along the side of the bed as a rush of vertigo hits me all at once. My breathing is shallow but fast, and I cannot seem to control it as the pain shoots through my temple. I reach with shaky hands to the glass of water on the nightstand and dribble some out over top of the rim as I bring it up to my lips.

I moan as another wave of pain bursts from behind my eyes. What the hell is happening? I pull myself up from the bed and wobble to the bathroom. I pull open the medicine cabinets and all of the drawers. I just need something to dull the pain. Anything. *Please* let me find something here.

Shivers run through me as I rummage through deodorants and Band-Aids and toothpaste in order to find some pain relief. At this point, Tylenol would be welcome. I cannot be choosy right now.

Nothing. I slam my hands down onto the vanity and stare up at my lifeless eyes. My heart rate quickens, and the sound of the door squeaking draws my attention to Graham who is taking up the entire frame with his muscular body.

He hesitantly moves closer to me and wraps his arms around me. His knowing look reflected back at me makes me want to scream. He knew I would be struggling, and he's just allowing it to happen.

"Why?" I demand, turning and waving a finger at him.

"You are detoxing, Angie. The next couple of days may be rough on you. But we are going to get through it. I am taking some time off to help you. Let's go for a walk."

"A walk?" Hatred boils in my blood, snaking its way

through my veins, until it finds my heart—which is about to explode in anger. "I can barely see and you want me to go on a flipping walk?"

"Yes."

I throw my hands up in the air and knock over some supplies I placed up on top of the vanity. "I can't do much with this headache, Graham." My eyes well with tears. "I need help for my headache."

"Exercise will help. Go get dressed, and I have a light breakfast for us downstairs that we can enjoy before we get out into the fresh air."

I stare in utter shock as he pivots and leaves me to this mess that I created. Why is he so chirpy and cheerful? Is he really that deluded to think that a walk is going to help me right now? I don't want to go for a walk. I just want to lie in bed and sulk. I force myself into a pair of leggings and a cotton long-sleeved sweatshirt. I pull my hair back into a messy bun and then set out to find Graham.

Propped up on an island stool eating a piece of whole wheat toast, he looks calm and collected—exactly what I am not feeling at the moment. I feel on edge, like my skin is crawling with need. My heart rate quickens over the realization that I won't be able to find relief for this headache through pills. It's as if the only exit door is locked with one hundred deadbolts, and by the time I get each one unlocked, I will be too exhausted to even feel the relief of victory. Is this even worth it? Just one magic pill can make this all go away.

But then I will have to start from scratch again.

I can't keep running from this. I have lived in denial too long. Now I have to come to terms with my addiction. I never wanted it to get like this. I was naive in a way to think it would never happen to me. I just worry that my taste of addiction is deeply rooted into my psyche now, and getting myself truly clean will cause me to not recognize who I am anymore. Or even like her.

Mr. Sunshine reaches out a hand to me, coaxing me closer. He is all smiles and joyful. "Come have a bite to eat."

I nod and move closer. My plate is already fixed with fresh fruit, a Danish, and two slices of bacon. I look toward the stove to see if he fixed this himself and see the pan cooling off on the side.

"Thank you."

"Of course. Sit."

I take the stool next to him and hesitantly pick up the fork. I'm really not hungry. My mouth is dry and my appetite is completely gone. The smell of bacon used to make me get up in the morning. Now, it doesn't even have a scent to me other than the smell of grease. But I try to eat, if just to humor Graham. I stab a strawberry and bring it to my lips. It is sweet and juicy despite the peak season for them being months away. I nibble at each item but do not nearly finish.

"I'm sorry," I say, turning to Graham. "I just can't—"

"Hey," he says, taking my hand with the fork and placing the instrument on the counter. "Baby steps. Okay?"

I nod. "I can only try."

"That's all I'm asking. This is going to be a long journey to recovery."

"I hope I can even recover."

"You will. Just stop looking so far ahead. Just focus on an hour at a time."

I take a sip from the glass of orange juice and then slide off the stool. We throw on light jackets and sneakers, then enter into the empty elevator car. Collins is in the lobby and greets us with a single nod. I almost don't recognize him in nondescript street clothes. He walks over toward us, and Graham points to a chair for me to rest on while they talk business in private.

I sit down and look back over my shoulder to see the stern look on both of their faces. I imagine that it has not been easy on the security team with me being back with Graham. When I am around, drama finds me. Mark and his goons are probably back to thinking I am a huge target again. Maybe if I told him I am going to probably fail my semester and not even have any work to show for it, it would get him to not care about me anymore. But I doubt it. Because I do still want to find the answers, even if just for my own peace and for the sake of the victims.

Graham finishes up his conversation and saunters over to me. He extends his hand and I accept. We walk hand in hand out the lobby's door. The cool air hits me like a slap to the face. I should have been expecting it, but I never am prepared—even though I have lived in Oregon my whole life. It is a good way to wake up to the day, especially when I already feel like shit.

I let go of Graham's hand as we find our pace on the sidewalk. The city is bustling, with dozens of people on the street entering buildings for a work shift. I let him lead, and I follow beside him as we walk along the block behind the penthouse.

"There's a pathway not far from here that goes around a small park. You game for walking there?"

"Sure," I say breathlessly, feeling the burn from my lungs already. Graham was serious about actually walking. This is not a leisurely stroll; we are actually working out. He picks up the pace even more, and I find the motivation to keep up.

We stay like this for thirty minutes, walking and barely talking. The park is lovely and peaceful. There is a small path that borders the grassy plain that has benches and flower gardens—albeit everything is in the dormant phase right now. We walk around the perimeter four times and then make our way back to the city streets.

Sweat beads on my forehead and my skin feels clammy. My thighs burn from the exertion and I feel oddly refreshed, while also feeling like I could collapse at any moment. Graham's version of a walk was more like a jog. And although we did not track the distance, it definitely feels like we conquered a few miles.

"How do you feel?" he asks, slowing his pace down.

"Out of shape," I huff.

He chuckles and fixes a piece of my hair behind my ear. "Never too late to make a change."

His words pack a punch. I am not new to change. Most of the time, I resist it.

I shrug. "I guess so." I'm not really sure why he decided that a walk was in order for this morning, but I am glad he suggested it. Once my breathing returns to a less dramatic state, I do feel great.

"Want to go grab a coffee?"

"Sure." I check my phone for the time. "I have to work this afternoon."

"About that…"

I stop the slow pace and look up at him. "I didn't go in yesterday. These are my only two days I actually work."

He nods and then looks off into the street—at what, I have no idea.

"Well, I guess I'll be drinking a lot of my calories today."

I narrow my eyes at him. "You don't have to do that."

"I do if I don't want to look like a weirdo stalker." His smile beams across his lips and I burst out laughing.

"You are something."

"Better than being a nothing."

"True. But what about your work?"

"Playing hooky."

I move in closer to him and press my body up against his. Warmth radiates from his torso. I step a few inches closer just to partake in the benefits of having a personal body heater.

"That seems mighty irresponsible of you, Mr. Hoffman."

He plays it off cool. "I know the CEO." He holds up his two fingers and crosses them. "We are tight."

"Hmm," I hum. "Wonder if he is as hot as you are."

His eyes darken and he pulls me forward. "Quit flirting with me on the streets," he says into my ear. "Don't think public sex is a nonnegotiable for me."

His growl makes me shiver. I look up at him and bat my eyelashes seductively. "Who says it's one for me either?" I yip and jump as he bites my ear lobe. I glare at him and smack a hand against his chest. "Hey!"

He just smiles and pulls me into a coffee shop that is new to me. Once inside, he proceeds to pull me toward the family style bathroom that is in the back of the shop. He then guides me inside and locks the door.

"Not so bold now, are you?"

I turn to look at the sex-crazed man that guards the only exit and giggle, which is probably not my best move. But at least I stay true to my character.

"Here? In a coffee shop bathroom?"

His sexy grin makes me laugh more. "Are you biased against this bathroom for some reason?"

I shake my head dramatically and look around. "Seems good enough for me."

I watch with bubbling anticipation as he walks closer to me and grabs me by the waist, pulling me hard into his groin and grinding me against his muscular thigh. My head flops back as I succumb to the sensations that only he can bring out of me. It is like my body is an instrument that only he knows how to tune. It is a heady feeling, knowing that I was made for him.

I save him time and start lowering my leggings. I kick off my right sneaker, remove one of the pant legs, and then slide the shoe back on.

"Someone's a little eager."

"Last thing I need is you creaming your pants prematurely." I try to keep a straight face, but my smirk breaks out before I can reap the full effect.

Graham shakes his head at me. "What am I going to do with you?" he asks, pulling me to him.

"Hopefully fuck my brains out."

He throws his head back with a hearty laugh, and I

know that if anyone is in line for this restroom, they will know we are up to some sort of shenanigans.

I fix the collar of his coat and smile up at him. "What is that twinkle I see in your eyes?"

"Admiration."

The humor washes out of my expression. "Hmm, why?"

"You are the only woman I know who can make me want to rip her clothes off and fall to the floor in laughter within seconds. I have never had this much fun with anyone else in my life before you."

"Gotta keep you interested before you trade me in." It is a half joke. But if there is any thread of truth to my statement, I will claw her eyes out. There is no way I am giving him up now. Our journey to find each other has not been easy, but it sure has been worth it.

"Well, you better start putting out then," he jokes.

"Hey!" I say, smacking his arms. "Easier does not imply better."

His eyes dance with mirth. "Prove it."

I bite my lower lip as he reaches between us to undo his belt. He pulls the entire strip of leather through his loops, and I glance up at him in confusion.

"Want to have a little fun?"

I give the okay with a nod, although I am not really sure what he has planned. However, with certainty, I trust him.

"Put your wrists out."

I do as I'm told. My breathing picks up as Graham loops the buckle around my wrists and then tightens the strap to secure them into place. He lifts my arms to admire his work and then drapes my restrained hands over his neck.

"Keep them there."

"Yes, sir." It feels weird playing these games we do. However, when I relax my mind and allow him to boss me around, I enjoy it. Graham stares down at my panties. They are a peach shade. My leggings are dangling from my left leg, and I imagine I look hideous.

He finishes undoing his pants, grabs my ass, and lifts me up. I have nothing to brace against other than to balance my upper body against his chest and wrap my legs around his waist.

"You are so fucking wet," he says breathily against my ear. "I can feel you seeping through your satin panties."

"Maybe it's just sweat."

"It's possible," he agrees, "or maybe you like this idea of fucking in a public restroom. Does this remind you of when I took you up against the wine barrel in the vineyard?"

"I just hope you don't go easy on me now like you did th—"

I hear the rip of my panties before I see the scrap of material fly into the air. I gasp as he lifts me up and impales me onto his hard cock. His low growl resonates in my ears, and I toss my head back to succumb to the sensations of pleasure.

Graham takes his position of control up a notch and walks us back to the door. He presses my back up against the smooth surface and bends his knees to thrust upward. The sound of the door jostling makes my heart rate quicken. We are going to be caught. How could we not? The thrill builds within me at the pleasure that he siphons out.

I have had orgasms from him before, but this one is different. This one is raw and like a tidal wave that surges through me. I throw my head back and slam it on accident against the metal door. I grind my hips into his, as Graham pumps inside me. I scream out and, unlike in the past, do not get muffled with a kiss. Instead, I get bit. Hard. On the neck.

"Graham!"

"Is this how you like it? Hard and rough and against a door?" Each word is pounded into me with his rhythmic thrusts. I feel my walls clenching as another orgasm overtakes me. I chant his name and clench my inner walls until he releases inside of me with his own rivaling scream.

When we come back to earth, Graham undoes the belt and massages my wrists. He helps me back into my leggings, sans panties. He broke those. Just like he has destroyed numerous other pairs. It is his thing. He fixes his pants and laces the belt back through the loops. I will never look at that belt the same way again.

I turn and fix my hair in the mirror. My hand covers the mark on my neck that he just made.

"Graham!" I scoff, pointing to it.

"Hmm?" he says casually. "Consider it like a temporary tattoo."

"Oh yeah, this totally looks like a butterfly or dolphin."

"Actually"—he drags a finger slowly over the sore skin—"it looks like a perfect replica of my teeth."

His words come out so seriously that I burst into laughter over his literalness. "I'm going to need a lot of makeup to cover it up. It's already turning purple."

Graham moves behind me and wraps me in his arms. His lips kiss my mark and lick along the barely bruised skin. I would be lying if I said I didn't find it hot. The mark. The kiss. Everything. His animalistic side is one I try to bring out. So, for me to complain over the ramifications of me making him lose control would be silly.

"I love seeing my mark on your pale pure flesh. Do not cover it up."

I turn in his arms and stretch up to give him a kiss to the lips. "Pretty sure the world knows I'm taken." I just hope they will relearn that it is by him. The whole fake engagement thing has probably thrown everyone for a loop.

"Good. But that still doesn't stop assholes from trying to get you to notice them."

I'm not really sure if he is speaking of some specific asshole or just the generic ones. We finish tidying ourselves up and walk toward the exit. Graham opens the door, stifles a gasp, and reaches for my hand.

14

I glance up to see four people waiting in line to use the restroom we are now exiting. The three guys in line give us knowing grins. The woman looks like she is disgusted by our actions that I assume she heard. Dang. I keep my eyes on the floor as we walk past the line, while Graham leads me out into the actual eating area.

"Is this what they mean by the walk of shame?" I grumble, once we are in the clear.

"Wouldn't know."

I peek a look up at him and wonder if he is referring to differences in genders or if he just has never partaken in a sexual romp that left him embarrassed. I skip inquiring because we are next in line to order; plus, I'd really rather not know. I examine the menu and decide a hot beverage would taste good since I am starting to feel the chill from my body coming down from the high.

"What would you guys like?" the teen worker asks.

Graham rubs a hand along my lower back to encourage

me to order first. "Can I please get a medium gingerbread latte with skim?"

"And you?" the worker asks.

"Make that two lattes and add a large cinnamon roll."

"Heated?"

"Please."

Graham finishes paying and we find a place in the corner to sit. Our order gets delivered and we do what normal couples do—enjoy each other's company doing mundane things like visiting coffee shops.

"Thanks for taking care of me," I say softly.

He reaches across the table and squeezes the hand that is not holding my drink cup. "Always, baby. Always. And I enjoy doing it."

I give him a half smile in return. I really hope he is telling the truth. Because this year has not been the easiest on me, and I am taking way more than I am giving back. I wonder if I will ever catch up to my IOUs. But that is not how Graham treats me. He never acts like I am indebted to him for anything.

My phone vibrates, and I fish it out of my jacket pocket to see that Claire has sent me a message and pic. I open the app and laugh at her pouty face selfie.

Claire: I'm in need of a Girls' Night. You game?

We have a lot of catching up to do. When I was at the safe house, we video chatted nearly every day it seemed. Now life is getting back to normal and things get in the way. I type out an info-seeking response.

Angie: When and where?

I see the dots that indicate she is typing and wait patiently for her to reply.

"Something definitely has you preoccupied," Graham says, eyeing my phone. "Everything okay?"

"Umm, well," I start. I don't know why I am nervous about telling him. It's not like I need permission. I just know how possessive and overprotective he can be. "Claire wants to have a girls' night. I think she missed me while I was quarantining."

"Can you have it at the penthouse?"

"With you hovering around the corner?"

"Pretty sure someone will be hovering no matter where you guys decide to go," he says casually. "It's not safe for you to be left unaccompanied. And I don't think drinking is a good idea right now while we try to figure out everything else."

I glance down at my phone with the incoming text. "She wants to hit a dance club this Friday. Hasn't given me a name. I can promise to only do mocktails."

Graham sighs. "Accept an entourage and make sure it is a reputable venue and not the dive bar you like to attend."

I scrunch my face up at his hoity-toity attitude. "How will I know it meets your standards, Mr. Hoffman?"

"Keep it up with the fake formalities and I'll throw you over my shoulder, skip the line to the restroom, and fuck you on top of the vanity this round."

I stare at my nails in boredom, then glance up at him with innocent eyes. "You make it sound like that would be a punishment."

"Insatiable," he hisses.

"You made me this way."

Graham takes a sip of his gingerbread latte. "Guilty."

I laugh and get back to business. "How about the new place that just opened a few months ago on the south side? Stride? No, um, Spark? That's not it either."

"Slay?"

I hit my hand on the table. "Yes!"

He takes his phone out of his pocket and places it up to his ear. "Angie wants to have a girls' night at Slay. Yes, that's it. Thank you." He shuts off his phone and then takes a bite of the cinnamon roll that I have been picking at between sips of my coffee.

"So?"

"I'll let you know once Collins checks it out. If it seems like they actually follow fire code, have multiple exit routes, and train their employees on emergency procedures, I will consider."

"You realize how silly this sounds, right?"

"You realize I don't care about a lot of things, but your safety is something I do care about? I won't budge on this."

"Fine."

"Fine."

"Maybe it will be the night they bring in the male strippers," I tease, but try to keep my tone nonchalant.

"Then that will be the night that you do not attend," he says blankly, as if he knows my comment is just meant to try to poke at him.

Graham throws away our trash, stuffs a few bills into the tip jar, and escorts me out of the shop. It doesn't take us long to get back to our building, and when we do, I am on edge. My skin starts to crawl with need now that the distractions are gone. Graham pushes the call button for the elevator once we cross through the lobby. He glances down at me, concern in his eyes.

"These first steps are the hardest. But food and exercise will help."

"Is that why you are skipping work? To babysit me?"

"It's called support," he says sadly.

"I'm sorry. I don't mean to take out my frustrations on you. I'm starting to feel like my body is bubbling with need. My head is starting to hurt."

He takes my hand and we walk into the elevator together. He tugs me to him and lets go of my hand to instead wrap his arm around me. I kick off my shoes once we are in the foyer and am surprised to see the door into the main part of the house open. I look up to Graham for answers but am just greeted with a look of indifference.

"What's going on?"

"Dr. Saber is here to check you out and do a blood test."

"What? Why? I feel a lot better." And I do. I don't understand why I would need a blood test or any of this fussing. "I'm doing everything you say. I'm drinking water and eating and going for fast-paced walks."

"Baby, I'm not doing this to punish you. I just think it's for the best."

I glare up at him. "Then why not warn me?"

He bends to place a kiss on my forehead, tugging me to him. "Because you would have obsessed over it all morning and defeated the purpose of taking your mind off the need crawling through your body."

I bite my tongue as tears start to fill my eyes. But I

swallow down my fear and allow Graham to guide me into the living room.

"Hello, Miss McFee. Graham," Dr. Saber says from the corner of the room. He is rummaging through his briefcase to find his notes.

"Hi," I say quickly, but then turn my attention on Graham who feigns nonchalance. Maybe he doesn't trust me.

"Graham, step out of the room for a bit while I examine her. When it comes to the needle prick, I will call for you."

He reluctantly leaves, and I move to sit on the couch. "Is this even necessary? I am starting to feel a lot better."

"It's an illusion. Your body and mind are resilient. They want you to cope, and having you think nothing is wrong is a powerful strategy."

"How do you know?" I question.

"Because I've been doing this for a while. And I saw some warning signs."

My mouth opens and closes. "What kind of signs?"

"You would ask for higher potency pain meds when the injury did not justify the risk of taking said meds."

"Oh." Was I that transparent? I would have done anything to get my hands on some pills. But will I resort to those means now? I seem to be back on my feet again.

"Just sit and relax, while I take a look at you."

"Okay." I sit still, but I can't help my fidgeting. I have been on edge since leaving the coffee shop—my anxiety at a barely manageable level.

"How do you feel?"

"Great," I lie.

His eyes narrow at me. "Your head feels fine?"

I feel the lump forming in my throat. "Well, no. Not exactly."

"Your mouth isn't dry?"

I swallow but feel the scratchiness deep in my throat. "Just a little."

"You feel like your skin is crawling?"

Shit. How does he know? And who am I fooling? Not even myself.

"Angela, this isn't a twenty-four-hour success story. This is a journey. You're going to have to come face-to-face with your addiction and go through the steps to heal." He shines a light into my eyes and jots down a few notes. "This is not the time in your life to cut corners. You did not get to this stage overnight. So, do not expect to get better overnight."

I nod my head and sigh. "I honestly have no idea how I got so bad."

"That's what happens to so many people. It's not like one day you wake up and decide to develop an addiction. It is often gradual. But what you have been taking alters the reactions in your brain, and your body craves higher dosages. That is how people move from self-medicating for relief to full-blown addiction."

"So, what am I supposed to do?"

"I'm going to draw your blood and test it in the lab. Those results, you will need to sign off on for the release to another doctor. I want you to see someone who specializes in addiction and psychological counseling. I am not your best fit. However, I can monitor vitals and take routine blood to make sure your overall health is taken into consideration."

"Okay…"

"I'm also going to give you a couple of books to read and a journal to write in. Staying busy and understanding how you got to where you are today will help you dig your way out. Some days will be harder than others—know that. You have a man by your side who would move heaven and earth to help you. It's okay to lean on others for support. In fact, I recommend it."

I nod my head. "He is my rock."

"And I'm sure you are his."

I shake my head. "Not so sure about that."

Graham's throat clears, and I turn to see him lingering in the hallway that leads to his office. "Everything okay?"

"I'm going to draw some blood, recommend a new team of doctors, and leave Angie with some reading materials."

Graham walks over to me and sits down beside me on the couch. I lean into his shoulder and rest my head. I am not in the mood for a conversation and am glad he doesn't force one. Dr. Saber puts on his latex gloves, ties a tourniquet band around my arm, and gets the needle ready.

I close my eyes and listen to Graham talk about his plan to take me to his parents' house to celebrate Christmas in a few weeks. My semester will be over. I can either lick my battle wounds there or celebrate the start of something wonderful. Either way, I can find appreciation in the aspect of getting away together. While the last holiday spent in Hillsboro was fun, there was the lingering threat and the box of secrets hanging over our heads. But has anything changed from then until now? Mark is lying low, but it is not like the target was ever really removed from my back.

The only thing changing is me and how I decide to cope

with the stress. I can either control my own destiny or allow the hardships of life to dictate the direction I travel.

"All done," Graham says, kissing my forehead.

I open my eyes and look down at the Band-Aid that is on my vein. Dr. Saber is extremely efficient at what he does.

"I'm leaving this stack of items for you to look through," Dr. Saber says, pointing to the pile on the coffee table. "I also left the name of the doctors who I recommend for your case. They work together in the same practice. They do not do home visits, but the office is right here in the city and you can probably even walk there. Appointments are usually booked six months out, but with some persuasion from your gatekeeper," he says, nudging his shoulder toward Graham, "I bet they'll make an exception."

"Thanks, Mitch," Graham says, reaching a hand out to shake his.

Dr. Saber walks over to me, pats me on the back, and wishes me well. He then exits right as Collins is arriving.

I glance at the time on my phone and see it is almost lunchtime and my shift at the cafe will be starting.

"I'm here to take you to work, Miss McFee," Collins says.

"Okay, thanks. I'm just going to run upstairs and change fast."

Graham follows me up. I move about the room getting ready for my shift, pulling clothes from hangers, and trying to find comfortable shoes to match. I feel the panic rising in the pit of my stomach as I want to climb the wall with my craving. It is like a shadow lingering in the caverns of my brain, waiting for me to crack.

"Can you call and ask Dr. Saber if I can at least have some Tylenol or ibuprofen? I forgot to ask."

"I know the answer."

"Well, what is it?" I snap. I don't want to play a game right now. This is information I need to know.

"No, Angela."

"You sure?"

"The answer is no."

"Ever?"

He lets out a sigh. "Just not right now."

I huff and stomp into the bathroom. I bend down over the sink and splash some cold water on my face. I feel the warmth of Graham's arms envelop me. I lift my head. Water drips down my cheek, and he grabs a clean hand towel to help me dry myself off. He looks at me in the mirror, and I feel weak and small.

"We'll get through this together. Okay? A step at a time."

I shake my head. "I'm not sure I'm strong enough."

"Yes, you are. You just need to give it time, and we need to keep busy so you have less desire to think about it."

"You removed everything from here, didn't you?"

"You already know the answer."

I nod. Of course he did. So, I guess there is no point digging through every nook and cranny when I feel at an ultimate low. I take a few deep breaths and move back into the bedroom where I have my clothes thrown on the bed. I slip on a red sweater and skinny jeans. I decide on a pair of brown ankle boots that are made from the softest suede.

Graham escorts me downstairs and hands me off to Collins. I am sure his men know of my condition and are instructed to keep me from supplementing in any way until I can fully detox. Quite frankly, I'm not really sure how bad it is going to get. I apparently am in the early phase still.

When Collins and I get into the parking garage, he guides me into the black SUV's backseat. I place my bag beside me and strap in.

"Collins?"

"Yes, ma'am?"

"Did you figure out if Slay is a good choice for Claire and me to enjoy a Friday night out yet? I really want to firm up plans with her and have been waiting to see if it is safe or not."

"I checked out the place this morning and it seems suitable enough. What time were you thinking of going there for the girls' night?"

"I'll let you know in a minute. Let me text Claire."

He nods into the rearview mirror as he pulls out onto the busy street. I open my text chain for Claire and send her a message.

Angie: My prince says Slay is suitable. What time? Want to meet at my place and head there together?

I wait for her to respond, but my phone buzzes with an incoming call from her instead.

"Hey you," I answer.

"Hey," she huffs, "I'm taking, ah, this killer abs, fuck! Class."

I giggle into the phone. Claire's dedication to going to the gym is neck and neck with my dedication to avoiding the place. While I had a lot of fun with her for those few classes we attended together, it naturally is not my scene. I stand out like a sore thumb. "Are you okay?"

"Yes, I'm fine," she grunts. "Hey! Yes, I'm chatting on the phone, do you have a problem with that?"

"Claire?"

"Just hold on, Angie, while I tell this broad bitch off." She growls and huffs at the other person. "I pay for these classes the same as you. You think you're better than me? Nope. Get over yourself. What's the difference between me making a simple phone call while this trainer here breaks my abs down or you making a live video to stream for all of your followers? Here, I'll help you out with the answer, you bimbo. There is no difference! So shut your face hole!"

"Claire!"

"I'm back. Now where were we? Oh yes, Slay. So it is winter wonderland themed night, and we are to dress in a themed outfit."

"Oh goody!"

"Save faking it for the bedroom. I know better."

"I suck at dress-up," I whine.

"Well, lucky you, your best friend is freaking amazing at it."

"You're going to make me look like an inappropriate snowflake."

"Probably," she agrees. "Or Santa's slutty elf."

I let out a breath. "Why am I agreeing to any of this?"

"Because deep down you love it."

"What time does this all start?"

"Seven."

"Okay, you going to come to my place?"

"Yup. And I'll bring your outfit, so you have less chance to veto anything."

"Bye Claire."

"Bye Angie."

I shut off my phone and slip it into my bag. I really do not like these dress-up themes due to the pressure to dress provocatively, but Claire lives for this type of stuff. How can I disappoint her? Plus, knowing Ethan's need to maintain an image, I am an easy target for her vision board that she alters weekly. If she can't dress him up, then I turn into her involuntary tribute.

"Collins?"

"Yes, ma'am?"

"Claire is coming over earlier on Friday but we plan to be at Slay around seven o'clock."

"Sounds good," he says, pulling as close as he can to the cafe entrance. "I'm going to leave you out here and make sure you get inside. I'll park and be around in case you need anything."

"Thank you," I say softly and exit.

I enter the cafe and wave to Paul. I then make a beeline for the cubbies, so I can set my belongings there. I pull out my work shirt from my bag and slip inside the restroom to put it on. After, I wash my hands at the sink behind the counter and punch in on the register so the owner knows I am on time.

"Hey," Paul says. "Everything okay with you? You missed yesterday, and I haven't seen you since before Thanksgiving."

"Yeah. I was just not having the best day yesterday," I say, but quickly add, "but am feeling much better now." The last thing I need right now is to explain any details. I just want to move forward.

"Glad you are better."

"Yeah, me too." Am I better, though? I feel like my cravings are manageable. But what if tonight they aren't? Then what?

I handle the influx of customers that arrive as a group. I punch in the orders, accept the payment, and then go to work making the drinks. Bills get stuffed into the tip jar, and I stay focused at my task.

Halfway through my shift, Graham gets in line and waits his turn. I can feel his eyes boring into me as I move about the workstation, adding ingredients to blenders and popping on lids. When he gets to the front of the line, he slides three one-hundred-dollar bills into the tip jar.

"You didn't even order yet," I scoff at his blatant disregard for the value of money.

"I'm gambling that it'll be the best drink I've had today," he says sultrily.

"Quit flirting with me," I warn, my voice low and gruff.

"Quit making me want you."

"You make it seem like this is my fault," I blanch.

"It is."

I prop my hands on my hips and try to think about what we are debating in the first place. When I come up blank, I start giggling.

"Are you even thirsty?" I ask.

He licks his lips subtly and stares blatantly at mine. "Oh yes, I am very thirsty."

"Then maybe a smoothie is just what you need," I say cheerfully. My boss walks past from the office area, and I hunch my shoulders in relief when he exits and doesn't notice anything peculiar as to why my line is not moving even in the slightest.

"Surprise me."

I punch in a medium make-your-own-creation, tell him the total, and swipe his credit card. I then move over to the workstation and decide to whip up a pineapple smoothie using fresh fruit, some vanilla yogurt, and juice. I blend, pour, top, and then get creative writing his "name"—which is basically a suggestive question—along the side.

Handing it over to Graham, I watch as his eyes zero in on the Sharpied words. "Hope you enjoy your drink, sir."

"Can't wait to hear back from you later on your little science experiment."

I click my tongue. "Who doesn't love a little taste test?" I am genuinely curious if the pineapple will have any impact on his flavor when I suck him off.

He stares down at my throat. "I hope you can handle me."

I suck in my bottom lip, trapping it between my top teeth. "I don't think my hands will be needed much."

He opens one side of a straw, puts the exposed end into his mouth, bites down, and then pulls the rest of the wrapper off. The simple act is very sexual. I suppose that was his purpose. Or maybe I am just going through withdrawals in that area of my life as well.

"Hope you enjoy," I say, backing away and then moving on to the next customer.

Graham winks at me as he takes a spot along the side wall. He opens his laptop and starts doing a bit of work—I assume.

"I'm going to take a break," Paul says from behind me.

"Sure."

The place is back to being dead, and my shift is going to end soon. I busy myself with wiping off tables, counters, and the workstation. When Paul moves over to the back booth with his phone, I glance over to the cubbies where his book bag is located.

My mouth waters over getting my hands on some pills. He has had them in his bag before, so maybe they are there now. I look over at Graham, and he is busy with his phone up to his ear and his fingers on his keyboard. I imagine missing an entire day at the office has underlying consequences.

I go back and forth in my head over what I really want and what I think I need. My head starts to throb and my teeth start to chatter with the growing craving running through my body. It penetrates every cell.

My feet slide along the floor until I find myself behind the bar, where the personal cubbies rest. With gentle fingers, I move Paul's bag and hear the rattle of the bottles. I unzip the side and take a peek. There are four orange bottles, all with little white disks. I look up over the bar's surface and find the men busy with their electronics. I squat back down.

Inhale. I pop a lid off and shake out a few pills into the palm of my hand. Guilt stabs at me. Exhale. I cannot do this. Inhale. If I do, I will be taking a hundred steps backward, instead of moving one step forward. I force the air out of my lungs that I hold. I put the pills back into the bottle and seal them up. I suck in a breath, as my forehead beads with sweat. I pull myself away from the stash and walk into the restroom to take a moment to myself.

My reflection in the mirror is one of weakness. That is how I feel. I feel powerless and borderline hopeless. One second I feel like I can conquer the world. The next? Deflated.

I stand in the same spot for a few minutes. Then I remove my work shirt and exit to find Graham.

"Hey baby," he says sweetly, getting up and wrapping his arms around my center. "All done?"

"Yup. Let me just grab my bag and we can go."

He walks me over to the bar, and I sneak behind to get my belongings. I stuff my balled up work shirt into the bag and swing it over my shoulders. I wave bye to Paul who seems to be getting ready to leave as well, now that the fresh workers have arrived. I really can't wrap my head around him being part of a drug ring. He seems so straight-laced and kind.

"See you next week, Angie," he calls out, as I walk beside Graham toward the main door.

Graham pushes it open for me, and as soon as we get onto the main sidewalk, a dozen or so men bum rush us. Some have video cameras on their shoulders. Others are flashing lights in our faces from their cameras. Microphones are thrown into our faces.

Dang.

15

My eyes dart up to Graham's as his anger boils to a temperature I rarely see from him—but when I do, it never is good. His tense stance makes me quiver a few inches behind him.

"Angela! Angela! Tell us about your boyfriend!" one demands.

"Mr. Hoffman, is it true you are cheating on Sophia? Does she know? What does she have to say about it?"

Graham grabs my elbow and pulls me to him so we do not separate.

"Angie, how does it feel to be the other woman?"

"When are you due? There's a baby, right?"

"Did this start out as an emotional affair or just a physical one?"

They all talk over each other and the words blast in my ears. Cheating. Other woman. Affair.

A baby?

What is wrong with them?

I tremble at Graham's side, as he tries to push us through the cluster of reporters, using his laptop as a shield.

"Miss McFee, how are you coping with your drug addiction?"

"Are you planning to go to rehab?"

"How did you get started?"

"Is your boyfriend your pusher?"

The questions radiate in my ears as Graham barks orders to "move" at the nameless faces.

"There are rumors that you're an escort. Can you confirm or deny?"

"Are you on the job now?"

"What is the hourly rate for a lady of the night?"

I feel my stomach start to cramp, and I fear the worst. I fear that I am going to throw up for the entire world to see. And judge. All of my sins are laid out in front of me. One after another. My shoulders hunch, and I want to curl into a ball to protect what is left of my dignity.

Hands grab at us, and I think Graham is going to punch someone. It isn't until I see Collins running toward the chaos that embodies us that I allow the relief to rush through my limbs. He gets to me and shields me from the chanting...the questioning...the insults—the truth.

My feet feel like they are stuck in cement as Collins plows through the crowd. He gets me inside the backseat and slams the door before I even realize I'm being transported.

Graham slides in beside me and sneers, "Fuck!" His phone buzzes and he pulls it out of his pocket. "Hoffman. Yeah. Shit. How did this happen? When did everyone start to care to this degree? I'll handle it." He glances my way. "No."

I watch as he hangs up, tosses the phone into the door's cupholder, and then pulls me toward him as Collins maneuvers the car, while the group of reporters try to stand in the way for another shot of us fleeing the scene.

Graham's phone buzzes, and he wrenches it out and answers in a fury. "Tell me you have answers." He tenses at my side. "Leaked? How certain? Insider? But who would have the motive? Yes, run internal investigations on every HH employee. And when you find out who did this, tell no one. I want sole knowledge of the culprit."

"What's going on?" I ask.

"I'm not sure," he says, kissing my forehead. "But I'll find out and they'll pay for their crime."

"You think it's a disgruntled employee at HH?"

"That's what my sources are telling me. Just not sure who yet."

"Someone you fired?"

"Possibly."

"I just don't get it. How does everyone know about my issues? I have barely come to terms with them myself."

"I half expected the press to have a field day with my supposed infidelity, although I'm shocked it's to this extent. But the drug use comments? That's way out of line and not many people would know. Regardless, whoever did this will be dealt with."

Tears fill my eyes as I think of all the implications of the things the world is going to learn about me. Breaking up an engagement—even if it is fake—and falling into the pitfall of addiction. This is probably the worst thing that could happen to me in terms of trying to graduate, be an investigative journalist, and get an internship. Who will want to take me seriously now when I am going to be the talk of the entire city? Probably no one.

That's the thing about rumors of half-truths—people tend to believe the worst and sometimes there is nothing a person can do to change that course of thought.

"Sweetheart, I will figure out who is at the bottom of this."

"Doesn't matter, Graham. That's the thing about rumors and reputations. Once accused, the seed is already planted. That seed will continue to grow in people's minds, and that is now how the world will see me. It's not even like it is false. *I am an addict*. Now the world knows."

He pulls me closer, and I break down into fits of sobs. How can this be happening? I am finally coming to terms with my own issues. But apparently other people knew what they were before I could identify them. Just as I am trying to resurrect a failed rough draft for my article to hand in to Dr. Williams, I will now look like a discreditable source. No one is going to believe anything I say.

"Am I going to be plastered all over the tabloids?" I whisper.

Graham looks down at me, gives me a squeeze, and then a hard kiss to the head. His non-answer is his answer. I groan and sink into his side.

"I contribute a lot of donations to this city. If I have any favors to call in, I'm going to do so. But as you already know, there is no real control over the media. We can sue for defamation of character or slander, but in the end, the stigma can only be removed from those who want to see others in a different way."

I cringe over the possible headlines that are being cooked up right now when the photographers bring their prized photos back to the office. It is ironic that I am going to get screwed over by the same profession that I am striving to enter into. There's a difference though—at least, that is what I am telling the rational side of my brain. Bringing awareness or enlightenment to important issues is vastly different than targeting me and trying to ruin my fore-seeable life.

Collins gets us safely inside the penthouse without being followed or confronted. Graham guides me straight upstairs into the master bathroom, where he starts to fill the huge tub with hot water and bubbles. Clothes get discarded into a pile on the floor, and we both enter into the water. I want to relax, I do. However, the tension in my entire body keeps me from truly being able to put my mind and body at rest.

"Come here," Graham says softly, beckoning me to him.

I slide over to him, and he turns me so I am sitting between his knees on the built-in seat. His expert hands massage into my flesh, and I lean my head forward as he rubs his fingertips down the sides of my neck.

"That feels so good," I moan.

"I'm sorry about today. I feel responsible."

I turn to look up at him with narrowed eyes. "Why do you say that?"

"It's not like you encouraged me to do the whole fake relationship with Sophia. And the media already has her labeled as America's Sweetheart."

"What a joke," I mumble under my breath.

"Things will clear up again. Just give it some time."

"What about all the drug comments and the escort questions? How am I supposed to move past those?"

"How have you managed to move on from all of the other pain you have encountered in your past? How did you get to where you are now?"

The corner of my lip retracts as I think about Graham's questions. "Things are different now."

"How so?"

"I have to graduate and secure an internship and eventually apply for a real job. You know that during interviews, they dig up your past and make sure you are a worthy candidate. Scan through social media pages, Google names, and ask for recommendations. Won't take long to type in my name after today and see what I'm all about," I respond sarcastically. "People judge. It's what they do."

Graham washes my hair as I ramble on. I am glad he is listening and not just trying to fix everything. Quite frankly, I am not sure how to dig myself out of this hole.

When the water is becoming too cool to enjoy it, we get out, dry off, and walk into the closet in search of comfy pajamas. Graham tosses me a T-shirt, and I look down at the lettering to reveal it is one of my creations, "Property of Graham Hoffman." He pulls his "Property of Angela McFee" shirt over his own head, pairing it with some jogging pants.

I smile at our reflection in the mirror. We look silly, and it is what I need to take my mind off wanting to self-destruct, like I have numerous times in the past.

"Want to have dinner in bed?" he suggests, wrapping his arms around my midsection.

"I'm not that hungry." In fact, I can feel the start of a migraine forming. When Graham looks like he is going to get angry, I quickly counter, "But I'll try my best to have something."

"I'll go get it. You go get settled in bed and relax."

On my side of the bed, I find my journal and a stack of books dealing with addiction. I grab the journal, climb under the covers, and retrieve a pen out of the drawer. I title the first page by today's date and start writing. It has been years since I wrote anything for myself—and not just for an assignment. I almost forgot how to do it.

I don't worry about spelling or formalities. I just write. And it feels liberating.

When my hand starts to cramp, I grab the top book from the stack that is titled *You Are Your Own Worst Enemy* by Nina McGraw. I peel back the cover and read the dedication. "To those who called me names, misjudged me, and made me feel less of who I am. Thank you for helping me see what really matters. It is not you."

I turn the page and start with chapter one.

I wake to the sound of paper crinkling. I jerk my body up and move my hands to try to find the source.

"You dozed off," Graham says, helping me to sit up.

I look down at the book and remember getting lost in the words. Then I must have shut my eyes.

"What time is it?" I ask, turning to see Graham propped up on a stack of pillows eating his dinner.

"Seven thirty. I made you a salad."

I grab my bowl from the nightstand and actually feel relaxed enough to eat without the fear of indigestion. "Thank you," I say, taking the first bite of chicken Caesar salad. "This is really good." I chew another bite. "Did you shave this parmesan cheese yourself?"

Graham chuckles and nods.

"Your mom would be proud of you, I'm sure. The presentation is spot-on."

"You know that woman sends me a harassing text at least every other day to make sure I am not jacking things up with you. I had to cave and tell them that all of the media attention over Sophia and me is fake. It was either come clean or face my mom showing up at HH unannounced and making a scene. You have made quite the impression on my parents' hearts."

I smile at him. "You have the nicest parents. I honestly don't even know why they have welcomed me so quickly into their lives."

"Sweetheart, you have that effect on people."

I shrug. "Not all people."

"The ones who matter, you do."

I let his words mull around in my head. I suppose they can be true.

I hate being one of those why-me people. I hate playing the victim card. But when life beats you down, it is hard not to want to hide and lick your battle wounds in peace. Between the drama with Dr. Williams, the downhill spiral into addiction, and the paparazzi beating me down, it is easy to slip into depression. Or maybe I have been depressed this whole time and never noticed it.

I slide from the bed and make my way into the bathroom. Every movement of my body makes my head throb. It is like someone is jackhammering a stake into my skull. I stumble into the vanity as I kick the door closed with my foot. My fingers white-knuckle grip the counter, but I lose my balance and fall to the floor. I groan as my hip hits the tile first. Shit.

Tears fill my eyes as I reach for anything to help me stand up. It is like grasping at water. I roll into a ball and clutch my knees up to my chest.

A knock sounds at the door. "Angie? I heard something fall. Are you okay?"

"Go away. Let me die here."

The door cracks open and Graham peers inside. "Baby? What happened?" he asks, kneeling at my side. His fingers hesitantly touch my back, but he doesn't help me stand up. He just lets me have my moment of self-pity.

"I'm a mess."

"Did you fall?"

"I think so. I just…" I can hear my heartbeat in my ears. Like a siren warning me of danger. "Need help."

"What kind of help?"

"Isn't it obvious?" I cry.

"I want you to admit it, Angie. Tell me how I can help you."

"I need to make an appointment with those doctors who were recommended to me. I can't keep on going through this battle without some expert to guide my steps," I admit. "If you weren't here—" I can't even finish my thought. "If you didn't clear everything out"—I gesture toward the drawers—"I would have gone back easily to the pills. I need them. I'm going crazy without them."

Graham whispers understanding to me and scoops me up into his arms. "Did you come in here to use the toilet?"

"Uh-huh."

He helps me pull down my bottoms and places me onto the seat. It is the most pitiful thing someone has done for me. It is not romantic. It is not what I read about in my romance novels. But it is the epitome of love. He loves me. Lots. To help me through this low in my life. To take care of me when I am struggling with even my basic needs. That is the love of a lifetime that my momma told me to wait for. This I know for certain. This is it.

Falling is a part of life. That is exactly what she said in the time capsule letter addressed to me. And those people who truly matter will be the ones to help me stand up again. But it starts with me. I have to accept the help.

Graham lifts me up, helps me wash my trembling hands, and gets me back into bed safely. He snatches his phone from the nightstand and makes a call.

"Now? At this hour?" I ask suddenly.

He just smiles and waits for the other end to pick up. "Hi, this is Graham Hoffman. Yes. I would like to make an appointment for Angela McFee. Tomorrow? Let me ask."

I look up at Graham as he puts the phone on mute.

"Does three o'clock tomorrow work for you? There's an opening."

I just nod. I can barely form words right now. I know there is not an opening in the schedule. How can there be when Dr. Saber said it takes months to get in just for a consult? I guess they knew Graham would be calling and made room for me. I suppose money has something— correction, *everything*—to do with it.

Graham gives my personal information needed in order to start the registration process. I just sit in silence as I listen to him do what he does best—take care of things.

I wake with the sun and the sound of Graham breathing. I snuggle in closer to his warmth and run my fingers through his chest hair. I rarely get this opportunity to enjoy him at rest, so I plan to have a little fun.

"Graham?" I barely whisper. His answer is a shift in his breathing, nothing more. So I probe, "What is your favorite color?"

"'Reen."

"Green?"

"Mm hmm."

"Do you like losing?"

"Nopes."

"Do you like Angie?"

"Oh yes." He moans.

"What's your favorite thing about her?

"Her perfectly pretty pink pussy."

I rest my body weight on my elbow and look at him with my mouth wide open. One eye opens, and a grin pulls at the corner of his lip, making me burst into fits of giggles.

"Were you pretending to be asleep or did you just reveal all your secrets to me?" I ask, smacking his chest.

He laughs and flips himself so he is lying on top of me, his body pressing me into the mattress.

"Why are you up so early?" he asks. "It's not even seven yet."

"I just can't sleep anymore."

"Up for another walk?"

"Sure."

We get ready and head downstairs to grab a quick protein bar out of the cupboard. I down a glass of water and tie my sneakers. With a glance out of the living room's row of windows, I see it is flurrying out. I check the coat closet for my gloves and hat.

Graham sets the pace for us once we are outside, and the bite to the air makes my lungs work harder as I try to keep up with him. It feels invigorating to exercise with him, and it is nice having something else we can do together as a couple.

"Want to come into the office with me and hang out before your class starts?"

"Are you going to take advantage of me on your desk?"

He fake scoffs. "I have very high morals, and I take offense to that question."

"Pfft." I stick my tongue out at him as we round the block and head toward the river walk. "Don't you have a lot of work to catch up on from missing yesterday?"

"Angela. I'm the CEO. I have employed plenty of people to handle things in the off chance I am not there. Come hang out. We can eat breakfast together. You can hang out on the sofa and read. Work on an assignment. Whatever you want to do."

"Okay, sounds good."

He smiles big and it's like he just won the grand prize.

When we get back to the penthouse, we shower and get ready for the day. I select a pair of black slacks, a deep purple cashmere sweater, and black boots. My hair gets twisted on top of my head after I thoroughly dry it. I move to my jewelry box, resting on the dresser in the closet, and find the dangle heart earrings that Graham gave me on Thanksgiving and the diamond necklace he gave me to wear to the winery in Washington state. It's too early for the piercing studs to be changed, but I can't help myself from lining Graham's creation up to my ears to envision what they would look like on.

Graham sneaks up behind me and helps me fasten the clasp around my neck. I put the dangling heart earrings back in the box for safekeeping. In just a few more weeks, I should be able to wear them. Turning around, I hug Graham as his fingers touch the necklace he designed just for me.

"You look lovely, Angela. Diamonds suit you well."

"Pretty sure any woman would wear them well."

He shakes his head as he examines each stone with his thoughtful eyes. "I'm certain no one would look as good as you do wearing them. You have the grace and the sophistication that they deserve."

I want to laugh at his compliment but refrain. I doubt that the rest of the world sees me as being sophisticated. But then again, he always seems to be sporting rose-colored glasses when he looks at me.

Graham's phone starts to blow up with texts and calls. He ignores them all until we are safely in the back of the SUV, and Collins is pulling out of the parking spot in the garage. The tension radiates from his bones, and I cringe over what it all must be over. I can only assume that the favors that were once owed to him no longer hold their value.

"How bad is it?" I ask sadly. "Can I even rebuild my reputation?"

"Anything can be rebuilt, Angie. Try not to think about this."

"How can I ignore it when I don't even know the scope?"

"The important thing is that you have made some important steps into getting help. Let's forget about the rest."

I frown over his lack of regard for my questions. This makes me furious. "Just tell me!" I snap. "How many articles are printed?"

"At least six."

My face pales from the slap it just received. "Six?" And counting. Shit. "I want to see what is being said."

"No."

"No?"

"Let's just get through the day. Please. Let's forget about this for a few hours."

Collins pulls to the side entrance of HH where the parking garage is located, only to find the area swarming with reporters—completely blocking us from access. He curses, and the sound of the single word is so foreign to my ears from someone who is usually so even-tempered.

"Sir," he says to Graham, "all entrances have people staking out."

I feel Graham's body tense and mine does too as a result. "We'll have to go through the lobby."

Collins backs up with efficiency and pulls up to the main entrance where security is already pushing back photographers and reporters. I imagine some were hanging out at the apartment building but could not get access to the parking garage in order to harass us. So, here's their chance.

"Graham?" My voice quivers.

His eyes soften at my unease. "Baby, no matter what anyone says or thinks, I'm yours. Take a deep breath. We are in this together."

Collins gets out of the driver's seat while the car idles, opens my back door, and flanks me along with Graham. Both men escort me inside off the street, while obscenities are thrown my way.

"Fuck," Graham sneers at the group gathered, who are trying to get a new story to take off for the next lineup of entertainment headlines—starring me.

I ignore all of the chanting and questions and comments. I just keep my head low and walk straight into the safety of HH. Is this new layer of chaos going to be my new norm?

Graham turns to one of his building security men and calls him over. "Take Miss McFee up to my office. Make sure she gets there safely while I take care of a few things."

I start to argue but am quickly silenced by his stern look. I watch as he exits his building.

"Miss McFee?"

From the glass window, I can see him address the reporters and photographers. What is he doing?

"Miss McFee?"

"Hmm?"

"Let's get up to the office," the guard instructs.

I don't want to make any problems for him and his job, so I comply. He escorts me to the elevator bank, calls the car, and then presses the number for Graham's floor. He is smart enough to stay in the lobby so I cannot escape.

When the doors open on the correct floor, I exit and get granted access.

"Hi Kylie," I say with a wave.

"Good morning, Miss McFee. What can I order you for breakfast?"

"Oh, you don't have to do that. I can just find something on my phone and call it in."

"Then I wouldn't be doing my job," she says anxiously.

I am taken aback that she is that worried over her job. It is just breakfast. "Oh, umm, maybe some home fries? And a hot chocolate."

She nods and then rummages through her desk. "I'll have it delivered soon."

"Can you order Graham something? Maybe a miniquiche and coffee?"

"Of course."

I walk down the corridor that leads to Graham's main office and find the door already cracked. I knock—only out of habit—but push it open. Sophia is sitting behind Graham's desk like she's second in command and has newspapers and magazines sprawled out on the polished surface. Several televisions are on with the news shows broadcasting their findings.

"What are you doing here?" I ask, crossing my arms over my chest.

She rolls her eyes. "I work here, Angela. What do you think?"

The way she says my name makes me tense. "Last time I heard, you were simply a model. You know, the ones who simply have to wear layers of makeup and then smile. The no-opinions-needed type."

"I'm not sure why you have such a beef with me."

"Please don't play the victim card, Sophia. You have been gunning for me since our paths first crossed and you realized Graham was interested in me."

"It's a phase."

I shrug as if her comment means nothing and look at my fingernails. "Sure is a fun phase."

"One that is costing him his reputation." She motions with her hand for me to come closer to the desk. "Here, take a look."

I stare down at the newspaper articles that have not-so-flattering pictures of my face plastered across the front. Speculative headlines. Eye-catching rumors. Hell, *Hear Say* tabloid says it best with just one word—ADDICT! In bold red script, like a scarlet letter.

I steady my heart rate as best I can, given the stress over what the world sees and thinks of me. But I keep my head held high, at least in front of her. "Hey, sometimes bad publicity is still good publicity."

"Except for Graham who is trying to build his jewelry line. You are single-handedly ruining his career."

The door behind us opens, and Graham is holding a takeout bag and drink carrier. His angry expression startles me.

"Sophia, what are you doing in my office?"

She looks baffled by his question. "I, um, wanted to see how you were doing after all of the controversy surrounding Angela."

He steps into the room and places the drinks and food on the table. "Remind me again how this is any of your concern?"

I glance over at Sophia when Graham dismisses her. His cold demeanor toward her is vastly different from his reception to her in the past. Maybe he is catching on to her constantly harassing me. Taunting me. Making me want to punch her in the face.

"It's just that when I saw what was being printed, I worried you were going to be painted in a bad light by your proximity to Angela."

He turns to stare her down. I watch as a visible chill shakes her body. "This is not your concern. Leave it be."

"Very well."

Graham glances down at the plethora of articles covering his desk like a tablecloth. Sophia turns to leave, but glances over her shoulder to shoot me a look of disdain once Graham is perusing the news clippings. I move over to him as the door shuts harder than what is necessary.

"I'm sorry if I'm making things complicated for you. I have no idea how to fix this or even overcome it. I feel like I am drowning in drama that I have zero control over."

"I don't give a damn about my image. People are going to believe what they want to believe to suit whatever narrative they concoct in their head that seems the most interesting. Going to judge who they want to judge." He straightens his posture and pulls me into a hug.

My body molds to his, and it feels like I just found the missing piece to a puzzle I have been working on for years. "I'm still sorry."

He places a gentle kiss on the span of skin between my eyebrows. "I care about you. How are you dealing mentally with all of this?"

I shrug while still in his warm hold. "I don't know what to do."

"Let's focus on the things we can control. Everything else, let's say 'screw it.'"

"There's not much I *can* control," I say, pulling back from him to look him in the eyes. "Everything is so crazy right now."

"Angie, you can either let this all bring you down or you can face it head-on."

I nod and try my best to hold back the tears. "I just want to get myself the help I need."

Graham smiles and kisses my forehead. "We are in this together." His words are another reminder of what he said in the SUV prior to arriving here, and the more he says them, the more I start to believe him.

I play with the waistband of his pants, staring up into the blue abyss of his eyes. "I just don't want to mess things up for—"

He places a finger on my lips to silence me. "Stop. Stay focused. Quit worrying about what everyone else thinks."

"Okay." My voice is barely a whisper.

Graham pulls me to him, and we walk over to the table where our breakfast waits. I'm not that hungry, but I know I should at least try to eat. He takes out all of the items and passes me my hot chocolate. I take a sip. It is the perfect temperature. We move to the couch, and I relax into a pillow while I eat my home fries.

"That's all you wanted?" he asks, taking a bite of his quiche. "Here, have some of mine."

I hold my hand up. "I'm good, really."

"Did you bring enough stuff to keep you busy before class?"

"Yeah. I'm going to journal and try to resurrect my failed article from the grave. Oh, and read more from the book Dr. Saber gave me."

Graham's brow furrows. "You're not going to keep pursuing Tanner, right?"

"I have no time to do that even if I wanted to. I am just going to use what I have and try to get the victims to email me again." Even though Dr. Williams is pretty pissed off at me, I need to have something if only to satisfy my ego.

"I wish you would just drop this whole thing altogether, but I'm also trying to respect your need to pursue your own career."

"I appreciate you trying." I smile brightly. "I know it's very difficult for you to be dating such a strong-willed feminist."

"Worst feminist ever," he says, swooping in to capture my lips. "You need me in your life—like the ocean needs the shore."

"Or candy needs my mouth," I counter with a giggle.

"Or your pussy needs my cock."

My hands run down his chest and settle on his leather belt. He looks mighty fine in his power suit. "That is not false," I concede.

"And you love it when I boss you around."

"Only in the bedroom though."

"Hmm, okay. Want to test this out and see who is telling lies?"

I swallow hard and then nod. "Yes, sir."

16

"Stand up."

I place my empty takeout container on the end table next to my hot chocolate and then get up. My hands twist in front of me as I listen to my next directive.

"Strip down to just your bra and panties."

"Graham—"

"Quit thinking."

I frown. That is pretty much impossible for me.

"Do it."

I glance back at the door, knowing that it's not locked. My heart rate increases as I start pulling my sweater over my head and removing my pants. "What if—"

"Your mouth needs to be gagged." Graham starts undoing his pants and sliding them and his boxers down to the floor. He kicks them off, and my mouth dries at the thought of someone walking in on us or hearing. It is a thrill I have come to enjoy. The heady feeling of knowing we could be caught mid-act.

When I am wearing just my gray lace and satin bra set with pink trim, Graham sighs and mutters some expletives of approval under his breath that my ears do not quite catch.

"Turn around, spread those legs, and bend to touch your ankles."

I hesitate but only for a second to repeat his words back in my own head. When my fingers curl around the girth of my ankles, he lets me know with a moan that I must be doing well with his orders.

"All these lies you tell yourself about not wanting to be bossed around," he starts, "but here you are, my little kitten, dripping from your core with cream that's meant just for me. I can smell your juices from here."

I shift my weight from foot to foot to maintain my balance. I hear a sound behind me of what I assume is Graham standing up. A hand cups my mound and squeezes, making me struggle to stay in position from the sudden pleasure surge. He helps me to stand back up, turns me to face him, and then kisses me sloppily on the lips. It is raw. Primal. Our tongues invade each other's space, and his hands grab at my neck to pull me closer, like he can't get his fill of me. Like we are each other's source of oxygen.

Graham pulls away, but just for a moment and then is back on me, his hands grabbing my ass and squeezing so hard that I scream out in unexpected pleasure. "Dance for me," he directs.

"What?"

"Don't be coy. You heard me."

I look at him through my eyelashes as he gets comfortable on the sofa and grips his cock in his hands as he waits for the show to start. I struggle to find a rhythm in my head that will help me remain graceful. By the need evident in Graham's eyes, I am pretty sure I can do anything and he would find enjoyment in it.

I swirl my hips and saunter closer to him but stay out of reach of his touch. I turn around and bend to touch my knees and sway my body to the music in my head. I used to hate when he would make me "show off" but now I've come to enjoy the release. I feel empowered knowing that someone finds me this desirable. I don't even have to try hard, and he will find anything I do sexy.

When I can no longer stand it, I turn back around and climb right up onto Graham's lap and start grinding my panty-clad crotch onto his bare cock. His hand smacks my ass playfully, and I bear down harder onto him, rocking my hips back and forth—driving us both wild.

"You are such a fucking tease," Graham bites out, reaching down between us to slide over the edge of my panties. "Lift up and sink down onto me. Show me how sopping wet your pussy is for me."

I do as I'm told and enjoy it. He's right. I love when he bosses me around. I get off to it. My body stretches to accommodate his size, and I close my eyes at the sensation of him filling me up. He thrusts upward, and my eyes flash open to catch his gaze. So many emotions are wrapped up in this one look. Need. Love. Desire. And most importantly —understanding.

Graham pumps upward into me as I push myself down. We keep this rhythm for several minutes before we both have had enough, and I squeeze my inner muscles to propel him into a powerful orgasm that rivals my own.

"Fuck, Angie!"

"Ahhh!"

"Yes. Give me it."

His fingers grip my hips, and he moves me himself as another wave builds. His semi-hard cock regains its strength as he wrings out more pleasure from my body—even when I think I have no more to give. I want to stop. It feels too good.

It starts in my toes—that feeling of euphoria—and works its way to my core. My body tenses as he takes from me the last few ounces I have left to give. My body flops forward onto him, and my sweaty face melts into the side of his neck.

"How's my girl doing?"

"I'm ready for a nap," I say with a groan. "And the day isn't even half over."

"And I need to be ready for a meeting, when all I can concentrate on is how my dick smells like you. I don't want to wash off your scent."

I curl myself onto him like a little kitten, while he slips out of me as he softens. "I want to stay here like this. Just have your meeting here while I nap on you. I bet no one will notice."

"Ha, I'm sure you'll change your tune when you are greeted by a few dozen employees in about"—he shifts his arm from around me—"twenty minutes."

"Don't care."

Graham's chuckle makes me smile. I have so much fun with him that time seems to fly by. I don't even have a chance to worry about all the struggles on my mind.

After several minutes, I lift my head and kiss Graham on the lips.

"So what's the verdict?" he asks.

"Hmm?"

"Seems like you like to be bossed around outside the bedroom too."

I give a weak shrug. "I think we need to conduct more research before we can draw an adequate conclusion."

Graham growls with desire. I jump from his lap and dart across the room. I love teasing this man.

He stalks toward me as I take a stance behind his desk. "I'm going to be late. So, you better make it worth it."

My sore body makes its way into the classroom for Human Behavior. Collins dropped me off right on time, despite Graham making it difficult for me to leave his office space. That man is insatiable. But so am I when it comes to him.

I make my way down the steps and find Bryce already in our usual seats. His pink shirt showing a llama wearing a Santa hat makes me laugh.

"I can't tell if you're laughing *at* me or just *near* me," he says with a smile, handing me my beverage.

"What's this?" I ask, looking at the side for a description but finding nothing.

"It's a surprise."

"Oh boy."

Bryce smiles. "You could use a little excitement in your life."

I take a sip of the warm drink. It is delicious and tastes of nutmeg, cinnamon, and vanilla. "How do you figure?"

"You look," he says slowly, looking thoughtfully at my face, making me feel self-conscious, "tired."

This is true. Graham had me on every surface of his office this morning, and when we almost got interrupted by Kylie during round three, I nearly had a heart attack. It didn't stop me from reaching my climax, though. At that point I lost count of how many I endured.

"How have you been?" I ask.

His smile says it all. "Good. Really good. I'm officially off the market."

"What? Really? Who's the scarf-wearing queen?"

"Very funny. But I have upgraded my tastes in women, after I realized I could harness my charm and use it for the greater good."

"This is exciting. So you're done pining after Professor Turkey Neck?" As soon as the words leave my mouth, she arrives through the side door and makes her way to the podium, clearing her throat and greeting the class.

Bryce leans over and whispers to me, "Pretty sure Turkey Neck will be joining us—in a figurative sense—inside the bed."

"That's"—I try to look horrified—"weird."

"You can meet her after class. She's meeting me here."

I nod. "I can't wait to see if she exists."

He makes a scrunched up face and sticks out his tongue at me.

Class goes by nauseatingly slow, and the sound of the professor constantly clearing her throat into her microphone makes me have a headache. She may have the start of bronchitis. My mind wanders during the presentation, and I start to freak myself out over going to see the doctors today. Despite feeling a lot better than I did days ago, I know I still need to work through my addiction. If I skip some steps along the way, I may relapse and find myself even further into the hole than before.

Class ends and Bryce walks me out into the fresh winter air while we wait for his girlfriend to arrive. And she does.

"Angie, this is—"

I turn to see her walking up the sidewalk. "Hanna."

"Yes, Hanna," Bryce answers with a curious tone to his voice.

"We met before," Hanna interrupts with a fake smile. "Hello, Angie."

I force my lips to curl up at the awkwardness of this meeting. The once pixie brunette with a flirty retro style is now a fierce and fiery redhead, with wavy locks, dressed in modern-day overalls and a sweater. She looks cute. Like she moved on from being Graham's assistant based on the glow to her skin. The last time I saw her, she was crying outside HH, and I was bleeding from her broken picture frame.

I want to ask her if she still blames me for her losing her job. I never wanted that to happen to her, and yet I feel the pangs of guilt. I want to apologize, but I also want to forget about the whole situation entirely.

"How are you doing, Hanna?"

"Well, this is bizarre," Bryce interjects. "How do you guys know each other? Did you two"—his smile elongates into a straight line—"date?"

My mouth drops at his question. "What? No!"

"Her boyfriend is my ex-boss."

I nod to confirm as Bryce places a hand on Hanna's lower back. She is being very formal and direct—despite calling me by my shortened first name. I can see through her layers, and at the core she is still bitter toward me.

I never saw Bryce with a girl before so it is an unusual sight. He has also toned down his flirty ways. He must actually like her.

I glance out into the parking lot and see Graham's car idling at the curb. His door opens and he is about to exit it, so I wrap up this awkward gathering and excuse myself to go to him. I don't need to add him to this situation. I am sure Hanna will act even colder in his presence. She may have moved on, however, I imagine she still harbors some resentment toward him.

Graham greets me with a huge hug and a kiss to my forehead.

"How was class?" he asks, looking behind me at the building.

"Not as riveting as you would imagine a Human Behavior class to be. Quite boring today, actually. I had other things on my"—I bite my bottom lip—"mind."

He chuckles at my response and helps me into the passenger side. He walks around the front, winks at me through the windshield, and then settles into the driver's seat. "Want to grab a light lunch before your appointment?" He starts the engine, and the soft purr is barely audible over my racing heartbeat.

"Um, my stomach is in knots."

"Then, let's just get a snack. Maybe a pretzel?"

"From Let's Get Twisted?" There is hope in my voice. I really do love a good soft pretzel.

"Yup. There's one that just opened up right downtown."

"That does sound good. I'll have to tell Claire one opened." That woman may claim she is a slut for margaritas and pancakes, but I think soft pretzels would also be welcome to join her food orgy. I guess it depends on how gourmet they are.

Graham smiles and pulls away from the curb. It takes us just ten minutes to get back across the bridge and parked along the street a block away from the new pretzel shop, which specializes in gourmet soft creations.

He helps me out of the seat and keeps his hand in mine as we walk along the street together. A group of people holding cameras up ahead makes my heart rate quicken, but as we approach, I learn that the people are just tourists.

"Why am I no longer being harassed by reporters and photographers?"

"Because I went to the heads and struck a deal after they printed what they did. I couldn't put a stop to everything but I sure tried."

"What type of deal?"

"One involving a large sum of money. And some exclusive future interviews to be cashed in." He shrugs. "I did what any good businessman would do. I negotiated."

I look up into his eyes and am in awe that a man loves me so much to go through such lengths to protect me. "Thank you," I mouth. Sometimes I wonder if he is going to wake up one day and question whether or not I'm worth it. "But your reputation is tarnished by looking like a playboy."

"Society is weird, Angie. I just want you to ignore the press and focus on your short-term goals. Okay?"

"Okay."

Let's Get Twisted is crowded with a line stretching outside the store. I have ample time to look at the menu and settle on the twisted nuggets sampler with six different flavors—ranch, cheddar, maple bacon, sweet cream cheese, apple pie, and garlic herb. The line moves fast, and we manage to snag a table near the window to enjoy the doughy goodness.

"I want you to relax, Angie. You seem so uptight," Graham says, taking hold of my hand. "You are not alone on this journey. And these first few steps are likely the hardest."

I swallow my bite and nod. "I'm just so nervous. Vulnerable."

"Those aren't bad emotions. Just think of the positives about today."

I smile and dip another piece of the apple pie flavor into the caramel dip. "Did you know Hanna is dating one of my classmates?"

"Hanna, my ex-assistant?"

"Yup," I mumble, as my mouth is stuffed full of pretzel.

"No. This is news to me."

"Same."

"I usually don't keep tabs on former employees," he adds. "So, I'm not surprised I wouldn't know this."

"I figured as much. But the meeting was, of course, awkward."

"How so?"

"Well, for one, I'm pretty certain you fired Hanna solely because of me. At least that's how she is making me feel."

Graham looks off to the side. "There's more to it than

that, Angie. Please don't feel guilty over this. You don't need to fill your head with these types of worries."

"But it was my fau—"

"It's business and as simple as that. If I can't trust my workers, then I do not have a place for them in my company —or my life. Hanna broke trust. So, she was let go with a respectable severance package. She should be thankful she even got that. My generosity only extends so far to those that step that far out of line."

Pretty sure Hanna may have moved on with Bryce, but she did not move on from having anger toward me. I could feel it radiating off her in the way she looked at me, her posture, and the tone of her voice.

"Why else was it awkward?" he asks.

"I never thought my friend Bryce would find a girl-friend. He seems to be the guy who is chronically single and everyone's best friend."

Graham nods and takes a bite of the cheddar pretzel dipped in a habanero sauce. When it is standing room only in the little place, we decide to squeeze out the door and get a little fresh air.

"What time is it?" I ask, not wanting to dig out my phone in the bottom of my bag.

Graham glances at his watch. "Twenty to three."

"I imagine I have a lot of paperwork to fill out," I grum-ble. "Should we head to the office building now?"

"Yeah. That's a good idea. We are just five minutes away."

We walk in silence a few blocks until we reach the private offices of Dr. Lucian and Dr. Westinger. The building houses several different specialists, each taking up their own floor. We head up to the sixth floor and are greeted by a kind receptionist who hands me a packet of papers to fill out—mostly on my current health and reasons why I am here.

I fish out my driver's license and insurance card to hand over. My insurance is basically to keep me from a hefty bill if something bad were to happen to me. Otherwise, it is useless, and the copays are so steep that I usually just suck it up if I am sick.

"Oh, I'm sorry, I thought you were informed already. We don't accept any type of insurance."

Graham, who was allowing me some privacy, walks up behind me and hands over his black card. "Just charge it. Go ahead and store my card on file to use for Miss McFee for any appointments here with or without my accompaniment or knowledge."

I turn back to look at him and furrow my brow. His hand on my lower back calms my nerves. Why is he not even caring how much it's going to cost?

"Don't worry about it, Angie," he whispers. "I got it. Okay?"

I exhale and move over to the couch to work on the packet. It is boring work, going through my medical history and listing everything out in writing.

"Umm," I hum, looking over the last form.

Graham leans over and reads the title to himself. "You can use me, sweetheart, as your emergency contact."

"Thank you," I whisper. "For the past four years, I have listed Claire down for things like this." And she did the same for me.

Graham kisses me on the side of my temple and watches

me finish filling out the document. When I am done, he walks my paperwork up to the receptionist and then takes his seat beside me again.

"If you could have three things for Christmas—money is no object—what would you want?" he asks, rubbing the palm of my right hand with his thumbs.

I tap a finger to my chin. "Hmm…"

"Surely you have thought about this before now."

I shake my head. "No, actually. I mean, I never gave it much thought. Claire, Zander, Blake, and I exchange gifts every year with each other, but the price is usually around twenty bucks per person. We are supposed to give ideas for what we want, and I struggle even to do that. If Claire picked my name, she would always go off the sheet and get me something way above the price point. But that's just what Claire does."

I can tell he is absorbing everything I am saying, genuinely interested. "Why did you struggle coming up with ideas?"

"Because everything I want doesn't have a price tag."

Graham gives me a lopsided smile and nods. "The things in life that mean the most do not cost money."

"Exactly."

"You helped me realize that, Angie."

His confession catches my attention. "What? Really?"

"Before you, I would throw my money around to get my way. I still do, of course. It is a great bargaining chip. But, you were the first person I have dated who didn't want me for my money or to improve their social status. You also were the first person who could not be bought."

"Ironic, huh? Considering you did buy me when I was still working that job."

"Any sensible woman would have taken the damn money and run."

I bite my bottom lip, letting it pop from my teeth. "Pretty certain by now you should have concluded that there's nothing sensible about me."

I am careful not to reveal too much in a public place, but based on the realization passing over Graham's facial features, I know he is catching what I'm saying.

"Frustrating as hell."

"Poor you. Must be so difficult walking through life and not being able to buy all the things."

He nods exaggeratedly. "See, you get me."

I giggle at him.

"Angela McFee," a nurse calls.

I stand up and bend down to give Graham a kiss, while he squeezes my hand.

"You okay going back by yourself?" he asks hesitantly.

I look from him to the nurse and then back again. "I think so."

"If you need me, just tell the doctor. I'll be here waiting for you, baby. I'm not going anywhere."

"Thank you." I slowly walk toward the nurse but turn back around to flutter my hand to Graham for one last goodbye.

"Hi. Hope the wait wasn't too long." She opens the door and moves her hand in the direction she wants me to go. "Right this way."

I walk down the hallway and into a small room where she takes my temperature, blood pressure, weight, and pulse. I am instructed to give a urine sample in the attached restroom and then come back to wait for the blood draw.

"Why do I need more blood taken if I just had this done by Dr. Saber?" I ask.

"This is just our protocol. It's a good baseline to have as well," she explains. "It helps the doctors to know how your body rids itself of chemicals by comparing the results."

"Okay."

It only takes a few minutes between when I get out of the restroom to when the medical lab technician arrives to draw my blood. I close my eyes the entire time and listen to the elevator style music being broadcast through the speakers. I open them again when the Band-Aid is in place.

Dr. Kim Lucian arrives with a cheerful smile. She is a kind middle-aged general physician who provides me with a thorough physical examination, checking for any signs of organ distress from my concoction of medication I was taking. Her silence while looking over my chart and then taking her own notes is unnerving.

"Angie, before we really get started in the session, I thought it would be helpful to provide some information about opioids to you that many people do not realize. This is not meant to sound patronizing. It is simply meant to educate."

"Okay."

"Opioids adhere to opioid receptors in the brain, digestive tract, and spinal cord. Whenever opioids link onto these receptors, they employ their effects. What many people who take these types of drugs do not realize is that the brain actually manufactures its own opioids. This is the body's way of coping with pain, anxiety, and often depression. By having the body produce its own, these stressors are often prevented."

"Then why aren't people overdosing on their own without anything added to their system?"

"The body never makes an abundance. Nor does it make enough to counter the painful side effects of, say, a broken ankle. The drugs that get prescribed mimic what the body is already capable of making."

"I get that I may have taken a bit too many pills when I was dealing with extreme headaches, but maybe I'm not as bad as I thought."

Dr. Lucian gives me a knowing look. "Your headaches are a withdrawal symptom. Be real with me for a moment."

"Okay…"

"How long have you been medicating yourself?"

"Few times a month for four and a half years. But recently, almost daily."

"Prolonged use of these types of pills alter the nerve receptors in the brain. You become desensitized, and thus need more to produce the same euphoric feeling of being pain-free. This is what causes accidental overdoses. Most of the incidents where Narcan is administered to overdose cases are from people who have legitimate prescriptions and just do not realize the withdrawal and overdose symptoms."

"That makes sense when you explain it like that."

"Have you received any street pills?"

I shake my head. "Um, I don't think so."

"Just to be clear, I will go ahead and lump in any pills not prescribed directly to you or administered from a licensed pharmacist in that category. Many people think that street pills have to be bought in some shady alley. Drug distribution has gotten way fancier than that with the invention of the Internet and social media. Plus, with the offering of two-day shipping from major retailers, along with access to the international market, people can basically make their own chemical compounds at home and pass them off as the real deal. It's easy to purchase potent drug components, just as one could order socks from a clothing store."

"So um, well, I have gotten pills from other people they were prescribed to," I explain. "I doubt they were counterfeit."

"Are you one hundred percent sure they were legitimately acquired from a pharmacy in the United States?"

"Umm, well—"

"The reason I ask is because pushers are able to put pills in prescription bottles and make it appear they are authentic. Some even create deceptively authentic labels. But instead of these drugs being a certain measured dose, they can be laced with other added ingredients set out to make you powerfully addicted and then seeking their services for a refill."

"I never really thought of it like that. Why would someone go through the trouble of putting pills in actual pill bottles? Seems like a waste of time."

"It all boils down to money. If a buyer believes they are getting authentic medication, they somehow feel better about it. When in reality, a lot of the knock-offs are highly addictive and stemming from other countries where the wholesale value is vastly cheaper."

"Do you think I was given phony pills?"

"We just met, so it is hard to say. However," Dr. Lucian says, glancing down at my chart, "I would say yes. And recently. Have you taken anything in the past forty-eight hours?"

"No. No, I haven't. I wanted to, but I resisted. How long do drugs stay in my system?"

"It depends on several variables. I can't be certain, but based on your blood results, I would say within a few days' time you were given or you voluntarily took a cocktail of drugs."

I shake my head in confusion. "I don't even feel like I am under the influence of anything. How can this be?"

"Tolerance levels change. You may need much more to react or even feel it in your system. Again, this is how overdoses happen."

"I'm just so confused. I have been trying to stay clean for days and here you are telling me I had a relapse and don't even know about it."

"I'm just going off of current blood results. I may have to run your labs every visit just to look for trends in the data. Your body may just be holding on to the drugs longer than the average person does. Everyone's body reacts differently. I am just glad you made the first steps to come here. Between Dr. Westinger and me, we'll get you back to having the control you lost along the way."

Her words strike me. I guess I did lose control. And yet this whole time I thought I was medicating to seek out control.

Dr. Lucian flips the page in my chart to look at some results underneath. "Also, with your permission, I acquired your results from your visit to the hospital a couple of months ago. I also ran some tests on the pills Mr. Hoffman had in his possession that he said you have stolen—and I assume—consumed.

"Okay…"

"So, you were found to have Lorazepam in your blood when you wound up in the hospital. The drug is extremely powerful and often used to treat seizure conditions. It can cause memory loss, coordination issues, and alter your ability to make logical choices. Mr. Hoffman was right in worrying about you. Were you using at this time?"

"Yes. But I think in hindsight that something else was slipped to me at the bar. I was in a car accident over four years ago. I was prescribed pain killers, and I did not use them all then, so when I was having some issues with my anxiety, I would take a pill and it would calm me down. I never had anxiety medication like what you just mentioned."

"I also saw that there were other traces of drugs in your system at the time. Nothing that would have ever been prescribed to you by a licensed physician. Please understand that anything that is not prescribed can be warped. Different dosages of active chemicals can be molded into the pill, and you would have no idea how much of each substance you were actually getting."

"Wow."

"Think of it like this." Dr. Lucian grabs her notepad and starts drawing a diagram of a container. "Imagine putting all of the ingredients to make a certain pill into a jug. Then it gets shaken up." She continues drawing on her notepad to add in a few more details. "However, the mixture might not be uniform, so one pill could have a lot of the active ingredients and another pill from the same batch could have none. This is how some people die."

I frown. "I never thought about this before."

"It would be like buying an iced coffee and splitting it in half to share with a friend. One person will always have more ice than the other."

My thoughts scatter as I think about all of the pills I have consumed and where I got them from over the past several months. It scares me to think that I could have caused organ damage during this time.

"You may have been slipped something in your drinks. In general, these pills could alter your mood, cause severe depression, and could lead to suicidal thoughts. Without a qualified psychiatrist's guidance, you could end up in serious trouble. Plus, the rates of overdoses are much higher with street pills because of the analogies I described. Consuming a nonuniform pill that is spiked with a deadly amount of a drug can be fatal."

"Is it possible I got hooked on something unknowingly?"

"Anything is possible. Someone may have groomed you or seen you as an easy target."

"Well, I can only control what I put into my mouth knowingly."

"That's very true. But if addiction was that black-and-white, no one would have trouble just stopping their behavior."

"So what do I do now?"

"Dr. Westinger is one of the top psychiatrists in the nation. She is at the top of her career and can further counsel you on the right medication and remedies to help if you have debilitating anxiety or have the illusion that you have residual pain stemming from an accident five years ago. I can find you a physical therapist if that is what you need. We will work as a team. Dr. Westinger even has a rehabilitation center that has gained celebrity status with clients all over the world."

I don't want to be sent away and locked up.

"Oh Angie, don't cry, dear. We will get you straightened out. Just remember, I am sharing options. Not all of these things will be part of the plan."

I wipe at the flowing tears that roll down my face. I feel like a weakling, and I wish that the cushioned chair would swallow me up. My mom would be devastated if she knew that my life had veered this far off the path.

"I know that right now you probably don't think that you have a serious problem. But you do, Angie. Your blood results show a high concentration of the drugs that you took recently. It is the urine and saliva test, however, that always shows the presence over a longer period of time. I'll let Dr. Westinger break down the reasons as to why you felt the need to take them in the first place. I'm simply trying to let you know that your liver and kidneys can't take this abuse for long before you start to have permanent damage."

I nod and continue to try to dry my eyes.

"Angie, if you think someone is slipping you drugs—for whatever reason—I would advise you to inform the police."

"Are you going to report this all back to Graham?" I ask, embarrassed. I fear he will go crazy if he thinks I am, yet again, being targeted. I need to tell him on my own terms.

Dr. Lucian takes my hands in hers and gives them a

motherly squeeze. "Heavens no, dear. Despite Mr. Hoffman footing the bills, he doesn't have access to any of your files. There are some levels of privacy that money can't buy. This is one of them."

"Thank you."

"Just doing my job," Dr. Lucian responds with a nurturing smile. She rises from her chair and embraces me in a big hug. "I'll have the receptionist schedule a follow-up appointment for two days from now. We can do more blood work and see how everything is coming along with Dr. Westinger."

"Okay," I respond meekly. I imagine Graham is forking over a small fortune to get this practice to squeeze me into the schedule.

"Follow me out, and I will take you to Dr. Westinger's office."

When we get to the new office down the hall, it has a more homey—and less clinical—feel. A wall water fountain runs and adds just enough background noise to mute my own pounding heartbeat.

Dr. Lucian waves to her colleague and then leaves me there, shutting the door.

"Hello, Angie." The forty-something silvery-blonde-haired woman stands up from her chair and reaches out her hand for mine. "Dr. Westinger."

I shake her hand and admire her grace and elegance at how she carries herself. She definitely doesn't look her age. She gets settled back in her chair, resting her clipboard on her lap. She extends her hand toward the sofa and I take my place.

I stare up at the diplomas and awards perfectly displayed

in bronze frames in a diamond pattern on the adjoining wall. A beautiful bonsai plant rests on the coffee table, and the room suddenly fills with silence. My silence. I freeze up and instantly feel vulnerable. I expect her to judge me, and maybe that fact is making it harder for me to accept my responsibility.

I watch the water flowing from the fountain and wish it was louder. Anything to break her watchful silence. I don't want to face my fears. Or the truth. Or the past. Yesterday I wanted to. But at this moment in time? No.

"Why are you here today?" she asks. Her question is blunt and in complete contrast with her sweet voice.

"Dr. Lucian sent me," I answer meekly, suddenly losing my voice.

"Not good enough."

Excuse me? I raise my eyebrow.

"Why are you here, Angie?"

"Because Graham and his personal doctor think I have a problem with the painkillers I have been taking."

"I don't care what Graham thinks. Or his doctor." Her response is almost like a slap in the face. "I want to know why *you* are here today. Because as far as I can tell, you came in willingly." Her arm gestures toward my attire, as if highlighting the fact that I am not bound.

What the hell is her problem? And why is her tone in contradiction to her intrusive questions? It is extremely unnerving.

"Remember, Angie, everything you say is protected by doctor-patient confidentiality," she reminds me.

I get up from my solo couch and pace in front of the coffee table. I don't know how to answer the question. I definitely don't know how to give her a response that will make her move on to the next part of the interrogation.

"I'm here because I have a medication problem."

"Quit sugarcoating."

"*Drug* problem."

"Keep digging."

I turn and stare back at her. Her eyes are a soft gray. "What?"

"Surely there was some turning point in your life that started this whole thing. It's not like you woke up one day and decided to take some painkillers and some antianxiety drugs. So, keep digging. And maybe"—she taps her pen on her clipboard—"just maybe, we will learn something of value today."

"I don't even think I remember taking any antianxiety meds. If I did, they were never prescribed to me." I pause and look at the doctor who is simply listening. "I think someone is drugging me," I whisper.

She nods. "Maybe. But before that happened, you made several choices all on your own. I want to know what led to those choices. Tell me the backstory. Tell me how you got to where you are at this very moment."

"I don't know."

"Yes you do. And only you know the answer. So, I have no one to ask but you. If you want my help, you have to come clean."

Come clean.

"My mom died when I was twelve. Six years later, my twin brother, James, died in a car accident. I was the passenger. I watched him die. I never got over it. Doubt I ever will.

I was not myself after the accident and started to cut. I had injuries I was coping with."

"So, why not start abusing drugs then? Seems like that would be the logical time for this all to start. In addition, you had easier access to the medication."

I shrug. "I guess I didn't need to cope then as much as I have needed to recently."

"That doesn't logically make sense," she points out.

My eyes narrow at her. "Excuse me?"

"Oh, I am just calling bullshit on your answer. That's all."

"I gathered that."

Dr. Westinger crosses and uncrosses her legs. "Let's dig deeper, shall we? Why did it take so many years after the accident to decide that you need the pills? Physically and emotionally, you should have been at your worst the days right after the accident."

"I was emotionally numb then. And physically, I think I welcomed the pain."

"Yeah? Tell me about it." Her eyes stay fixated on me. Expectant.

"What's there to say?" I answer with a bit of attitude. "How would you expect for me to act after my twin brother died in front of me?"

"A lot of people deal with tragedy, but not everyone gets hooked on pills. We need to figure out why you fell into that type of darkness. If we don't know how you got there—beyond just that you were sad—then getting out will be harder."

I shrug and slump into the cushions. My temple is starting to pulsate, and the telltale signs of a headache brewing are in the background of my mind. "I guess I am just weak."

Dr. Westinger dismisses my flippant comment with the wave of her hand. "Sometimes guilt and grief are two emotions that often compete with one another. Did you get a chance to grieve for the loss of your brother?"

"I attended the funeral. I visit James's grave every time I go back to my hometown. And I think about him often—even in my nightmares."

"But did you have a chance to get angry? To cry? Scream? Place blame?"

"I'm still angry. I never stopped being angry. I still cry. I still scream. And as for placing blame? I still don't know who killed James. I have these fragments of memories. They are buried deep in my mind. I thought it was a drunk driver who fled the scene. For years that is what I believed. I was the only surviving witness besides the driver who hit us. But then I went through a box of memories from the hospital. I also went back to the crash scene on Monday, and I keep having these memories…"

"Tell me more. Don't stop."

"It was not an accident that we crashed. We were being chased down after someone tried to drug and rape me at a college party. I called my brother to come get me, and we were going to go to the police station to report the attempted crime."

Dr. Westinger takes a few notes. "Angie?"

"Yeah?"

"Do you blame yourself for the accident?"

I think about the question. "Yes. How can I not blame

myself? I called James to come rescue me like he always did. I lived. He died."

"What if I told you that you were both victims? That the only person who is to blame is the person at the party who did you wrong."

"Sure, logically, I know that is true. But deep down, I have this guilt."

"Guilt for what?"

"For surviving," I admit.

Dr. Westinger points the end of her pen toward me. "Bingo. You just diagnosed yourself."

I furrow my brow. "What?" I am struggling as is keeping up with her rapid-fire questions, let alone understanding her when she is rattling off comments.

"You have something called survivor's guilt, which is a symptom of your PTSD."

"I am an addict."

Again, she waves her hand, as if my words are just unnecessary commentary on my part. "You are a survivor who feels guilty for living while a person you love died. You became an addict years later. And we are on our way to discovering more as to the reason why."

I rub at my forehead as I feel the migraine starting. "I get migraines."

"Withdrawal."

I want to reach over and hit her. How can she be so certain? "That's exactly what Dr. Lucian pointed out," I mumble.

"Good. We are often on the same page. Why else do you feel guilty? And what brought this on at the moment in your life where you felt the need to abuse pills?"

I dig deep into the pit of my soul. Tears fly out of my eyes, and I feel lightheaded as I strip myself down to an emotionally raw level. "I think I was finally at a stage in my life where I was starting to live again and not just go through the motions. I was turning a new page. Trying to find happiness. And the happier I am, the more guilt I guess I feel. Probably because I know that James's life ended too soon, and he will never be here to have the things I have now." I wipe at my eyes that suddenly are leaking tears. I choke on the ball forming in my throat.

"And what makes you happy, Angie?"

"Graham."

Her smile is warm. She nods. "You aren't alone. There are many people who experience PTSD and survivor's guilt. Surviving victims of school shootings. Sole survivors of house fires. Soldiers who go to war zones and make it out to talk about it. What you have gone through has changed your life forever. But there is nothing you can do that will ever bring your loved ones back. How you react to this realization is what you have control over. You can choose to be happy or choose to be miserable. You can choose to skip to the next chapter, or you can choose to keep rereading the same page over and over again. These are things you have control over. And if you can make these decisions, then you will not need the drugs to compensate for your guilt."

Wow. Dr. Westinger's words shake my heart.

"You can't fix heartache with medicine, Angie. You can only fix it by embracing possibility."

I furrow my brow over her words. "What do you mean?"

"That's what we are going to discover within our

sessions. Sometimes the most devastating experience is the catalyst for the greatest door to be opened. I want to leave you with a parting thought. Where would you be today if your mom and James never died? Do you have a journal?"

"Yes."

"I want you to write in it daily. Or even multiple times a day. I want you to search your heart for the answer to that question."

"Okay."

"I'll see you in two days."

"Thank you."

I stand up from the couch a little lightheaded. It feels like I just had my entire brain dissected by Dr. Westinger. I may have had my doubts about her at the start of the session, but she really got me to open myself up—something I haven't even done in the silence of my own thoughts.

I walk out with her to the lobby where I have to sign some documents. I feel mentally drained. Sharing my past was the easier part of the session. All of the emotions she dug up have left me with even more stuff to think about later. Damn, she's good at her job.

Graham greets me at the receptionist cubicle, completely private from everyone in the waiting room. Sensing my exhaustion and mood, he resists asking me questions and just pulls me to his side.

We walk out of the office space holding hands and enter into the elevator we used to come up here hours ago.

"Want to go for a walk?" he asks. "We can go anywhere you want."

I shake my head *no*. I don't feel in the mood for anything.

"Ice cream?"

"Can we bring it back to the penthouse? I just feel very" —I bite my bottom lip—"I don't even know."

"Sure. No need to explain, sweetheart. We can do anything you want."

"Right now, I just want to lie in your arms and eat empty calories."

"Then that is exactly what we'll do."

17

"I don't deserve you," I whisper.

Graham tucks a piece of hair behind my ear as we lay cuddled up on the sofa watching our second chick flick of the evening. Empty ice cream bowls litter the coffee table. We decided to eat dessert before dinner, and because we couldn't decide on a flavor and therefore bought a crazy amount of minis, we are now barely wanting real food. So, sodium-enriched TV dinners for the win. Graham is not a fan. He is kind of a snob when it comes to food—if you ask me.

He kisses me on the forehead and places his empty plastic tray onto the table. "You are everything that I never thought I needed in my life, Angie. And now that I have you, you are my entire world."

I hug him and tuck my head under his chin. His citrus woods scent surrounds me, and I breathe him in. "I feel the same way about you."

The movie finishes up with the iconic grandiose gesture of love, which Graham scoffs at.

"What?" I ask, turning to look at his expression.

"It's not realistic, Angie. Plus, these men have zero game."

"Of course it's not realistic, Graham. It's a movie."

"Then why watch it or read it?"

"An escape."

"Next time let's pick something more relatable."

"Like the news?"

"No. Like sci-fi."

I burst out laughing. "Oh yeah, because the chances of aliens overtaking the world in the next century is a likely possibility."

He laughs and gathers dirty dishes from the coffee table. I grab the trash and follow him into the kitchen to dispose of it.

When I get upstairs, I brush my teeth and then decide to just forgo all of my clothes and crawl into bed naked. It has been one of those days where my mind is completely fried and even making the simple choice of what to wear to bed is too much for me.

"I could get used to this," Graham says, gathering me in his arms.

I lean my head against his chest and curl up beside him. "You're so warm."

Graham gets me tucked into the covers and reaches over into the nightstand to pull out my tattered book that we both have been guilty of reading. Me for fun; him for research. Or so he claims. He must have snagged it from my side when I wasn't home.

I watch in awe as he flips open to a section I have already read and starts to recite the lines.

"*Trent grabs my chin and kisses me senseless. Just like he did when we first met. Eight months later and he still has the same effect on me. We breathe as one. My arms circle up over his neck, and his hands bury themselves into my hair. He pulls away and my lips instantly mourn the loss of his touch. He smiles at my pout.*"

"I love this next part," I whisper. "Keep going."

"*Maintaining eye contact, Trent gets on one knee and pulls out a tiny pink velvet box from his back pocket. My eyes fill with tears as he reveals the solitaire diamond ring. 'Margaret Marie Carlson, I freaking love you. Will you marry me?*'"

"Yes," I respond absentmindedly. I sit up and bend down to kiss Graham. Our tongues connect as he tosses the book toward the end table, missing it completely.

"For someone who doesn't do the whole romance thing, you sure know how to make me melt," I comment.

I lie back on the pillow and savor the sweetness of such an action. Lying in bed with a man who makes me weak in the knees, having him read romantic lines from a novel, as I snuggle into his side under the dim light of a lamp and fall asleep in his arms.

"You smell so good," I moan, my voice hoarse from sleep.

"You feel so good. Especially when you are…" Graham flips me under him and presses his weight between my parted thighs. His bare chest, strong and tanned, is perfectly defined in the morning glow of the sunlight sneaking through the curtains. I can't keep my hands from touching him.

"Helpless?" I interject.

"No, not helpless," he disagrees with a shake of the head. "*Cooperative.*"

"I'm always cooperative."

"Lies." He nuzzles my neck with his nose and licks up the side, until he finds my waiting, deprived lips. "Hmm."

I can feel his erection awaken with a twitch and lengthen along my bare thigh. Hell, he feels good.

I squeeze my way out from under him and sit up. "Let's chat."

He rolls to his side and eyes me suspiciously. "You want to chat?"

"Are you going into the office today?" I ask. "I think the weather is going to be cooler. I am wondering if I should work at making a grocery list. Thoughts?" I feel his eyes bore into me, as I grab my phone to pull up my weather app. It takes everything in me not to burst into a fit of giggles. I stretch my legs out, and my knee bumps his cock and makes him jerk from the unintentional attention. Easy boy.

"Angie?"

I glance up from my phone. "I think I'll wear jeans and my knee-high boots. What are you going to wear today? Oh and do you actually go into stores to try things on or do you just get a bunch of stuff sent here and then yay or nay it?"

"Angela—"

"Did you know that honeybees have acrobatic—in the air—sex? Like there is one queen in a colony of two hundred male drones, whose sole life purpose is to get it on with the main girl and all the female worker bees. Isn't that crazy?"

"Nuts."

"And the best part is that the drone's reproductive parts get torn off."

"What?"

"Basically his testicles explode." I bite my tongue as Graham cringes and rolls to his back. But when he groans up at the ceiling, I cannot contain myself anymore and burst out laughing, throwing myself on top of him like a floppy bunny.

"You doing this to me on purpose?"

I force myself to sit back up and plaster on my serious face again. "Just giving you some fun facts, that's all. Not my fault you take things so personal."

"Talking about the weather and outfits and then exploding testicles. You are evil."

I fake scoff. "Harsh."

"And another fun fact is that if you don't get over here," he says, pointing to his side of the bed, "my testicles might mimic your graphic science documentary descriptions."

I crawl over to his side and run my hands over his chest. He smiles and grabs my ass, squeezing the meaty flesh, as his lips kiss my neck. He trails a wet path down to my breasts and buries himself in the valley.

"Ahhh..." I moan-yell, arching my back up from the mattress as his mouth suckles and nibbles at my sensitive peaks. While he attacks one with his tongue, the other is squeezed and kneaded with his hand. "That feels incredi...ohhh!"

He treats each globe fairly with equal attention. I wrap

my lower half around his waist and pull him in toward me with a thrust.

He kisses and licks my flesh. "You are the most beautiful woman I've ever seen."

"I want you," I breathe, enjoying his light kisses.

Graham pulls back suddenly, unlocking my ankles and shifting his weight off the bed. His hand moves to his mouth, wiping the moisture from the corners.

"What the hell?" I ask, moving up on my elbows. Suddenly shy of my naked form, I cover my chest with my arm. "Why did you stop?" Does he no longer want me?

Graham makes it a huge production to look at his watch that he has resting on his nightstand. "Wow, what do you know? It's time for me to get up and get dressed." He rolls out of bed and meanders into the closet. "What did you say the weather was again?" he calls over his shoulder.

I watch his bare ass retreat and sigh. This whole fun plan of mine backfired. I follow him inside and jump onto his back when he bends over to look for a tie.

"Ah, Angie!" he yells, stumbling to the floor but shielding me from the impact.

"Got you," I laugh into his ear, rubbing my crotch onto his thigh, as I pin him to the floor with my lower half. "In my scissor hold."

He laughs. "Sounds scary."

I gather his wrists up into my hands and place them above his head. "There. Right where I want you. Now be good and stay."

"Now that you have me, what do you plan to do to me?"

"Just admire the view from above."

"That's it?"

"It's a mighty fine view." I glance down at his erection. "And suck you off," I say casually, making him laugh. "But if your hands move from where I placed them, it's all over."

A wicked smile breaks out over his lips. "You play hardball."

I ignore his comment and slide down his body so that my mouth is lined up over his cock. I hold my breath and slide him into the back of my throat on the first suck.

"Fuck, baby! You better not be practicing elsewhere," he snarls. "Your talents are for me only."

As soon as I feel his hand in my hair, I pull back and get up. "Well, that was fun," I say sweetly, looking down at his shocked face.

"Angela…"

"Too bad you broke the rule. The *only* rule. Ya couldn't just lie there and look pretty, could ya? And you messed up my science experiment to see if the pineapple you've been eating this week has made any impact on"—I gesture toward his crotch—"your taste."

I turn and walk out of the closet, leaving him in a desperate state on the floor. This is too fun. Except, I only make it about two yards before I am thrown over his shoulders and my ass gets smacked hard, making me yelp.

"What are you doing?"

"Being the bad boy you crave."

He tosses me onto the bed, and I bounce from the impact. I get up on my knees and dart toward him and knock him back.

"You seriously want to wrestle?" he challenges. "You forget that I was an All-American wrestler?"

I kneel back on my heels and keep my face as straight as

I can. "That was like a decade ago. You are slower now. Older." I allow my eyes to lazily stroll along his body until they stop at his cock. "*Softer.*"

He shakes his head at me and laughs. Then he darts toward me and has me pinned underneath him before I can even let out a yelp.

"Damn," I exhale, letting the word drag to a hum. "I'm in trouble, aren't I?"

"Let's see what this old man of yours can still do."

Graham and I enter HH with to-go cups of coffee in hand and a takeout bag of pastries. We squeezed in a mini-walk, post-walk sex, and shower sex all before nine o'clock. I feel energized and ready for my day.

"Lots of meetings today?" I ask, waving to the regular security guards. I am starting to get used to them and see them as less judgmental of me than I did weeks ago.

"It's a pretty packed day. I'm about to launch an idea for a new line."

I look up at him as we wait at the elevator bank. "Oh yeah?"

"Yup. One that is more affordable."

I giggle at his megawatt smile. "You have all the good ideas."

"Best idea I ever had was to pursue my current girl-friend. I should introduce you to her, because in fact, this was *her* idea. She is pretty amazing and smart and knows how to see things from a different perspective. She is also

296

stubborn, very intelligent, and determined to make me lose my mind on any given day."

I smack his arm as we enter the car. I love that he is taking my opinions to heart. That my voice matters. That I matter. "She better be good in the sack."

"Only complaint I have is that she wants me all the damn time. Can't keep her hands to herself and basically treats me like her personal sex toy. She's going to rub me raw."

I gasp and glance around the empty confined space—as if someone is going to hear. "Shush!"

"It's okay though. I'm fine being objectified. Whatever keeps her happy." He winks. "Plus, she is super hot. And her pretty pink pussy is"—he gives a chef's kiss—"divine."

I blush over his comments. He has a talent for making me uncomfortable but in a good way. Keeps me on my toes.

Once we are in his office, I relax on the couch and enjoy my breakfast. Graham sits at his desk and rummages through files and documents that are situated in the corner. I throw away my wrappers and settle in at the conference table with my new laptop that Graham got for me, my notepad with the start of my newly revised article for Dr. Williams, and a list of agency girls who have been drugged.

"Graham?"

"Hmm?"

"Can I get a list of all the girls in the Entice database?"

He looks up from his computer screen and eyes me with concern. "I don't want you involved anymore. I need you completely disconnected from all of this. Mentally and physically."

"You said so yourself that I have this ability to see things from a different perspective. Maybe I can help."

"You are striving to be an investigative journalist who wants to report on a case that is ongoing with the FBI. This is a direct conflict."

"Well, is the FBI even considering—"

"Stop," he interrupts. "Please."

"I think someone is drugging me. In addition to my own bad choices."

"What?" He gets up from his desk and moves over to me.

"When Dr. Lucian ran my blood, there were a lot of substances in my blood and urine."

"Where have you gotten the pills you were taking?"

"At first, they came from an old prescription that a doctor gave me for my injuries endured from the car accident. But then, I would get my refills from a classmate who had an injury. Or from bottles I found at a party. Some came from your supply you had stored in the filing cabinet."

Graham's eyes grow dark as he absorbs all of this information I am dumping onto him. I don't think I ever really admitted my persistent behavior to him on how I would acquire my fixes. And now that I'm trying to get clean, all of my shady methods are glaring back at me. I hid behind my research and used it to mask my poor choices to those around me but also myself.

"You could have killed yourself or overdosed. All the pills I had in my possession have been for the purpose of trying to decode the chemicals and origin. I would have some girls, who I hired through Nic, work for me undercover in the agency to gather evidence."

I remember him divulging this information. At the time, I thought his gambling with other people's lives was too risky. Now, I am desperate to figure out how everything ties together. I am angry. Exhausted. And nervous about what this means for my future career.

"I was gathering my own evidence too. I just didn't know that we were basically working against each other, despite having a common goal."

"No more. I beg you. I need you clean. Healthy."

"I promise you I won't take any more pills. I am done. I think back to how I got to this stage in my life and am disgusted with myself. All these bad choices I've made and yet somehow, you have managed to stick by me in my despair. I feel like I am trying to find some good out of the ashes of my life."

Graham pulls me up into his arms. "I'm always here for you, Angie. You are it for me. And just remember, your choices don't define you. You have the power to change."

His soft kiss to my forehead makes me melt into his arms. His phone buzzes on his desk, which he ignores. Then there's a knock at the door.

"You're being summoned," I playfully tease.

"Has to be by someone other than Kylie. She knows better than to interrupt me when you are here."

"Yeah, she is probably terrified of seeing her boss caught with his dick in someone."

His fingers tip up my chin. "Not someone." He wiggles his eyes. "You." His mouth captures mine and I melt a little more. Pulling back, he stares into my soul. "There will never be anyone other than you, sweetheart. You are my life."

The knocking persists, but this time louder than the previous round.

"Sheesh," I mutter. Way to ruin the moment.

"Let's see who I'm going to fire today."

"Graham—"

"It's a joke."

"You have a bizarre sense of humor." I giggle as he tickles my sides.

I sit back down at my chair as Graham answers the door. I have so much work to get done before my lab class starts. The sound of laughter makes me turn around to see who is at the door.

"Have you ever heard of texting?" Graham teases, welcoming his friend inside.

I wave at Logan and am surprised to see him in a button-down and khakis. When I was in his piercing chair, I don't recall what he was wearing—however, I know it was less formal. That's if button-downs and beige pants can really be lumped into that category.

"I came to invite you in person, since you have a bad habit of not answering your phone when I call."

"You gave me thirty seconds to pick up. So, I would not classify that as avoidance, you asshole."

Logan shrugs and flips Graham off. Never in a million years would I have pegged these two men as being friends. They are on completely opposite ends of the spectrum. I guess outsiders may say the same thing when it comes to me and Graham as well.

"Hey, Angie," Logan greets.

I wave back. "Hi."

"How's your ears doing?"

"After my infection and two trips to the ER, they seem to be—"

His eyes grow large. "Wait, what?"

"Just teasing!"

"Oh, that's evil." Logan turns his attention back to Graham, who is resting his backside up against his desk. "Dude, you have your hands full with that one."

"Oh, don't I know it," Graham agrees, giving me a smirk. He focuses his eyes on me, completely ignoring his friend.

What's up with his excessive watching? It is throwing me off my game.

"You know it is a workday," Graham says. "Get on with it. What's this invitation you speak of?"

"Poker."

"No limit?"

Logan sighs. "Not all of us are made of money. There's a cap at two hundred."

"So we are basically playing with M&M's again. What night?"

"Tomorrow night."

Graham glances over at me as I tap the end of my pen against my lips. "I'll be gone for girls' night anyway. Remember? With Claire."

He nods and accepts the invitation, which I am glad about. He needs to relax and hang out with his friends. Loosen up a bit. "Want me to host since I have the table?"

"Sure, but I'll bring the beer. Tired of your shitty seltzers you like to serve."

Graham shakes his head chuckling, obviously entertained by Logan's joke.

After Logan leaves, Graham heads out for a meeting, while I work for another thirty minutes on my article before I have to head over to campus for my class. Like the loyal bodyguard and chauffeur that he is, Collins is waiting for me in the main lobby to escort me out of the building into his idling SUV.

Lab class is interesting with an experiment involving the analysis of nervous tendencies for people in high stress situations. I always find the hands-on part of class the most intriguing and beneficial for my line of career. It helps to be able to read people, detect lies, and then use intuition to decode the real emotions of a person.

Since last week, the professor has moved us away from partner work and has made it more individual. I actually prefer it this way, only because now I no longer have to carry the weight of Bryce who seems to just be along for the ride—and the easy credits. I think he has completely checked out and is ready for the semester to end. I'm ready too. It's just that so much needs to be done before I can do a victory lap. No point celebrating anything until my diploma, with my degree stamped on the front, is in my hand.

We walk out together, and like yesterday, Hanna is waiting for him outside.

"Hi, Hanna," I greet, earning just a singular nod from her. She wraps her arms around Bryce, and he soaks up the attention like a sponge desperate for water. It is a bit over the top and forced. But who am I to say? I'm just merely an outsider looking in on a fresh relationship. "Well, I'll see you next week." I wave goodbye and make my way to the parking lot where Collins is waiting.

I get inside the vehicle and am taken back into the city.

Except instead of being dropped off at the penthouse, I find myself in front of Hoffman Hotel.

"What are we doing here?" I ask.

"Mr. Hoffman wanted me to drop you off here. He has instructed me to tell you to go to the front desk and ask for him."

"That's it?"

"That's it."

"Okay. Thank you, Collins."

I exit the backseat and walk nervously across the sidewalk. The doorman greets me with a bright smile and opens the door for me to enter. I haven't been here in months and the last time was with Mark—who basically has fallen off the face of the earth.

I make my way to the line of desks and find several friendly faces all waiting for me to get closer to speak.

"Hi. I am here to meet Graham Hoffman."

"Right this way, ma'am," the male worker instructs, motioning with his hand to follow him.

I allow him to lead me up a ramp and through an employees only door that leads me through a corridor and the back entrance to the spa. When we get to the other side of the room, the worker opens up another series of doors that leads into a private dressing room.

"Please get undressed and put on the robe that is hanging on the hooks near the door. Your personal items are safe inside this room and it will be locked upon your exit."

"Thank you," I say shyly.

I have never been to a spa before, so I'm not sure what to say. Do I keep my panties and bra on? I am just glad I am pretty well-kept and that I shaved where I needed to prior to coming here. This is how rumors start…

"Mr. Hoffman wanted you to have this," the worker says, handing over an envelope. "Enjoy your afternoon, Miss McFee."

I watch as he exits the same door we arrived through. I stare down at the envelope in my hand and turn it over to find a little gold heart sticker on the back flap. I run my finger under the seal and rip it open. Pulling out the card, I read Graham's handwritten note.

Sweetheart, I wish I could join you for the entire afternoon, but I have business to tend to… Please enjoy a spa day on me. Oh and by the way, we own this hotel now. So, if you hate the service, tell them. -GH

I stare at his words and reread them three times until it sinks in and I start to believe it. We own this entire building? Did Graham inherit it from his relative? Buy them out?

The knock at the door on the other side of the room startles me, and I nearly jump out of my skin.

"Yes?"

The door hesitantly opens and a pleasant, petite woman steps inside. "Hello, I am here to help guide you through your spa experience, starting with your massage." She looks down at my outfit.

"Oh, sorry, I still need to change." I suck my bottom lip between my teeth, gnawing on the soft skin.

"Is everything okay?" she asks nervously.

"Oh yes, of course. I just didn't know how much to take off and what to keep on. I'm kind of new to all of this."

She smiles warmly. "It's fine. Go ahead and take everything off. However, stick to your level of comfort. Today is a pampering experience, and Mr. Hoffman wants you to be spoiled and refreshed."

I smile over her words. "Thank you. I'm pretty excited actually."

"Good." Her face is so kind and welcoming. "I would be very excited too. Mr. Hoffman planned an amazing menu for you to enjoy. I'll be waiting for you outside." She points toward the door. "Just come out whenever you're ready to start."

I wait for the door to fully close and then I start removing my boots and clothing, folding them and placing them on a wooden bench. Soft instrumental music plays through the speakers, and the smell of vanilla is prevalent.

I slip on the pair of cloth slippers and make my way out to find the worker, right where she said she would be waiting for me.

"Please follow me."

I do as I am told, and she leads me into a room that has water fountains, dimmed lights, and a long cushioned table in the center. Despite lacking most of my wardrobe, I am still warm and cozy.

"You are going to remove your robe, lie down on your stomach on the table, and cover up with the sheet. Your therapist will be in soon," she explains, closing the door to give me more privacy.

I place my robe and slippers on the chair in the corner and climb up onto the table. Nerves get the best of me as my trembling fingers grip the cloth sheet behind me and pull it up over my back. Three knocks at the door alert me of a new arrival.

"Come in."

"Hi, Miss McFee. I will be taking care of you today."

I wave and offer a mouthed "hello."

"When you have gotten massages in the past, what did you like best or least?"

"Oh, um, I've never had one done professionally before."

"Well, then, you came to the right place. I have been a massage therapist for the past twenty years. I specialize in post-recovery massage and prenatal massage. However, I particularly love hot stone massage."

"Wow, that sounds very cool."

"Do you have any injuries currently or ones from the past?"

"Yes. I was in a car accident several years ago," I explain. "I suffered several injuries but was dismissed from my physical therapist." I point out my problem areas and try my best to remain calm.

"If at any time during the session you feel pain, you let me know. Sometimes pain is expected during introductory sessions as your body adapts to the sensations. However, today is not meant for that. Today is to help you relax and feel cherished."

"I really do appreciate it."

"It is my pleasure."

I sink into the cushioned table and wait for the therapist to get her supplies ready.

"During the session, feel free to close your eyes and fall asleep. I'll be using the stones, heated essential oils, and some hot towels to help you to enjoy your experience. Again, if anything hurts, please let me know."

She starts at my shoulders and works her way down my back, sliding down the sheet as she goes. I thought it would feel weird, but it doesn't at all. She is professional and respectful. I melt into the table and my mind drifts as she works her magic on my tense muscles.

When my eyes are heavy, I close them and submit. My muscles melt, and I allow my body to go boneless, molding itself to the table.

I float in and out. I have moments of being present and submersed in the pleasure of having my entire body cared for, and I have moments where I don't even feel like I am here. It is a euphoric feeling.

"Miss McFee?"

"Hmm?"

"This ends the massage portion of your package. Once you feel comfortable, please place your robe on and meet me in the hallway."

I open my eyes, and they take a few seconds to adjust to the light. I must have dozed off. I feel limber and gushy. Like my arms and legs are made of the best kind of noodles. I could get used to this royal treatment.

I tie the strap of my robe around my waist and meet the therapist in the hall. She guides me down another hallway and into a room that is set up with polishes and foot baths.

"My coworker will help you with getting a manicure and pedicure. Hope to see you back here again soon. It was a pleasure meeting you."

"Thank you so much." I want to give her a tip because I

am so impressed with her talent but my belongings are locked in the room.

After a minute, a middle-aged woman greets me. "Would you like a glass of sparkling cider while you look over the color choices? Mr. Hoffman instructed me to give you the full package. All the glitz and the glam." Her excitement is contagious.

"Sure, thank you." I accept the glass she offers and take the first sip. Oh, this is fun. The flavor of the beverage is so good that I don't even miss the alcohol that would normally be in it.

I scan over the hundreds of colors and am stuck with whether to go flirty or dramatic. I hear the sound of the door behind me opening and turn to see Claire walk through with a big smile. She is wearing a knee-length denim dress and looks so cute with her hair piled high on top of her head.

"Hey!" I say, giving her a big hug. "What are you doing here?"

"Graham invited me to join you. Plus, we both know you could use my help," she says with a laugh.

"This is true," I admit.

The worker hands Claire a glass without even asking if she wants any.

I can't keep from smiling. "This is so fun. I'm so glad you're here."

"Me too. I miss you. But two days in a row you get to experience all I have to offer. Lucky you."

I nod. "Lucky me."

We spend the next twenty minutes debating colors until we finally just pick one. I settle on a frosty silver shade called the Tin Man. Claire selects a pretty sparkling red shade that is titled Get Glittery With It.

The nail technician guides us to the private VIP section in the back of the shop that has a buffet set up with cheeses, cold meats, and mini pieces of bread. Fresh fruit, nuts, and preserves are also offered, along with an assortment of chocolate truffles.

Claire stares at the display. "Keep him."

I giggle. "He sure knows the way to my heart."

"Right through the stomach."

"Exactly."

We fill up our plates and set them on tables that are beside the foot baths. Our assigned worker refills our glasses and introduces us to Claire's attendant. We sit back, allow our feet to soak, get massaged, and get exfoliated. We giggle over being tickled with the cheese grater type tool, munch on food, and talk about the most stupid topics—like Doomsday bins and what we would do if we switched bodies for the day.

Our technicians snap silly pics of us with my phone, as Claire and I show off our nails.

"Wait until you see your outfit I picked out for you for tomorrow's night out."

"Please tell me it did not come from the Juniors section of the store."

"Oh, no. This was a special order ensemble. Pretty sure you are going to melt the ice from a few hearts."

I groan over her excitement. She is acting like she just won the lottery and bouncing around the space, waving her freshly painted hands in the air.

"Is Graham going to allow me to leave our place with me wearing it?"

"Oh, good thinking! I can bring a conservative top layer to trick him. Just like I used to do in high school. Look at you, making me bring back all these memories. Speaking of your overbearing man," she says, pointing over to the doorway where he is standing, watching us chatter.

"Hot damn, he looks good," I mutter, throwing back the last of my bubbly cider. His eyes catch mine, and I blatantly ogle him in public, licking my lips. He grins at me and his eyes glance over my robe knowingly.

"Get it, girl. This eye-sex thing you guys are doing is making me a bit uncomfortable, though. It's like I am part of a surprise threesome. Get a room. I'm out."

I lean over to give her a hug. "You sure you don't need a ride?"

"I'll just call a cab, no worries."

Claire thanks Graham, waves a quick goodbye, and exits in a hurry. I am so entranced, watching every movement he makes on his way toward me.

"Hey you," I say with a smile.

"Ready for a little fun?"

18

––––––––

"What kind of fun?" I ask suspiciously. "The kind that results with me underneath you yelling ahhh…ahhhhh…ohhhh?" I make my exaggerated O-face and then burst into tears laughing at my own jokes.

Graham's eyes darken and narrow. "Teasing me never ends well."

"Or maybe you will fuck me right here." I cover my mouth with my hand. It must be my deprivation talking. I'm not usually this bold in public. Correction, I am *never* this brazen.

He reaches for my hand and pulls me toward the front of the shop. He fishes his wallet out of his pocket and tosses a handful of one-hundred-dollar bills to the worker behind the desk.

"Cancel the chocolate bath," he says and then drags me out of the spa area.

"Graham!" I yell, trying to slow him down. "I want that chocolate thing. I love me some chocolate. What type of chocolate experience is it? Was it a couple's thing? Do we get to sample chocolates? Why are we canceling it?"

"Another time, Angie."

"Where are we going? I don't have clothes on under this thing," I say, waving my sash around, accidentally exposing my bare thighs in the process. "My belongings are—"

"Fine. They are fine. Let's go."

Graham takes me through several doors that require his keycard that he has tucked away in his upper breast pocket of his suit coat. I guess being an owner makes it easy to avoid the general patrons who visit the hotel. He tugs me along to a private elevator and smashes the number for the fifteenth floor.

"Where are we going? I love chocolate." I pout. "Now I'm craving chocolate. No part of this seems fair!"

"Well, then you should have thought twice before you got bold and horny."

"You think the latter is a choice or something. You show up looking mighty sexy fine in your power suit with your brooding eyebrows and your chiseled jaw and that look."

"What look?" he asks, obviously amused.

"*The look.*"

His eyes smolder. "This one?"

I nod. "You look like a caveman."

He chuckles and flips me up over his shoulder like a sack of potatoes.

"Hey!"

"Just fleshing out your fantasies, sweetheart. You wanted caveman. I'll give you caveman."

I yelp as his hand smacks my ass, making me jump. He

is in the best kind of mood right now, and the anticipation of what he's going to do to me has me excited.

The elevator opens, and he carries me down the hall to room 1565. He opens it with a new card and walks us inside with such ease that I want to ask how many times he has done this before. But why ruin the moment now?

The place is spacious and immaculate. The color scheme is all neutrals, with punches of red.

"You had this planned the whole time?"

"What makes you say that?" he asks slyly, placing me back on my feet.

"You have a key!" I call out, pointing to it, like I just discovered the big mystery.

"I knew we would end up here, yes." He moves toward the master bed and starts removing his coat, tie, and belt. "But you rushed all my plans."

"No, I didn't," I say, my hands propped up on my hips.

He turns and rakes his eyes down my body. A fierce need radiates from him. He is hungry. And I think I know what he wants his food source to be.

"I wish I knew what you're thinking," he says, quirking a brow.

"Just thinking that you need a sandwich."

"A sandwich?"

"Yup. You look so hungry. Want me to call room service?"

"No, Angela."

He takes a step closer and I reciprocate. Another step. And another. When we are pressed up against one another, I help him unbutton his white shirt, pulling the ends out from the waistband of his pants. He spreads his legs and I move in closer, my breath picking up from the anticipation. I fall to my knees, but Graham grabs me before I can hit the floor. I look up at him in confusion.

"I appreciate the sentiment. But tonight is about you. And your needs."

"What happens if my need is to get you off in my mouth? To taste you sliding down my throat…"

"My need to claim your pussy is greater. I promise not to disappoint. Are you going to deny me?"

I shake my head. I can't refuse him now. I doubt I can refuse him ever. He has managed to take my heart hostage so that the beating of it coincides with the rhythm of his own.

"Good."

Graham stands, removes the rest of his clothes, then starts untying my robe. It slides to the floor, and his audible gasp of approval is music to my ears. I am thrilled he likes what he sees. He always makes me feel like I am the most beautiful girl in the world.

He helps me back up on the bed and props one of my legs up on his shoulder. I am wide open for him. His fingers slip inside me first and stretch my opening with my own juices. I moan as he shocks my body with the sudden plea-sure. He knows exactly what to do to get me on fire.

Next, Graham's mouth descends and licks me from my pussy to my clit. And then repeats that move—a dozen more times.

"Graham!"

"Do not come."

"What?" I burst out. What kind of nonsense is he speaking of?

"If you come, you will be punished."

"What the hell?"

I can feel his lips curve from down below into a smile. Oh, the nerve of him!

After several minutes of the slow buildup toward an orgasm, Graham stops abruptly and works his way up to my breasts. His cock settles between my legs, and I thrust upward to grind against him. I need friction, and the loss from his fingers and tongue places me in the desperate category.

"Patience," he warns.

"Any other day, you want things hard and fast. But today? Nope. You want to make me go crazy."

He sucks a nipple into his mouth and ignores my whining. I can tell he is having fun and doing things his way. Shocker.

Something hard presses against my entrance, and the vibrating pulses make me jerk up from the bed at the sudden intrusion and my own sensitivity.

"Fuck!" I yell, trying to get away from the pulsing toy. "What is that?" I try to sit up and look at the device he is using on me, but he just holds me down. "I"—gasp—"I"—gasp—"won't be able to—"

Off.

He shuts the damn thing off!

"That was fun," he mutters calmly, obviously proud of himself.

"Graham," I snarl in anger.

"Patience," he reminds, kissing me on my fucking nose.

"Have you lost your mind?"

His eyes twinkle. "No. But you're about to. And I'm going to enjoy every fucking second of it."

I pant, out of breath as I deflate back into the bedding. I am going to combust. I can feel it in my heart. In my toes. In my panicked breathing.

Then the vibrations start again. I squeeze my thighs together to endure the pleasure, but Graham just wrenches them open more. I cannot hide. My head sinks back into the pillows, and I whimper with a pleasure so intense that it borders on being too much. Just when I think I will explode, the device is shut off.

I am not shy about toys—I own several. However, engaging in this type of edge play has never even crossed my mind. I thrust upward as the vibrations start again, in unison with Graham sucking on my nipples. I can feel the moisture leaking from me as if the dam has been broken. There's no going back.

"I'm going to—"

Off.

I let out a cry and admit defeat, just as Graham pushes himself inside me from tip to root. He pulls out and sinks in again.

"Give me your all," he permits, sending off an orgasm so intense inside of me that I almost black out from the force of it.

When I am down from my high and can form coherent thoughts, I give Graham the biggest hug. "That…"

"Was fun?"

"Hell," I mutter, pinching my arm to make sure I am still alive.

He nuzzles my ear. "You take my breath away."

"Thank you for my special day spent here at your hotel."

"Our hotel," he corrects.

"Didn't know you were in the business for buying," I say, sweeping my hand around, "this."

"I'm always looking for business ventures where investing money will help me make more money. However, this hotel was owned by my uncle, and with his age approaching seventy, he needed to pass along the torch. He is still an influential partner—as is Nic. I am simply the owner. It is not my pet project. I have managers and other associates who will be running this place. However, I get final say and the right to veto anything."

"It's nice that you don't have to change the name."

Graham laughs and kisses me on the nose. "True. Let's go on a little tour, shall we?"

"Does this tour require clothes?"

"If you want onlookers to keep their eyeballs, yes."

I stare down at my naked body and am about to ask for him to send someone for my clothes at the spa when he intercepts my thoughts.

"I have a dress for you hanging in the closet."

"Oh. Seems a bit fancy for a tour."

He just smiles and rolls out of bed to get himself dressed. Inside the closet, I find a long red silk dress and a pair of matching shoes. A lightweight white fur coat hangs beside it. Wow. This is way fancy.

In a box on the floor, I find a strapless bra and panty set in red. I slip those on first and the dress follows in line. Everything fits like I would expect for someone ordering it who is obsessed with my body. I move into the bathroom and find my personal hygiene products in travel sizes. I touch up my makeup and brush through my hair, spraying the sides in place.

Graham sneaks up behind me in the mirror and wraps his arms around my midsection.

"You look exquisite, Angela."

"Thank you. You look amazing as well," I say, eyeing his solid-black suit. He looks dashing. And all mine.

He brushes all of my hair to one shoulder and kisses my newly exposed neck with his mouth. His eyes catch mine again in the mirror, and he bites down on a sensitive spot at the base, making my eyes close as I succumb to the sensation of pleasure and pain. When they open again, Graham is simmering with need—his erection poking me from behind.

"I'm trying to be gentle with you. To be less controlling. But I struggle sometimes, Angie. Sometimes, I just want to lock you away and keep you all for myself to enjoy. To explore. Eyes other than mine do not deserve you, and I refuse to share."

I turn and lean my butt against the vanity. "What's this about? Me going out tomorrow night with Claire?"

He turns away from me and runs his hands through his hair, pulling at the ends. "I'm already dreading it. Bastards staring at you and imagining what it would be like to have you. It drives me wild to be away from you. Makes me go crazy."

"I'll be fine. I can handle myself, Graham. I have been taking care of myself for years before you ever forced your way into my life."

He stalks toward me. "Pretty sure you forced your way into mine."

I narrow my eyes and cough to muffle my smirk. "You hired me," I tease with a shrug.

"My asshole brother, Nic, hired you—despite my advice to blacklist you."

"Seems like he sucks at taking orders from you too."

Graham growls, his nostrils flaring. "I was forced to go along with it or blow my cover at the time. But my days of taking orders from anyone are over. Nic may still be a puppet," he says, shaking his head with anger, "but he has less to lose. And I have everything I have ever wanted standing right here in front of me."

"Am I worth it?"

"Fuck, yes."

"You sure? I can be quite sassy and stubborn and insub-ordinate."

His thumb plays with my bottom lip. "You are definitely all of those things. And still worth it."

I smile and bite down on his thumb, and for a split second I think I draw blood from the shocked look on Graham's face. And when I look down, I confirm that I did. Oops.

He pulls back his hand and sucks his wound. His eyes heat. "Even if who I love makes it her life's mission to drive me to my breaking point."

"How about we just skip this tour you had in mind and you fuck me here on the bathroom tile. I have," I pause, while I think of the right word, "needs."

"Oh no, my little tiger. You are getting the damn tour. We can both suffer through a little edge play. That way when I do fuck you raw later with just your shoes on, you will remember who owns this body."

His eyes rake over me, and I shiver from the implication of his words.

"Good. I don't want you to be soft and gentle some-times," I admit. "You make me crave things I didn't think I would want."

"Like what?"

I blush. Graham has that way of making me open up with things I didn't think I would ever share. He is my first sexual partner. The man who I will always remember as taking my virginity. All of my desires and fantasies are wrapped around him performing them. If things do not work out between us long-term, I have no idea how I will ever be able to move forward with anyone else. My body might eventually get used to having another person's touch, but my mind and heart will never accept it. For every time my eyes will close, I will only be able to visualize one man— · my man—Graham Xavier Hoffman.

"Angela?"

"Hmm?"

"I asked you a question."

"What was it?"

"Like what?" he tries again, eyes full of determination.

I stare up at him with genuine confusion. "Like huh?"

"What do I make you crave?" He pulls me closer and sucks on my bottom lip.

"Oh. You know—" My words come out muffled from his hold.

He squeezes my ass and plops me up onto the vanity. "You want to play some games? Sure, then. We'll play some games. Let's go."

His words are sobering. He always plays so dirty that I

know I am doomed. Ugh. The anticipation of what he has planned is going to eat me alive.

I follow Graham out of the hotel room with the slam of the door. I drape my fur coat over my arm, not sure where this tour will start or end. I have been to this hotel before, so I already have visited some of the restaurants and seen the lobby. He holds my hand as we walk down the hallway, passing by several couples, all dressed impeccably.

"Where are we going?" I ask softly.

He brings my hand up to his lips and kisses my knuckles. "I told you. Just a little tour."

"Why are we dressed so fancy then?"

I see Graham's smile from my periphery as he keeps his lips shut. His secrecy is unnerving.

"Did I tell you that you look stunning?" he asks.

I nod. "Yes, yes you did."

Graham leads me into the waiting elevator car and we go to the main lobby, through another hallway, and then through two massive wooden doors with intricate designs carved into the surface. Several other couples follow us inside, some greeting Graham with a knowing pat on the back or a simple, "Good evenin', sir. Miss." I struggle to keep my composure as my heart rate quickens. What are we doing?

Nothing on the walls or the doors gives away why we are here. Everyone, however, is dressed to impress. I might stick out with my inability to adapt to this rich lifestyle that Graham is part of, but at least I can fake it with my attire.

"Come," he says to me, motioning for a security guard who is standing in front of a metal door to open it.

He allows me to enter first and mutters something to the

worker that I do not catch. We walk holding hands down a long dimly lit hallway until we enter a large room surrounded by huge thick red velvet curtains. The echoing of a mic fills the space, and several people enter our area from behind the wall of curtains.

"Mr. Hoffman, you are up next," one says. "Time estimate four minutes."

I stare up into Graham's eyes. "What is going on?" I mouth.

"There is a private charity event going on that HH contributes toward. I would like you to accompany me while I make an appearance on stage and announce the singers. All proceeds go toward the cause."

"What's the charity?"

"Together is Better."

I rack my brain to think of what this would benefit, but don't have to think long because Graham clues me in.

"It's a charity to help families cope with drug addiction."

"I—"

"I have been donating toward the foundation long before we met. I know it is a bit ironic. But I thought you accompanying me on stage would be a positive step for you."

"I hate being on stage. I sang with Zander at The Shack and made myself sick over it."

"That's because you had time to obsess," he theorizes.

"I'm not prepared for this at all. My hair and makeup and—"

"You look amazing. This reaction is precisely why I didn't tell you ahead of time. It's still your choice. I just know that you are very upset over how the media is portraying you, and this may be a step in the right direction to help build your image."

"One minute, sir," a stagehand announces quietly to us.

"You just need to stand with me. No need to do anything more than smile and hold my hand."

I nod as another worker motions for us to walk out. I drop my fur coat onto a nearby bench and walk out with Graham, who looks impeccable and at ease. His confidence oozes from him. The man never ceases to amaze me. The overhead lights are so bright that I can barely see the audience, which actually helps with my nerves. There could be two people present or two thousand.

Graham keeps my hand in his and is my forever anchor. He adjusts the microphone when we get to the center spot.

"Good evening. It is my utmost pleasure to introduce the next artists who have been rising on the billboard charts for the past two weeks with their single, *I Say I Do to You.* Please help me welcome the amazing duo couple, Grace and Jace."

The crowd erupts with applause as we move off to the side and down the steps that lead into the audience. We take our place in the front row, at a little table with a candle lit in the center. The curtain lifts on stage, revealing a band set up in the background and a couple perched on stools. Jace has a guitar and Grace is holding on to her bedazzled microphone.

The look the pair gives each other is unmistakable. They are undoubtedly in love with one another.

Everyone in the audience is on their feet and swaying to the song that starts with Jace singing, while Grace harmonizes. It is like we are witnessing an intimate moment that is reserved just for them. I want to look away but can't. They are captivating.

Graham moves behind me and whispers how much he loves me in my ear. He places his hands on my hips as he moves us to the music. I stare mesmerized at the stage while the couple delivers an amazing performance of one of their hit songs. I have never been to a live concert—let alone been in the front row to enjoy it. I lean my head back to his chest as he descends onto my lips with a passionate kiss.

It is like we are the only two people in the room. The music dulls to just a hum in my ears, and I smile up at Graham who makes all of the struggles I endured through my life worth it—because it all led me to him.

And then it hits me. Dr. Westinger asked me to reflect on a question. Where would I be today if Mom and James never died? Well, I wouldn't be here. The only reason I moved to Portland was to get away from the memories and the pain of living in a small town with all the reminders of what I no longer had. If I never moved to Portland, I would have never met Claire—who was also going to the city to escape her neglectful family in Virginia. We became soul-mate friends. If I didn't break up with my boyfriend Russell, lose my job at the bakery, and fail my last semester, I wouldn't have been interested in getting hired at Entice.

I would have never met Graham.

Our paths would have never had a reason to cross.

All of the pain and suffering I encountered over the course of years prepared me for the hurricane force that is Graham Hoffman. While I would give anything to have a minute longer with Mom and James, I would give up everything to have a life with Graham.

I turn to look at my man who is so wrapped around me, I feel like I am his greatest gift. "I love you," I whisper. "With everything I have."

His eyes smolder, as he places a hand on the small of my back and guides me from our barely noticed table to a hidden door along the edge of the room.

"We're leaving now? Is it over?" I ask when we are away from the noise.

"I never planned for us to stay. I just wanted you to enjoy the song. This hotel has a whole events team, and you can get front row seats to anything that is hosted here."

I smile a stupidly happy smile. "Wow."

"Why date a filthy rich bad boy and not reap the benefits?"

I laugh over his wiggling eyes. "True. And man, is it a good benefits package."

"Quit flirting with me." Graham's eyes are serious but I know he is teasing.

"Stop encouraging me by looking sexy."

"It's not my fault," he fake scoffs. "Blame it on genetics."

We take the elevator up to the highest number, get out and then climb three flights of stairs. I want to ask questions but know it is pointless. Graham uses his keycard and pushes open a heavy metal door that leads to the rooftop. Several strands of outdoor bulb lights are lit and strung on tall poles surrounding a beautiful table. A vase of white roses acts as the centerpiece. They are simple but sophisticated. Space heaters border the setup and provide the necessary warmth for being so high up and outside.

"Wow," I exhale, turning three hundred sixty degrees as I take in the entire scene.

Graham lifts his hand, and out of the shadows a waiter reveals himself with a bottle of sparkling grape juice, which he pours into two flutes.

"I'm not twelve," I mutter, taking a sip. "Surely a little indulgence won't hurt? Especially now, when you have me so on edge with anticipation."

"Oh…" he says leaning into me, "I plan to indulge."

"I'm too sober right now to appreciate your sense of humor." I giggle as my sides get tickled, making me almost spill my beverage on my dress. "Stopppp…"

We walk along the edge of the roof, looking out into the night sky at the beautiful city of Portland. Boat lights sparkle in the river, along with the neighboring lights from the buildings.

I shiver from the cold drink and the breeze blowing through the silk of my thin dress. Graham calls a second waiter over to us and instructs him to retrieve my fur coat. I vaguely remember leaving it behind stage on a bench; I think my handbag is with it. He wraps his arms around me and settles them on the small of my back. We dance to nonexistent music and enjoy each other's touches.

Graham nibbles on my ear, making my goose bumps multiply like rabid bunnies. "Spoiler alert. I'm going to fuck you on this roof, Angie."

I jerk myself away from him in order to analyze his face for sincerity. "Are you serious?"

"I'm also going to fuck you in the stairwell."

"Okay…"

"And in the elevator."

"Damn," I mutter under my breath.

"There's no part of you that I do not desire. Even in my sleep, I yearn for your touch. You infiltrate my conscious and unconscious thoughts. You have changed my life for the better and yet I still feel like the best is yet to come."

"Graham," I say, looking up into his eyes. "Every part of me craves you." I wrap my arms around his neck and kiss along his jawline, until my lips settle on his. I pull back to look at him. "You make me want things I have never expected to want." I continue making out with my man, as we run our hands up and down each other's backs.

"If you want to keep your dress on, then you better start answering the question you keep refusing to answer."

"Hmm?" I look up at him with confusion and take a few steps back if just to break our hold so I can think straight again.

He saunters closer, as I shuffle my feet to slide back away from him. But where am I going to run? I glance at the exit.

"I hope you decide to run," he says, his voice gravelly. "Chasing you will be all the fun."

"What was the question again?" Did he even ask a question? I can't think or even remember. I prop my hands on my hips. "Maybe you didn't even ask a question and are bluffing."

He looks away and stifles a smile. At least he is entertained by me.

"You will forever be unpredictably amusing," he comments, running a hand down the side of his face.

"Can you repeat the question that I am not quite sure you even asked?"

"What do I make you crave, Angela?"

I think about the question. "Maybe crave is too"—I pause—"generic." I sigh.

"Care to explain?"

"You have awakened this sexual energy and drive inside me that was buried under years of self-hate. Maybe that is why I couldn't achieve an orgasm on my own. Maybe that is why I chose the wrong guys. Probably was my way of coping with the fear of being happy. Then you came along, and all I can think about now is how we can get closer. Physically and emotionally. You make me crave having a future."

"There's more. Keep going."

"I crave you bossing me around. Telling me what to do to please you, but in return, it really pleases me."

"I'm a selfish bastard, Angie. So, trust me, it fucking pleases me too."

"But I never thought I would like it."

"Your body was waiting for me to command it, sweetheart. It was a gift to be your first."

"You are such a contradiction. And I love it. But it confuses me. You say something so sinfully sexy and then call me sweetheart. It is like you can go from soft to hard within a breath's time."

"Does that make you wet? Do you love the anticipation of not knowing whether or not I will fuck you with witnesses or let you hold on to an ounce of your modesty? It excites you, doesn't it? To know that I can take you when and how I want and your body is a prisoner to the pleasure that only I can give you."

"Yes."

"Take off your panties."

I stare at Graham and then my eyes bolt over to the door where the waiter is going to come through at any minute with my coat and bag.

"Heed my warning. Hesitate again and I'll video us in the act so you can watch yourself come later. I dare you to step out of line, because either way—I win."

I swallow over his promise. My pussy clenches with need.

"You are such a dirty little girl, aren't you? My ideas for punishment are really your hope for pleasure."

I shake my head *no* but neither of us believes it. I lift up the long hem of my dress and peel down the red strip of fabric. Swimsuits cover more. I am happy to get them off, only because every move was causing tantalizing friction to my nether regions, just adding to my edginess.

"Sniff them," he demands. "I want you to know how good you smell to me."

I move the panties up to my nose and breathe in my scent. It is intoxicating to know that he finds me so desirable and that my body loves what he has to offer.

"Now go place them on the table beside your napkin."

"But someone wi—"

"You want the video we make to have a different cameraman other than myself?"

I shake my head frantically.

"Then do as you are told. You aren't in control. Quit trying to defy me. Unless your body really craves the punishment. Are you going to be a good girl or a bad girl tonight, sweetheart?"

I let the question mull around in my head, but not for

long because Graham's eyes are burning holes into my dwindling clothes. "A good girl."

His smirk is playful. "Not sure that is possible."

I turn on my heel and walk my panties over to my place setting. I let them fall from my hands onto my napkin, right as the worker opens the door and hands me my coat and handbag. "Thank you," I mutter, not making eye contact with him. I know he is glancing at the panties that are sitting like a red stain on top of a solid white background.

I turn to move back to Graham with my head down but walk straight into him. His hands steady me at my hips, his fingers shooting electric pulses toward my limbs.

"Easy," he whispers. "Just give in to my needs and your own desires will be fulfilled."

One finger gets placed on my bottom lip and pulled downwards to open my mouth. He swoops in and the kiss makes me want to faint. He impedes my oxygen supply, and I feel lightheaded from his sudden intrusion. When he finally pulls back, I am gasping for air.

His fingers undo his belt and pants with ease—like he could do it one-handed if he tried. I swallow hard, knowing what is coming next. He moves to sit down in one of the chairs at the table. He spreads his legs and pulls his erect cock out, pumping it twice. Fuck, he looks like he hopped out of a porno—except there is no part of him that is cheesy or rehearsed.

The heat from the lamps coupled with my own simmering arousal keep me from turning into an ice sculpture. At least the man thought ahead. I should expect nothing less.

With the curl of his fingers and the subtle lick of his

lips, he beckons me toward him and I comply. I have no choice. Not because I am being forced, but because I cannot help myself. The body wants what the body wants. No matter how many times in the past I have pushed him away, it is me that I hurt the most.

"Lift up your dress. Let me see what's mine." I start to turn toward the door, and his startling voice shakes me. "Eyes on me. Worry your mind with nothing but following my orders. Let my wishes halt all of your impulses."

I bend at the waist and slowly pull up the bottom hem of my silk dress. The fabric glides over my thigh highs, and when I get to the exposed skin at the top of the lace, I shiver from the cool air whisking around at the top of the building. I stare down at his hardening cock as he pumps it a few times.

"Turn around and back your sweet ass up to me."

"Graham—"

"Do it."

I slowly move so my behind is to him, and I step a heel length backward. And then another. I hear the muffled sound of him spitting and then the feel of his hands on my hips, pushing me down.

"Spread your pussy lips. Get yourself ready to accept all of me."

I reach down under my dress and pull my lips apart for him.

"Now sit down on me. And take all of me," he clarifies. "Oh, and hurry before the waiter brings out our food."

I squat down, bracing one hand on the table and the other on my lips to stay open for him. My legs spread over his muscular legs. Graham pushes inside—already well lubricated—as I sit farther down into his lap. His arm bands around me. It takes me a minute to adjust to this angle.

The sound of the door opening startles me and I jump, almost dislodging him out of me.

"Easy, sweetheart," he says into my ear, fixing my dress to cover a few more inches of my thighs.

The waiter walks over and doesn't even act like it is unusual that we are sitting at the same side of the table. Glued at the hips. I watch as he places two plates on our side of the table and refreshes our drinks.

"Would you like fresh ground pepper on your chicken, ma'am?" he asks, holding up this wooden device that I am assuming has some sort of black peppercorns inside.

Graham vibrates behind me with amusement as I struggle to make a decision. I clear my throat to try to mask his reaction, discreetly elbowing him in his chest to get him to stop.

"I, um, I'm fine," I answer.

Graham's lips tickle my ear. "That you are."

"Sir?"

With the wave of his hand, Graham gets the waiter to retreat back into the building through the door. I guess he is willing to gamble that his food is seasoned correctly from the chef.

"So, we are just going to sit here like this and eat, while your cock is stuffed deep inside me?"

"Sounds like the perfect way to spend a Thursday night," he answers jollily.

"You are insane."

Within seconds, I am swung around, hoisted up, and

carried over to the edge of the building. My ankles clutch at his back for fear that he will get weak and drop me.

"You want insane? Well, I'll give you insane. I hope the buildings surrounding us get their fill of your beautiful ass as I fuck you for anyone to see. He lifts me and thrusts deep inside, while pulling me back down onto him. Over and over, he takes. And takes. And even when I think I have nothing left to give, he takes just a little bit more.

My hands reach back and grab the cement wall behind me. I arch my back. "Graham!"

His growl is in my ear. "Do not come."

But it is too late. My thighs clench and my inner walls spasm. I twist and turn in his arms as my treacherous body disobeys.

"I was hoping you would do that," he says, satisfied.

My eyes open to his twinkling ones.

"You can't be serious."

19
_____

Graham's eyes twinkle with possibility.

"What are you going to do?" I ask.

"Right now? Finish dinner."

I swallow hard at his brooding and edgy mood. He did not get off. But I did. And while he seems quite pleased with himself, I know it is only a matter of time before he reveals his hand. He sets me back on my feet, and I teeter nervously on my too-high heels. His hands steady me and help put my dress back into place. He is tender and loving, despite being mysterious.

He walks me back to the table where our stuffed chicken and mashed potatoes with creamed spinach wait for us— along with my panties. I cross and recross my legs. I can feel my moisture leaking into the silk of my dress. I start to feel chilly after the high Graham had me on and slip my arms into the fur of my coat.

I stare at my food and rake my fork three times through

the potatoes. I swirl into the spinach and poke at the chicken.

"Eat, Angela."

I look up at him across the table. He places a piece of chicken into his mouth and chews. Using his fork, he points it toward my plate and reminds me again to eat.

"Here, I'll give you a clue, since I can already tell your brain is working overtime." He reaches into his pants pocket and pulls out a shiny silver device that has a rounded point at the end. He sets it down onto the table, flat side down with the rounded tip up. "There. Now eat."

I stare at it but dare not touch it. "How is a doorknob a clue?"

Graham quickly grabs his cloth napkin and covers his mouth with it.

"You're laughing at me," I point out, pushing my chair back to get up. I don't need this right now. "Your clue sucks. What are we doing—rekeying locks?"

He holds his hand up to stop me. He places the napkin down on the table and clears his throat. "All apologies. I am sorry. It is just that you catch me off guard sometimes— many times—and I do not expect it."

"What is it, Graham? And what is it for?"

I can tell he is holding back a smirk, and why he tries to hide it with the back of his hand beats me, when it is so obvious.

"It is a butt plug. And it goes in—"

"I can fill in the blanks!"

"Very well."

"The answer is holy hell no." I am not shy around sex toys. However, I am not adventurous—or brave—enough to try something like *this* on my own. The doorknob *thing* looks daunting. There is no way I am going to enjoy metal shoved up my butt.

"It was never a question," he says blankly, his eyes studying me.

"Hell to the capital no. And quit looking at me like you are going to convince me otherwise."

"You have obviously never tried it, so why write it off as being a negative thing? Surely you are a bit curious."

I point my empty fork at his idea of fun. I open my mouth to speak but the words escape me. I furrow my brow and shake my head no.

"No?"

I look up into Graham's eyes. "It's not going to fit."

His smile is soft. "It will."

"No. It won't."

"Is that your main fear?" he asks in a serious tone.

"Maybe."

"Angela. Do you trust me?"

"I did until this very moment."

He sighs. "I brought lube. Doesn't that make you feel better?"

"Sure, let me just bend over this table and plop that thing into me now."

"My only regret is forgetting a gag. Would come in handy for your sassy mouth."

I glare my eyes at his. "Next time." My words come out as sarcastic as I intended for them. "What's the point of it anyway? I can't imagine it is going to feel good."

"We shall see."

"So it's decided?"

"Yes. Now, eat your dinner."

I guzzle my flute of grape juice and silently wish it were wine. At least a buzz would make all of my anxiety seem lesser than what it currently is. As soon as my empty glass hits the table, a waiter is at my side to refill it, but I shoo him away before he can do so. This is beyond awkward. We are sitting here with some table accessory that belongs in the bottom drawer of my nightstand—not beside the salt and pepper shaker.

"Touch yourself," he says.

I gawk at him.

"If you aren't going to eat, then you might as well let me enjoy dinner and a show."

"I'll eat," I surrender.

"Good."

I stick my tongue out at him before sliding a bite of mashed potatoes between my lips and sucking longer than necessary on the fork, all while batting my eyelashes. Yup, that is a big mistake. I can tell as much right in the moment as Graham's eyes turn to the dark shade of blue. He then picks up the metal paperweight and smiles into it—as if he is admiring himself in the mirror. Ugh. Pretty sure my butthole clenched and muttered "No, thank you." And that thing is going to be cold. I just know it.

The waiter refills my beverage glass, this time with water. Apparently he wants me super hydrated for the circus as well.

"Quit scandalizing me," I warn.

"Or what?"

I shrug. "You may be using your butt toy on your own

tonight. Pretty sure assholes are universal and do not discriminate from intruders."

He bursts out laughing, takes a sip of his drink, and then wipes the excess from his lips with his napkin. "What am I going to do with you?"

"Apparently get something lost inside my butt and have to take me to the emergency room and then, well, that will be a huge ordeal and the entire medical staff will have something to talk about for years to come. I'll become some legend and will have a secret nickname there that no one tells me about—but obviously will be referred to behind my back. Lost Buttplug Girl or Ass Abyss or something equally horrifying."

His eyes twinkle with mirth. "You have been watching too much porn."

I choke on a bite of chicken and reach for my glass to only be reminded of the fact that it is just water. "Sounds like horrible porn!"

"Pretty sure all porn is horrible. And trust me, I have seen"—he makes an exaggerated face—"a lot."

"Ew."

"No use for the fake stuff anymore. I now have my own personal Porn Princess."

"Wow. You didn't think that one through very well in your head. That still sounds horrible. Like I'm a sex doll."

"At least dolls argue less."

We laugh until we are in tears. This is what we do. We are huge weirdos.

"You excited to hang out tomorrow night for poker with your friends?"

"No."

"No?" I press.

"I'm going to probably lose some money because my focus will be on you and what trouble my men are going to have to endure. Hopefully none get fired or hand in their resignation the next day."

"No need to worry your pretty head over me. I am basically an angel most days."

"But your best friend has an awful habit of getting you involved in her crazy need for drama. She is a magnet for it."

I nod. "Yeah, we do usually end up passed out drunk in an alley, taking rides with guys who are not actually taxi drivers, or searching for the shadiest tattoo parlor that is open at three in the morning. Just another Friday night in the slums of Portland."

His face darkens and a growl vibrates through his throat.

"Teasing, Graham. Thought that was obvious."

"You do not have a good track record to even joke around right now. Literally every time you guys go out, something horrible happens. So, appreciate the fact that I'm allowing you this opportunity, despite my better judgment."

"Oh wow. Guess you have no idea how chauvinistic you sound right now."

"Guess you missed the part where I care about few things more than I care about your safety."

"I'll be safe," I promise.

"You better be," he snaps. "No crazy skits. No running away. No dodging your security detail."

"You probably will have a full army watching over me."

"Pretty much." He shrugs, not even trying to look apologetic. "And no flirting."

"I can't promise you that last one."

"Angie?" he growls.

"Flirting is definitely in the eye of the beholder. I cannot be responsible for other people's free will, Graham. But, I can promise not to bump and grind with any dicks on the dance floor. You're welcome."

He shakes his head at my taunting and flies around to my side of the table to bend down and kiss my lips. Yum.

Who needs to flirt with a rando at a bar when I have this man waiting in the wings?

He pulls me up from my seat and removes my coat with ease. I gasp at how fast he has his hands up the back of my dress and my bra flinging off behind me to the concrete ground. The air hits my bare ass cheeks, and I squeeze them together as his hands slide down my back.

Graham nibbles at my ear. "I bet I can make you come undone faster than you ever thought possible. You just have to trust me." He runs his finger along my crack—from top to bottom. "Relax your muscles."

I hesitate. I overthink.

"Do it, Angie," he says, smacking my cheek lightly.

The sting feels good, warming my area. I try my best to let go of the tension I am holding in my body. When I relax enough to suit him, he picks me up. I wrap my arms around his neck and my legs around his waist. My dress bunches around my midsection, completely exposing my ass to the night's air—and anyone trying to sneak a look. My nipples harden under the thin layer of my dress, no longer having the protection that my bra once afforded.

With one arm braced under my ass, his other moves beside us, making me look down. He fishes out a tiny bottle of lube from his pocket and brings it up to his mouth. Biting down on the cap, he removes it and spits it out into the air. The sound of the tiny piece of plastic hitting the ground and rolling distracts me for a few seconds while he removes the safety seal with his teeth. He looks savage.

I clutch onto him as if he is my lifeline, even despite him being the one to soon administer some pain in my back-side. I assume it is going to hurt. I have read enough maga-zine articles and heard enough stories to know that this is going to be unpleasant. It has to be, right? In theory and all. It just seems very unnatural to me and makes me wonder why he would want to do this in the first place.

It is just a toy.

A simple, harmless toy.

Graham squirts a generous amount of the product onto the bulb part of the plug with one hand, coating it all over with his palm. I bury my face into the side of his neck. I feel like a broken bird being rescued by my hero, but then also getting my wings torn off at the same time. It seems so contradictory.

"If you do not like this at all and want to stop, we will. I may be a bossy son of a bitch, but you definitely have a choice. Okay, Angie?"

I nod.

"But if you trust me and give me a chance, I will make you feel so good, baby. Just give me a chance."

"Okay."

"Take a deep breath and let it go."

I inhale until my lungs are at max capacity and then exhale.

"Keep doing that and relax. This will feel foreign. But

just keep breathing through and give yourself time to adjust. Then I will make you feel amazing."

I focus on my breathing and stare out at the twinkling lights of the city. I feel the cold bulb at my back entrance and tense up involuntarily. Graham runs it up and down my slit until I stop clenching as much. He then presses it gently against my opening and pushes it in.

It is cold and uncomfortable—but not as horrible as my mind told me it would be. I think the angle helps and the fact that my legs are spread around Graham's waist, naturally opening me up.

"It's not going to get lost, is it?"

"No, Angie. You are safe."

I imagine that he would not have gotten me one from some chintzy website with a bunch of fake reviews. My guess is that this also did not come from the local big box store.

"How do you feel?" he asks, turning the plug.

"Full."

"Well, you are about to feel even fuller, because I am going to stuff my cock in your pussy and fuck you hard."

"Damn."

He carries me into the stairwell and as soon as the door shuts, has me smashed up against the concrete wall. He sets me on my feet and spins me around.

"Hold on to the handrail."

Every move I make jostles the plug and sends a tingling sensation to my pussy. Graham flips up my dress, positions my hips back, and slides himself inside.

"Ahhh!"

"You are so full. Stuffed."

I don't think I can take all of him. There's no way. I look between us to see that he is only a third of the way inside. My hair falls around my face, and I jerk my head back to toss some onto the one side. I look up at Graham and see his smoldering eyes. Sweat beads on my forehead, and some of his drips onto the exposed skin of my back. He pushes an inch more inside, adjusting my hips to accommodate him.

"You look so fucking hot right now, sweetheart. Your ass stretched to take the plug that I made specifically with you in mind and your pussy at max volume, trying desperately to accept every inch I have to offer. You are going to come so hard on my cock, and I can't wait to shoot the load I've been saving for you deep inside your womb."

I pulse at his dirty words. I shiver at the thoughts of someone seeing us in mid-act. His hand reaches around me, and I hear the sound of buzzing before I feel the effects.

"Graham!"

The tiny vibrator hits my clit in the right spot as he pulls back and thrusts forward. I anchor myself on the handrail to keep myself from crashing into the wall. My orgasm builds from deep within my core. It is unlike anything I have felt before and feels like a tidal wave approaching shore in record speed.

He turns the plug, pulls on it a bit, and thrusts into me hard.

"You feel so good, baby. Give me your pleasure."

The vibrator pushes down hard on my clit, and I explode right as Graham pushes himself deep within me and unloads with his own violent climax. He pulls me upright by an arm bounding around my chest and bites my neck as we both scream out in pleasure.

343

Our sweat droplets merge together to form little streams sliding down my face and my neck and my breasts. I collapse into his arms, as he pulls out his cock, removes my plug, and pockets all of his toys. Once both of his hands are free, he scoops me up and carries me down the few flights until we are at the elevator. I close my eyes and enjoy the afterglow.

I wake up without any bearings in a pitch-black room. I feel around on the bed beside me and am met with a palm of chest hair and muscles.

"You feeling me up, sweetheart?"

"What day is it? I am so confused." My eyes try to adjust but all I can see is the light coming in from the crack at the bottom of the door.

I hear the click of the lamp and squint over the artificial light source. I look down at my naked body and feel the soreness between my legs from the roof sex. The amazing roof sex.

"You promised me elevator sex too," I pout. "Did I miss it?"

His deep chuckle makes me smile. "You are insatiable."

"I'm horny. How am I supposed to go about my day with these needs you unlocked inside of me?"

"Want to wear the plug inside you all day?"

My eyes widen. "No. No. How will that help at all? Will probably just make me want you more."

"Maybe it will get you to cancel tonight's girls' night. I

can tie you to my bed, and you can be my sex prisoner. Don't worry, I will take care of all of your needs."

I close my eyes over that fantasy. "Don't tempt me."

"You are such a bad little girl. You have the good girl outward appearance. But in here," he says, tapping my head gently, "you are wickedly naughty."

"You like it."

He swoops down to kiss my lips and then my nose and then both eyelids. "One hundred percent, yes, I like."

I lean over and look for my handbag. I am so disoriented on where my belongings are. Do I even have belongings here? I arrived here not even twenty-four hours ago and got whisked away to the spa. Then the charity event. Followed by public rooftop sex. And somehow I managed to get myself back into the hotel room and put to bed.

"Where are my things? I think I have a handbag somewhere."

Graham points over to the dresser. "I had a worker retrieve all of your belongings that you forgot about at dinner."

"Oh silly, forgetful me," I joke. I glance over at the pile of items on the top of the dresser. My fur coat, panties, bra, handbag. Everything is all there. Lovely. I bet whoever he pays to be the gopher had a fun night putting these puzzle pieces together about me.

I slide out of bed and go to find my phone. Every step I take is a reminder of where he's been. How am I going to get through the day? It is Friday and seven fifteen in the morning. I have my therapy session with Dr. Lucian and Dr. Westinger today before my big winter costume reveal—

courtesy of Claire. I can only imagine what she will come up with.

"Come, let's get a shower," Graham suggests, kissing my naked shoulder, "and we can hit up the coffee shop down on the first floor."

"Let's just stay in bed," I whine. "I'm not sure I can stand the friction of having clothes on."

He chuckles behind me, splaying his fingers out across my belly. "Cancel tonight and come play poker with me. Or just sit on my lap and be my good luck charm."

I turn my head to look back at him. "Pretty sure I would end up under the table with your cock pushing down my throat. And everyone else suddenly canceling last minute."

His eyes darken with need. "There. It's settled."

"Ha, I bet the guys will never let you live that down. Bringing your girlfriend to a guys-only poker night."

"I can handle the ribbing."

"Unfortunately, I can't handle Claire if I desert her. Have you met her before? She would hunt me down. And then you."

He shrugs. "Still worth it."

"I can't."

"Fine. But let's have a little shower fun before we head for breakfast and then the office."

"Sounds like the start to a perfect morning."

20

Graham's phone buzzes on the cafe table. I glance at it and frown. This is the third call within a minute that he has ignored.

"You better just answer. It's probably important."

"Always is. I'm just preserving these last moments of serenity before we head over to HH."

"It has to be tough trying to manage your empire."

His grin lets me know he got my attempt at lightheartedness. He picks up his phone and finally ends the caller's misery. "Hoffman."

I take a bite of my fruit salad and sip my smoothie. I feel so refreshed and alive this morning that I forgo my typical caffeine indulgence. Maybe I can break that cycle too. Pretty sure Graham has been working overtime at distracting me from my past behaviors. It is successful. Instead of craving what a pill can give me, I am becoming addicted to him instead. If that was part of his big picture plan all along, then he would be a very clever genius.

I watch intently as he swipes the hair from his forehead and rubs at his temple with his fingers. Something is wrong. We had such a perfect twenty-four hours that it was only a matter of time before a shoe dropped.

"Get Collins and Austin here. There is a private back exit along the west side of the building. We'll meet you there in about five minutes." He shoves the phone into his pocket and plasters the fake look of calm on his face.

"Something is obviously wrong. I can tell you don't want to talk about it right now. But just know that I really wish you would let me know anyway."

He tosses his trash into the paper bag and leans back in his chair. "Let's just enjoy these last few moments together."

"And pretend nothing is wrong?"

"Excellent idea."

I am no longer hungry, so I gather my scraps and toss them into the trash near the main doors of the shop.

"I think I'll just hang out at our place if that's okay? I really need to focus on my article. The semester is winding up, and I have to just wait for my professor to let me know when I can submit my work for the final review. Plus, all of my notes and files are at the penthouse already."

"You can work in one of the empty offices at HH. You can have an entire floor to yourself if you want quiet. We can swing by and grab what you need."

I shake my head. "I just need to spread out comfortably."

"Okay," he says with a nod of his head. "I'll have one of the men drop you off."

"Thank you."

Graham guides me through several corridors and doorways until we are on the west side of the building. Idling at the curb is Collins, followed by a fleet of other similar looking vehicles.

I glance up at Graham and get the *not now* look. There are way too many cars here to take just me and him to our separate locations. Collins is out of the SUV, cell to his ear, and walking around the front to retrieve me from Graham's hold on my arm. What is going on now?

I am flanked until I am safely inside the backseat.

"Hi, Miss McFee," Austin greets from the passenger side.

"What's going on?" I ask directly. "Something is obviously going on."

"Nothing that we can't handle, ma'am. Do not worry." He passes me a bottle of water, which I accept.

"Being in the dark makes me worry," I snap.

Sipping my water, I watch Collins and Graham chat on the sidewalk. I glance to the end of the street and see a mob of photographers rushing toward us. The men disperse and Collins throws himself into the front seat. He pulls from the curb within seconds, doing a three-point turn and speeding off in the opposite direction.

I turn to look out the back window and see another SUV not in our fleet following us. Collins whips through the Portland streets and manages to get us into the parking garage without being noticed. He escorts me up to the penthouse and alerts whomever is on the receiving end of the Bluetooth device in his ear that I am home safely.

The adrenaline charging through my veins makes my head feel like it is going to burst. Something obviously happened this morning that is making the paparazzi want to attack me—again. I am not some movie star, so it is hard to justify to myself why they even care.

I flop down on the couch in the living room and text Claire.

Angie: I was just a part of a high speed chase and have not a clue as to why.

Claire: Google your name and today's date.

Angie: Is this going to stress me out?

Claire: Just go see for yourself. And I'm sorry.

Oh shit. I close out the text app and open up the search engine, doing as she suggested. There are so many articles that are time stamped within the past four hours that I don't even know where to begin. "McFee is a McFake" is one title. "Drug Addict Turned Charity Case" is another. But the one that slashes my heart the most is the one with the title, "In the Life of a Hypocrite."

Damn. These are brutal. When I click on the articles, I see myself at the charity event that Graham and I attended yesterday. My red silk dress. The cause in which we went to support.

Society once again shits all over me, and I have no way of rising above it. Graham said he handled the press with money. However, there is no stopping photographers when the chance of becoming famous is at stake. I guess that's why the streets surrounding Hoffman Hotel were bustling with excitement at the chance to confront me face-to-face. How much more of this can I take?

I sink into the cushions and close my eyes. Why does a night full of amazing memories have to be tainted with the morning after dosage of reality? Last night, nothing could touch us. No wonder why Graham didn't want me to come back here and have time to think and clear my head. He knew I would have this opportunity to sulk and do the whole why-me thing.

I guess, like most things in life, I have two choices— feel sorry for myself or feel sorry for them.

I scrape myself off the couch and meander into my sewing room. Despite the sticker shock, I ordered a crazy ton of storage cabinets and a huge table to set up shop for my projects. On nights I cannot sleep well, I sneak down here and work on Christmas projects. There's a peace I find in this room, the only sounds being the buzz of my sewing machine or the errant thoughts running through my head.

I sit down at my heat press and find my latest line up of to-do items that are awaiting their fate. My shopping list this year for the holidays has grown massively with the introduction of Graham's family. I am not bringing in much money from the smoothie shop, and asking Graham for an allowance to buy him a gift seems so backward to me—so homemade for the win.

I spend just a half hour in here. It is just enough time to refocus myself, clear my mind, and provide me with some solace. I hide the few finished products, shut off the lights, and head back out into the hallway.

I glance down the other end toward Graham's office and startle at the man in the shadows. My hand flies up to my chest, and I stumble sideways into the wall from the shock.

"It's just me, Angie."

"Oh, hi Owen. I wasn't expecting you."

He laughs. "I can see that. Was just doing some business for the boss. Malcolm is here too"—he glances behind him —"somewhere."

"Everything okay?" My breathing slowly returns to normal.

"Of course. Nothing for you to worry about."

I nod. I imagine Graham has briefed his men on making sure I am not tainted with too many things. He is forever trying to shelter me.

I move back into the living room and spread out all of my schoolwork on the table, the couch cushions, and onto the floor. I decide that if I am going to have a shot at my journalism career, this is my make-it-or-break-it moment. I am days away from graduating, and even though I will have to wait until the spring to walk with my class in a ceremony, I will gladly celebrate my own victory if I land an internship of a lifetime.

After several fails at an actual rough draft, I decide to generalize my topic of research. I use the online campus channel to post as anonymous and ask questions to female students.

Do you feel safe on campus as a female college student?

Have you been drugged while on campus or off campus during your college years?

Have you ever blacked out at a party and not known what happened to you when you woke up?

If you informed the university about any drugging incidents, what has their response been?

I hit submit on my post and cross my fingers for a few responses. Maybe broadening my topic will be a positive thing. The good thing about our campus channel is that you can change your name to anything you want for any post. This allows students to voice their opinions, thoughts, and fears without any backlash. Of course, this makes the admins' jobs harder because often they have to go in and clean up the trash talk that sometimes happens when students get drunk and think they are keyboard heroes.

I make my way upstairs to use the bathroom and grab a sweater to put on over my shirt. I trot down the stairs and rub at the back of my neck as a headache starts to develop. The downfall of being away from Graham is that I have more time to think about my bad choices in life. It is in these moments that I want to go find some pills to cope with the ache. For the past few days he has managed to get me through a withdrawal period where he kept me so busy and addicted to him that I did not crave what I once did.

I imagine that Graham locked all of his medication up somewhere safe when he discovered my taste of addiction. I do want something to take the edge off. I hate how I feel when my head hurts. However, I also know that if I back-slide now, the road to getting clean again will be even harder.

When I get back down to the main floor, I jump at the voices coming from the kitchen. I turn and see Owen propped up on a kitchen stool, eating an apple. Malcolm is beside him looking his jolly self, and Parker is standing guard at the door near the foyer.

"Miss McFee," they each say with a bow to their heads.

I wave awkwardly, wondering if the addition of Graham's men inside our home will be a regular occurrence when he is unable to be here with me. It will definitely take an adjustment period on my part.

"Everything okay?" Malcolm asks.

"Yeah, just a headache," I say with a weak smile.

Owen frowns, tossing his apple core into the trash. "Want me to alert Mr. Hoffman?"

"I think I'll just get some water and take a rest."

"Here, go lie down and I'll bring a glass to you," Malcolm offers. He is always so polite. "Can I get you a snack as well? The fridge is fully stocked."

"That is really kind of you, but I am good with just the drink."

I move into the living room and check my channel post. Holy shit. One hundred eighty-six posts within twenty minutes. I glance over the comments.

"I've woken up at a party and have no memory of the night before. It is the single biggest event that has shat-tered my life."

"Campus police have been useless. They even refused to submit a statement to the state or city police departments."

"I wish I never went to the frat party that changed my life."

"I am now in rehab and attempted suicide twice since I woke up and found a guy over me after I passed out in my dorm room."

"Not knowing what happened to me is the hardest..."

"I was a virgin when I was raped on campus. I now have no hope for humanity."

"I am four months pregnant after being hospitalized after a dorm party. I have no recollection of how this happened. Now I am finishing up my semester and maybe will complete the rest of my degree at another time."

"Having a voice that is not heard is worse than suffering in silence."

Tears roll down my cheeks as I skim through these comments. I rub at my temples and accept the glass of water that Malcolm hands to me, taking a big sip. I copy and paste a few of the comments into a blank document and then lie back on the cushions to rest my eyes.

"Can I get you anything else, ma'am?" he asks politely.

"No, thank you so much. I think I just need to take a break from the screen."

"The others and I will be just out of the doors in the foyer if you need anything. We are scheduled with you today until the boss picks you up."

"Okay, thank you."

I must have dozed off for about a half hour, and when I wake, it is now approaching lunch time. I slip back down to the floor and open up the channel to read through more of the comments and—

Where is my post?

I search the entire page for my original list of questions. Nothing. It has vanished. I look at the admin page and shoot all three people who are working under alias names a private message—asking why that particular post was deleted. When sending private messages, my real name appears, but I leave out the fact that I started the post. I guess this is one way to verify members' authenticity and keep outsiders from posing as students who are not even attending the university. I understand that there would be a need for a checks and balances type of system.

I get a response back from an admin within a minute with a canned message.

"Any post that defames our university is outlawed from this page. Please check the rules and featured posts before submitting any controversial material again."

Every feminist hair on my body stands on end. To me, this sounds like women are being silenced, and it raises more red flags than ever. I open up my email and at the top of the list see that Dr. Williams is giving me the date at which I am to meet with him for my final paper. And it is Monday.

I groan as I look at my materials scattered about. I have nothing concrete. Even after months of trying, I have nothing. I feel deflated and defeated. While I still want to help protect agency girls from being drugged, there is a bigger umbrella issue here that I cannot uncover in two days' time.

I have failed.

I sense it.

I know it.

I just need Dr. Williams to confirm it.

Instead of writing about anything of meaning, I grab my laptop and start writing about the downsides of being a female investigative journalist in an industry that is dominated by men. I bare my soul on paper and talk about my struggles of writing this final paper for a class. How one paper is determining my grade for a repeated semester of struggles, sweat, and sabotage.

It may come across as whining, but at least it is therapeutically good for my soul. The closure alone will be medicine for the wounds. Maybe to some I have given up. In a way, I have. There's no easy route to success when the laws of the universe are ganging up against me. Even Dr. Williams has pushed me into changing my topic. So here it is... My topic change.

After I have bled my words onto the page, I upload them into the journalism document, save it, and go off in search of a printer. I am not taking any chances this go-around with my work getting lost. Even if I predict it not being good enough, I at least want the opportunity to share my thoughts with my professor in charge of my future.

I make my way out to the foyer and find the men at their post, right where Malcolm said they would be.

"Hey," I say, peeking around the door. "Is there a printer here? I need to print a few pages."

"Mr. Hoffman has one in his office. I can open it up for you," Owen says.

"Okay."

I follow Owen into the main part of the penthouse and down the hallway. With the turn of a key, we are inside Graham's office, and it feels weird being in his space without him being here.

"There's a cable lying beside the printer, just place it into your USB port, turn the printer on, and go to town."

"Seems easy enough," I mutter, moving over to where he points.

"Just let me know when you're done and I can lock everything back up."

"Sounds good."

I watch Owen retreat and am left to my own devices.

I hook up my device, turn on the printer, and set it to print two copies—just because I refuse to take any chances. My curiosity is at full volume, and it is hard to be in Graham's space and not want to snoop. But I resist. If I want to move forward with Graham, I have to respect his privacy.

With the printed articles in hand, I head on out to the living room and find Owen relaxing on a chair.

"I'm all done," I say.

He nods and stands up from the chair to lock Graham's office back up. I spend the next twenty minutes cleaning up my workspace and head back up to the bedroom to freshen up before my therapy session.

Graham is prompt, as usual, and meets me and Parker in the parking garage. I enter the front seat and give him a kiss, waving goodbye to one of my many bodyguards who stays back.

"Not walking today?" I ask softly.

He stares intently at me. "No. Not today."

"I can handle reporters. I'm sick and tired of the media world I am trying to enter keeping me from having my own voice."

"These people are not looking to speak any truth, Angie. They are looking to destroy your reputation and attack you. They have some narrative to follow. Trust me, I've tried to make it financially worth it to them to shut up."

"Let them spew their hate."

"Not while I sit and watch."

He pulls out of the parking garage and barely dodges the camera people on the street. Lovely…they know where I live too. Nothing should surprise me anymore and yet it does.

"I *am* a drug addict. I may be in my recovery phase. But I am one, nonetheless."

"I do not want you to have any setbacks."

"I don't want that either, Graham. I have so much on my mind, trust me. Now would be the perfect time for me to have a relapse. But I have my head looking ahead. What is in the past needs to stay there. I have a future that I want to enjoy."

His hand squeezes mine, which is nervously pulling imaginary fuzz balls off my jacket. "Have I told you how proud I am of you?"

I shift my weight in my seat to face toward him. "Your support means everything. I got into this mess on my own, but am so thankful I have you to lean on through my journey out."

"I'm always on your side."

His words and actions match. This is how I know I can trust him.

It takes minutes to park, enter the elevator, and sign in. Graham sits beside me, and I use my wait time to journal in the little book Dr. Saber gave to me. I have entries for every day—some even double or triple depending on my mood.

My phone buzzes with an incoming voice message. I hold it up to my ear and listen as Beth, Dr. Williams's work-study student, informs me that I am to send my final article electronically for review. The professor will be out of the office all of next week and requests my document prior to Monday, if possible.

Saved on my new email account, I open up my file and submit it directly to Dr. Williams's account. There. It is all done. I have nothing left to do but wait.

The nurse calls me back, draws my blood, tests my urine, and calls for Dr. Lucian after the results are ready.

"Hello Angie," she says, glancing at my chart. "How have you been feeling?"

"Good, actually. Minor headache today."

"Did you take anything for it?"

I shake my head. "No. The thought crossed my mind. But I resisted."

She nods and then smiles, but it doesn't reach her eyes. "If we are going to move forward, I need you to be one hundred percent honest."

Tears fill my eyes. "I am being honest. I've been struggling, yes. But I haven't slipped up. Not even once, I promise."

"It's just that you have residual traces of Fentanyl in your system still."

"I was never actively taking that."

"Remember, any street pill could—and often does —have it."

"Okay. I just wish I knew how it was entering me. I've been very careful."

"I would have expected you to have detoxed from this substance already—especially in your bloodstream— which is the first to get cleansed. Urine is next, followed by hair. I am going to analyze your hair, with your permission."

"Sure, yeah." I think of all of the places I have been in the past two days and all of the ways someone could have slipped me a low-dose drug without me realizing it. Maybe my body is holding on to the chemicals longer. I just know that I personally have stayed clean.

"I'm going to get a hair follicle from your head sent to the lab here and maybe that will provide a bigger scope of what is going on with you. In the meantime, let's head down to see Dr. Westinger."

After losing a hair to the plucking, I follow Dr. Lucian out of her office and get situated on the couch of truth. I am twiddling my fingers under Dr. Westinger's watchful eye, feeling exposed and vulnerable. This woman doesn't miss a beat. I feel bad for her husband; he probably can't get away with anything.

Our appointment seems to fly by with just a back and forth question and answer session. She follows up on the question that was asked at the end of last visit and accepts my answer.

"I think we are moving in the right direction, Angie," she says happily.

It is the first time I have really seen her smile. "Thank you. I know I'm not the easiest client, but I do appreciate all of your efforts."

"In addition to what I can offer you here, I think joining in group therapy would help you bond with others who have similar struggles. It can do wonders for your spirit and growth. It is confidential, and those who attend follow a code they live by to keep it that way."

"Okay, I can try it."

"I'm going to leave you with one parting question that I do not want you to answer today. I want you to think about it, journal about it, and then report your answer back to me next week."

I bite at my bottom lip. "Okay."

"If you could exorcise the self-hatred from your body, what would you find there instead?"

I stare at her while I dissect her question in my head, so I know I understand her correctly. I send myself a text with the question so I do not forget and depart her office with a quick wave.

I run my fingers through my hair. Today has been very intense. I am really looking forward to hanging out with Claire and letting loose on the dance floor tonight.

I meet Graham in the lobby and melt into his open arms as he wraps me up with them. "How did everything go, sweetheart?"

"Today was pretty draining. I just need a few moments to decompress."

"Sure, want to go back home and take a quick nap together before you need to get ready for your ladies' night?"

"Cuddling sounds amazing," I agree.

The sound of my phone vibrating wakes us up from our slumber. I roll and stretch. The nap did wonders on my headache and mood. I feel rested and ready to have fun. I glance at the screen and see that it is a text from Claire alerting me that she's on her way.

Graham sits up and leans his weight onto his elbow, bending down to capture my lips. "I want you to be careful tonight. No taking chances."

"Okay. I'll be on my best behavior."

"It's not you I'm solely worrying about. It's who you hang around with as well."

"She's my best friend."

"I know," he says with a nod, "that's why I bumped up security."

I shake my head over his ways. What once used to drive me crazy, now is endearing.

"Enjoy guys' night. Win some money so I can justify the amount I spent on my craft room."

He makes a silly face, as if my expenses even put a dent

into his bank account. "I'm going to step out and handle a couple of business matters while you guys get ready here. But I'll be back before you leave with Collins to say goodbye and set up for poker."

"And approve of my outfit?"

"Sure."

"Graham!"

He doesn't even hesitate or laugh, which really solidifies my suspicions. "Claire better hope she stays on my good side."

"Pretty sure that girl doesn't care about pissing you off. But the mani and pedi sessions yesterday had to have helped soften her view of you."

"That was the plan."

"You are so manipulative," I comment with a snicker. "You don't even try to hide it."

Graham shrugs, throws on a pair of overly worn jeans and a T-shirt, and slides a solid-black hat over his wayward hair. He is looking mighty fine and all mine.

"You look hot and mysterious," I comment. "Why don't you dress like this for me?" I wrap my arms around his neck, tip up his hat, and stretch to kiss his lips. "Hmm."

He kisses me deeper and moans, grabbing my ass with both hands and squeezing. "Quit flirting with me. I'll never leave."

The sound of the doorbell ringing lets us know Claire is here. I trot downstairs ahead of Graham. I'm still wearing only his boxers and undershirt, never bothering to change after my nap. He slaps my ass before we round the corner, and I glare back at him for his blatant teasing.

"Hi, Claire," he greets with a small smile.

Despite whatever he wants to pretend, I know Claire has taken a spot on his "Like List" after a record-breaking two months on the "Dislike List." He has warmed up to her and has accepted that she will forever be in my life. We are sisters from different misters. Friends forever. He may not approve of ninety-nine percent of her ideas, but at least she is predictable at having bad ones—like tonight's costumes, no doubt.

"Hey, Graham," she says with a wave. She is already sprawled out on the living room floor surrounded by costume paraphernalia chaos. She is in her element and, despite the ridiculous makeup palette she just reveals from her bag, I know she will come up with something amazing. Overly sexualized, but still amazing. "Oh and Graham?"

"Yes?" he asks, while hugging me and kissing me on the nose. It is so feathery soft that I giggle.

"Hey!" Claire yells, hopping up from her place on the floor, clapping her hands together to get our attention back to her. "What I wanted to say before you both started groping each other was thank you for the spa date yesterday, Graham."

"Of course. Anything for my Angie to relax and spend time with her best friend."

Claire eyes him speculatively. "Something going on?" She points from me to him and back again. "I can sense it. It is like you guys are maturing in front of me."

I laugh at her serious expression. "Pretty sure my maturity will be dwindled down by whatever you plan to dress me in," I say, pointing my chin to the mess all over the furniture.

"I'll be back to say goodbye. Have fun, ladies."

"Oh, we will," Claire calls out, grabbing my hand and pulling me over to her makeshift workstation. "So, first off, I took your direction."

"My direction?"

"Your suggestion. Actually, plural—*suggestions*."

"Enlighten me, Claire," I deadpan.

"Drumroll, please!" she announces but doesn't wait for me to do anything, because I refuse. She uncovers my costume. "You're going to be a sensually seductive snowflake. And me?" She pulls the trench coat's flaps back to reveal her red velvet and white fur outfit. "Santa's ho!"

"You didn't."

"Oh, I did. And it's done. Settled."

"I was completely joking when I said these ideas, mind you."

She shakes my shoulders, jostling me from my once peaceful state. "Get excited! Go nuts. Yay! These were your best ideas to date."

"You know Graham is coming back, and he won't let me leave this place if I am just wearing some snowflake pasties."

Claire's hand flies to her chest. "Gah, show your master some respect."

I laugh over her fake disgust. She is something else.

The next hour is a whirlwind of fabric and makeup and open gawking. Claire dresses me in an outfit that is entirely white and blue. She laces a white corset up my spine that has silver and blue snowflakes attached to the rim at my chest. A flaring skirt with a fur trim slides up my hips, paired with knee-high shiny pleather boots with pom-pom balls attached to the lace ends.

Claire adds silver, white, and blue sparkles to my hair—twisting up half into a cute curly snowflake clip. My eyebrows get brushed with glitter paint, while my mascara is a pasty white. She adds several layers of eyeshadow in different shades and makes my eyes look icy.

Claire hands me a mirror and steps back to get the full view of her handiwork. "Wow," I gasp, "I look like I just came out of the freezer. You really know how to make my eyes pop. Thank you!" I honestly was not expecting to like what she had planned, but with the exception of the too-revealing outfit, she kept it super classy.

"I can see you're trying to give Graham a heart attack."

Claire and I jump up from the couch over the masculine sound coming from the entryway. We both glare at Nic, while holding our chests. Glitter shakes out of my hair from the force of my movements, making me sneeze.

"Next time warn us!" Claire yells, barely able to catch her breath.

"Hi," I say, running over to give him a hug. I haven't seen him since Thanksgiving at his parents' house. "Graham is out doing something for work. He'll be back soon."

Nic looks at my attire. "You know Graham is going to go ballistic, right? I mean, when it comes to you, it doesn't take much for him to get crazy and controlling."

"Oh, so you met the man before," Claire says, rolling her eyes. "Pretty sure if I wasn't the best friend, I would have been thrown into the river by now."

Nic eyes her as if seeing her for the first time. "You do bring on the trouble."

I glance down at my outfit, earning a smack on the arm from Claire.

"No, don't you dare feel guilty for how you are dressed," she snaps. "You look freaking hot. I'm telling you, I would bang you if I had a dick."

"They make devices like that you know."

"Ugh, Angie! You have such a fertile imagination!" she accuses.

"Probably because some of your humor has brushed off on me."

"Well, I only speak in facts. And the fact is, that man of yours is going to cream his pants when he sees you."

"Or kill us both," I counter.

"Yeah, I vote for that one," Nic chimes in, looking like he is going to enjoy the showdown I am sure to have with his brother.

Claire's huff echoes in the room. "You guys exaggerate too much. Maybe he will be so distracted by my awesome makeup skills that he will completely miss what she's wearing."

"Right," Nic says with mirth.

Claire has never really told me if the two of them have had much interaction. I mean, technically, he's her boss. But I am not sure of what the agency was like before I joined. Seems like a lifetime ago. So much has happened since I first walked into Entice Escort Agency for an interview with Nic. I was a different person then. Someone who lacked self-esteem and still saw the good in most people. Maybe a part of growing up means losing some of my naivete.

I clear my throat. "Let's all just remember that I'm the innocent one here."

"Do not play the victim card, Angie." Claire scoffs. "You love it when your man gets all obsessive and jealous.

You guys are into all that kinky shit where you try to get each other to go insane. Then the clothes will start-a-flying and then"—she crosses her arms over her chest—"poor Claire looks like a hussy. When in reality, I am the hero."

My mouth flies open over her fictional description. There is no way that is actually accurate. "Hero? Really, Claire?"

"Yes, really," she says, moving her hands to her hips.

I glance at Nic who is leaning against the wall, taking this all in like a sponge. I can't tell his mood—maybe amused? Perhaps he is enthralled over the whole dynamic of me and Claire.

"I'm the hero," she continues, "for helping the two of you meet in the first place. I'm basically the greatest match-maker on the planet. So you owe me a lot more respect."

"You know Graham is not going to let me leave like this, right? He is going to sabotage our night out and will be trying to put the blame on someone."

"You think I don't know this?" She scoffs in exasperation, growing more annoyed with me by the second. "Watch and learn, people, watch and learn." She pulls out a can of vanilla cupcake scented sparkle spray and mists it into the air, shooting the perfume all over the place. "Now, walk through it," she says, shoving me into the sparkle storm.

I choke, as I get covered in the sweet smelling scent and the glitter. "Is this necessary?" I yell.

"Yes." She looks at the can. "It might even have pheromones in it, who knows. Not that you two need help in the attraction department. But the scent should distract him."

"You're going to need to do better than that," I grind out

between my teeth. I think some of the sparkles are stuck on my tongue and caught between my gums. Moving to cleaner air, I stand closer to Nic who cannot stop trying to resist laughing. Yup, he is entertained.

"I obviously came prepared. I'm not some idiot," Claire says, draping me with a glittery chiffon cloak. She places it over my shoulders, ties it at my neck, and flares it out around my arms like a veil. "There. Just keep that wrapped around you and he won't bust a nut letting you leave."

The sound of the door opening causes all three of us to look toward the noise.

"Let the fun begin," Nic responds with amusement, knowing exactly how Graham is going to react.

Graham gives Nic a pat on the back and then makes a beeline toward me. He wraps me in his arms, as I struggle to get mine free from the cape that Claire just added to my costume last minute. His lips are at my ear and his five o'clock shadow has me tingly. "I'm going to fuck you so hard in this outfit later and make my ice princess melt."

I giggle over his mix of sexy and cheesy words. He is such a contradiction sometimes. I love it, though.

He pulls back from me, clears his throat, and announces, "There's no way you are leaving in this. It's too sexy. And" —he sniffs the air—"who baked cupcakes?"

"Just for the record, this was all her idea," Claire chimes in.

"Yeah, right Claire. You basically took something I was making a joke about and turned it into your little pet project —again."

Her hands prop on her hips and it pulls the hem of her

skirt up two inches, revealing an obscene amount of bare leg. "Again?"

"Remember when you signed me up on a dating site without my permission?"

"Oh yeah, that thing. You really do hold grudges, Angie. You should work through some of that animosity."

"You did it behind my back." I stomp my foot down, making it snow more glitter all over the penthouse.

"For your own good. I mean, it got you back together with Teddy Graham. You guys basically owe me."

"How about the time you tricked me into attending a stripper pole class?" My mouth is dry from arguing. I walk into the kitchen and grab the glass of water I had poured earlier from the counter.

Claire stares down at her nail polish, admiring the new paint job from yesterday. "I'm failing to see the negatives here, Ang. Pretty sure Graham reaped the benefits from your newly acquired skills."

"Still am," he admits, making me spit out my mouthful of water.

"I'm wearing this," I say, holding my ground and channeling my frustrations back to Graham. "No negotiations. No discussions."

"I definitely went on the more conservative end of the spectrum," Claire comments. "You should have seen my original plan ideas."

Graham's expression is indifferent. "Fine."

I throw my arms around him and give him a kiss on the cheek. "Distance will make the heart grow fonder"—I stretch up for just his ear to hear—"and make the cock grow hornier."

"Watch it, woman."

"I expect to be ravished later."

"Oh, trust me, you will. If I can find your body under the layer of glitter later."

"Promise?"

"Promise."

21

The sidewalk outside of Slay is packed with people trying to get in. Graham supplied us with a limo for our girls' night out—demanding that if he couldn't be with us to watch over me, at least he would be able to function easier if he knew I wasn't out lying in a gutter or something equally overly dramatic.

No one can say the man lacks an imagination.

Collins is in charge of keeping an eye on us, although I have already thought of multiple ways to put a kibosh to his hovering. Parker—the uptight backup man—has never been prepared to deal with this much estrogen at once. That I am sure. And his ninja warrior skills need to be sharp.

"At least we are pregaming it before we enter that mob," Claire says, clinking her glass with mine.

"Cheers!"

Claire hits the button for the privacy screen to scroll down, revealing the men in the front seat, looking uncomfortable and edgy. "Cheers, boys!" she says, throwing her glass up into the air and only catching half of the drink before it sloshes over the edge onto Parker's suit coat. Why did he even wear something so not blendable? He is going to be banished from the club for not looking the part. "Oops, sorry!"

"How are you drunk already?" I ask stupidly.

"I skipped dinner."

"Claire... You know this place is not serving food, right?"

I can feel Collins's stare through the mirror and look up to catch his look of disapproval. I shrug and try to look innocent, but most likely I just come across as impish. I promised Graham that I would tone down my fun tonight with mocktails at the club, but a little bubbly won't hurt.

Pulling away from the curb and back onto the street, he ignores our hollering that he is going the wrong way. We bang on the glass, pointing at the club that seems to be getting farther and farther away.

"Really? You need to fill up the ol' gas tank now?" Claire asks, her anger showing. "We were right there!"

"Parker, go get a pizza and two bottled waters," he orders his coworker.

"Ooo, I like-y this idea!" I say, clapping my hands together. "Quick Mart pizza is so delish."

Claire scrunches up her nose with distaste. "I hope they use organic cheese."

"I'm sure they *only* use organic cheese."

"You are the worst liar on the planet."

Parker opens up the side door and hands us a box of pizza and some waters after several minutes of waiting. I know that Graham is not just having two of his men watch us tonight. There has to be a couple more hiding among the patrons at the club. He has been too paranoid to trust me with just two.

Claire and I each pull a slice out of the box. Taking a huge bite, the cheese stretches like a rubber band from my mouth to my hand.

"Dis his oo wood," I mumble, enjoying the best gas station food in the three-mile radius.

Collins tries to avoid eye contact in the mirror as we make sex noises in the backseat over the amazing food.

"You guys are the best babysitters eva!" Claire compliments, making me spit water out onto the limo's window. "Oh no, she sprung a leak!"

I laugh harder, but my corset is cutting off my air supply if I do it too much. Ouch.

I hold up my phone and set it to selfie mode. I slide next to Claire and make my best animal noise that gets both Collins's and Parker's attention, just as I snap the pic—including them in the background. "Nailed it!" I chant, fist pumping the air.

I send the pic to Graham with the caption—*Slumming it with my homeboys.* I even managed to capture my slice of pizza in the shot.

He is not as humored by it as I predicted, because it is only a moment later when he is giving Collins the riot act through his Bluetooth.

"Our boss has a temper," I announce—not even earning a smirk from the men. Sheesh, everyone needs to lighten up.

My phone buzzes with a text.

The Boyfriend: Behave.

Welp, that is direct and to the point. I am feeling brave from my liquid courage, so I text back.

Angie: Maybe.

The Boyfriend: I will come get you.

Angie: Fine. I can pretend to be good.

Collins drives back to Slay and valet parks the limo across the street at a private garage, not affiliated with the dance club. He nearly has a heart attack when I forgo my cloak and walk out of the backseat with half the clothes on than he probably expected.

"Mr. Hoffman is not going to like this," he warns, not elaborating on his meaning, although it is obvious. He probably hopes I'll reconsider my choices.

"Stuff it, Collins," Claire interjects, tugging me toward the crowd waiting to get inside the club.

We manage to jump to the head of the line with a quick exchange of some Ben Franklins. Collins follows us inside —probably on strict, finely detailed orders—and looks as comfortable as a father giving his daughter the infamous sex talk for the first time. He has a perpetual scowl on his face and eagle eyes. Parker lingers outside. Neither man thought it was necessary to wear an outfit to blend in with the crowd.

Glancing around, I spot Malcolm along the back perimeter of the room. I wish he would have at least stuck with the winter theme when he chose his suit for tonight. He is big enough to be confused as a bouncer but nice enough to pose as the greeter.

Claire leans into me and whispers, "I think Collins could have used some pizza. He looks hungry for a fight."

"He does seem pretty angry," I mutter, making him look at me and glare. "Oops, you heard that."

The entire club is vibrating with techno Christmas carols. Snowflakes are strung from the ceiling on long wires, sparkling like flattened disco balls. There are three separate bars, all lit up with frosted blue lights. The club is two levels with the top one wrapped just around the perimeter, with private viewing booths and a personal waitstaff.

This is definitely not the type of dive that has the little bowls of cocktail peanuts for everyone to spread their germs in on the bar. This place is too classy for that kind of snackage.

Along the side of the dance floor, huge ice sculptures are carved into a winter scene, decorated with up-lighting and moving parts. Claire grabs my hand, pulling me toward the far side bar that appears to be less crowded. The bartenders are all male and all dressed like strippers. Low hung white pants, no shirt, and a white bowtie make up their uniform. Oh, and a six pack of steel. Let's not forget that.

We order the signature Snowflake Martini drink which is colored Caribbean Ocean blue. The rim is decorated with white chocolate and shredded coconut flakes. It is like a luxurious liquid dessert, despite mine missing the alcohol.

"Do these things even have alcohol in them?" Claire asks, staring at her empty beverage. I know mine doesn't. "I need something that'll make me feel alive."

"Well, I got just the thing," the bartender says, filling up a shot glass with something clear.

"This better not be bottled water," she teases, earning a wink. She throws back the shot—squinting over the throat burn—slamming the empty glass down onto the bar's surface. "That ain't no bottled water," she whisper-yells, looking dizzy from the surge of alcohol to her system.

We order another drink, chat about stupid shit, and laugh until our bellies hurt.

Feeling in the dancing mood, I grab Claire and push her toward the blaring music and the polished floor. We enter with our drinks in one hand and the other waving around obnoxiously in the air, probably not even in beat to the music—although I think my rhythm is right on the tempo.

With each song change, we either shout compliments to the DJ spinning the sounds or scream our request on what should be played next. My corset rises as my arms fly into the air—exposing more bare belly than I probably realize. My flaring skirt is fun and flirty, swishing side to side with the sway of my hips. I shake my ass and get into the groove, ignoring everyone in my vicinity. I feel pretty and just let go and breathe in the atmosphere.

While I give him credit for being discreet, Collins is still here watching my every move. It's a bit daunting when I am able to slow my mind down enough to think about it. When Claire flinches beside me, I follow her gaze down to her phone.

"What's wrong?" I yell, trying to get my words out above the music.

"Nothing."

"Pretty sure your face says otherwise."

"It's just that I thought Ethan would be home tonight waiting for my return. Instead, he's going to do a campout with his son at the ex's."

I frown over her disappointment. She's not acting like herself, and I worry that she is putting all of her eggs into one basket with a man who might not be worthy of her. I just want my best friend to be happy.

"I'm sorry," I say, giving her a half hug, all while trying not to dump my beverage down her back. "Let's forget the guys for the night."

"Sounds good."

We clink glasses, throw the rest back, and place the empties on the side table that lines the wall. I don't need to be drunk to have fun. I just need to be around my bestie.

My attention is back to shaking my ass and singing at the top of my lungs to the music. I mess up the lyrics on numerous occasions and laugh at the silliness of my improvising. The grinding of a guy behind me and the hands on my hips make me freeze. I see Collins moving across the room—ready to explode his fury on the poor dude—and before he can make it to me, I turn to look the offender in his eyes.

"Let go. I'm not interested," I announce loudly, feeling the need to scream over the music.

"Oh, come on, babe, don't be like that."

Ugh, I hate when guys use that line of persuasion.

"I came here to dance, not get an STD."

"Don't be so frigid."

"Leave me alone before my bodyguard breaks your face."

He shrugs and moves on to someone easier, mumbling

something about not wanting any trouble. I turn to catch Collins grabbing my elbow. "Are you okay, ma'am?"

"Yeah, of course," I huff, swaying on my feet. I pat his arm. The man always wears a suit. I would bet he sleeps in one too. "Relax. Go grab a drink or something."

"I don't drink when I'm working. Ever."

"Oh. Well, go search for one of those sand trays with the rake or something. I am good. I can take care of myself."

"Yeah, just chill," Claire says, dusting some snowflake confetti from his arm, giggling over her own inside joke.

We take several dozen silly pictures and selfies in our costumes. Even the security detail gets their images captured involuntarily.

Every time some guys get too close, we find ourselves flanked by Parker and Collins, while Austin and Owen verbally growl at them.

"I feel like I am part of a surprise orgy," Claire announces, doubling over and laughing her ass off.

I laugh so hard I fall down, despite being surrounded by the man crew.

Claire helps me stand again. "Seems like your ninja reflexes have worsened with age," she fake scoffs, pointing at each man individually.

The whole display is comical. We must look like royalty to anyone paying attention, with our security detail ready to slay any dragons that come our way.

"Gotsta use the pee station!" I announce unceremoniously, participating in the fit of giggles that spring out of my throat. I sound demented. I sway to the influx of the alcohol that must finally be reaching my nervous system from the bubbly on the ride over. I feel light and airy.

"Go before you leak," Claire warns between breaths, only fueling the unending fit of giggles.

I excuse myself to go to the restroom. As I walk into the crowded space, I squeeze past everyone to find a free stall. I check my text messages and see that Graham sent me one.

The Boyfriend: I miss you, sweetheart. I want to wrap myself around you.

I type out a message quickly, hearing the water running outside and the hand dryer blowing. I think the room is finally clearing out, and I feel less claustrophobic in the space and in my thoughts.

Angie: I prefer you buried deep inside me.

The Boyfriend: I am going to fuck you so thoroughly when you get home. I like you sore. So you have a constant reminder who you belong to. I ache for you, sweetheart.

As I type out my next message, I see an email alert pop up on my screen from the university. I open the app. At the top of my inbox list, I find a message from Dr. Williams. I hover my finger over his name and click it.

Miss McFee,

I am sorry to inform you that I cannot ethically allow you to move forward with graduation with a journalism degree. You did not meet the qualifications for this class. On a professional note, I advise you to search for work in the English field and take some basic journalism classes online postgraduation.

On a personal note, I would advise you to take responsibility for your actions and not push your own gender insecurities onto others. Society is already flooded with these false notions and accusations that lack the finesse that facts often bring to making a difference in the world. Accepting responsibility for your own inadequacies should be your first priority.

While your name will still go into the running for various internships if you submit your entry to the master link that I emailed you weeks ago, I would expect a denial based on the competition here at River Valley and the quality of work that you have submitted for review this semester. Enjoy your graduation and your future. You should be proud of the degree you secured, regardless of whether or not it was your end goal.

He is failing me. Dr. Williams is failing me. I read and reread the typed words. My second chance was wasted. I still did not achieve what I wanted to achieve.

"Miss McFee, are you in there?" Collins asks from the doorway. I catch some anxiety in his voice.

"Be right out!"

I stare down at the screen, as if somehow I can make the words change—my *reality* change—if I just pray hard enough. All of the work I put in. All of the hours I endured. Just to have the past four and a half years culminate to one final verdict—failure.

Fuck.

Sitting on the toilet, alone in my thoughts, I try to think of what I will do next. What my future will look like.

My head spins, and I crave the buzz that only the pills can give me. My taste buds crawl with need. My mouth dries with thirst.

No.

I have come too far to go hunting right now for a temporary fix to a permanent problem. The problem is I need to accept that life can be cruel. Fucking cruel. And the things I thought I want might not be the things I actually need.

My mind clouds with regret and grief and—

Heartbreak.

I feel utterly and thoroughly broken.

Dazed and a bit fuzzy, I focus my attention back to my screen to see that Graham is messaging me.

The Boyfriend: Baby? Everything okay?

Angie: I wan u to make me forget my name.

The Boyfriend: How much have you been drinking?

What's that supposed to mean? Ironically, I have only had the bubbly at the start of the evening. For once, I am making better choices for myself, despite the fact that I really could use something to numb the pain right now.

Angie: Enough to think you are prettttty.

The Boyfriend: Thought so.

Angie: Why all the self-rightnessous?

I stare at my words as they blur along the screen. I think my brain is just confused and worn out from the realization that my future is now once again undetermined.

A few angry tears blot my screen, turning into little streaks. Graham seems as if he is ignoring me. So, I wipe and flush, exiting the stall. I wash my hands and fix my dance-crazy hair, trying to put the email news behind me. If there is one thing I am good at, avoidance is it.

"Miss McFee?"

I let out a groan. "I'm coming out now," I promise. I wash my hands again, wipe at my eyes, and shuffle my feet out the doorway.

"Ma'am?" Collins asks, concern evident in his voice.

I glance up to see both Austin and Owen hanging out behind him. "I'm fine," I brush off. How many men does it take to look after me? Graham seriously has a security fetish. More men keep coming out of the woodwork. It seems a bit overkill.

Ignoring their probing looks of concern, I head to the dance floor to find Claire. I use dancing as my therapy and get lost in the steady rhythm of the songs. I do not want to think about anything other than this moment in time.

Claire catches my mood change within the first five minutes and pulls me over to the bar, using some excuse about needing to hydrate our fire hydrants—or some bull-shit like that. I tell her everything. Dr. Williams's email… About my failure.

I specifically order a water, and Claire follows suit.

"I'm sorry," she says, pulling me in for a hug, "but I don't see it as a failure at all."

"And why not?"

"Because maybe not getting exactly what you think you want will eventually bring you everything you need."

"You are speaking in poetry."

"I'm serious, Angie. Don't let a fancy degree determine your self-worth. You are better than what any document might represent."

I give my best friend a hug. She's always so wise. "Thank you."

"Want to do a shot?"

I shake my head no. "I just don't want alcohol to murk up my brain tonight when I am still recovering from the—"

She nods, knowing where I am going with my train of thought without me having to say the words in public. "I'm proud of you, Angie. I really am."

It feels weird hearing the words, but they do not sound condescending. Eventually, I will be able to accept them freely, knowing that all of the hard work I've done to stay clean could be part of someone else's inspiration. But right now, I just can't bring myself to feel the same pride toward myself.

"I'm sorry if I've been a bad influence tonight by partying a bit too hard."

"You aren't," I promise. "It's just that I've been having cravings. And I don't want to make them worse by adding in other distractors."

"I never want to be that for you." She pulls back and frowns. "I think I've been using alcohol to cope with some of my own drama. It's hard being here knowing that my family back home doesn't care if I ever even travel back to see them."

"You deserve better than that. You deserve love, Claire." It kills me inside that her parents don't show her the love that she needs.

"Plus, as graduation approaches, things start to get real."

I sip my water, taking in her words. What am I going to do now with my life? Right now, I just feel deflated. I can only hope with time, I will figure things out.

I catch a shiny green dress in my periphery, followed by the wisps of red hair. When I turn my attention to the beautiful woman at the bar, she gives me a once-over and snickers. I know her. But from where?

"Angela McFree?" she slurs, her posture straightening on the stool.

"McFee," I correct, knowing that her slip was most likely a planned insult. And then I place her. "Britt?"

She swirls her hand into the air, taking a half bow. "The one and only."

I look behind her, half expecting to see her bestie Sophia lurching in the background.

"I bet you feel mighty proud that Graham cheated on Sophia with you."

He never cheated on anyone.

"Who are you?" Claire asks, giving Britt the once-over.

I'd be surprised if Claire doesn't in fact know her. She seems to know everyone in town.

Britt narrows her eyes at us. "Sophia's best friend."

Claire smirks. "Oh, so a nobody." She clicks her tongue and gets up from the bar, tugging my arm to pull me with her. "We don't need to sit here with Miss Judgment. C'mon, Angie."

Before I leave, Britt looks me up and down—making me feel dirty. "Never knew what Graham saw in you."

I shrug. "I wonder that sometimes too."

My admittance catches her off guard. Good.

"He had the second highest chip stack when Sophia texted me a picture."

My eyes twitch over her comment. *Do not react. Do not react.*

She smiles wickedly at me. "I think she's his good luck charm."

Claire barrels around, seething at the mouth. "Quit spewing lies. Nobody has time for this shit."

Britt holds up her phone, flashing the picture of Sophia with the table of men in the background. After we get a good look, she drops her phone onto the surface of the bar haphazardly.

Damn. Why is she there?

"Who would have thought that the whole—" Britt stops midsentence, putting her drink up to her mouth to silence herself.

Something seems off. It always has with Sophia. Without thinking, I snatch Britt's phone from the bar before she has a chance to stop me. A warning pops across the screen stating that the battery life is low. I hurry and open up the text app to find where Sophia texted her the photo and skim through the back and forth messages.

Sophia: This whole fake stalking scheme that we constructed has been life changing. I think Graham might actually take me back.

"Hey! Give me back my phone!"

I keep reading, as the acid from my stomach burns my throat.

Britt: Just don't get caught. Last thing you need is for this to blow up in your face.

Sophia: I would be back with him by now if it wasn't for the wench that stole my man.

What the hell?! I thought she was making this whole thing up, but to actually see the proof is too much. Britt's phone slips from my hands as my fingers can't stop from trembling.

"She lied," I squeak out.

Claire links arms with me. "Lied?"

"You have the nerve to steal my phone!"

I clear my throat. "Sophia lied about the stalking and the texts and the impending danger. She lied about it all."

"What a fake bitch!" Claire yells, more to Britt than to me. "Who does she think she is?"

Britt's eyes widen with fear, probably stemming from the rampage Sophia will be on once she realizes how I found out the truth.

I need to clear my head. "Let's go," I tell Claire, allowing her to guide me across the room toward the dance floor.

We stop once we are clear of Britt's gaze.

"I swear to you, Angie, the few times I was near Sophia, I didn't think she would go this far and be this type of evil whore. She can really play the victim card. She has so many people fooled."

I can feel my eyes twitching and my nostrils flaring. "I've suspected it for weeks. Something always seemed too convenient about her text messages and stalker fears. Oh, the nerve of that bitch! I want to punch her face in and finish what we started back at the safe house. I never had such violent tendencies until I met her." I shift my weight from foot to foot. "I mean, I wanted to hit things after Mom and James," I choke, my eyes watering. "But, never a human being as much as I do her."

"She's asking for it. I wouldn't blame you."

"And she's probably still at the penthouse now, lurking around with her boobs popping out, trying to get Graham to notice and worry about her."

"Well, there's one way to fix this whole mess…"

I straighten my posture and push back my shoulders. I can only hope that Britt doesn't have time or battery life to warn her best friend. "You in?"

Claire's smile widens. "Wouldn't miss this epic show-down. If only we had time to go grab some popcorn. I could use a salty snack while I watch this unfold."

I bark out a laugh. I appreciate Claire lightening the mood, despite the adrenaline pumping through my body like an uncontrollable fire. "Let's go."

We head toward the front entrance, signaling our suited entourage to follow along. My head is starting to hurt and no amount of water guzzling is going to fix it. I just want to sleep and wake up from this craziness. However, I've been pushed around enough by Barbie Bitch and the time is now that she hears exactly what I think of her.

We make it outside and the night air is frigid. It feels like it could snow, it is so cold out.

"Where to now?" Collins asks, probably confused as to why we are leaving so soon from a night out that should have lasted longer.

My throat clenches, but I force down the lump to not give off any warning signs. No one is going to stop me from delivering my message.

"Can you take us back to the penthouse? Claire left some supplies there that she needs to grab from our costume making. Plus, I'm rather tired and want to lie down."

"Sure thing, ma'am."

When we get to the parking garage, Malcolm is waiting at the limo to open the door. He must have left Slay early. He waves to me, offering up a cheerful smile. He definitely has the personality that the others lack.

Collins takes up the driver's seat, while Owen joins him on the passenger side. I watch out the window while Parker and Austin slip into the back of an SUV, while Malcolm moves behind the wheel.

"Gang's all here," I mutter impatiently, playing with the hem on my skirt. I clench my knuckles and bite at my tongue, growing anxious as Collins pulls out of the garage and onto the road.

I'm coming for you, Sophia.

And you won't even know what hit you.

22

I am out of the backseat of the limo before Collins can exit fast enough.

"Slow down, Miss McFee," he calls to me, but I am running toward the elevator as fast as I can, only Claire being able to keep up the pace.

I slam my hand onto the call button, feeling the pressure of the guards closing the distance on us.

"C'mon, dammit!"

The doors finally open and I thrust myself inside, followed by Claire. I slap the close button, then shove my keycard into the slot that allows me access to the penthouse floor.

"Well, if it isn't Tweedledee and Tweedledum."

My jaw clenches as I glance to the side corner of the car to see Sophia dressed in a fitted red dress, looking like the devil she is. How did I not even notice her? She takes in our appearances, casting her judgy eyes on our outfits.

"What are you doing here?" I ask, but I already know

the answer. She can't stay away from my man. Been trying to stuff herself up his ass since before I even came onto the scene.

"Oh, you know, hanging out with a good"—she pauses for dramatic effect—"*friend.* But considering you kept me from exiting into the parking garage, it looks like we'll be spending even more time together."

"Don't you get exhausted trying to squeeze yourself into relationships where you aren't welcome?"

"Don't you get bored playing house and dress-up at Graham's expense?" She looks at her pointy, red-painted fingernails. "You'll never be the woman that a man like him desires."

"Except she is," Claire says matter-of-factly. "And he is pretty much obsessed with all things Angie."

"He's just confused."

As I pass in front of her to move to the back of the car, my foot catches on hers and I know that it is intentional. I stumble and touch my knee to the dirty floor.

"You okay, Angie?" Claire asks, concern evident in her voice. She rattles off a string of swear words to Barbie Bitch, reaching for my elbow to help me balance.

I pick myself up, and wheeling around, I see red. I dart toward Sophia's frail, perfect body, shoving her shoulders until she hits the car's wall. The elevator stops as our bodies crash into one another, bumping into the button panel.

Claire ducks to the side, trying to be my backup support. The small space is already feeling claustrophobic, as limbs swing at each other.

"What's your problem?!" I bellow.

My arm is resting at the hollow of Sophia's throat,

pinning her. She's not even fighting back, and there's humor dancing in her eyes. And that infuriates me the most. She is taunting me with her fearlessness. Tormenting me with the growing doubt flooding through me that even if Graham learns the truth, that he may not actually believe it.

I want to punch her. To throw her down and tell her to stay away. Far, far away. To tell her that Graham is *mine*. Everything that I have endured and tolerated over the course of all these months is finally coming to a boiling point. I have put up with her blatant flirting, her comments over me being a fling, and her bullshit lies over having a stalker just to gain Graham's attention.

Enough is enough.

Sophia's nails dig into my arm, making me wince from the pain. I release my hold on her, stumbling back. I rub at the wounds she created, drawing blood from my arm.

"Apparently money can't buy you everything," she spits out. "Class is something you are born into, my dear, not something that can be purchased."

"Stay away from him," I snarl.

"Or what? You'll hit me, Angie? Because if you haven't noticed, Graham is a very powerful man"—she pauses and laughs even louder—"who knows what he wants." She throws her head back and looks up at the ceiling. When her eyes join mine again, they sparkle. "And he wants me to be his company's signature face. You hurt me, his business associates and board of directors will sue your ass. So if you want to deal with the fallout, then you better lawyer up. Because the marketing team was not happy I came into work after Thanksgiving break with a bruise on my face from where you took a swing at me."

Her perfume burns my nostrils as I struggle to find clean air to breathe.

"I know the truth, you bitch." I sneer at her, as the sparkle in her eyes dulls into a look of disbelief.

"What truth?"

I watch as her bottom jaw trembles and she swallows. "I'm sure it hurts to go from being at the middle of his list to the bottom," I say nonchalantly. "And pretty soon, the only list you'll make is the blacklist."

Her hands fly to her hips. "You cause that man so much stress, you know that? He can do better, so much better."

I keep my temper at an even level and deliver my next question with crystal clarity. "Do you get tired of being used goods to him? You keep pining after a man who has already cast you aside. He's done with you. Give it up already."

"Oh, honey, it's better to be used by Graham than to not be used at all. We have had many intimate moments, and I'm sure he'll grow tired of trying to preserve your innocence and come back to me for the excitement I can offer him."

It takes everything in me not to punch her bleached teeth out of her mouth, right here, right now. "You know nothing about our sex life."

"I'm just hoping he got tested after his time with your skanky ass," Claire mutters beside me.

Sophia glares at her. "I know that he'll grow bored. Always does. You can't ride the gravy train forever. Eventually he'll catch on that the juice isn't worth the squeeze."

I swallow hard and hope that she cannot see how much her comment has affected me. She somehow has determined one of my fears of being used and then pushed aside. While

Graham claims I have the potential to destroy him, I know that he can equally do the same to me.

The elevator starts to ascend, resuming its climb toward the penthouse. Claire must have hit the button.

"I'll never understand why he ever found you appealing," I mutter. "He usually has impeccable taste—except when it comes to you."

On the surface, Sophia is the epitome of perfection. The thought of the connection they share in both the professional and personal realms of his life nauseate me. Well, tonight that ends. I am done with the bullshit this woman spews.

"But don't worry, honey, you are the *it girl* of the moment. The media loves you," she teases, her tone sardonic.

"Did you leak things to the press, you bitch?"

Her face genuinely looks surprised, and I can tell in this instance she is not the person who is trying to sabotage my reputation. "Hell, no. But I would enjoy the attention anyway. While it lasts. Graham does love a damsel in distress. He has been helping to keep me safe, making sure I am cared for. I'll be waiting for him to have his fun with you but return to me when—"

"There is no when!" I yell. "I know you have lied about your stupid text messages and have been using Britt to help you. It's all over, Sophia. Tonight's the night where my *boyfriend* finds out about how you have deceived him."

Her smile is fake. "Your word against mine. Wonder who our beloved Graham will believe?" She takes a step closer and pushes her shoulder against me, challenging me. Testing my self-control.

And I accept.

My hands tangle in her hair, as the ding of the elevator sounds. She pulls at mine as Claire pushes us both out of the elevator before it shuts on us.

"Let go!" Sophia yells as Claire holds her arms for me, so I can take a swing at her.

The three of us stumble into the foyer door, causing a loud sound to erupt from a picture on the wall crashing to the floor. Broken glass sprinkles the floor like little crystals.

"What the hell is going on?" Graham calls out, trying to separate the three of us from killing each other.

Sophia breaks free first and darts into the living area of the penthouse. I run after her, jumping on her back as she falls face-first into the poker table. Cards go flying, followed by the skittering of poker chips on the tiled floor. Claire joins us on top, as she tries to hold Sophia down.

"Chick fight," one guy calls out, jumping from his seat.

The sound in the room is so loud that I struggle to even make out the words being screamed from all of the men.

The smell of beer permeates the space, as bottles come crashing to the floor in the craziness.

Strong arms bind around me, pulling me off of the Barbie Bitch.

"I'm not done with her," I yell, trying to wiggle loose.

"What the hell is going on?" Graham yells, trying to keep me from breaking free and hurting myself.

Nic has Claire contained, despite her struggling against his force. "Let me go. That Barbie Bitch has it coming," she screams.

"I've been assaulted," Sophia cries, putting on an Oscar-worthy performance.

Collins—who finally makes it to the scene—grabs her

before she can start round two.

"Let me go," she demands. "You all see this? Angie attacked me."

"You deserved it, you liar!"

The room is surrounded by Graham's friends and security detail, as they take in the mess. Guilt stabs at me for interrupting their poker night, but I've had enough of being emotionally pushed around by Sophia. It is time for everyone to know what I discovered.

"Lying about what?" Graham asks for clarification, his attention moving between me and her. His hands trail down my arms, where Sophia's fingernails have made crescent shaped cuts along my skin. "She do this to you?"

I nod. I take a deep breath and round my shoulders. "The stalker texts are a lie. Her friend Britt has been helping to execute the whole scheme. All of it has been a lie to get you to worry about her and hopefully go back to her."

"Well, that's never going to happen," Graham says confidently, disgust evident in his tone. He turns his attention to the disheveled princess who looks like her crown just got tarnished. "Is this true, Sophia?"

"She's lying."

"No, I'm not," I counter.

"I have proof," Claire calls from across the room. "I took screenshots of Britt's phone."

What? When?

"I don't need proof," Graham says flatly. "I trust Angela. And it's not like the thought hasn't crossed my mind before." He looks directly at Sophia. "I was just delusional to think that your soul had some goodness to it. Well, I was wrong."

"So you aren't going to hear my side?" Sophia says in shock.

He lets go of me and walks over to where Collins has her restrained. I watch from the sidelines as he stares right into her eyes. "After all I've given you? After all I've done to support your modeling career and your endeavors, you do this? You fucking disgust me. Do you hear me?"

"I can—"

"Get out."

"Graham…"

"Get out!"

"Don't do this," she begs. Her eyes move around the room looking for a lifeline, someone who can bail her out of the shit situation she created for herself. But there is no one.

"I mean it, Sophia. Get out. You are fired, effective immediately. Never step foot on any of my properties. If you get within a few yards of my *girlfriend*, you better turn the opposite way, or I will slap a restraining order against you. Do you understand?"

"Grah—"

"Don't approach her. Don't look at her sideways. Don't talk to her. Don't even utter her name."

I watch in awe as tears rush out of her eyes. Seeing her have this much real emotion is actually hard to witness. Sure, Sophia deserves what she is getting served, but now that the excitement has worn off, I actually feel a bit sorry for her. She is losing the best thing she thought she ever had —Graham.

Too bad he belongs to me.

That is something I will never feel sorry for.

Owen and Collins escort Sophia out of the penthouse. Graham moves over to my side, wrapping me in his arms.

"I'm sorry that went on for as long as it did, and that I never figured out the truth on my own."

"I thought maybe she was the one who fed the press information about me," I say softly. "But when I confronted her about it, she looked genuinely surprised over the accusation."

"Knowing now what she is capable of, it's not hard to think that is a possibility. I'm sorry, sweetheart." He places a kiss to my forehead. "I'm sorry that this whole debacle has caused you unnecessary stress and pain. She is out of our lives for good."

I lean up to kiss him on the lips.

"My biggest regret is not videotaping your woman in action," Logan chimes in from across the room. "That was hawt."

We all laugh, appreciating the lightening of the mood.

Collins and Owen come back, and we all pick up the mess that I had a hand in creating.

"Sorry I ruined poker night."

"Yeah," Nic says, "but you basically just turned it into fight night instead."

I laugh over his laid-back mood. He always has a way of making me feel comfortable, despite the situation being stressful.

"I'm pretty sure I had the highest chip count," a man I don't know says, his lips curling up into a smirk.

Nic laughs. "Dude, you had the *lowest* count."

"But I would have won the pot if Graham's warrior princess didn't come here to show him who's boss. And to think he's the one with the actual wrestling experience." He turns his attention to me. "Pretty sure you can teach your man a few moves."

I smile. "No doubt."

"In and out of the bedroom," Logan chimes in.

"Hey now," Graham warns. "Don't be thinking about my woman in any bedrooms."

"Territorial much?"

Oh, he has no idea just how much. Graham tickles my side, making me squirm.

Glitter is scattered across the poker table, making me realize I am still dressed like a snowflake. The night didn't turn out like I expected, but at least I got the conclusion I wanted on one thing. I'm sure in the morning, the realization of me failing Dr. Williams's class will be harder to swallow.

I move into the kitchen to grab a drink, allowing the men to finish with the rest of the cleaning. Claire joins me, as I pour two glasses of pineapple juice from a pitcher in the fridge. My hands tremble as I bring the glass up to my mouth, taking slow sips as I come down from the adrenaline high.

"I'll be back," I mutter to Claire. "Going to go to the bathroom."

I head toward the hallway, deciding to use the spare one instead of going up to the master. One glance in the mirror, and I shudder at my appearance. My hair looks like it barely survived a hurricane, while my makeup looks like it didn't survive at all. I dampen a tissue, swiping the cloth under my eyes to soak up some of the runny mascara.

Once I am done freshening up, I return to the group,

who has already lost a few of its members. I find my empty glass on the counter, so I refill it and continue to hydrate my body.

Claire is camped out on the sofa, with her legs curled up under her. She looks comfy, and seeing her relaxed makes me want to go join her. I feel like I've been on my feet all night.

As I make my way over to the sofa, it feels like the floor is moving. I feel my body drifting and flopping, as a chill runs up my spine.

"I don't feel so g—"

"Miss McFee! Miss McFee!"

Collins. I hear his voice but it sounds like it is underwater. Everything is happening in slow motion. My body goes floppy, and I feel like my limbs are too heavy to keep me upright.

"Stay with us."

It is Graham. I open and close my eyes as his face blurs.

"Fuck."

"I've got the Narcan!" It is Owen's voice.

"She is on something," Graham bellows. "Someone get an ambulance here!"

"Right on it."

There are so many voices that I can no longer tell which belongs to which person. My vision clouds, as I feel my heart rate slow down and—

Breathe. Just breathe.

The last thing I see in my vision is the boy who tried to drug and rape me at the party, the night James died.

Help! Help! He has a knife! He's going to kill me!

And then everything fades to black.

23

"Angie?"

I jerk up from whatever surface I am lying on, thrashing my limbs around, trying to find solid ground.

"Calm down, sweetheart. Everything is okay."

My eyes fly open, and I throw my arms around Graham who is leaning over me, eyes full of worry.

"I know who killed James. I think his killer is connected with the agency druggings and I also think—"

"What? What are you talking about?" he asks, looking back and telling everyone to clear out. I am in a room at the hospital. All three of my private doctors are hovering along the sidelines, most likely waiting for me to wake up.

"I saw him."

"Who?"

"The guy who tried to run me and James down the night he died."

"Who is it?"

My head hurts and I try to remember the image. But it is

lost. No. How can that be? I just had it in my memory. Now I just have a ghost still haunting me.

"Sweetheart, did you take any pills last night?"

"No. Nothing. I swear!"

We stare at each other in silence for a minute.

I get my pulse checked, my IV bag changed, and my pupils examined. None of the doctors communicate with me and just exit the room as a trio when they are finished with their examination.

"What happened to me?" I whisper, once the room is empty. "I remember dancing at Slay and being with Claire. I remember Sophia and me fighting on the poker table. But then my brain is foggy."

"You overdosed. We had to give you Narcan," he says, looking over to the window. When his attention returns to me, he looks heartbroken—like the light inside of him turned off. "You could have died."

"I never took anything. I swear it."

Graham's eyes look sympathetic but hollow. "You can tell me the truth, Angie. Your blood results do not lie. A whole slew of substances were found in your system."

"Graham!" I try to sit up farther in my bed, struggling to find the strength to get my arms to work, while not dislodging any cables. "I did not take anything." Why is this not making more sense to him?

"Okay."

"I think someone is drugging me. And I think it is someone on the inside," I whisper. "Who else would have that kind of access to me? I have not been taking anything voluntarily since Baker City. I swear. I think the person who hit James and me is connected to the big ring. I know it sounds crazy, but I think this all ties together. I didn't think about it before, but there are too many coincidences. Or maybe nothing is a coincidence at all. Maybe this has all been part of some greater plan, and I missed all of the warning signs. Something scratching at the back of my head has me wondering if I'm missing something right in front of my nose."

"Angie," he says hesitantly. "I'm very worried about you. We all are."

There is a knock at the door. My eyes follow the sound and then look at Graham for an explanation.

"Come on in," he calls, sitting down in a chair close to my bedside.

Collins enters first, followed by a whole lineup of others. Claire and Blake give me a worried smile, while Zander hovers in the background. Everyone surrounds my bed, making a semicircle, staring at me with pity.

Claire rocks on her feet, swaying back and forth. "I guess I will start." Her voice is so sad that if I wasn't watching her mouth move, I might not recognize the source. "Angie, you're my very best friend, and I want you to know that my life has been made better from the very moment we met. You have…"

You have got to be kidding me… I drown out Claire's voice from my mind as she continues talking, scanning each person's face as I go around the room.

Blake continues with pleasantries but keeps his gaze focused on his shoes. His voice drones on as I stare at him in disbelief. "You're such a good friend…"

Then it hits me like the force from a gust of wind. This

isn't a come-see-how-I-am-doing type of visit. This is a fucking intervention!

Zander starts talking, but I am too livid to even hear him. And Graham? He looks like he just ate razor blades. Fuck.

"I didn't take any drugs," I growl, cutting off Collins who is apparently next in line. I try to get myself out of the bed. I thrash around as Graham tries to keep me still.

"Stop it. You're going to hurt yourself."

"You don't fucking believe me." I point an accusatory finger to each person in the room. "None of you believe me."

"I told you," Claire shouts to Graham. "I told you she didn't do this and yet you forced me to participate."

Collins clears everyone out of the room, not even getting a chance to finish his speech. I feel the prick of pain in my arm and cringe as I pull out my IV in the scuffle.

"Please calm down," Graham begs. "We'll get you more help. I'll do anything it takes."

"I don't need help."

"You relapsed, Angie. Now you have to get clean again," Dr. Lucian says, walking briskly into the room. She disconnects my IV and bandages up my sore arm. "The sooner you are honest with yourself, the better your chances at overcoming this added hurdle."

"But I didn't do it this time," I say adamantly. "I didn't take anything. I haven't all week. I promise."

She nods. But I know from her demeanor and her glance to Graham that she thinks I am just trying to protect my addiction. That I would do or say anything to cast responsibility on anyone but myself.

I shouldn't blame them. In the past, I would lie and steal and do anything I could to get my fix but mask the extent of my cravings.

"I need a moment to myself," I demand. "Please, everyone go."

"Sweetheart, I—"

"Go. Get out!"

I wait until the last person leaves, and I curl my knees up toward my chest. I let the tears fly from my eyes.

No one believes me. The reality of that revelation stings.

I throw myself back on the bed and close my eyes. Everything is such a mess. Yet, I know how I got here. I managed to break trust in others and now no one believes me.

My eyes are so heavy that it hurts to try to open them. I sink into the cushions of my hospital bed and allow my mind to drift. And drift.

Until the only thing I see are my worst nightmares coming true.

I wake to my hands being secured with Velcro straps. Stop! I try to scream but my mouth is covered with a strip of tape. I throw my arms out but I am completely tied down.

"Hello, Angela."

From the shadows, dressed like a doctor, Mark Tanner reveals himself. "Did you like your slumber?"

I moan behind my tape, shaking my head side to side.

"I heard you had a little setback. My sincerest apologies."

"Mhmph."

"Tell Graham I'm coming for him. There is nowhere to hide anymore. As for you, your time is fleeting. The Prophet is not happy. You'll have to answer to him sooner or later."

The Prophet? Who the hell is The Prophet?

Mark removes my hand restraints. I frantically pull the Velcro off my legs and rip off the tape from my lips, crying out as the sting burns my delicate skin, but when I look up—

He is gone. Vanished.

I stumble out of bed and go to the window to look out. I check behind the curtain. Nothing is out of place. Mark is like carbon monoxide. You can't see him, but you know eventually he will kill you.

With shaky legs, I move out into the hallway where my team of nonbelievers are having a meeting about me—without me—in an alcove.

"Sweetheart, you need to be in bed," Graham says, rushing to my side.

"I'm not safe here. He got to me. He was here."

His eyes show concern. "We need to have a hard conversation."

I shake his arms. "Mark was here."

"What?" He pushes me into the room and back into bed. "No, I think you are just confused. Maybe you had a bad dream?"

"He must have climbed into my window. Or you missed him entering and exiting the door? He had on a white coat." I furrow my brow and look up into Graham's eyes. I see something there that I have not seen before—pity. "You don't believe me, do you?" I whisper.

He leans down and kisses my forehead gently, tucking the sheet under my chin. "Sweetheart, I have some of my men hunting down Tanner in Reno. Been chasing after him since last night."

"Nevada? No." I shake my head. "He was just—"

"Dr. Lucian said a major side effect to the drugs you have been taking is hallucinations."

"I'm not taking drugs. I mean, I did. But not now."

"When you were brought here, we found several pills in your skirt pockets. Where have you been getting them? They are knock-offs. Highly potent and laced with who knows what."

What? No. This can't be happening. I shake my head violently back and forth. "I never had pills. I promise you." I feel like I am being framed.

He sits his butt on the bed and picks my hands up in his. "We are going to sort this all out. Together. Just as I promised you."

"He tied me down."

"Who?"

"Mark." I am growing irritable, my tone aggressive. "With straps."

Graham sighs, running his hands through his hair. "Your bed has Velcro restraints. It's designed that way in case patients get combative. Maybe you saw them and your mind took off with an idea."

"No!"

"Okay, okay, there's no point arguing."

I look over at the trash can and see a bunch of tape hanging over the side. It's the same tape that I thought Mark used on my mouth. The same tape that was used on my arm to secure my IV. Am I going crazy? Or is everyone else oblivious to what is really happening?

"I want to go home."

"We're going to take a little retreat together."

My eyes narrow. "Where?"

"The house in the woods. I won't leave you this time."

I nod. I just want out of this hospital. If agreeing to go with him gets me out of here, then I am all for it. I need to feel safe again. Staying here is not helping matters. I glance at the window again and back to the door that is my only exit from this hellhole. I rub at my temples. What is happening to me?

Graham signs all of the documentation that places me in his care. Dr. Lucian and Dr. Westinger inform us that we can video conference while I am away for the weekend to detox —again. They are on retainer, so I'm sure if I call, they will come running. I slip on a pair of sweatpants and a sweatshirt that were brought for me.

After everything is handled for my release, Graham and Collins escort me into the back of the SUV. I lose track of time as I stare out the window at the winter wonderland. Snow and ice cling to tree branches, making the entire scene look majestic. We make our way through the gate and then up the driveway, stopping in front of the safe house.

"I want to go for a walk to the field," I request, as soon as my feet hit the ground. "I just want to clear my mind and journal."

"It's cold out," Graham says. He is stressed out. I can tell by the fine lines deepening at the corner of his eyes.

"I'll wear a coat then," I bargain, looking at the snow-covered trees. I begin to sob. "I'm suffocating with my thoughts. I feel trapped in a nightmare where I scream but no one hears. Please. I just need—"

He nods and then helps me into his coat. He then grabs a blanket from the trunk. We walk around the house and up through the patch of trees until we find the clearing. We don't talk. I think Graham is afraid to break me. He is treating me like a delicate flower, ready to wilt with any sign of tension.

I don't have my journal with me, so I use my phone to email myself my thoughts. I sit down on the blanket and let Graham hover from the sidelines while I lay back, typing out all my emotions.

I am so alone.

No one believes me.

And I could have died.

I lie in silence and listen to my own breathing. A few flurries fall from the sky, and I try to catch some on my tongue. It seems like a lifetime ago that I was last in this open space in the field, still as lost as I am now. When a shadow moves over me, I turn on my side to see Graham. He crouches down and helps me sit up.

"How are you feeling?"

I shrug. "I really don't want to talk about it. I just need some time to process everything."

"Can we go back inside and relax?"

I nod. My fingers and toes are starting to burn from the cold. It is frigid out. And I worry if I stay out any longer and avoid having a real conversation with Graham, my heart will harden as well. He doesn't trust me, and that is what hurts the most.

I allow Graham to lead me back to the house, even

though I have a fond memory of this field and know my way around here.

The buzzing of his phone and the stiffness of his shoulders as he checks his messages let me know that relaxing is not what he'll be doing back at the house.

"Is everything okay?" I ask, watching as his entire body language changes.

"I have to run into town, but I'll have some of my men here with you."

"You said you weren't going to leave me."

"Something came up that needs to be handled. It won't take long. Maybe you can nap or—"

I force a smile. "It's fine." Yet, not a single thing really is. Everything seems wrong. And I don't have a single clue how to fix it.

Once inside the house, I meander to my bedroom and shower. Opening my closet, I find just a handful of outfits—mostly pajama style—and some footwear. I put on a pair of light-pink leggings and an ivory-colored sweater, then make my way downstairs to the library. It feels weirdly eerie being back here. I have good and bad memories during my previous quarantine time.

I lie in my overstuffed chair near the window and play with my phone to pass the time. I pull up pictures from last night that Claire and I took. We were so drunk—her on alcohol and me on the disappointment of failing my assignment—that half of the ones in my storage I don't even recall taking in the first place.

Scanning through the lot, I find one that has a ton of dancers behind me showing off their moves. Zooming in, I see someone on the sidelines who I didn't even know was there. Paul. Why was he there?

I open up my facial recognition app and run the picture of me and Claire through the software, highlighting each face just to see what pops up. As the search engine thinks, I start to wonder if Paul is drugging me. We work together at the same cafe that Resa visited the night she was chased. It was the same night that I learned from the local police that other girls were getting drugged. He definitely has the means to do so, and despite always being nice to me, he is shady about his reasoning for being at River Valley when he already went to college under a completely different name.

Paul has been on my radar ever since I first saw him with Mark Tanner on campus doing a hand-off. However, he always seemed to be on the sidelines of my suspicion and not at the forefront of my mind.

When my phone finishes the search, I look at the photos and am alarmed when I see a group one with Paul, Mark, and a third man who I barely recognize due to the blurring effect from him moving. It looks to be a security footage photo from a back alley meeting. I have no idea how it got on the Internet. But it is here. I look closer at the men, zooming in. Holy shit. I know the third guy.

It is Owen.

The same Owen who is working for Graham as one of my bodyguards.

I start a new search with just Owen's face and allow the app time to work.

Three new pictures load featuring what the algorithm assumes is him.

I study the first picture in the lot. Fuck. He is with

Bryce. And they are in Baker City. I can tell by the clock tower in the background because it is iconic for the small town. Both men appear to be much younger. Attached to Bryce's belt loop is the pink Swiss Army Knife. My eyes water.

It is him.

Flashes of memories fill up my vision like a strobe-light slideshow.

The party.

The attempt at drugging me.

The almost rape.

It was Bryce who tried to chase me down the night James died. It could be Bryce trying to drug me in all of the coffees we consume during class. Owen could be helping him. No wonder he was quick in offering me pain medication during my first stay here at the safe house. Getting me to feed my own addiction made it easier to slip me whatever he wanted into my system—voluntarily. And then Bryce had his own pills for his supposed injury. Pills I stole. Pills that were concocted of who knows what ingredients.

Damn.

Maybe Bryce and Owen are friends. They could be working together, trying to shut me up or keep me from remembering my past. All this time, I have been trying to keep above water, and they are both trying to drown me.

I am not crazy.

I was forced into a relapse that I never asked for. Not only did these men have ample opportunity to execute their plan, they also had the luxury of those around me not trusting me. These men exploited my weakness and are trying to keep me from bringing them both down.

Sneaky bastards!

I need to find Graham and tell him. I remember. I remember it all.

My phone comes alive with an incoming text alert from an unknown number.

Unknown: I knew this moment would come. I have prepared for it. You are going to finally meet The Prophet.

I read the text as bile rises in my throat. Dammit. I glance around the room. Someone is here. I have to get out.

I frantically send Graham a message.

Angie: Owen Paul Carson Tillman Bryce Help

I need to find Graham or Collins and tell them about this. I take a few deep breaths and think about what I should do next.

I quickly dial Graham's number and get sent straight to his voicemail. He must have his phone off. If he does, my text won't be seen for a while. I try Collins's. Same thing. I search my contacts for Dominic's number. I never changed his name in my list.

"Angie?" he asks. "I'm sorry I couldn't visit you in the hos—"

"Owen's a bad guy and is working with one of my class-mates to drug me. Graham and Collins left me at the safe house. I need help."

"Just take a few deep breaths and calm down. You are hyperventilating."

"He's going to kill me if he finds out I know."

"I need you to find Austin and Malcolm." Nic's breathing changes, as if he just started running. "They should be outside patrolling the house. Do not give away that you are onto Owen. If he is playing on both teams, he won't hesitate to use force if he feels threatened. I'm on my way."

I am on the cusp of remembering everything. And the closer I get to learning the truth, the more my life is in jeopardy.

I disconnect the call, get up from my chair, and walk toward the door when—

I see him.

I stumble back a few steps, nearly losing my balance.

"Oh hey, Owen. I wasn't expecting to see you here," I say with a bright smile. I have no idea if I am acting weird or not. Now that I know he could be dangerous, I try to keep my cool. I just need to buy time until Graham or Nic get here.

But something seems off. It's in his eyes. In his breathing. The way his jaw tics and his fingers clench as he eyes me.

My phone buzzes in my hand, startling me and making me almost drop the device. I glance down at the screen and see that someone sent me an image. I open up the app and gasp. Both Graham and Collins are tied up and gagged.

I am in danger. And whoever sent me that text wants me to know it. The air leaves my lungs, making my throat constrict with fear. *Think Angie, think.*

I have to try my best to stay calm and to keep up the pretense that nothing is out of the norm. I need more time.

Time for Nic to get here. Time for Graham and Collins to get free.

"I have a craving to make brownies. Just like old times. I know that this is last minute and all, but I hope that some of the baking ingredients are in the pantry from last visit."

I swallow down the lump in my throat that keeps growing in size with every beat of my heart. I fear I am going to pass out before I can warn the others. At this point, I have no idea who is safe—except for Graham, Nic, and Collins.

Nic alluded to Malcolm and Austin being good guys, but what if he misjudged them? Graham trusted Owen enough to hire him to watch out for me—and he is slowly starting to look deranged.

"I actually was just looking up a recipe on my phone," I say, holding up my screen so only I can see it. I dial Nic again, but turn the volume completely down.

"I'm not sure if anyone can leave here," Owen says with a shrug, "to get your supplies."

Up until now, Owen has never really sought out my company. He has primarily stayed in the shadows and never really made his presence obvious—except at the penthouse when he was there after one of the paparazzi events. Has he been watching me this whole time? Spying on me by pretending to be my bodyguard?

"Do you think Malcolm or Austin can run into town?"

"They are tied up at the moment."

The way Owen says the word *tied* instantly makes me know the hidden meaning. He finds this humorous. Sicko.

"Okay. Well, I think I'm going to go hang out in my room."

"I can't let you do that."

"Oh? Why not?" My voice reaches a higher octave, and I inwardly cringe that I am sending off warning bells for him to see. Graham always says I lie like shit. And maybe he is right. I am just buying time. Maybe Nic will be able to figure out the missing clues by listening in on our verbal conversation. I just hope Graham and Collins can get free and not get hurt. Every second counts. Stall. Delay. Keep him talking.

"Because my boss has given me other orders."

I fake a giggle, knowing that he is referring to someone else entirely. "Well, we both know how bossy Graham Marshall Hoffman can be." I hope my mess-up of Graham and Nic's middle name, Xavier, is a tipoff that I am in danger.

Owen snatches the phone from me, slamming it against the wall. He narrows his eyes at me as I quiver. "Quit being so coy. You know damn well that I'm not who I claim to be."

"Why are you doing this?" My mind races at what to do and how to alert the others.

"We're going to take a little field trip. Does that sound like fun?" he asks, his voice rough and now full of menace. He no longer looks like my bodyguard. Instead, he looks like a madman who just discovered he won.

As his body moves toward me, I take my fist and slam it against the bridge of his nose, using the technique Collins taught me just a few weeks ago. Never in a million years did I expect to need to defend myself from a man who vowed to protect me.

And then I hit Owen again. The loud sound of my

huffing fills the air as he stumbles back. His hands fly toward me as he gains his bearings. I dodge and dart out of the room, bumping my shoulder into the wall as I frantically try to get ahead of him. I open my mouth to scream, and it's as if my voice is frozen. The only sound that escapes my lips is air. Stale, dry air.

All my fears rush through my body, causing me to think of nothing except for how to survive. To get out of this hellish mess and to alert those I love of the betrayal.

I make it into the living room and weave myself between furniture, knocking down lamps and vases with each bump of my legs. I make it past the last couch when arms grab my waist and pull me back to a hard muscular chest. My flightless scream gets silenced by a hand, and I am lifted up and transported toward the foyer. No! I twist and try to wrestle my arms free when the front door comes into view.

I kick and wiggle with every ounce of my strength, as adrenaline surges through my body. I can't leave here. I have seen so many of those crime shows warning about never getting into the kidnapper's vehicle. If I do, I will surely die. Everyone dies.

I throw my head back and connect with Owen's face. He lets go of me for a second, and I bolt toward my room to hide. I make it up a step, and then slam my chin onto the stairs as he grabs my leg and tugs me toward him from behind.

"Dammit," he sneers. "You sure are feisty. Too bad keeping you as a pet isn't part of the ultimate plan. Breaking you would be all the fun."

I see the shoes of someone coming down the hallway,

and I scream as loudly as I can. "Help! Someone help me! Helllllp!" My voice. It is back. I scream at the top of my lungs. Someone is here. Someone will hear me. My voice breaks into a crackling sound as I run out of stamina. Blood drips down my chin. I glance up to see some splattered against the wall, as the shoes become legs. Then a body. And a face.

Mark Tanner.

Shit.

I wish I was hallucinating. I wish this was just a bad dream. But from the sinister look in his eyes to the way his Adam's apple bobs in his throat, I know that I am in the presence—once again—of a madman.

"Good seeing you again, Angela. The hospital room visit was too short. How does it feel to have the love of your life not even believe you? I mean, granted, I have an awesome body double taking part of Graham's security forces through half of Nevada. So, we should excuse his stupidity this time, right?"

"Ugh…" I groan. I knew it. I knew I wasn't going crazy. He was at the hospital. I was not hallucinating.

"But to leave his woman in her time of despair…" Mark makes a shame-shame motion with his fingers. "Seems mighty careless."

My teeth grind together. "What do you want?"

"What I've always wanted," Mark bites out. "For no one to interfere with my ultimate plans."

My nose flares as I see all light shut off from behind his eyes. "And who drugged me last night?"

Owen pulls me up by my hair and binds me with his arms. "That was me," he snickers in my ear. "You make being a drug addict look so fun. Livin' the high life." He dodges my head as I try to connect with his face again. This cannot be happening. Tears well in my eyes as he forces me to look at Mark's cold ones.

"You drugged me when you were watching me another time at the penthouse too? In my water?"

"I couldn't let you get clean yet," Owen laughs. "What fun would that be? I needed Graham to doubt you. You made it too easy, though, really. You wanted drugs and would seek them out like a kid wanting candy. You even took my knockoff ones you thought were prescribed to me from a dental procedure. Made my job super easy."

I am going to die in this house. They are going to murder me and then bury my body in my beloved field.

"You just couldn't leave things alone, could you?" Mark asks, moving closer to my bound body. He reaches a finger to my cheek, trailing it along my jawline and then my throat. "Graham's little security squad thinks I'm in Nevada. Austin and Malcolm are incapacitated outside. And Graham and Collins got tricked into leaving you here all alone. Isn't this all just cute?"

"Help!" I scream. "Help me!"

Mark cups my throat with the palm of his hand, tightening his grip to block out the sound flying out of my mouth. I struggle against Owen's hold, my efforts futile.

"No one is here to help you, my dear. Only people here are a pack of vulturous villains, ready to pay homage to The Prophet by delivering you to him. You, my dear, are the sacrificial lamb."

I feel my face go numb from the lack of oxygen. I go limp in Owen's arms as Mark takes a step back, releasing his hold on my throat. I gasp for air, sucking in as much as I can, worried that it will be my last chance. I am surrounded by madmen, and there could be more lurking about the house.

"Who planted drugs in my pockets last night?"

Owen's snicker lets me know the truth. "Yours truly." His lips kiss my cheek and I feel like I could vomit. "Oh, and let's not forget the ones I put in your nightstand drawer back at your townhouse. I mean, in all honesty, we didn't have to do much to get you flying high. You were such a willing little druggie."

"But you weren't part of the scene the other times I think I got drugged," I hiss.

"That would be my buddy. You know how it is… Team-work makes the dream work."

Bryce. It was Bryce. He had access to me at The Shack the night I sang with Zander. It was also the night I self-medicated on my own. He had access to me at the Halloween party and so many other instances. He got to Monica easily. And he had access to Gossip Girl Tracy.

"Your boyfriend has caused me a lot of problems," Mark states freely, joining back into the conversation. "But if it wasn't for your silly quest at justice over the recent drug-gings, I would have been able to move more product and secure more territory."

"How could someone as insignificant as me cause you anything?" I ask, trying to get him to talk.

"You knew from our first date," Mark answers, "that I was up to something. You have been recording meetings ever since. At first I thought Hoffman hired you to spy on me. But his attraction to you couldn't be hidden. Exploiting you as his weakness was almost too easy. And there was no way he would use someone he cared about as bait—even if it was a means to bring me down."

"Is that why you constantly tried to talk in other languages? To get me to not know what you were doing? Probably worked on less intelligent girls, huh? You did like the concept of handpicking your dates. Sucks that you wanted me. I could see through your bullshit."

"Who in their right mind has enough balls to actively try to investigate a crime boss like myself? Do you even know who I am?"

I shrug. "Apparently not." I look him up and down. "Your semiauthoritative demeanor doesn't exactly translate over to boss status. Oh, and I'm nearly positive that you aren't calling any of the shots," I taunt.

"Little bitch has some jokes," Owen snickers behind me.

"Which one of you tampered with my car, sent me threatening text messages, and tried to terrorize me? I was followed and made to feel scared, just like my friend Resa. Cowards. You guys are fucking cowards!"

"Our secret weapon was the executor of those fun acts, including almost running you over while you were out exercising."

Damn. I even forgot about that. All this time I've been tormented and didn't even realize to what extent. Nothing was a coincidence. It has all been planned. "So, it was Bryce," I answer simply. I look into Mark's eyes as he realizes the depth of my discoveries. "Oh, you thought all this time I was just some stupid girl?"

His smile is wicked. "Oh, you're definitely stupid."

I twist against the hands holding me hostage. "And you,

Owen, followed me to Baker City and played the hero coming to rescue me."

I can feel his chest shaking with laughter. "I play the good guy character well, don't I?"

"Just wait until Graham finds out what you all are doing to me. I would be scared."

"The whole point is for him to find out. We're counting on it," Mark sneers. He removes something from his pocket and holds it up to show me. "And finding you will be the best part. The main event, if you will."

My eyes focus on the little black bracelet that has a blinking green light on the top. Shit. I am the bait.

I struggle in Owen's arms as Mark wraps the band around my wrist, clicking it into place. It is different in structure than the one Austin used at The Shack when there was a riot. This has a more permanent feel to it and is heavier.

"Okay, story time is over," Owen chuckles into my ear. "It is time to say buh-byes. Road trip time. Lucky you, The Prophet is excited to see you and make you pay for the destruction you have caused to his organization by your meddling."

"The organization where he drugs helpless girls and uses them as test dummies?"

"You women are all the same," Mark says unfazed. "You want the status recognition of being with someone powerful for money, but then can't handle the consequences of how that power is obtained."

"You're a delusional asshole."

He steps closer to me, grabbing my aching jaw to force me to stare up at him. I feel the spray of liquid before I can distinguish that it is coming from the back of his mouth. I close my eyes and try to turn away from his nastiness, only to have him wrench my chin back to face him.

"Too bad there's not a drug that exists that we can slip to you that will erase the vileness from your body. Lucky me, I get off to nasty bitches." Mark bends down to capture my lips in his mouth, making me thrash in Owen's arms. He releases my lips, while licking his own. "I chew them up and spit them out."

His words pierce me, freezing me into place.

"Save some for me," Owen says, making his accomplice chuckle maniacally.

"Sickos," I hiss under my breath.

With the nod of Mark's head, Owen carries me toward the front door. I jerk and kick and fight with all my might not to make it outside. But it is the feel of fresh air on my face that lets me know that my current fate is inevitable. There is no one here to save me.

I am just a pawn in their game of chess.

From the corner of the house, I see a flash of movement. My eyes narrow as Paul reveals himself. What the hell is he doing here too? I don't know whether to rejoice or fear for my life more. I go limp in Owen's arms and try to be so cumbersome for him to hold that he cannot get me in his vehicle. My eyes catch Paul's again, and he reaches for his ankle gun.

I flop to the ground as Owen struggles to keep hold of me. The dampness of the snow soaking into my pants sends shivers through my body.

"Quit stalling," Mark grunts out, entering the driver's side and slamming the door.

"Dammit," Owen bellows. "Get the fuck up and walk."

When he bends down to lift me, I push my fingers into his eyes, making him fall to the ground with me. I roll and am almost free, when I feel his hand grip my ankle. I kick as hard as I can and scramble away on my knees. I dash toward the house, just as Paul blocks my path.

I look up at him with confusion, not knowing what he plans to do. He frowns and mutters, "I'm sorry," just as the handle of his gun connects with my forehead, knocking me—

I hear a rushing sound of water. I am going to drown. It is a sickening feeling knowing that my efforts are going to be hopeless.

That soon...

I'm going...

To—

24

"Oh good, you're alive."

My head hangs to the side as my eyes slowly open. I try
to move my hands, but they are bound behind my back, with
rope I am assuming from the bite I get when I move them.
"Bryce?"

"Would be a shame if you died before I can wipe out
Hoffman's bank accounts. Who would have thought our
previous connection from the car accident that killed your
brother would make me a future billionaire? Life can be so
unpredictable, can't it?"

"Why are you doing this?"

"For funsies really." He looks deranged. His eyes are
bloodshot and his mood seems manic. Like he is one breath
away from losing his cool and going complete unhinged.
"You know how frustrating it is to chase you down? You've
been walking around for months with a secret army
protecting you. And all it took was Owen drugging you at
Slay and the penthouse to push things forward with the plan.

The planting pills in your pockets was an added bonus to put the seed of doubt in everyone's head that you couldn't stay clean. While I didn't have a hand in executing that part, it was my idea." He takes a bow, as if wanting a standing ovation.

"Noted." *Asshole.*

"Then, bam!" He smacks his hands together in front of my face. "A little Narcan... Now, he looks like the hero, and your army dissipates. You made it so easy, you know? Allowing me to get you coffee each week. Low dosing you just to keep you craving more. Oh, let's not forget me faking an injury that scored me the good drugs. I mean, they were constructed using our little drug cocktail methods, but still."

"You've been drugging me from the day you introduced yourself to me in Human Behavior class? Pretended to be my friend. Called me *Teach*?"

"No, I'm not some monster." Bryce fake scoffs. "I was just setting the stage for gaining your trust. Ironically enough, you were already on your way to craving the buzz all on your own. I could have just handed you pills and said 'swallow' and you would probably have salivated over them. So, don't blame all of this on me. You have to take responsibility as well."

I ignore his condescending comments. "What about Hanna? She your accomplice too?"

"She fell in love with my charm," he says proudly, "and convincing her to share Hoffman's habits was too easy. It is almost like the universe is working for me. Ya know?"

I shake my head, trying to absorb all of the information he is freely sharing. I look around the dark dungeon-like room, with the only lights coming from the lanterns hooked to the walls on rusty chains. "Where are we?"

"In the pits of hell."

I thought hell would be hotter than this. And less damp.

The door creaks open and in walks Owen. I half expect Paul to be accompanying him. My head still throbs from where he hit me.

Owen's eyes are void of remorse. It's like someone pulled the plug on the emotional compartments of his brain. I am surrounded by two sociopaths—and probably a fleet more waiting in the wings.

"Just tell me what's going on. Please," I beg.

"It's cute when you beg," Owen says, pervasive meaning seeping through his word selection.

"No harm in doing story time," Bryce says with a shrug. "She already knows too much. The Prophet can fill in the rest of the gaps later."

"Who the hell is The Prophet?" I snap. I wiggle my hands, trying to break free with all my might.

"Now, now, now," Bryce fake soothes. "Everything will be revealed soon."

"Huh," I say, looking at him with pity. "You don't fucking know, do you?" I watch as his face drains of color, confirming my suspicions. "Oh my gosh! You are allowing some mystery dictator to call the shots, and you guys haven't even met him yet? Or her?"

"It's a *him*," Owen yells, disgusted by my revelation.

"You all are risking going to prison and don't even know the mastermind behind all of this lunacy. You bunch of dirty douche bags." I start laughing, so much so that I cry a little. "Idiots."

"Are you done running your mouth, bitch?" Bryce's voice is sinister.

"You are just a pathetic puppet, who refuses to look up to see where his strings are attached."

"Do you want to be gagged?" Bryce snaps, his annoyance showing.

"Just get on with your story time before I lose interest." I need to keep them off their game until I can figure out what their plan is, where we are, and how I am going to get out alive.

"So, once upon a time," Owen starts, in an octave higher than his normal voice, "there was this young teenager named Angie. She was a very naive teenager who attended a college party late one night with a friend. Big bad wolves Owen and Bryce were into having some *fun* with the lady folk."

"And by *fun*, he means that we drug and rape them for pleasure," Bryce interjects. "Just your normal college boy hobbyists."

"But Angie took a wrong turn at the party and put her nose where it didn't belong. She accidentally found our little laboratory where we had our pill presses and makeshift pharmacy. We were running a huge network of drugs through Baker City and no one knew that two college-aged, C-average students could make a name for themselves in such a small town."

Bryce clears his throat. "You found everything. Our receipts, our scales, our list of contacts. You just kept snapping pictures. I tried to drug you. I wasn't even going to snatch your innocence. I just needed you to forget. But you fought me. Made a scene. I tried to cut you to subdue you with my favorite pink dull knife—the one that has a horrible entry into flesh. But instead you got ahold of it and used it as your ticket out of the party. You told me you were going to the police and that there was nothing I could do to cover this up. So you fled with your ride."

"You chased us down. You murdered my twin brother!" I yell, thrashing around in my seat, almost wobbling over.

"You murdered him," Bryce corrects. "If you would have just let me drug you so you would have memory loss, things could have been different. So I had to stop you. And I thought I did. Except—"

"I survived."

"Unfortunately," he sighs. "But, wait, plot twist. You didn't have any memories anyway from the accident. So I lucked out. When we saw how you were handling the media attention, we knew that you had no idea what happened to James McFee that night. We kept tabs on you. You dropped out of community college, and enough time passed where we could stop worrying over the past."

"We were amateur rapists, really. We were not running a date rape factory," Owen interjects. "We were primarily running a mini drug lab. We were like born-again chemists and highly respected in a small town."

Bile rises in my throat as I think of all of the people they must have violated. "Why did you come to Portland?"

"We got discovered by a big drug pusher," Bryce explains. "Offered a deal of a lifetime. One that neither Owen nor I could refuse."

"From The Prophet?"

"Yes and Mark Tanner," Owen responds. "He saw potential in us."

"Did you guys know I was here?"

Bryce clears his throat, crossing his arms at his chest. "No. We continued keeping very weak tabs on you. We figured after we watched you go on your little escapade around Baker City searching for justice for James without finding anything valuable, we were in the clear. Our clientele expanded. We were young enough to blend in with college kids and still be able to test product. We joined forces with Tanner, who was under the guidance of The Prophet."

"Who has ties to the entire West Coast. A celebrity and role model," Owen adds.

"And someone who you haven't met yet," I point out. "So, to summarize, Bryce was brought to Portland to sit beside me in class and drug me. Owen, you needed to infiltrate Graham's security team and gain his trust."

"No easy feat either," he chimes in.

But what is the big overarching connection? Seems that whoever hired them hand selected them for this particular job. But why? "At any point during your hiring process, did you stop and wonder why there was a coincidence between me and what you both were hired to do? Seems like that would have been the first thing I would have asked myself. Why was I magically sent across the state to help drug a girl I had a prior connection with?" When neither answers, I continue. "You are both just little minions. Expendable, really. Whoever hired you handpicked you for this job based solely on our connection, not your lame-ass drug-pushing skills. And at no point did you worry that me being around you would make it easier for me to remember the trauma I endured by your evilness?"

"Shut up," Bryce sneers, raising his hand and smacking my mouth so hard, my whole chair falls over.

I feel my lip open up at the corner, making blood drip onto my sweater. I wiggle my fingers, trying to get feeling back into them. They are going numb from lack of movement.

"Don't hurt our insurance policy," a masculine voice calls from the doorway.

I look up through teary eyes as Paul saunters over to me, yanking my shoulders to sit me back up again. When our eyes connect, I notice his aren't as evil as the other two. He might actually have a bit of compassion left in him.

"So, how long have you both been trying to follow me, drug me, or terrorize me?"

"You make it sound so personal," Bryce snaps.

"It is personal." Why is he not understanding? Everything about this is personal.

"I was hired to attend Human Behavior with you, slip you a little something-something from time to time, and—"

My eyes narrow at his. "Pretend you were my friend?" He called me "Teach" and all this time I thought it was just an innocent joke, when in reality he knew I was an education major while studying at Baker City Community College. He knew me from a previous life.

"Sure. That."

"And what about you, Owen? You were hired to infiltrate Graham's security team and gain his trust? Continue drugging me when Bryce couldn't... Pretend to rescue me... You must have sabotaged my computer and destroyed all my research and work too." Planted that keylogger thing...

Owen shrugs. "Yeah, pretty much. You nailed it, princess." His smile is evil. "Oh wait, one more thing. I also fed the media the rumors of you being an addict. But, ironically, that was not a rumor at all."

So, Sophia didn't do that after all, like she denied. "Hope you know how your story is going to end. Graham is going to kill you when he finds you."

"Oh, he'll find me," he answers confidently. "You have a tracker on you, after all. You are Hoffman's weakness. His kryptonite. You're going to be the reason he dies at the hands of The Prophet. But, not before he leads his entire team here so we can take care of everything all at once."

"Sounds ambitious. Why all the beef with Graham?"

"Ever since his sister, Penny, became a victim," Paul interjects, "Hoffman has been set on destroying our entire operation. Before him, no one came close to figuring out the underground network that has been happening all up and down the West Coast. He has to pay for his crime of interfering in business he has no right to involve himself with."

It wasn't that long ago that I tried to convince Graham to utilize my skill set and accessibility to help him find out who drugged Penny. He made it clear that I would never be sacrificial bait for his mission in seeking justice. This is why I got laid off and forced out of the agency. It is ironic how I now find myself in exactly that scenario that he promised me he would never put me in.

Has this always been inevitable? A situation that was destined to come to fruition?

"You see, Angie," Owen explains, "there's going to be a big bonfire soon. Maybe even some fireworks. I get a hard-on for fireworks. Remember the night at The Shack?"

"That was staged by you?"

His eyes come to life with pride. "I had to create some fear in Graham's head so I could get further and further into his business. The fireworks were just a decoy. Something for funsies."

"Is Austin a bad guy too?"

"No, that pissant is too loyal to ever switch sides. He'll learn where the big money is at eventually. Young and stupid."

"Sounds like you are describing yourself." I purse my lips, looking at each of the three men. "I honestly don't think you guys are smart enough to pull off anything profound. I have sat beside Bryce for months and he's just not—"

"Bitch," he snarls, charging toward me, only stopping from pummeling me when Paul pulls him back.

"She needs to be coherent," Paul warns. "Don't be foolish when we're moments away from the grand finale."

My eyes squint at the light coming in from the hallway. When my vision clears I see a man standing in the shadows.

"Good, you boys managed to keep her alive," Mark snickers. "Thought I would find all three of you with your dicks hanging out with this hot piece of ass." His eyes trail over me, and it makes me feel nasty.

I hear an audible buzz. All four men check their watches in unison.

"It's go time, boys," Mark announces, rolling his shoulders and cracking his knuckles. "Paul, you're on babysitting duty. Owen and Bryce, come with me." He turns his attention to me, smiling a megawatt smile. "I'll see you soon, sweet Angie. Rest up. You're going to be the main attraction, until the fire at least." He chuckles like a demented clown and heads out with the other two men in tow.

As soon as the room clears, Paul rushes to my side, kneeling down on the ground before me. "We have no time, Angie. The whole entire place is going to be set on fire as soon as Graham arrives with the team."

My eyes water with tears. "I can't believe you're doing this. I suspected you for months. Your name is Carson Tillman. I know!"

"I'm a good guy, Angie. I promise. I'm going to get you out of here, but we have to be fast."

"Don't lie to me," I cry. I can feel blood dripping down my cheek from being smacked around. "I heard that one before."

"Owen is a traitor."

"No kidding," I bite out. "In more ways than one."

"I'm not. You can trust me. I've been trying to keep you safe all this time, despite how reckless you've been with your life."

"How have you been keeping me safe?"

"I've been signaling Nic of your involvement in spying and trying to gather evidence through our mutual ties. He doesn't know I'm FBI. Tanner has been on to you from the start, and I've been carefully trying to get you less involved."

"Mutual ties?" I whisper.

"Yes."

"Does anyone know?" I ask. It's all starting to make sense now. Paul must have squealed on me when I sent Claire to the Hideaway to spy. Somehow the message got back to Nic.

"Nic knows as of today, but only because I had to tell him for his own safety. I didn't know what Tanner had planned, but when I saw him show up at the safe house, I knew that this was going to end. He was finally making his big move. So, I had to come clean with Nic, who I knew was working undercover. Because of rank, he didn't know I am FBI."

"How long have you known about Bryce and Owen?"

"Bryce revealed himself at the Hideaway, but Owen had me fooled all this time. He had to keep a very low profile, I imagine, as to not alert anyone from Graham's security team of his true nature."

"Sick bastards. They killed my brother James back in my hometown of Baker City. I think they were brought here to Portland for a specific reason involving me."

"It's not out of the realm of possibilities. I've been working for two years trying to bring down the kingpin, and I'm moments away from finding out how the entire operation has been running underground, but I cannot let anything happen to you. I'm sorry for hitting you with the gun, but I was buying time. We would have both been killed— including Collins and Graham. Even Austin and Malcolm's lives were at risk. If I didn't do something to preserve my cover, it could have been very bad. Can still be."

"They are tied up. I got a text sent to me," I whimper, thinking about the image that is burned into my head. "I can't lose them." Graham is my life. And Collins has become family to me.

"I know," he says with a nod, "but we have to be smart about this. Graham and Collins will get loose and be able to track you here with your bracelet. They probably were only restrained long enough to buy Tanner some time to get things set up here."

I look down at the blinking light. "Take it off me. It's too dangerous for Graham and Collins to be here. It's a trap."

Paul sighs. "There's probably something built in to it that will set off an alarm. I need everyone to think I'm the bad guy, so I can get you out of here alive."

"What are we going to do? Can you call for help?"

"I did when we were above ground, but it's tricky. If I call in the infantry, we could all die. I'm sorry you are involved. There's no cell reception down here. We have these watches to communicate."

"Who the hell is The Prophet? Do you have any clue?"

Paul growls. "No. But he's been calling all the shots and will be here soon."

"Well, what's the plan now? I'm not just going to sit back and wait to die." I have too much to live for.

"We need a diversion. I need to get Bryce and Owen back so I can lock them in here," he explains. "Once they are restrained and we are less outnumbered, I can get you back up to safety."

"Untie me."

"They will know I'm not on their side."

"Untie me. I have a plan." When Paul has my arms and legs undone, I wiggle life back into them. "Give me your knife."

"Angie…"

"Trust me."

With hesitation, he hands over the blade he used to undo my straps, and I pull down my leggings revealing my scars

437

of my past that are barely visible anymore. Maybe my outlook on life has changed so much that they are no longer at the front of my mind.

I take the knife and—

"What the fuck, Angie, no!"

Blood bursts from my skin. I slice the same area where I almost killed myself by accident the last time. I slide my pants back into place, shocked that I could even go through with it after my warped view on pain.

"Go tell them something is wrong with me," I insist. "I'll keep my hands behind the chair so they don't notice."

He glances back at me as he opens the door. "Guys! Get in here. Something's wrong with her."

Bryce and Owen rush into the room, slamming the heavy door shut as they survey the scene. I am losing a lot of blood. My light pink leggings absorb as much as they can, forever staining the fabric.

"Uh man, is she on her fucking rag?" Bryce asks, glancing down at my bloody crotch and thigh.

"Think so," Paul says, looking like he's disgusted. "I can't be in here, I hate the smell of blood."

"You're such a pansy," Owen teases.

"Going to have to suck it up, sweets. Should have come prepared," Bryce says, turning to leave.

Paul waits until Bryce's view of us is blocked and leaps at him, knocking him down with the handle of his gun. I jump up from my chair and shove Owen. He stumbles forward but doesn't lose his balance. Instead, he whirls around and charges at me. His hands grip my throat and squeeze. I stare up at his eyes, dark and glassy—like he isn't even here. Like he is someplace else. He chokes me, fingers pressing into the bones of my neck. I kick. I push. Nothing. Just when I think he's going to let loose, he just presses tighter. My eyes droop. I see darkness swallow me up, as I start to lose consciousness.

And then the band around me snaps. I gasp for air. Panting. Doubling over. I suck in as much as I can.

My fingers move up to massage the bruises at my neck. I look to find Paul striking Owen with his fist. He reaches into his jacket, pulls out a handful of zip ties, and binds the men together on the floor. He then secures them to a hook on the wall, completely immobilizing them.

Paul grabs my hand and pulls me from the room, locking the door with a metal latch. Slicing off a piece of material from the bottom of his pants, he ties a tourniquet around my upper thigh, adding pressure to my self-inflicted wound.

Damn, it hurts.

"You are brave," he says, looking me directly in the eyes. "Keep your head clear. We're going to get out of this alive."

We travel through an underground maze. "Do you know how to get out of here?" I ask him, barely able to catch my breath.

"Yes."

"Where are we?"

"Underneath the university. Apparently there are secret tunnels and storage areas that date back a half a century."

"What are we going to do?" My heart is about to fly out of my chest. Adrenaline and fear pump through my body as I think of ideas on how we are going to survive this.

"I need you to keep your hands behind your back and

act like you are my hostage. I need to get you out and then I need to find the kingpin and end this saga. I've waited two years for—"

"Well isn't this nice," a menacing voice echoes through the halls behind us. It sounds familiar in an odd way, but not so much that I can easily place it. "Taking another field trip?"

Paul and I whip around and come face-to-face with a shadowed man. My eyes squint, trying to make out his image. My shoulders round, my jaw twitches, and the pulsing of my thigh makes me lightheaded.

"Let me introduce myself," he says coolly.

I feel Paul stiffen and hear his breathing speed up.

With the rise of his lantern, I wait with anticipation as the man's face lightens with the glow of the flame. Just when I think I cannot be any more shocked, I feel overcome with sickness, deep within my stomach, twisting and turning until I am moments away from retching.

"Holy shit." The words rush out of my mouth as the blood drains from my face.

Holy shit.

"I am The Prophet."

25

"Dr. Williams?"

His smile is menacing, his eyes extra dark. "Being a professor is my side gig. This is where the real money is at." He looks at me from head to toe, like he is seeing me for the first time. "My fans refer to me as The Prophet. Are you going to be a fan, Angie? Or a foe?"

I can't answer. I am frozen stiff.

I wish I was hallucinating. I wish this was all a bad joke.

"And Paul—or shall I say Carson—it's nice to finally know what a traitor looks like." He claps his hands. "Kudos to you for fooling me this long. I have special plans for people like you."

Disgust fills my body. "What are you doing here?" I ask stupidly. I stare at the pistol he raises and aims at my head. I didn't even know he was armed. He looks like a completely different person. His dressed-down clothes and evil eyes make him look like the villain I never expected him to be. My mind hurts from all of this information overload.

"For over a decade, I've been running an underground empire." He looks around at the cavernous space. "But in a more figurative sense. I did this, barely ever going noticed. I chose my clients carefully, as well as my victims. I had the perfect cover and the perfect job that linked me to the media outlets—and all their top stories. I was highly respected and basically untouchable."

I seethe at his arrogance, wanting to lash out and initiate my own war.

Dr. Williams lowers his gun, toying with the handle with his thumb. "But then something went wrong during one of the operations between my second in line and a fragile young girl. It was unfortunate, really."

"Penny."

"Oh yes," Dr. Williams hums. "I forgot what a small world it is. You are dating her annoying big brother. You can blame him for setting this all into motion. If it wasn't for Graham Hoffman, I wouldn't be in this mess right now. You see, Miss McFee, when Mark Tanner saw Graham's reaction to you, he knew you were his weakness. His only weakness. You are the one person he is willing to die for. And he will. Soon." He clears his throat, holding back a laugh. "I quickly found out everything I could about you. Discovered you were famous for a tragedy in your home-town. I was able to uncover who was responsible and then hire those predators to help execute my own bigger plan here in Portland. You became my ticket to bringing down the man who wanted revenge for his sister's mishap. And what better way to do that than to use the two guys who had a special past with you from Baker City? Can you at least appreciate my attention to detail?"

"You are sick."

"I mean, some things were purely coincidental. Being my student was just a bonus and your choice as to what topic you wanted to focus on was simply stupid on your part. In my defense, I tried to warn you. If only you knew what I've been trying to preserve for all these years. Think I would allow some naive young student to interfere with my drug network?"

"You're not going to get away with this," I threaten. "Everything is going to stop tonight."

"Oh, there will be an end. But it won't be how you've envisioned."

"What did you do to Penny?" I ask, not knowing whether or not I can trust whatever is said next anyway.

Dr. Williams turns and motions with his hand. "You all know my second in command."

Mark Tanner steps out, an evil smirk plastered on his face. "Penny was the one who got away," he says with a tone laced with nostalgia. "Our attraction toward one another was obvious. I was helping her with her modeling endeavors. Some girls just want to be famous, but when the spotlight is on them, they get stage fright." His eye winks. "She needed to be loosened up."

I snarl. "You are evil."

"Now, now, sweet Angie. Calm down. If I'd known how much trouble Penny would eventually cause me in the form of her big brother, I would have at least made it worth my while and raped her when I had the chance."

"Sick bastard." I dart forward, but Paul pulls me back, tucking me slightly behind his body. So, Penny wasn't raped. I should feel more relief, but it's hard when I don't know whether or not I will make it out of this alive to tell her the truth.

"Always so noble, Paul," Mark snickers.

"You're going to get caught." I feel dizzy from all the blood I am losing. "You *are* caught."

"I have a backup plan," Dr. Williams says confidently.

"And what's that?"

He smirks. "I figure I can tell you since you aren't making it out of here alive."

"Then tell me, dammit!"

Dr. Williams shakes the barrel of his gun in the air back and forth, warning me who has the upper hand here. "I just need Graham and his posse to get here so I can knock everything out in one go. I am efficient like that. Did I tell you we're going to have some fireworks—extra emphasis on the *fire*? Oh, and Paul? You had your fun fooling me. Hope you say hello to the devil when I send you to meet him." He waves his gun around between me and Paul, his hand trembling as if he can't decide whether to shoot us or wait to execute his original plan.

I glance around the cold and damp hallway. I need to buy time. Time for Nic or Graham to find me—if they are even capable now of doing so. "Where are we?" I've already been filled in, but I need to keep Dr. Williams talking so he can lose focus.

"Literally underground," Mark answers first.

"Decades before River Valley was built, there was a subway that ran under the city. But funding stopped and it never really got completed. Having top secret meetings in an abandoned underground location seems so glamorous, doesn't it?" Dr. Williams's eyes twinkle with mirth.

"You both are demented."

"Thank you," my former professor says with a smile. "What about you, Paul? Aren't you going to chitchat with me?"

I glance at Paul who is silent. His eyes are zeroed in on Dr. Williams. "Angie needs medical attention."

"But why?" he says with a fake frown. "She's not going to *make it* anyway."

I catch a shadow behind him and see Nic hiding behind the corner. He uses his fingers to count down.

Three.

Two.

One.

Everything happens so fast that my brain can't keep up. I am pushed hard backward, as Nic flies on top of Dr. Williams. The scuffle knocks me against the cement wall, causing me to crumble to the damp floor. I can hear my own voice yell out in pain, but it's like I am watching from a dirty window. I struggle to sit up. Gunshots blast through the confined space, echoing in the chambers of my ear drums.

Strong hands pick me up, pulling me away from the scene. My attempt at a scream gets stuck in my throat.

"Angie, it's me."

"Caa, caa…" I moan. It's Collins. He is here to rescue me.

"I'm getting you out of here."

"Graaaa…!"

I look back as Collins pulls me away, watching as the men fight it out. My heart burns with fear as I see Graham join the scene, brawling with Mark.

And then I see it. Flames. They start at the corner of the room and then ignite through the dampness of the stone floor. How did I not notice it before? The smell. It is gasoline. My clothes reek of it, as well as the entire space.

The fire rages through the tunnel as my vision of the men blurs from the force of it.

Collins runs as fast as he can, carrying me as cargo. Shots ring out in the distance, as I hear the sound of screaming bouncing off the walls. When he gets to a dead end, he pushes me up a ladder first, shadowing me from behind. At the top, he hits the latch and opens the panel.

"Crawl out, Angie."

"But Graham! What about Graham?"

"Get out, dammit!"

I pull myself out the rest of the way, looking back as Collins jumps down into the abyss, leaving me. I hoist myself up, just in time to see several people charging my way.

Police, the SWAT team, and firemen all surround me as they evaluate my appearance.

"Help them!" I yell. "Hellll."

My head feels dizzy as I point toward the trap door I just exited. With every ounce of energy I have left, I let out a roar so loud that it causes me to black out—

"She's stirring."

My hands go to my forehead. The pain is so real inside my head that it feels like it doubled in size and that my brain is going to explode. I try to move, but my neck cannot possibly withstand the weight of it, so I slump back into a darkness of my mind and drift back off.

The echoing sound in my ears doesn't help me determine my whereabouts. I just know that I am not alone, yet I am not in immediate danger. With my eyes still closed, I try to sit up and can't get my body to move. Every attempt sends a jolt of pain to my thigh. Thoughts flutter through my brain like a slideshow set on high speed.

The facial recognition software. Discovering Owen. Mark Tanner. Trying to get free. Seeing Paul—*Carson*. Learning about Bryce. Cutting my thigh. Dr. Williams. The gunshots. Fire. Raging flames. Graham!

Where is Graham?

I pry my eyes open and instantly shut them from the blast of light that burns my pupils. My hands move to rub out the pain with my balled up fists.

I groan and try to move again. Nothing. It is like I am boneless.

"Try not to move, ma'am."

Ma'am. Never would I have ever predicted that the sound of that title coming from Collins's mouth would sound so good. It is like music to my ears.

I am safe.

I am safe.

I am safe.

"Graaa," I say. My throat is dry and the sound is gravelly.

"He's getting bandaged up now," Collins explains.

We are at the hospital—again. The sterile smell gives it away. I hate hospitals. I have visited more times within the span of a couple of months than I have my entire life. My tracker bracelet is no longer on my wrist. It is now replaced with the plastic one that is labeled with my identity and a barcode.

"Is he hurt?" I whisper.

"He will heal just fine. Do you not remember? Maybe that's a good thing."

My eyes open slowly, adjusting better to the light this go around. "I remember." I clear my throat and look at his arm bandages. "Did you get burned? Shot?"

"Fortunately, just some minor scrapes and a few stitches."

"And Graham?" I choke out.

There's movement at the doorway. "I just checked on him and"—Paul enters the room—"he's doing great. He'll be here to see you as soon as he finishes up with his doctor."

"How do I ever thank you both for saving me?" I ask, tears running down my cheeks and soaking into my hospital gown. "I could have—" My body shudders as it all becomes real.

Both men cast their eyes downwards, as they know my next word.

"I'm just glad we got there in time," Collins says softly.

Paul offers me a weak smile. "You were so brave, Angie."

"I'm sorry I disrupted your mission from the moment I became aware of the druggings. I could have gotten myself killed for the sole purpose of aiming for a career in a field I am not even sure I am cut out for."

"We are just glad you are safe, ma'am."

"Is it over? All the bad guys caught?"

"Yes," Collins says with a smile of relief. "It's done."

"Did anyone…" *Die?*

Collins shakes his head. "Everyone you care about made it out of the underground tunnels safely."

"I remember being there, but I don't remember the ending. Everything is a bit fuzzy. You carried me away. I kind of remember the ladder. Climbing to safety. But then I blank."

"Graham and Nic had a showdown with Tanner and his crew. Paul, I mean *Carson*," Collins corrects, "got banged up quite a bit. We're just glad he was able to protect you for as long as he did. The FBI moved in and several members were arrested without bond. Including the main leader, The Prophet, who was really…"

"Dr. Williams," I whisper, still trying to wrap my head around that piece of information. "It is crazy how his prestigious influence allowed him to get away with pushing drugs and orchestrating all of these nefarious acts without getting caught for so long."

"You are a hero, Angie."

"I don't know about that. I feel like I messed up along the way not coming clean with my intentions from the very beginning. I'll always wonder if all of this could have really been avoided or if it was always inevitable. But I wouldn't call myself a hero. Just stubborn."

"You helped Graham and Nic find you and gave them just enough information to be warned before getting to you."

I rub at my eyes. Wetness coats my fingers, and I suddenly feel cold. A blanket gets pressed to me, as I drift into the hollows of my own dark thoughts.

The beady eyes of Owen. The mystery of The Prophet. The pain and helpless feeling of trying to scream and not being able to make a decibel of sound.

I hover here, in this unknown, negative space. Like I am trapped. A victim to my own fears, as I doze off again.

———

"Graham!" I yell and bolt up.

"Calm down, Miss McFee."

I open my eyes to see Collins's concerned face looking at me. His hands push me back into the mattress of the hospital bed. A damp cloth dabs my forehead, and I cough up the phlegm that collects at the top of my lungs.

I am safe from my nightmares.

"Here's a drink."

I look up at the glass of water held out to me by Nic. His warm smile makes me want to cry. "Are you okay?" I ask, looking at his face bandages. I quiver back into the mattress and look to Collins for reassurance.

"Just a minor scrape," Nic says softly. "Could be worse."

"Did anyone get burned in the fire?"

"Nothing major on that front," Collins answers. "Luckily we were able to run into another passageway before things got really bad."

"I'm sorry," I cry. "I was so...scared."

"It's okay, Miss McFee. We were all pretty scared," Austin says, rounding the corner. He is shirtless with a bandage wrapped around his upper arm. He has another one

—but much smaller—on his ribs. I look at his stacked body and then back up to his eyes.

"You and Malcolm got hurt at the safe house," I conclude. "I didn't even see you guys there."

"Yeah, it was all a clusterfuck." He sighs, running his hands through his hair. "Sorry for the language."

"What happened?"

"Just part of the job," he says with a shrug. "Been hurt worse. Owen and Tanner knocked me and Malcolm out—after I put up whatever fight I could. They definitely had the element of surprise in their favor. I regret blindly trusting the traitorous bastard."

"Anything broken?"

"Just a few cracked ribs. Nothing to worry about, Miss McFee."

I close my eyes as more tears flood out.

"We're all fine, really," Nic reassures.

"Is Owen being handled?" I ask, fear still evident in the shakiness of my voice.

Collins clears his throat and rubs his hands over his forehead. "I'll forever live with the guilt of not seeing it sooner. He has some balls."

I turn to see the tall figure in a hospital gown at the edge of my room. "Graham?"

He walks over to me with a walker, tears in his eyes. "I'm so sorry. I should have believed you when you were telling me Tanner came to terrorize you and that someone from the inside was a bad guy." His hands brush against the sides of my cheeks, leaning forward despite the cringe of pain to kiss me gently on the lips.

"This isn't your fault."

"Yes it is. It is very much my fault. I could have gotten you killed."

"You had reason to distrust me. I was self-medicating for so long, Graham."

"You were clean though, and those fuckers were slipping you pills. Tanner had a whole lab with pill presses, prescription bottles, and imported Fentanyl. He would manufacture his own medication and push it out for testing. All my agency girls were just test dummies. You knew it. You had it almost all figured out. That's why Dr. Williams kept steering you away from the truth. I wish I could have taken a hit on that man."

"Owen said he was the one that kept tipping off the press about my drug addiction."

"He doesn't deserve to keep breathing air," Graham snarls.

"It's all over, right? The FBI got the key players?"

"Yes, sweetheart. And they are putting the fear of a huge prison sentence into any lower level pushers' minds to encourage them to give out names and information surrounding the entire ring. This is all out of our hands now."

"Benjamin, Samson, and Edward?"

"They've all been arrested. In fact, there've been over fifty arrests so far in just the past twenty-four hours. Dr. Williams made the mistake of not having his burner phones destroyed prior to entering the tunnels. I don't think the man ever considered losing."

Collins and Austin dip their heads, while walking out of the room. It pains me to see them bruised and a bit ragged, all because they were trying to rescue me.

"Bryce tried to rape me in college and drug me. He and Owen were running a whole ring on a smaller scale back in Baker City. They tried to run me over when I got away after a party and was planning on going to the police. James died."

"Sweetheart, I am so very sorry."

"I'm just glad this is all over and we are all safe again," I say, squeezing his hand. It is over.

"Thank God the FBI decided to plant someone else into the mix who was trustworthy and not a fucking traitor," Graham snarls. "I owe Paul for saving your life."

He holds onto my hands and continues to examine my face. His fingers graze my chin, and for the first time I realize I have a bandage there from where I hit the step hard when Owen pulled me down. And where I was slapped over in the chair while restrained.

"How did you know Owen was a traitor?" Nic asks me. He is hovering along the edge of the room. "You knew it before I did. He had us all fooled. And you thought Paul was on their side too."

"I had been taking pictures and audio recordings of all the dates I was on with Mark. Business meetings and solo dates. During some of the meetups, his associates spoke in Spanish and Russian—and maybe even a few more languages. Hard to tell for certain. During the last meeting before Thanksgiving, I sent Claire to spy for me."

"We were aware of that fiasco," he responds, a bitterness to his tone.

"Because of Paul. He was at that meeting. He tipped you off about my involvement. Anyway, Claire got more pictures. During my Internet research phase, I discovered something called reverse image search, which led me to a variety of facial recognition software programs. I was in the library at the safe house analyzing the images from my girls' night at Slay. I plugged the photos into the software to see if any from the web would align. My search results completed, and I discovered some with Bryce and Owen. I saw Bryce with the Swiss Army Knife. It was the same one that was in my hospital bag from the hospital after the car accident that killed James. It was what was triggering some of my memories. So I knew he and Owen were after me during that time in Baker City. I just couldn't remember at the time of the car accident. Maybe part of me didn't want to live through it again."

I swallow and want to stop. The memories are just too much. I went from college student to an unofficial informant basically overnight.

Graham looks like he is going to be sick.

"It's not your fault," I promise. "You didn't know Owen was going to switch sides."

Graham flinches. "He was never on my side. Fabricated all of his credentials and even had manufactured voice recordings from his recommendations list to fly completely under the radar. His sole purpose coming to Portland and getting hired for my security team was to destroy me. Granted, Dr. Williams was the master pimp, getting these assholes to trust him enough in order to risk their lives for the cause."

I hate seeing Graham this broken. This isn't his fault. "I completely misinterpreted Paul's intentions. All this time I have been following him around and keeping tabs on him, and he wasn't even a contender," I say to myself, rubbing my hands into my hair.

I think back to the Halloween party, the cafe training, and the meeting where Claire spied for me. With my stubbornness, I could have sabotaged the entire FBI operation and blown Paul's cover before it was time or safe. I could have gotten him killed—Nic too.

"So you didn't know he was FBI, Nic?" I ask.

"I was almost positive he was," Nic says with a sigh. "As an informant, I'm not privy to a lot of valuable information. It helps to keep the chances of being compromised lower. Plus, some informants end up being traitors. I kept getting pressured to get you out of the operation. Far away from it. I would get tabs on you and how Tanner and his gang knew you were watching them. Now, it's obvious that those tabs were being done by Paul."

"Did Mark ever have a clue Paul was on the opposing side?"

"No."

"So I was quarantined after Thanksgiving to protect his image unknowingly? He knew it was only a matter of time before I would figure it all out," I conclude.

"Angie, you were putting your life in so much danger that it was impossible for me"—Nic pauses—"or I imagine Paul to do our jobs. Sure, we were working toward the same goal without realizing each other's roles, but you were way too risky with your life."

"That is something I can finally agree on."

"Thankfully this is all over now," he sighs. "At the rate you were ignoring all your self-preservation signals, I was about to have a heart attack."

"Mark told me in the tunnel that he never raped Penny. I could tell he was being honest, because he didn't have any reason to lie, fully believing I was going to die with the truth."

Both brothers clear their throats as they look at each other, tears welling in their eyes but not escaping. It is like a sense of relief washes over them at this news. I lean up in my bed and open my arms for them both to join me.

"I'm sorry Penny got drugged and is mentally paying for the sins of those bastards, but maybe—just maybe—she can move forward faster now."

After several seconds, Nic straightens his posture and takes a few steps back. "If I haven't said it before, I will say it now. Angie, you are the best thing to happen to my brother. And..." He looks off to the side of the room, appearing to be coping with some deeply buried emotions. "I"—his lips pull up into a smile—"you know."

Graham's eyes soften, as he tucks me to his side on the bed.

"I feel the same way, Nic," I say, battling my own unleashed emotions. "I love you too." I have never seen him this tender before and it just further solidifies the fear we all faced.

Nic heads out of the room, closing the door gently. Graham's eyes connect with mine as he processes everything. He looks tired, with his worry lines on his forehead more prominent. It is during this lull in conversation that I am able to understand the stress he must have been under while we were constantly working against each other to try to conquer a common goal.

I reach for his hand, giving it a squeeze. "My lying and risking my life days are over."

Graham sighs and bends down to kiss my lips. "I'm just glad we all made it out of that hellhole alive."

"When I got a text with you and Collins tied up and gagged, I was so scared. How did you get free?"

"Collins was able to undo the knots in the rope before it was time. We were being guarded by one of Tanner's minions, so I imagine he was going to release us when he got the call. Collins is a real Boy Scout when it comes to survival. That's the only reason we were able to get to the tunnels as fast as we did. Thank God we weren't too late."

"If something would have…" Tears well in my eyes as I think of the worst case. "I just…"

Graham swipes the pads of his thumbs against my damp cheeks. "I can't do life without you in it."

"My life is finally worth living again because of you. You make everything better. I never want to lose you. You are my forever."

He slides up farther into the bed to lie beside me. "Forever is not long enough."

26

"I can't believe we're officially moving out of here," I say to Claire, as we pack up the last of my belongings into boxes. We are in my room, sprawled out on the cold floor—trying not to cry.

A donation service truck is scheduled to arrive later today and pick up some of my old furniture that I no longer need. Campus is cleared out already. The dorms are empty for the long winter break, and those graduating are packing up for good.

"There have been so many good memories built here."

"Some of the best," I agree, glancing around my room.

"Remember when you threw all of asshole Russell's stuff out the window?"

I nod. "One of the highlights, for sure. How about when you forgot to put the lid on the blender with daiquiris and started it?"

Claire bursts into a fit of giggles. "Wasted forty-two

minutes of my life trying to scrub the stains out of my clothes before finally deciding to trash the whole thing."

"I'm going to miss sharing space together. I still can't believe this chapter of our lives is over."

I put on my graduation cap and hand her the one I made for her. We decided to forgo the ceremony scheduled for next week—it's not like we have family who would attend anyway. I am not big on crowds and everyone staring at me. Plus, the official graduation will be in the spring, but I doubt I will attend that either.

I secured my English degree. But other than that, there's not much to celebrate. It sucks that the past four plus years resulted in something that I did not predict would happen. However, I am happy that I feel like I was a part of something profound with the bringing down of the drug ring. I can't brag about it due to the case needing to go to trial, but at least I know that my determination for the truth paid off for the better—even if I have nothing to show for it.

Claire grabs her phone to use as a mirror as she fixes her hair under her cap. "You did a good job on the design of these. I'm impressed."

"We can still go, you know, if you're sad to miss it," I say looking at her expression. "It's a big deal getting a master's degree." I watch her distract herself by wrapping a few picture frames and placing them into an open cardboard box.

She shakes her head. "Nah, I am just reminiscing in my head over the good ol' days where it was still socially acceptable to work mediocre jobs because you are a student." She holds up one of her gym T-shirts that made its way under a pile of my romance novels. "Now we embark on the journey to the real world where all our dreams stay dreams and reality is less than stellar compared to how the big kids made it seem when we were still young."

"Okay, okay, okay," I say, holding up my hands. "What gives? You're not usually this—"

"Honest?"

"Pessimistic." I sigh. It is hard seeing my bestie this unhappy. "Usually those feelings are reserved only for my repertoire of emotions."

Claire shrugs. "I just have a lot of things happening inside my head that I need to work through."

"I have time to listen. I always have time for you."

She leans over and gives me a hug. "I got accepted."

I pull back to look at her face, trying to figure out her meaning. "You're going to have to be a tad bit more descriptive than that."

She extends her arms behind her and leans back to rest her weight on her hands. "To the facility in California."

"For the internship?"

"Yup."

"When did you find out? This is so exciting," I squeak. I try to force the pain in the pit of my stomach to go away. I know I will miss her so much, but I cannot allow my own selfish feelings to keep her from blossoming into the flower I know she can be. So, I fake it. I slap on a cheery face and try to share in her—

Why is she not excited?

"A few days ago. I got the notification in the mail. I was shocked seeing it, actually. Part of me just expected the answer to be a no."

I sit up straighter, pulling my bent knees up to my chest.

"That's wonderful!"

"It's a dream to go back to Los Angeles and work toward my career goals. This internship will definitely make my resume sparkle—especially since I landed it fresh out of college."

"When do you leave? How much time do we have to make more memories here in Portland together?"

"I haven't even made the final decision on whether or not I am accepting or rejecting the offer."

"Oh, I just figured…" I don't know how to complete the thought. I study Claire's face for answers.

She shrugs, looking toward the light coming in from the window. "I have to make a final decision soon. I made four vision boards to weigh the pros and the cons. But I'm running out of time. I have to accept or decline."

"What's the holdup?"

Claire lets out a long sigh. "I'm struggling to choose between progressing forward with my life here in Portland or starting fresh again with my dream job in LA."

I give her a squeeze to the arm. "Whatever you decide, it will all work out. You will make it work out. You are fierce and strong and brave."

"Some days I feel like none of those things," she says sadly.

"What else is bothering you? There's more. I know it."

Claire finishes packing a hoodie and looks up at me. "You scared me, Angie. And the fear of losing you in my life sent me into a rabbit hole of what-ifs."

It has been over a week since I was kidnapped. My wounds are barely visible, and thankfully nothing appears to have left a scar that wasn't already there. My heart, however, still carries a burden of knowing that things could have gone vastly wrong that day—for a lot of people. It is rare to get a second chance at life. It is even rarer to get a third one.

"I scared myself too," I admit for the first time. "I'm done with drama. I need some time to be boring."

"I can stand behind that idea," she laughs. "What do you plan to do next?"

"When we first met, I was still very much broken from the loss of my mom and brother. I spent my entire college journey chasing demons. I used the pain of my past to push me forward into what I thought I wanted for my future. But what happens if it was all for nothing? *Is* all for nothing?"

"Angie, maybe you didn't accomplish what you set out to accomplish. And that's okay. Maybe instead of searching for the right path, you simply just make your own."

I let Claire's words settle into my heart. She is so wise that I don't even think she realizes her impact on my life. I nod my head. "I may not have all the answers now, but that's what life is all about, right? Learning lessons as we go. Trying our best to make good choices?"

"Or bad ones," she giggles. "Sometimes those can be fun too."

I laugh. "True."

"Whatever you decide to do next, promise me you are done with the lifestyle where you jeopardize your happiness or put yourself in danger," she begs. "I can't do this life without you. You are my emergency contact. You are my bestie and I love you."

I squeeze her so tight that we both fall over, laughing as our graduation caps poke each other in the forehead.

"Ouch!" we say in unison.

The doorbell ringing halts our box stuffing. We trot down the stairs and open the door.

"What are you guys doing here?" Claire asks, welcoming in Blake and Zander.

"Figured you two could use some extra emo-ness as we say farewell to your bachelorette pad," Blake says, looking around at the emptiness.

"I prefer the name She-Shack better," Claire teases, making us all laugh.

Zander gives me a smile as he adjusts his guitar on his shoulder, looking hesitant but hopeful. Slowly, things are going back to normal. We've been texting more and already have plans to get together before he heads back to San Diego after winter break.

"I'm glad you came," I say softly, initiating a hug that he accepts.

"Good seeing you, Angie."

His smile is friendly. Platonic. So much is said with just the lopsided curl of his lips.

"Here, these are for you ladies," Zander says, revealing two bouquets of roses from a bag I didn't even notice he was carrying.

"Congrats on graduating, you two," Blake says, giving me a hug and then Claire.

I bite my bottom lip to keep my tears at bay. "You guys are graduating too," I comment. Everyone has a master's degree but me. I am lucky I even have a degree at all—even if it is not exactly what I set out to accomplish.

"Thought we could all say goodbye to this place together," Blake says. "I brought a few of my friends."

"Please tell me one is Jose!" Claire chants.

"You're in luck," he says, pulling out the bottle of tequila, followed by all the mixers.

We make a circle on the floor in the living room that is stripped of its furniture. It feels so empty here. Some other people will move in, most likely in a month, and make their own memories.

Blake serves up the margaritas into plastic cups, passing us each one. Zander busts out his guitar from his case and we all join in singing, "Memories Don't Die."

When the last box is loaded into the car trunk, Claire and I linger on the steps in an embrace.

"I'm going to miss this place," she says tearily.

"I sure am too."

"Claire. Please tell me what's wrong. You can tell me anything. What's on your mind?"

We are sitting in Ethan's apartment while he is at work, day drinking and celebrating our entry into adulthood. For someone who is a businessman, I am a bit surprised over his meager residence. His style seems polished but minimalistic. Maybe Deena cleaned him out during the divorce, and if that's the case, I hope he has some funds to give Claire the life she deserves—assuming they try to make it work no matter where she ends up living.

Claire and I have a bit more free time on our hands as of late and are taking advantage of getting together more often. Her gym hours have been cut to make up for the limited attendance due to the winter holidays. I resigned completely from my job at the smoothie cafe. Between the limited hours and the paparazzi lingering on the street to harass me, I just could not justify the hassle for a minimum wage salary. Plus, the smile bursting from Graham's face over the news was enough to make it all worth it.

But that still leaves me without a big plan for the future. While to Graham it would be acceptable for me to lie around and spend his money, I need to contribute to society in some aspect to feel content. I may not have all the answers now, but I will eventually figure it all out.

I refill my glass from the communal wine bottle. We are sprawled out on pillows in the center of Ethan's living room, tossing organic cheese puffs into each other's mouth. They taste considerably worse than the non-organic processed cheese ones, but I would never break Claire's heart with my menial analysis.

She clears her throat, rolls her shoulders back, and announces, "I'm running out of time."

"Can you be less vague?"

"The internship. I still haven't decided."

"What? Why?" Ever since I saw the accidental mail stating that Claire applied to the LA facility, I just assumed if she got accepted, she would go. Now I'm not so sure. Not many people get these types of once-in-a-lifetime opportunities. It never occurred to me that she would put her dreams on hold like this. And for what?

Or who?

"I just feel like my head is one big puff of smoke and no matter how hard I squint, I can't see what is ahead of me."

My lips press into a hard line. "No one can see into the

future, Claire. Just trust your gut with your decision. That's all you can really do."

"Have you gotten official word from the university regarding your degree?"

"They are having a team of reviewers look over my work from my previous semester and this one. I had to resubmit several assignments, answer dozens of questions, and now it's just a waiting game to see if my degree will change. But it doesn't matter."

"Of course it matters."

I shrug. "Not really. I missed the deadlines on securing an internship. Plus, when I had another failed project and no endorsement from the deciding professor at the time, I was overlooked for all of the good positions—that are now filled. I am at the bottom of the list, and everything available now would just be scraps."

"So, what are you going to do?"

"I'm no closer to knowing that answer than I was months ago."

"I highly doubt that, Angie. You have experienced a lot of growth the past few months. Don't discount that. Quit letting your fear of falling keep you from taking another step. If you constantly look back at the past, you will miss all of the beautiful things that are going to happen in your future."

"When did you get so wise?"

"Probably when I lost the safety net that was college. We are in the real world now. So, repeat after me... *I, Angie.*"

"I, Angie."

"*Promise to.*"

"Promise to."

"*Always listen to my best friend.*"

"Always listen to my best friend."

"*Because she is amazing.*"

"Because she is amazing."

"You feel better already, don't you?" she asks, throwing a cheese ball at my mouth.

"One hundred percent," I say with a smile, trying to find where it rolled. "I'm glad we can spend this time together."

"You pretty much are stuck with me for life, no matter where I move or what I decide to do."

I hug her to me. "Friends forever."

I slip into my softest pair of yoga pants and sweatshirt after my shower. Lying on the bed, I grab my journal from my nightstand and scan through my numerous entries—reading my own words that I bled onto the paper. Words of sorrow, of grief, of self-reflection, and of triumph.

I am more than what I limit myself to be. I am greater than the image that the media continues to paint of me. Nothing really has changed with their view of me, and as much as I tell myself to ignore it, it is hard not to read what is being published. The effect from Owen alerting the news outlets of my wrongdoings will be hard to undo. But maybe there is another way to fight back.

What if my fear of falling is keeping me from growing? That all of my anxiety about fitting into a certain mold, or having a specific image, is keeping me from allowing myself a chance to speak out. Good girls stay silent. I could deny, deny, deny what is being printed.

Drug Addict.

Pill Popper.

Self-Harm Princess.

Or I can confirm publicly that I am all of those things. I can embrace my journey and share it with others who may be struggling with addiction. I can be a role model for those who think vices define worth.

There is hope in the ashes of our pasts. Even flowers can grow in chaotic conditions.

I grab my laptop and start typing.

I Am a Drug Addict

By Angela McFee

I AM A DRUG ADDICT. AND I AM GOING TO BE OKAY. BUT BEFORE THAT HAPPENS, I AM GOING TO BE RIDICULED, MADE FUN OF, CALLED NAMES, AND BE MISUNDERSTOOD. FEW PEOPLE ARE GOING TO WANT TO HEAR MY STORY OF TRIUMPH. MANY ARE GOING TO WAIT FOR ME TO FALL.

THAT'S THE THING WITH HUMANS; THEY GRAVITATE TOWARD THE FLAME OF DRAMA. THEY WANT YOU TO BREAK. THEY WANT YOU TO LIVE WITH SELF-HATRED AND LOATHING, NEVER ANALYZING THE DAMAGE THAT CAN BE DONE BY SEEMINGLY SIMPLE WORDS.

I AM A PILL POPPER.

I AM A DRUG ADDICT.

I AM A SELF-HARM EXPERT.

EVERYTHING YOU THINK OF ME IS TRUE. MAYBE YOU
WANTED TO BREAK ME. PROBLEM IS, YOU CAN'T BREAK
WHAT IS ALREADY BROKEN. I HAVE BEEN HIDING BEHIND A
PREVIOUS INJURY FROM A CAR ACCIDENT AND USING THAT
PAIN TO JUSTIFY MY NEED FOR DRUGS. I LIED. I STOLE. I
HURT NOT ONLY MYSELF, BUT EVERYONE WHO STILL
DECIDED TO CARE ABOUT ME DESPITE THE SHITTY THINGS
I DID.

DRUG ADDICTION SUCKS. IT IS NOT GLAMOROUS. IT IS A
VILE SNAKE THAT INFILTRATES YOUR VEINS AND DOESN'T
STOP STEALING YOUR OXYGEN UNTIL YOU EITHER ARE
SNUFFED OUT OR YOU WAKE UP ONE DAY AND DECIDE TO
GET HELP.

I AM GETTING HELP. I MADE THE CHOICE, AND I MAKE THE
CHOICE EVERY SINGLE DAY TO NOT USE A PILL TO COPE
WITH THE THINGS THAT HAUNT ME. THERE IS HELP FOR
THOSE WHO FEEL HELPLESS. IF YOU ARE USING ANYTHING
TO MASK THE PAIN YOU FEEL INSIDE, KNOW THAT FOR
EVERY PERSON WHO TRIES TO KNOCK YOU DOWN, THERE IS
ANOTHER WAITING TO HELP YOU STAND UP AGAIN.

When I am satisfied with my work, I submit it to every
online media outlet I can think of in the state of Oregon. I
also post it on all of the social media platforms I am a part
of and any blogs that allow submissions. While the article is
very therapeutic for me, I want others to read it and know
that there is hope for the hopeless.

Sure, Owen and Bryce tried to make me look senile by keeping me drugged. However, I was the one who got that ball rolling. I am responsible. It is about time my true story gets heard. I am tired of trying to hide what has happened to me when my story can easily help others learn to rise above.

I close my laptop and take a few cleansing breaths.

"Is everything okay, sweetheart?" Graham asks from the doorway to our bedroom. His shirtless body covered in a sheen of sweat lets me know he just finished up one of his workouts.

"It is better than okay," I say with confidence. "I'm just glad you found me when I needed you most." I am referring to the first time we met outside at the mansion's pool. But he has continued to find me on several other occasions.

He always finds me.

Graham saunters over to the bed, leans down, and kisses my lips. "If you haven't heard me the other dozen or so times I have told you, I will say it again. I am proud of you. You can do anything that you set your mind to."

And for the first time in forever, I actually believe it.

27

"You promise this isn't weird?" Claire asks me from the comfort of the backseat of the SUV.

Graham and Nic are riding in the front, deep in conversation about potential job possibilities now that everything with the FBI is settled. Thankfully being informants protects them from ever having to testify or reveal their identities to the general population.

"I promise. Please stop obsessing," I say, reaching over to squeeze her hand to emphasize my words. "You are family to me. I just wish your biological one would see what they are missing out on. How incredible you are. Selfless and kind."

Tears roll down Claire's cheeks.

"Got any tissues up there?" I ask, catching a glance back from Nic. He looks between me and Claire, sighing. He is about as uncomfortable with a girl crying as probably shopping for tampons. His trepidation is written all over his hard facial features. "This isn't a show; just pass me some tissues."

"Here." I accept the napkins that he pulls out of the glove box, helping Claire dry up her face. "And as for Ethan brushing you off, I have no words."

"I get it, I do," Claire swears. "He has another family and a son who needs him. I just thought by now I would have integrated into his life better than I have. I feel like a square trying to fit into a hole meant for a circle. I think we just need time."

"Have you decided?"

She bites her lower lip. "I think so. But I want to still sleep on it a few nights."

I squeeze her hand. "Regardless of what happens or what you decide, I'm here for you. No matter what."

"Friends forever?" she asks through teary eyes.

I smile. "Friends forever."

I look out the window as we head out of the city. A light blanket of snow covers the trees. It is a winter wonderland. I catch Graham's watchful eyes in the rearview mirror, and I see love reflected back at me. He has given me a reason to love holidays again.

"Did I tell you how excited I am to give you all your Christmas gifts?" I ask loudly enough for the entire crew to hear. I am bouncing with energy, about to blurt out what they are.

"Only about a dozen or so times," Nic says with a chuckle.

"Pretty sure it cannot top the gift you have already given me," Graham says.

"And what is that?" I ask, leaning toward the front seat

so I can hear.

"Your love."

"Oh my," Nic says, looking at his brother like he just grew a second head. "When did you get this cheesy?"

"Yeah, I have to admit, that comment was pretty cheese infested," Claire says with a laugh.

"At least I got you to smile, though, right?" he responds, looking at her in the mirror. "No more tears, okay? We are excited to have you with us. So, cheer up before my mom sees you and gets you drunk on her cranberry juleps."

"That doesn't sound so bad," I mutter to myself.

I've gotten my drug addiction under control, and the doctor said I can incorporate responsible drinking back into my lifestyle. Avoidance was my actual coping mechanism— not the actual alcohol. In just a short amount of time, I have learned about my triggers and methods to safely cope with what has happened in my past. It has been very enlightening to witness my evolvement from unhealthy to healthy thoughts just by writing in my journal. However, I am very much a work in progress.

"Oh no, sweetheart," Graham warns, "you're not allowed to get drunk with my mom."

"And why not?" I say, crossing my arms over my chest. "That sounds like fun."

"Because when Mama gets drunk, out come the family albums, DVDs, and secrets."

I wink. "Oh, then I'm definitely getting toasted."

"Do it and see what happens."

"Ew. Stop," Claire announces, covering her ears dramatically with the palms of her hands. "Make it stop."

"We are here," I say with a clap to my hands, watching

out the window with anticipation as the house comes into view.

Donna and Germain's home is decorated to look like a scene fresh out of a home magazine. Thousands of lights stretch over the roof, windows, and landscaping. It had to have taken days to achieve this masterpiece. I open my door and slide out, standing in awe at the view before my eyes.

My trance is interrupted by a joyful Donna bursting out of the house in a pair of red and white slippers. She hurries to greet me in a warm hug, telling me and the others how thankful she is that we are here.

"Penny just arrived about five minutes ago from Seattle. This is perfect timing. Oh, you must be Claire," she says, wrapping her arms around Claire's frail form.

I hate how delicate her emotions are right now. I want her to have the best holiday with us. She deserves it.

"Thank you for having me, Mrs. Hoffman."

"Oh no," Donna says, pulling back, "you call me by my first name or we will turn this into a fun drinking game for every time you mess up."

Claire looks at her with confusion and then bursts into a fit of giggles. "I like you already."

"Mom, have you been pregaming it?" Nic asks, embracing her into a hug.

"It keeps me young."

"That's not a thing, Ma," Graham says, joining up with the group.

"It most certainly is," she scoffs. "And after all the stress you boys have caused me recently, putting your lives in danger, I hope you have settled into a less *exciting* lifestyle."

"I'm ready to be boring," Graham jokes.

"I've always been boring," Nic chimes in, only making his mom smack his arm over his casual behavior.

I know they both are thankful to have the whole thing over with and are just trying to keep the mood light right now, as we all mentally recover from the trauma.

The men unload the truck with all of the bags and wrapped gifts, while us women meander outside looking at all of the lights.

"This looks spectacular, Donna," I say.

I know I am wearing a weird grin on my face, but I cannot keep myself from smiling. It feels so good to be in Hillsboro. It is like a retreat away from the city and from the pain of knowing that the goals I have been working toward are just melted dreams.

But, I can choose to be sad or choose to be happy. As one door closes, sometimes three more open. I may not see it now, but with time the answers to my unspoken questions may be revealed.

Donna claps her hands together. "Come, let's go inside. I want to introduce you to two of my friends."

Claire and I follow her into the house. We kick off our shoes at the door and make our way toward the kitchen, where Penny is chatting with Germain and her brothers.

"Oh Angela, so glad you could make it," he says, embracing me in a hug. "And you must be Claire." He opens one arm wider, welcoming her inside his warmth.

Claire reaches for my hand and gives it a squeeze. I can sense her appreciation for being invited here. I know we both have grown up with less than stellar holiday memories. "This may be my favorite Christmas since I was a little girl," she says into my ear. "When being naive was actually a blessing."

Penny moves over to greet us. She looks so amazing. Her hair looks freshly cut and colored with lighter shade highlights. The sadness that once clouded her eyes is gone. She looks happy and healthy—definitely something worth celebrating.

"Ladies, come here, I promised an introduction to my two friends."

We shuffle over to Donna and get handed two glasses each. The rims are decorated with red dusting sugar and gold edible pearls. I look to where she has two huge glass drink dispensers set up.

"This is Merry," she says pointing to a beautiful red beverage with floating cranberries inside, "and this is Joy." The second dispenser is full of a festive green color.

Claire and I giggle. We fill our glasses with each liquid.

"Cheers," she says, double clinking glasses with us.

I try a little of each beverage. "Wow, these are really good. What's in them?"

"Hard stuff," Germain calls out over the multiple conversations being had.

"Easy, sweetheart," Graham warns. "You know how much of a lightweight you are."

"Hey," I scoff. "I can hold my own."

Penny has her arm around his back and is leaning into him. It is so good to have her here and doing so well.

"I cannot wait to see what you and Mom have come up with for the family games," Penny says to her dad. "I've been thinking about them since I left here on Thanksgiving."

"We have definitely outdone ourselves this holiday," Donna says thoughtfully to the group. "Pretty sure Germain and I are going to dominate the leaderboard, though."

Between the endless laughter, the warm winter smell of the candles burning in elegant jars, and the sight of everyone smiling, I know that my senses are in overload mode. And every second I endure is worth it. This is what a family looks and feels like. As sad as I am that my dad and I are on the outs, he is the only person missing from this picture-perfect scenario.

We move into the living room where a ridiculously huge charcuterie board is set up in the center on a long wooden table. It has to have twenty or more different types of meats, even more cheeses, fruits, nuts, and preserves. It is a masterpiece.

"Something for everyone here, so dig in everyone," Donna announces, passing us each a square plate with little pinecones and pine branches painted into the corners.

With the press of a button, Germain gets instrumental holiday music playing through the speakers. "Merry Christmas Eve."

We all echo his sentiments and fill our plates. Graham and I find a spot to sit on the floor near the Christmas tree and the blazing fire. I sit between his spread legs and lean my back on his chest. I feed him bites from my plate, popping toothpicks of cheese and grapes into his awaiting mouth. Every morsel touching my taste buds is fresh and at the perfect room temperature.

When my belly is so full that I can barely breathe, I relax like a jellyfish even more into Graham's strong body. He plays with my hair and runs his fingers up and down my sides in a soothing manner. I watch Claire interact with the family and then discreetly check her phone every ten minutes. If Ethan lets her slip through his fingers, then he is an idiot. And if she lets any man dull her sparkle, I will be very upset.

Claire has come a long way during her college years to erase some of the trauma from her past in Virginia. When we first met, we were both different people. Lost souls trying to find comfort in a world full of heartbreak. We bonded over coming to Portland to escape. The last thing she needs is to be here and yearning to run away again because of a man. He better do right by her—no matter what she decides.

We move into the sitting room where a huge grand piano is the focal point. We surround the huge piece, Germain taking the seat behind the keys. He starts playing the chords for "Have Yourself a Merry Little Christmas," one of my favorites. Donna initiates the singing and we all join in. I let down my guard and belt out the lyrics. This is the exact song we sang on our last Christmas we celebrated with my mom—except it was during the summer.

With Graham's hands splayed across my belly, I hold my own over my heart. I feel her and James deep within my heart. They have moved aside—no longer blocking the entrance—and helped stretch my heart to make room for the man who stands behind me. The man who walks beside me. And the man who is leading me into a future I have always wanted.

When the clock strikes midnight, we all say goodnight and disperse into our respective bedrooms.

"I need to talk to Penny," I say softly, stopping in the hallway outside his childhood room.

He gives me a kiss to the forehead, knowing what I plan to share with her. "How did I get this lucky to have someone like you in my life?"

"Not many women could put up with your *ways* like I can."

"I never wanted to be possessive of anyone else but you, baby. You captured my heart long before I could stop it from happening."

I bend up to kiss his lips and then cross the hallway to knock on Penny's door.

"Come in," she says softly.

I peek my head in from behind the door. "It's Angie."

"Hey."

I hesitantly walk in and join her at the foot of her bed.

"I'm so glad you weren't hurt like I was," she says sadly. "I never want anyone to endure what I think I went through."

"Penny, Mark didn't rape you." I place a hand on her leg, giving her a gentle squeeze. "He told me when I was kidnapped. He had nothing to gain from lying, so I think he was telling the truth."

Tears drip down Penny's cheeks, turning into sobs that shake through her upper body.

"Did you hear me? You were *not* raped."

"Yes I was." She turns her body so she can look at me straight on. "Mark might not have taken my body, but he raped my mind for months. Tortured me in my conscious and subconscious thoughts. He finds me in my nightmares and taunts me. So yeah, sure, he may not have possessed my body, but isn't it worse that he has shattered the hope I once had that a man can care about me for more than just sex?"

"I am so sorry." I pull her to me while she weeps, meeting her halfway with my own breakdown.

"He"—sob—"broke"—sob—"me."

It was a little taste of happiness that caused me to become addicted to my own self-sabotage obsession. Maybe as Penny progresses through therapy and learns how to reintegrate herself back into her normal life, she won't hold on to the pain that is keeping her from truly living her best life.

"You are so strong, and I'm grateful to know you."

Penny's eyes dry, and she gives me a gentle smile. "I needed to hear this tonight. I've been struggling, and I do want to get better. I can't rush my therapy. And I do want to change my outlook on life."

"You can," I say encouragingly. "I know you can."

She reaches over my lap and squeezes my hand. "Angie, thank you. You've given me hope."

"If there's one thing I've learned this past year, it is that hope is one of the many keys to happiness."

I give Penny one last hug and then make my way back to Graham's room.

"Everything okay?" he asks. "Have you been crying?" He gets up from the bed to comfort me.

"Yes," I confirm. "But it was necessary. I just needed to have a little chat with Penny."

"Yeah? And?"

"I think she's going to be all right. With time, of course."

"I love you, sweetheart. You have a gentle heart, and I promise not to take you for granted."

Graham helps me out of my outfit and then removes his. We crash into his bed and roll around until I am underneath his weight.

We make slow, passionate love, with the only light in the room coming from the moon and the decorations outside the window. I want to soak this moment in. I want it branded into my memory forever. For so long I tried to get my brain to forget, when now, all I want is to help it remember.

I wake to a tickle at my nose. My eyes pop open to see the boyish grin of Graham beaming down at me.

"It's presents time," he announces, giving me a little shake.

"Before breakfast?" I tease.

"Most definitely before breakfast."

"But not before coffee, right?"

"Negotiable."

"What do I need to do in order to get some of that Colombian coffee from your mom's friend?"

His eyes wiggle with boyish humor. "Lap dance?"

I rub my chin. "Hmm…not worth it. I can do without today."

"Blow job?"

"Ugh," I say making a face. "Too much work."

He laughs. "IOU office sex?"

I shake a finger at him. "Look at you using sexual favors as currency."

His smile lights up his face. "I learned from the master."

I giggle and slide out from underneath him to get myself dressed. "Seems pretty backward to be putting on Christmas pajamas that I have yet to actually wear."

Graham nods, raking his eyes over my bare flesh. "Yeah, this whole staging thing seems off. You should just go down naked."

"'Cause that won't be awkward."

I meander into the bathroom to do my quick morning routine. I separate my hair down the middle and braid each half, tying off the pigtails with a red band.

"Feigning the innocent look, I see," Graham says, pulling at each tail. "I cannot wait to grab a hold of these while I thrust into you from behind."

I turn around and place my bare butt against the cold vanity, glaring up at him. "Really? You're going to make us miss the entire day if you keep teasing me like that."

"I love that your drive rivals my own."

"Get dressed before I jump you," I warn.

We slip on matching red-and-black-checkered fleece pants, with shirts that have a male and female reindeer on the front. Walking out into the hall, we see Penny and Nic exiting their separate rooms. Nic has on a solid-black outfit, while Penny is wearing a powder-blue flannel set with snowflakes.

For the first time since meeting her, I notice a calmness about her body. It's like the tension in the chain has been released. I can only hope that our conversation last night had some positive effect on her, like it did me.

"I'm going to go check on Claire. Get my mug of coffee ready, please."

I find the other guest room and knock lightly on the door.

"Come in."

"Hey, you ready for some present opening?" I ask.

"I didn't go extravagant this year like I have in the past," she says sadly. "Money was a bit tight."

Claire has always gotten me crazy expensive designer items when we were roommates. She always said that the money her parents sent her in the mail was for managing their guilt for never visiting her—or wanting her to come back to visit them. The restaurant business sucks up all of their energy, and I think they blame her for moving away and not helping out with the family business.

"It's never about the money with me."

"I know that, but figured I would warn you anyway so you wouldn't be shocked."

"Come on, you worry too much." At least that's how she has been lately. Ever since she got notice of the acceptance for the internship in Los Angeles, she has not been herself. I want to ask her more about it. I want to find out if things are okay between her and Ethan. But now is not the time nor the place to put her on the spot. We'll just have to do another girls' night soon and really catch up.

Claire and I exit and make our way into the living room where the entire room is alive with anticipation and energy. Donna has hot drink dispensers set up along the side of the room on a rolling cart. Beside the dispensers, there is a mimosa bar. Where the charcuterie board was set up last night, in its place is a breakfast spread fit for an army. Pastries, breakfast meats, breads, fruits, and miniquiches fill up the entire wooden table.

Germain instructs us all to eat, standing back and admiring his family. He is giving me a window into the future of what Graham may look like in a few decades.

"Here, sweetheart," Graham says, handing me a mug of fresh coffee that he fixed the way I like. He brings a pastry up to my lips, gesturing for me to take a bite. I do.

"Yum."

He takes a bite along the place where I just did. "Yum," he agrees.

We then spend the next three hours snacking, opening up gifts, and taking a crazy amount of pictures. I laugh so hard as Graham unwraps his gifts from me.

"You really are like a twelve-year-old when it comes to gifts," I giggle, watching him tear through the paper like a madman.

He pulls off the lid of the huge clothing box, revealing a series of related items that I handmade with my heat press.

"Hold them up, let us see," Donna yells from across the room. "We can't see."

Graham unfolds the T-shirt that has my face printed across the entire front. Everyone laughs so hard.

"Because he is obsessed with me," I explain, as if anyone is really clueless to how he is.

"That I am," he agrees, admiring my work.

He holds up a tie that has dozens of little Angie faces all over it. Matching work socks. I even made him boxer shorts that are plastered with my face and then shiny lettering across the butt cheeks that says, "Angie's Man."

"Keep opening," I beg. "I got you more."

He takes the box from my hands and shakes it, placing his ear up to the side.

"Just open it," I whine.

Graham pulls off the paper into little confetti pieces, pops open the lid, and then removes the tissue paper to reveal a series of four custom mugs.

"What do they say?" Penny asks, watching her brother intently with his gift.

"Big Boss Man, Teddy Graham"—he pauses while everyone laughs at him—"Angie's Eye Candy, and In Love With the World's Worst Feminist. I love these." He kisses me passionately on the lips, making me blush an unhealthy shade of red, I am sure. "Your turn."

He crawls behind the tree and pulls out a huge box. I smile at it and start peeling off the paper. I hate having all sets of eyes on me—always have—but I just block everyone else out while I reveal a beautiful luggage set. There are three different pieces, each with a personalized luggage tag.

"I love it. I don't even own a suitcase," I say thoughtfully, looking down at the pull-out handle and the wheels. "These are great."

"And I bet it will come in handy on our trip."

I stop fidgeting with the custom tags and look up at Graham with confusion. "Trip?"

"Oh, I didn't tell you?"

My mouth drops. "No, Graham. You didn't tell me."

"As part of your graduation gift, I'm taking you to Florida. Key West."

"What?" I say, jumping up and throwing myself into his arms. "I am so excited!"

"I can tell," he says chuckling in my ear. "We will stay there a week and then I thought we could go to San Juan."

"As in Puerto Rico?"

"Yeah," he says, trying not to get whiplash as I thrash around in his arms. "That cool with you?"

I look up at him and kiss his lips so hard it hurts. "Yes, yes, yes."

"We leave a week after the new year."

"Sounds perfect."

After every gift is opened, we carry our new belongings back to our rooms and take a power nap before the family games. I wake feeling rejuvenated and still on a high from the knowledge that I get to go to Florida. I have never been to Florida. And I have definitely never been to Puerto Rico.

Graham and I join everyone who have already gathered downstairs in the dining room, sitting at the table.

"Sorry we are late," I mutter. "Is it game time?"

"That it is," Donna says, holding up a huge ball of saran wrap. "This game is called Unwrapped. The goal is to wear oven mitts and try to uncover hidden prizes from this ball of fun with a two minute time limit. Any prizes that you are able to unwrap are yours to keep. We will start with Penny and work our way clockwise."

Germain starts the timer feature on the mobile speaker and Penny goes to town, trying to rip the plastic away from the ball.

"Who comes up with these games?" Claire whispers to me.

"I have no idea. Probably Donna or Germain. They take family game night very seriously."

"I can tell," she says with a smile.

The ball gets passed to Nic, with Penny only barely getting the plastic started.

"Go," Germain yells, as we cheer on Nic, who manages to uncover a G-string thong and a lottery ticket.

"Really, Mom?" he asks shocked, holding up the piece of string from his finger. "Really?"

"That is called a—"

"I know what the hell it's called, dammit."

She tosses her head back and laughs so hard that she snorts. Graham places his arm along the back of my chair as we all break down into hysterics.

"I didn't know if you needed a refresher course," Donna says innocently.

"Just." Nic rubs at the scruff on his jawline, tossing the lace into the middle of the table. "Stop."

I stifle a laugh. I know Nic is single. From everything I've gathered, he plans to stay that way—permanently.

When Claire is up, she unwraps a one-hundred-dollar bill right as the buzzer goes off. She looks at it as if she just won the lottery. "Victory," she chants.

"Nice," I yell, patting her on the arm.

"Your turn, Angie," Graham reminds.

"Go."

I pull and tug at the little pieces of plastic wrap, trying so hard to get something from the ball of fun. Tug. Rip. "Yes! I got something."

"Keep going, you still have more time," Germain encourages.

I tear with all my might and release another prize from the ball. I am almost through another when—

"Time."

"What did you get?" Penny asks from across the table. "Show us."

I hold up a gold package and a lollipop, giggling.

"Ma, really?" Graham asks, looking at my prizes.

"That's a condom, son," she says. "For—"

"I know what it's for. Gah…"

Claire and I burst into tears from laughing so hard at Germain and Donna's sense of humor. They are a riot. I only hope that I am still this much fun when I get to be their age. They have a zest for life that is rare.

During Graham's turn he uncovers a tiny tube of lube and a few coins.

"I do not even want to know what is at the center of this ball," he says with a groan.

I pull off the wrapper to my lollipop while I wait for my next turn. Graham pulls me to his side and looks down at me sucking on the bright pink ball of sugar.

"You are as bad as my parents. You know that?"

"Worse," I say, smiling up at him, while popping the sucker out of my lips.

"Damn straight."

28

It is bittersweet saying goodbye to Graham's parents as we head out and back to Portland. They are both wearing their custom shirts I made them and sipping coffee from their personalized mugs. I am so glad they enjoyed their home-made gifts. I had so much fun making them.

When we get to the penthouse, I am excited to kick off my boots and relax. I didn't realize how much stress I have been holding on to with the ridiculous amount of expecta-tions I forced on myself. Now that Christmas is over and I am officially graduated, I can try to channel my energy into figuring out my next steps.

On the counter in the kitchen, a pile of mail rests. I dig through it and find two envelopes addressed to me. I tear open the bigger manila folder, revealing a cover letter and my new diploma. Highlighted across the front is the univer-sity's name, mine, and my new dual degrees—Journalism and English.

Wow. I did it!

I scan over the cover letter.

"What's this?" Graham asks, noticing my attention directed at the piece of paper in my hand.

"I can't believe it."

"Tell me," he encourages.

"The board acknowledged my current and past efforts in the field of journalism. So, my new diploma denotes the change." I hold up my embossed document. "See?"

Graham moves closer and reads my diploma out loud. It feels so weird hearing my recognition after going days believing I had missed the mark.

"Wow, baby, congratulations. This is what you have always wanted."

I smile as he spins me around in the kitchen. When he places me back down, I don't feel the same level of excitement that I thought I would have over this news. Maybe I am just in shock and once things settle in my brain, I will be able to make sense of everything.

I move back to the stack of mail. I pick up another piece addressed to me, ripping through the sticky seal. I pull out the folded letter. I open it and read through the words meant for me.

"Holy cannoli."

"What? What's going on?" Graham asks, rubbing at the back of his neck.

"They read it, my article. And loved it."

"The one you wrote for closure?"

"Yes. I cannot believe it. I just got asked to join the intern team at Pacific Press. This is all happening so fast. I wasn't expecting anything to change."

"Wow, baby, that's such a wonderful accomplishment."

I stare down at the words of acceptance. Days ago, it was a letter of being denied. But my article I wrote—for my own personal therapy—was valued by the right people apparently. "They like my raw honesty."

Graham leans in and kisses my forehead. "Because you wrote that article for yourself first."

I nod. "I stopped letting the expectations keep me from spreading my wings."

"Exactly."

I frown, folding the letter back into its trifold form and slipping it back into the envelope it arrived in.

"Is this what you want? What you *really* want, Angie?"

A sadness washes over me. "I don't know," I whisper.

"Sometimes it's okay not to have all the answers."

"Huh?"

"I know it sounds weird coming from my mouth, but you aren't the only one who is growing in this relationship. We are figuring it out together."

I smile, tears filling my eyes. "For over four years I have worked toward something I thought I wanted. I should be happy, right? Elated." I turn the envelope over and over in my hand.

"Why are you not then?"

"I cannot keep holding on to this fantasy, just because I think I can change the ending of the story."

"What's the fantasy?"

"This idea I had in my head that somehow I could find purpose in my life after James by focusing my attention on a dream I never really wanted. I let circumstances change my vision, instead of searching my soul for my own passions. I was at a fragile age, a time in my life that I was legally an adult but very much just a child trying to cope with a life without my brother and my mother."

"What are you saying, sweetheart? What do you plan to do?"

"I plan to take a couple of months to focus on myself. To dig deep within my heart and do some soul searching. To get through my therapy sessions and really think about what I want to do with my life. I know I did everything backward. I'm basically starting over again. I have two degrees and a formal education to at least show some credibility," I say with a shrug. "But maybe now is the time for me to really find out what my passions are and not let pain dictate the path to my future."

"With every new chapter comes the hope of possibility. I want to support you with whatever dreams you have. You have a lot of talents. Nothing is wasted, sweetheart. Never feel bad about growing—no matter which road you take."

"I could not do any of this without you."

"I'm your biggest cheerleader."

"Since we are in the whole open-all-the-envelopes mood, can we open up my cancer risk test results together? I have been holding on to them since I had my physical with Entice."

"Of course, sweetheart. Go grab them."

I jog into my craft room and find the sealed envelope buried in the back of my material bin. I am tired of hiding from the results. Moving back into the living room, I curl up in Graham's lap as we both tear open the flap.

"Wait," he says, stopping me from unfolding the results.

"Hmm?"

"Whatever you reveal, promise me we will handle it together."

My eyes move to his. "I promise." Then, I open up the letter and scan over the document. "I'm," I say, tears flowing down my cheeks, "negative."

Graham hugs me to his chest tighter. "Thank you for allowing me to be a part of this good news. We have the rest of our lives to celebrate every day we have together."

The next few days are a blur of lounging around the penthouse, finding new positions to twist my body in for our heated romps, and ordering takeout. The blizzard that hit a few days after Christmas barely has a speck of snow left on the ground as a reminder of its wrath. And by blizzard, I mean a three inch dumping of powder. The media sure has a way to get everyone fired up, burning through the store shelves for all the bread and milk people can pile into their carts. I know this because the day before the storm, I had a craving for cereal. Old-school, only-marketed-to-appear-healthy, cereal. Except, there was no milk to be found anywhere. While Graham insisted on sending out Collins to hunt a jug down from some dairy farm—okay, I'm being a bit dramatic—he also promised me that we were going to have a low-key end to our holiday break.

"I want to take you somewhere," Graham says randomly from the couch. We just finished watching a Christmas romance movie. The kind that always ends with the perfectly timed snowfall at a little sleepy town tucked away in the mountains.

"Umm, seems a bit spur-of-the-moment."

"Also known as spontaneous?" he teases, tickling my sides.

"What day is it?" I ask, pulling my knees up into my chest and yawning.

"This is exactly why we need to go out. You have lost all track of time."

I stretch my arms up over my head. "But seriously, what day is it?"

"New Year's Eve, Angie. One of the most romantic nights of the year."

"Wow."

"What?" he asks with genuine curiosity.

"It's crazy how inspired you can be from watching a little Hallmark movie. You are a changed man."

"Let's get dressed," he says, ignoring my teasing.

"Okay?"

"Come," he says, pulling me up from the cushions. "We can't be hermits forever. Eventually, someone will come check on us and make sure we're alive."

I groan as he drags me up the stairs. I smack his butt playfully on the way up, calling him soft.

"Soft?"

"Like a cuddly bear. You're losing your touch. I'm worried that my days are numbered where you rip my clothes off and have your way with me."

"We spent the entire morning with my cock buried inside your tight pussy. Your days aren't numbered. The count has just started."

"Tell my sex drive that," I whine.

As soon as my feet feel the rush of air, I yelp as he hauls my ass over to the bed, flinging me on top. Oh, here we go.

"Slide to the edge of the bed. I want to see your eyes when I thrust inside of you."

He stands at the edge, rips my pajama pants down, and lifts my ankles high up on his shoulders. Gripping my ass cheeks for leverage, he plows into me. I arch my back, accepting his demands. In and out. He pushes himself forward in powerful strokes, then pulls himself nearly out—hovering at my entrance. Then does it over again. And again.

"Graham," I scream, writhing with pleasure as he presses his thumb onto my clit and rubs it so hard that I lose all bearings. "I'm coming..."

"Yesss... Give me your pleasure."

By the time he is about to explode, I am on my second wave, thrashing around on the bed.

We scream each other's name in the quiet of our room. Graham collapses on top of me, panting out his breaths.

"Tell me that will satisfy you for a couple of hours."

"I can't make any promises," I say with a toothy smile.

"Woman, you are going to be the death of me."

"What a great way to go."

"That we can agree on," he chuckles. "Now, let's get dressed."

Inside my closet, I find a nice pair of gold-tone tights and a gold sparkling dress. I don't remember it being here before, but my memory is also not the best, so I don't even question it. I pair my ensemble with a matching pair of heels.

"You look nice," I say, admiring my man. He has on a

black suit and matching black tie. His stark white shirt makes him look polished and sophisticated.

"You look radiant. And all mine."

"Where are we going?"

"It's a surprise."

"Okay…" I watch as he rummages through his drawers until he finds what he is looking for.

"Will you wear this?" he asks, holding up a dark strip of fabric that looks like a tie.

I nod hesitantly. We have come so far together in our relationship that the level at which I trust this man is at full capacity. I know he would lay down his life for me. I know that he is my beginning and my ending.

Standing behind me, he gathers my hair to one side, bending down to kiss the skin below my ear. I moan over his gentleness. He can be so sweet. But I also love when he is impassioned and urgent and a bit rough. The sash covers my eyes, and within seconds it is tied securely behind my head.

"Ready to go?"

"Yes. I think so. Although, I have no clue as to where that is."

"Patience, sweetheart. Just trust me."

"I do, Graham."

He scoops me up into his arms and carries me through several rooms and into the elevator. My other senses are heightened, and I am able to map out the path we follow into the parking garage.

Graham carefully sets me on the seat, adjusts my outfit, and straps me into the belt. After a kiss on the forehead and a kiss to each concealed eyelid, I hear the sound of the door closing. Based on the amount of leg space and my knee being able to bump into plastic, I know I am in the front passenger seat, not the back.

After several seconds, I feel Graham's presence from the driver's side.

"You doing okay?" he asks.

I twist my fingers in my lap. "Yes. Just excited."

I lose track of time in the car and am unable to predict our route once we get out of the city. Or maybe we are still in the city and we are just hitting every green light at the right time.

I am disoriented and relax my mind of trying to think about where he is taking me. Instead, I think back to all of our good memories this year—and a few of the wild and crazy ones too. This is what I do almost every year as it approaches the end.

What has gone right this year?

What has gone wrong?

In the years since James has died, there were a lot of days where I just focused on my basic needs. I would eat. I would drink. I would shower. I would live for the sake of not actually wanting to die. I had a will to live, but not a will to actually do something with my life.

It was survivor's guilt, like I learned from my numerous and ongoing therapy sessions.

But now? I want to do more than just live, because my life is full of a happiness I used to fear. A happiness I didn't think I deserved or should experience. That's what guilt will do to a person. That's what depression does. It seeps into the cracks left in the heart after it has been broken.

I am a different person today than I was yesterday.

Tomorrow I will be changed as well. Each day I move forward is a day to do better, be better.

I have so much to be thankful for, and I attribute it all to Graham and his determination to see me as someone other than a broken weakling.

"What are you thinking about?" he asks, placing his hand on my thigh.

My hands join his, and I give it a squeeze.

"Just the good memories we have had this year."

"Oh yeah? Tell me."

"Remember when you tricked me into going on that first date with you?"

He chuckles. "I do remember, but you have the story a bit wrong."

"Of course you would say that."

"It was not a trick. Nic really was planning to go on the date and try to see if you were another FBI informant. I knew you weren't by—"

"How horrible of a liar I am."

"Yes, exactly. But he needed to visit Penny who was having a difficult time in Seattle, plus meet with a few associates for business."

"Then why not just cancel or find another guy to help me test-drive the agency?"

"Because I'm a jealous man and because in the beginning, I needed to find ways to quench my thirst and get my fix of you in a controlled setting. I had to learn to cope with my taste of addiction, because I knew from that night forward, one taste would never satisfy me. You were who I craved. Still are. I would have done anything in my means to have you."

"I'm glad you showed up that day to pick me up and not Nic. Plus, he's too much of a nice guy for me."

The car vibrates with Graham's laughter. "Oh wow, my baby bro sure has you fooled, doesn't he?"

"Nic is the most laid-back person I know. If he lays back anymore, he will be dead."

"Oh, Angie, your naivete is beautiful to me."

I look over at him even though it is pointless. "Please don't ruin this image I have of your angelic brother."

"You know I'd do anything for you, right?"

"Pretty sure you established that when I took you shopping for frozen pizza."

"And candy. Don't forget about your compulsive need to have something in your mouth to suck on."

I smack his arm, but not hard enough to cause a wreck. "You make it seem so dirty."

"I have been on the receiving end of watching your mouth molest a lollipop—multiple times."

"Remember when I called you to have video sex while you were—"

"At my freaking business meeting, sitting around a conference table, sporting a hard-on?"

"Yes! That's the one."

He bursts out laughing and I join in. "You are one of a kind, Angela Renee McFee."

"You bring out those sides to me that I never knew were there. I buried myself for years in my grief. You are the best thing that has ever happened to me."

He clears his throat but remains silent. We slow down and take a couple of turns.

"Did I say something wrong?"

"No, sweetheart, of course not. You keep saying that I changed your life for the better." His voice catches, and I wonder if he is crying. "But I want a chance to tell you how I feel too."

"Okay…"

"But we are here at our destination," he says, slowing to a stop and putting the car in park. I hear his door open and close, followed by mine. "Take my hand."

He pulls me gently from the car, keeping a hand on my head, as to not crack it on the roof. It is chilly but the air feels calming against my flushed skin. My nerves get the best of me and my breathing accelerates.

"Hey," he says, pulling me into a hug. "Relax, baby. I got you."

I smile. "I know."

Like before at the penthouse, he scoops me up and carries me up some stairs. It is so quiet here. We must pass through some building because the air temperature changes almost immediately.

When we get outside again, he places me on my feet, making sure I am balanced on my own. Then he steps away.

"Take off your blindfold, sweetheart."

I reach behind my head and undo the tie he secured, letting the scrap of material fall to the ground. He is standing before me, under a thousand little Christmas lights, in the exact place where our eyes first met.

I gasp, as my hands cover my mouth in awe. "Graham."

His smile is bright and his eyes sparkle—no longer bearing the mystery they once did four months ago. So many things have happened to us in such a short amount of time. And while we stand in the present, we both have a rich four-month past—full of memories and love—to look back on.

"We are coming full circle," he says softly, stepping toward me, sweeping his hand out at the patio and pool area that is decorated for a celebration.

Colored lights shine on the water making the surface look like a reflection of Aurora Borealis. Strands upon strands of lights cross overhead. It is like I am standing in one of those holiday light shows or my very own Hallmark movie.

Music is playing through a hidden sound system, similar to the night of the mixer event. Every "i" is dotted and every "t" is crossed.

I move a step closer and wrap my arms around him, hugging him so tight that it hurts. I look up at him and mouth, "I love you."

"You changed my life by walking into it four months ago. I did not know love until I met you. I did not know I was capable of change until I met you. You make me a better man, Angela. You are my past, my present, and please do me the honor of being my future."

I watch through a filter of tears as Graham gets onto one knee, reaches into his back pocket, and pulls out a ring that sparkles brightly under the canopy of twinkling lights.

"This ring is a symbol of my love. But the promise of forever is what my heart desires. Angela Renee McFee, will you marry me?"

"Yes," I yell, falling to my knees and crashing into him. "A thousand times, yes!"

Our lips lock and stay together, as he picks us both up

from the cold concrete, spinning me around. I feel dizzy from the emotion.

"I have one more thing to give to you," he says. "Stay right here."

He moves over to the table area and grabs a bag I didn't even notice from the chair. He carries it back over to me and reaches into the sea of tissue paper, pulling out a huge circular rainbow spiral lollipop on a wooden stick. He holds it up to me and turns it slowly, revealing the words, "She Said Yes!"

I hop into his arms, grabbing the candy, thrusting it into the air like a torch.

"She said yes!" he yells into the night sky. "She said yes!"

An eruption of clapping and chanting fills the area, as a rush of people flutter out of the French doors from the mansion.

"Well, thank God," Donna says, rushing toward me. "I gain another daughter." Graham releases me from his hold so I can be greeted properly. His mom squeezes me tightly in a loving hold, looking over to her son with pride. "Thanks for not messing this up, son."

I laugh over her bluntness. She is never one to mince words.

Claire and Blake clobber me with a group hug, nearly knocking me backward into the pool. Even Zander gives me a warm smile, and it feels like all of the tension we once had between us is finally ironed out.

"You are going to make the most beautiful bride," he 's, enveloping me in his arms. "You deserve to be happy, I'm so glad that I can witness it."

I lean up on tiptoes and kiss Zander gently on the cheek. "Thank you, Z."

I laugh as Graham's entire security team surround him. Congratulations are exchanged. Pats on the back. Handshakes. Fist bumps. It is overwhelming. These people are ingrained into my life in their own way.

"Angie?"

I turn to see my dad standing in the background. "Dad?"

"It's me." He takes a hesitant step forward. "Congratulations are in order."

I walk over to him and look into his solemn eyes. "I wasn't expecting to see you."

"It's part of my therapy goals to make amends with all the people I have done wrong."

"Therapy? You are—"

He nods his head, tears filling his eyes. "It was time. And that man of yours has helped me see all that I'm missing out on. You are very blessed to have found someone who loves you the way you deserve to be loved."

I look back at Graham, as he winks at me while making conversation with Penny and Nic. "He helped?"

"Came to visit me weeks ago to ask for your hand in marriage. I mean, first he had to officially introduce himself. I was in a very bad place. Have been for years. He got me into a rehab, and I've been working on myself slowly since."

"Oh Dad, I'm so glad you're taking these steps." I take a deep breath.

"Seeing you this happy is everything a father dreams for his daughter."

I hesitantly move closer. We haven't hugged in a long time. I can't even remember the last time. His arms open first, and I walk into them like I did as a little girl. The same little girl I buried deep within my soul on the day my mom died. Tears spring out of my eyes, and I shut them to prevent a flood. We stay like this, molded to each other, for several minutes. I sob. We both do. When I open my eyes, the entire patio is vacated.

"I'm glad you are here."

"I'm glad just to be a witness."

I rock on my heels. "I'm working on myself too, Dad. Every day. Making good choices."

"You've inspired me unknowingly to start living again, Angie. I'm so sorry for not being the dad I should have been for you, when you needed me most." He pulls back and looks at me. "Please forgive me," he chokes out between sobs.

"I do. I do," I cry, hugging him tighter.

"You know your mom would've been so very proud of you. James too. I miss them both with every ounce of me. I just had a horrible way of showing it."

"I miss them too, Dad. Every day."

"We just needed to learn how to walk again."

I look up at him, with a furrow to my brow. "What do you mean?"

"Going through a new life without your mom and James required us to take fresh steps, knowing neither was coming back, no matter how hard we tried to pretend. It is okay to not be okay, Angie. I was not okay for years. I want to do better. I want to be better."

"Me too, Dad."

We pull away, wipe our tears from our eyes, and just breathe. When my heart has calmed down again, we move ourselves into the mansion and are overcome with an engagement party fit for royalty.

Ice sculpture castles hold the cold appetizer options of shrimp cocktail, vegetable medley, and mini charcuterie cups. Waiters walk around the gathering with trays of hot foods for everyone to select bite-size portions. Along the side wall, there is a bar set up with huge glass containers filled to the rims with different candies.

A harp player sits in the corner, strumming pop songs on her strings. I love the enchanted feeling of hearing music I relate to without the lyrics.

I find Graham across the room with his eyes on me. Even in a crowded space, I can still feel his presence. That's how connected we are. He finishes up his conversation with his friend Logan and works his way over to me. I stare blatantly at the man of my dreams and smile as he approaches.

He leans his mouth into my ear. "You keep looking at me like that, sweetheart, and I'll end this party early just to have my way with you in every room of this mansion."

I look up at him and bat my eyelashes. "You make it sound like I don't want the same thing."

He taps me on the nose with his fingertip. "Oh, I know you want it too. Your drive is the only one that rivals my own."

I roll my eyes at him. "Pretty sure mine beats yours. You're getting old, after all."

"Keep taunting me and see what happens," he growls.

"I can get used to the idea of a lifetime with you as my boy toy," I tease, making him burst out laughing. He grabs two flutes of champagne from a waiter passing by and then tugs me outside again to have a private moment by the pool.

I hold his hand in mine and look out at the glistening water. He brings it up to his lips and kisses each of my knuckles individually.

"How are you feeling?" he asks, releasing my hand and wrapping his arm around me.

I take a sip of the bubbly. "I feel like a page is turning into a new book that has yet to be written."

"Except you do know the ending."

I turn and drape both my arms around his neck, smiling up at him. "I sure do."

"And we live..."

"Happily ever after."

EPILOGUE

"I'm staying back here," Claire says to me, as we walk toward the mailbox.

I stop midstride, turning to look at her. "Are you sure?" This is the first time I am hearing her official verdict and can't help but wonder if she is making a big mistake.

She shakes her head. "No. But my time is up to make the decision. So I made it. It's done."

I reach for her free hand and give it a squeeze. "Things have a funny way of working out sometimes." It is a weak point of encouragement, but I have no idea how to comfort my bestie on this major life decision.

"I can find a job and work toward a future with Ethan. He can't travel with me because of his visitation schedule with Finn. Long distance is never easy and is the kiss of death to most relationships. So, this is the natural thing to do."

"Oh Claire," I say, hugging her to me. I hate seeing my friend this unsure, but a part of me is relieved—for selfish reasons—that she is deciding to stay in Portland. I love Claire deeply. I just hope she won't later realize she has regrets.

She pulls back from me, tapping the envelope she is carrying into her free hand. "I'm just happy that the decision has been made. I hate having these things lingering over my head—and my heart."

"I'd be lying if I said I wasn't thrilled to have you closer. But I'm sad for you to miss a chance at something you've been striving for all along."

"Life is full of bittersweet moments," she says sadly. "Hopefully this will pay off." She turns the letter over and over in her hand, then slides it into the outgoing mail slot in the box. "Let's just hope more opportunities are available here for someone like me."

"Someone *amazing* like you," I correct.

"Where would I be without you?"

"Good thing you never have to find out. You're stuck with me for life."

Claire smiles until it reaches her eyes. "Good. Because life is so much better with you in it."

"Likewise, my friend, likewise."

Want more of your favorite *Entice Trilogy* characters? Follow Claire's journey in the *Toxic Desire Duet*.

ACKNOWLEDGMENTS

Dear Readers,

Thank you for taking a chance on a new author, who turned her hobby into a passion. Never in a million years did I expect to publish my books or expect anyone to enjoy them as much as I do. You've all given me hope that I can do this thing. I appreciate you being a part of my journey and sticking by me through all of the bumps in the road. You all bring such joy to my life, and I hope to make you proud with all of my future books.

For those of you who recommended, reviewed, beta/ARC read, and chatted about my books with others—*thank you*. Every little bit of buzz surrounding these books has helped new readers discover me.

Sincerely,

Victoria Dawson

ABOUT THE AUTHOR

Victoria Dawson is the creator of books with fiery heroines and possessive heroes. She thrives on writing stories that transcend the minds of readers, allowing them to get lost in the journey to love—and all the drama that entails. Prior to delving heart first into the romance writing world, she taught middle and high school students mathematics for ten years.

Victoria is a unique combination of hopeful realist and hopeless romantic. She is an iced coffee connoisseur, a reality TV enthusiast, and a habitual wearer of stretchy pants. If she is not chasing after her three active children, she is often found scouring social media for her next book boyfriend.

Having grown up in an itty-bitty town in Pennsylvania, Victoria is a little bit country. She currently resides in Maryland with her family.

Never miss a release or an important update by signing up for my newsletter.

Made in the USA
Monee, IL
05 June 2024

59472217R00301